Shadow Watch

Tom Clancy's
Power Plays

Shadow Watch

Created by
Tom Clancy
and
Martin Greenberg

PENGUIN BOOKS

PENGUIN BOOKS

Published by the Penguin Group
Penguin Books Ltd, 27 Wrights Lane, London W8 5TZ, England
Penguin Putnam Inc., 375 Hudson Street, New York, New York 10014, USA
Penguin Books Australia Ltd, Ringwood, Victoria, Australia
Penguin Books Canada Ltd, 10 Alcorn Avenue, Toronto, Ontario, Canada M4V 3B2
Penguin Books (NZ) Ltd, Private Bag 102902, NSMC, Auckland, New Zealand

Penguin Books Ltd, Registered Offices: Harmondsworth, Middlesex, England

First published in the United States of America by Berkley Books by arrangement with
RSE Holdings, Inc. 1999
Published in Great Britain in Penguin Books 1999
1 3 5 7 9 10 8 6 4 2

Printed in England by Clays Ltd, St Ives plc

Acknowledgments

I would like to thank Jerome Preisler for his creative ideas and his invaluable contributions to the preparation of the manuscript. I would also like to acknowledge the assistance of Marc Cerasini, Larry Segriff, Denise Little, John Helfers, Robert Youdelman, Esq., Tom Mallon, Esq.; the wonderful people at Penguin Putnam, including Phyllis Grann, David Shanks, and Tom Colgan; and Doug Littlejohns, Kevin Perry, the rest of the *Shadow Watch* team, and the other fine folks at Red Storm Entertainment. As always, I would like to thank Robert Gottlieb of the William Morris Agency, my agent and friend. But most important, it is for you, my readers, to determine how successful our collective endeavor has been.

—Tom Clancy

ONE

LATER, WHEN IT BECAME BOTH HER JOB AND OBSESsion to determine what happened at the pad, she would remember how everything had gone just right until it all went terribly wrong, turning excitement and anticipation into horror, and forever changing the course of her life. Astronaut, media celebrity, role model, mother—the world's easy reference tags for her would remain the same. But she knew herself well. There was the Annie Caulfield who had existed before the disaster, and the Annie Caulfield who eventually arose from its ashes. They were two very different women.

The morning had promised ideal conditions for the launch: calm winds, moderate temperatures, a clear blue spread of sky running off toward the eastern rim of Merritt Island, where the sun was shining brightly over Pad 39A at the ocean's edge. Annie would never forget that gorgeous sky, never forget looking out a window in the Launch Control Center and thinking it was like something from a Florida postcard or tourist brochure, the sort of roof NASA mission planners frequently wished for and rarely got.

Indeed, the preparations for *Orion*'s launch had gone without a hitch from the beginning. There had been no false starts, none of the frustrating last-minute technical snags that often caused countdowns to slip, and sometimes even forced missions to be scrubbed entirely.

Everything, everything, had seemed just right.

At T minus two hours, thirty minutes, Annie had joined members of the Mission Management Team and other NASA officials in accompanying the flight crew—*her* crew, as she'd called it, as she referred to all of the teams under her supervision—to the transport vehicle that would ferry them to the pad. While this was typically staged as a photo op by NASA's Public Affairs people, she was still a little surprised by the number of newsies waiting outside headquarters, their microphones covered with those furry wind baffles that looked like oversized caterpillars. There had even been a host from one of the network morning shows, Gary Somebody-or-other, who'd dragged her before the cameras for a comment.

In hindsight, Annie supposed she should have been prepared for the attention. NASA was intent on working the media, and she was aware that her strongly requested presence at the Center on the launch date, and to some extent even her appointment as Chief of Astronauts—a position very much at the upper level of the agency's organizational hierarchy—were calculated to draw a larger-than-normal press contingent. But she accepted her value as a PR tool, and sincerely believed the mission warranted its hype.

Long delayed due to funding problems, and of major importance to the International Space Station, the facility's first laboratory module was at last being sent into orbit, where it would be connected to the building-block segments already in place just two weeks before another research module was to launch from a Russian cosmodrome in Kazakhstan. Far beyond their political merits as concrete examples of East-West cooperation, the two missions were at the very heart of ISS's future scientific endeavors, opening up a new era in space exploration, and Annie was sure this was why she'd been so focused on their nuts and bolts and uncharacteristically oblivious to the surrounding hoopla. Together, they represented the largest step ever toward realizing a dream that had held her in its grip since childhood, and cost her dearly as an adult. With success for the ISS program within reach, Annie was hoping the pride she felt over her contribution might finally eradicate the guilt and pain that had been its lasting by-product.

But such thoughts had their proper time and place, and Annie's personal trials had been the furthest thing from her mind as she stood there outside the restricted-access buildings of Launch Complex 39, watching Colonel Jim Rowland lead *Orion*'s crew into the buslike silver transport with the circular blue-and-white NASA insignia on its side. Those five men and women had been scheduled to make history, and while her job required that she remain physically earthbound, Annie had felt as if a part of her would be going with them nonetheless.

They were her training group, her extended family.

Her responsibility.

She would always remember how Jim paused before entering the vehicle, his eyes scanning the crowd, seeking out her face amid the many others turned in his direction. The mission commander, and a fellow graduate of the astronaut class of '94, Jim was a strapping, vigorous man who seemed to pulsate with confidence and enthusiasm . . . and, at that particular moment, an impatience that only another astronaut who'd seen the Earth from 250 miles up could fully understand.

"Turnips, first and always," he said, knowing she'd be unable to hear him in the commotion, moving his lips slowly so she could read them without trouble. Grinning at her, then, he cocked a thumb at one of the breast patches on his carrot-orange launch/reentry suit.

Annie chuckled. Her mind flashed back to Houston, and the old training school motto they'd cooked up together, and the missions on which they'd flown as teammates. Ah, mercy, she thought. Once you'd been in space, it never stopped calling to you. Never.

"Terra nos respuet," she mouthed in Latin.

The earth spits us up and out.

Jim's grin widened, his eyes showing wry good humor. Then he tipped her a rakish little salute, turned, and entered the transport, the rest of the crew following him aboard in orderly procession.

Soon afterward, her functions as window dressing concluded, Annie broke free of the gathered reporters, ate a light breakfast in the commissary, and then headed for the mission's designated firing room, one of four expansive areas in the Center capable of directing a shuttle flight from prelaunch testing to takeoff, at which point operations would be shifted over to Mission Control in the Johnson Space Center, Houston. Filled with aisles of semicircular computer consoles, its enormous windows looking out toward the pad, the room was an impressive sight even while unoccupied. On launch days, when it bustled with ground controllers, technicians, assorted NASA bigwigs, and a smattering of guest VIPs from outside the program, it was something else again. For Annie, the atmosphere never ceased to be electrifying.

As she took her place in the Operations Management Room section of the firing room—which situated both the invitees and high-ranking personnel whose roles were nonessential to the countdown—Annie noticed the man seated to her right flick her an interested glance, instantly categorized it as the sort of I've-seen-your-picture-on-a-cereal-box look to which fame had made her accustomed, and then just as suddenly realized she was studying him in an almost identical manner. Not many businessmen were also household names, but only somebody who'd been sleepwalking for the past decade could have failed to recognize the founder and CEO of UpLink International, one of the world's leading tech firms and, most notably insofar as Annie was concerned, prime contractor of the ISS.

He extended his hand. "Sorry for staring, but it's a great thrill to meet you, Ms. Caulfield," he said. "I'm—"

"Roger Gordian." She smiled. "Our program's foremost civilian standard bearer. And just 'Annie' would be fine."

"First names all around then." He nodded toward the woman on his opposite side, a striking auburn brunette in a crisp business suit. "Let me introduce you to my Vice President of Special Projects, Megan Breen. One way or another, she's generally behind whatever good things our company manages to accomplish."

Megan reached over to shake Annie's hand.

"I hope you'll attest to hearing Roger say that when it's time for me to renegotiate my salary," she said.

Gordian gave Annie a wink. "Poor Megan's still got a lot to learn about the unshakeable loyalties between former warbird pilots."

All at once, Annie's smile became overlaid by something other than humor.

"You were downed over Vietnam, weren't you?" she said.

Gordian nodded. "By a Soviet SA-3 while on a low-alt sortie over Khe Sanh." He paused. "I'd been flying with the 355th out of Laos for about a year, and spent the next five on the ground at Hoa Lo Prison."

"The Hanoi Hilton. My God, that's right. I've read

how its inmates were treated. About its star chambers . . ."

She let her voice trail off. These had been rooms eighteen and nineteen of what American POWs called the Heartbreak Area, known as the Meathook and Knobby Rooms, the former for reasons that were self-explanatory, the latter because of the clumps of plaster that covered the walls to dampen the screams of the tortured. Say what you wished about the French, who had left Hoa Lo as a legacy of their colonization of the region—just as the notorious penal colony on Devil's Island was a historic testament to their rule of Guiana in South America—they had to be respected for having built escape-proof prisons that could impose behavioral modifications on the most hardened incorrigibles, the brutal inhumanity of those facilities notwithstanding. And quick studies that they were, the North Vietnamese had made full practical use of their inheritance.

"I've likewise heard about your exploits," Gordian said. "Six days evading enemy soldiers in the Bosnian countryside after an E&E from an F-16 at twenty-seven thousand feet." He shook his head. "Thank heaven you were rescued."

"Heaven, my survival manual, my radio beacon, and an iron stomach I've been razzed about my whole life, but that's uniquely suited to the consumption of grubs and insects," she said. "These days, with the GAPS-FREE recon and guidance systems you designed available on almost every fighter plane, it's less likely a pilot's going to be blindsided the way I was."

Gordian looked a bit uncomfortable.

"You give me too much credit, and yourself too little," he said, and then gestured around the room. "Though I'd bet we agree that *this* is really remarkable."

Annie nodded. Unless her judgment had gone totally awry, she'd just gotten a flash of genuine modesty from

Gordian—a rare trait for someone of his stature, as working around powerful men had taught her, often through lessons of a highly unpleasant nature.

"This your first launch?" she asked.

"Other than as a tourist, yes," he said. "When our kids were, well, *kids,* my wife Ashley and I got a car pass and took them to see an *Endeavor* takeoff from the public viewing site. That was spectacular enough, but to be inside an actual firing room . . ."

"Makes your fingertips tingle and your heart go pitter-pat," Annie said.

He smiled. "Guess I can assume you haven't gotten blasé about it yet."

"And I never will," Annie said, smiling back at him.

A moment later Gordian rose as NASA Administrator Charles Dorset arrived, clasped his hand, and bore him off to meet a group of officials in one of the adjacent rooms.

"So what's next?" Megan asked Annie, leaning across Gordian's vacated chair. "With so much going on at once it's hard to absorb everything."

"Don't sweat it. Sending human beings into space is a complicated process," Annie said. "Even the astronauts can't remember all their tasks without cue cards, and that's after years of training and a full dress rehearsal."

"Are you serious? About the cards, I mean."

"They stick 'em right on the instrument panel," Annie said. "One small step for man, a giant step for Velcro." She glanced at her wristwatch. "To give you a sense of where we stand, there's about an hour left till takeoff, and everything seems to be looking good. The closeout team's already secured the side hatch, and in a little while they'll be leaving the pad for the fallback area. Prelaunch checks started hours ago and are automatically sequenced by the computers, but there are a lot of switches aboard that spacecraft, and right about now the crew's going to be making sure they're in the correct positions."

"The number of personnel jammed into this room comes as a revelation," Megan said. "I've watched launches on television and expected we'd have plenty of company . . . but there have to be, what, two hundred people at the consoles?"

"Good guess," Annie said. "Actually, the total's a little higher, maybe around two hundred fifty. That's half as many as there were back in the days of Apollo, and a third less than were needed just a few years ago. The new CLCS—that's Checkout and Launch Control System—hardware and software we've been adding have consolidated most launch operations."

Gordian was working his way back from the aisle. "Sorry to have left in the middle of our conversation, but Chuck wanted me to meet some of his deputies."

Chuck to you, Mr. Dorset to me, Annie thought. In the future, she would remember trying to conceal her amusement out of concern Gordian might take offense. *I suppose it really is first names all around for some of us.*

Megan had turned to Gordian. "I wasted no time picking Annie's brain while you were gone. It's been quite an education."

"I hope one more eager pupil won't be too much trouble then," he said, taking his seat.

Annie smiled. "Not at all. As long as we keep our voices down, you can both ask any questions you'd like."

Which was precisely what they did for the next fifty minutes or so. Then, at T minus nine minutes, a hold was put on the countdown and a waiting hush fell over the firing room. For the most part, the ground controllers sat at their stations in silent readiness. Across the room, however, the Mission Management Team—a group of key NASA officials and project engineers—began having quiet, serious discussions, a few reaching for telephones on their consoles.

Annie noticed her new acquaintances looking intently over at them.

"The hold's altogether routine," she explained in a low voice. "Gives the astronauts and ground personnel a chance to play catch-up with their task list and see if any last-minute corrections are necessary. It's also when the managers make their final assessments. Some of them will want to teleconference with engineers in Houston before committing to the launch. Once they arrive at their individual determinations, they'll take a poll, see whether there's a consensus that it's okay to proceed." She motioned toward the lightweight headphones on her console, then at two additional sets in front of Gordian and Megan. "When the event timer starts again, you'll want to put them on and eavesdrop on the dialogue between the cockpit and ground operators."

"The polling you mentioned," Megan said. "Does it take very long?"

"Depends on the weather, technical snags that might have cropped up along the way, a bunch of factors. If one of the managers gets uneasy over something in his daily horoscope, he could theoretically force a postponement," Annie said. "Though I've never heard of that happening, there have been some oddball occurrences. Five, six years ago, for example, a *Discovery* launch was tabled for over a month, thanks to a pair of northern flickers."

Gordian looked at her. "Woodpeckers?"

"You know your birds." Annie grinned. "Unfortunately, these two were pecking at the external fuel tank's insulation covering instead of tree trunks. After it was repaired, an ornithologist was called in to scare off the little pests. I think he wound up hanging owl decoys around the pad area."

"Incredible." Gordian shook his head. "I don't remember hearing anything about it."

"Tales of the Cape. I can tell more of them than you'd ever want to hear." Annie chuckled. "But have no fear. Based on what I see, it'll be an easy 'go' today," she said.

And she was correct. Shortly after making her prediction, Annie saw the management team take their launch positions and reached for her phones. On the big wall screen across the room, a closed-circuit video feed showed what was usually referred to as "the stack"—this consisting of the Shuttle's two solid rocket boosters, its massive 150-foot external fuel tank, and the Orbiter—in its vertical launch attitude. But Annie knew the spacecraft from the inside out, knew it as only someone who had flown aboard it could, and saw other vivid, detailed images in her mind's eye: Jim and his pilot, Lee Everett, harnessed into their seats on the flight deck, the sun streaming into the nose of the vehicle and reflecting off the lowered faceplates of their helmets. Payload Specialist Gail Scott and Mission Specialist Sharon Ling directly behind them, the remaining three crew members below in the mid-deck. All of them in sitting positions on their backs to reduce the effects of g-forces on launch and ascent. Though she had never experienced space sickness, Annie knew they would have time-release scopolamine patches behind their right ears to alleviate potentially debilitating symptoms caused by acceleration and a microgravity environment.

Yes, in her mind, in her heart, she was right there in the spacecraft with them, *right there,* experiencing what they went through at every stage.

It was T minus five minutes and counting.

Annie listened to the voices in her phones.

"—Control, *Orion* here. APUs juicing up," Jim was saying. "It's HI green for one and two, starting three, over."

"Roger, proceed, over," the controller replied.

"Okay, we're three for three. Humming away."

"Roger, *Orion*. Beautiful."

Annie felt her eagerness building. What she'd heard indicated that the hydrazine-fed auxiliary power units that would gimbal the space shuttle's main engines—or SSMEs—during ascent were on and functioning normally.

They were down to the wire.

She continued listening in as the shuttle went to independent power and its external tank pressured up. Beside her, Gordian stared out the heavy windows facing the pad with rapt fascination. Only the controllers were speaking now; this close to liftoff, firing room protocols required absolute silence from everyone but those in the launch communications loop. The rules were strictly observed, although Annie guessed the overwhelming exhilaration of the moment would have rendered her speechless even if they hadn't been.

At T minus two minutes the controller declared they were okay for launch, and Annie felt the expectant tingling that had started in her fingers rush through her entire body.

She would remember checking the countdown clock on her console at T minus six seconds—when *Orion*'s three SSMEs were to have ignited exactly a half second apart in a sequence controlled by the shuttle's onboard computers.

Instead, it was when things went wrong.

Terribly, unforgettably wrong.

From the time Annie picked up the first sign of trouble over her audio link to the disaster's tragic final moments, everything seemed to worsen with dreadful rapidity, giving rise to a stunned, dreamlike sense of unbelief that, in a way, would almost prove a blessing, numbing her to the full impact of the horror, allowing her to cope with what might otherwise have been overwhelming.

"Control . . . I'm seeing a red light for SSME Number Three." The urgent voice belonged to Jim. An instant later Annie heard something else in the background, the piercingly shrill sound of the master alarm. "We've got a hot engine . . . LH2 pressure's dropping . . . smoke detectors activated . . . *there's smoke in the cabin. . . .*"

Shock bolted through the control room. Her eyes going to the video monitor, Annie reflexively clenched her hands into fists. As she'd glanced at the screen, an inexplicable streak of brightness had shot from *Orion* above its main engine nozzles.

The controller was struggling to remain calm. "We're aborting at once, copy? Evacuate Orbiter."

"Read you . . ." Jim coughed. "I—we . . . hard to see . . ."

"Jim, white room's back in position, get the hell out of there!"

Annie swallowed hard. She had performed the emergency evac drill many times during her flying years, and knew it as well as anyone. The "white room," a small environmental chamber, was at the end of the crew-access arm, which reached from the service tower to *Orion*'s entry hatch. Having automatically retracted soon after the ten-minute hold was completed, it now had been moved back into place. According to established abort procedure, the crew was to exit the hatch, then quickly pass through the access arm to a platform on the opposite side of the tower, where five high-tension slide-wires ran down to an underground bunker 1200 feet away. Each wire supported a steel basket that was large enough for two or three astronauts, and would deliver them to a nylon catch net at the opposite end.

But first, Annie knew . . .

First they needed to *reach* the baskets.

On the screen, she could see flames discharging from the SSMEs in bright orange-white bursts. Oily black plumes of smoke had enveloped the pad and were churning up around the spacecraft's aft section and wing panels. The blaze was hot, and it was getting hotter. While Annie believed *Orion*'s thermal shields might prevent its exterior fuselage from catching fire, the heat and fumes in its interior compartments would be lethal to their occupants. And if the fuel in the ET or solid rocket boosters ignited . . .

But she refused to let her mind go racing down that path. Her hands still tightly balled at her sides, Annie sat with her attention riveted on the monitor. Communication between Jim and the firing room had broken off, and she could scarcely make sense of the confused, anxious, overlapping chatter of the controllers in her headset.

Come on, she thought. Keeping her gaze on the screen, waiting for the crew to emerge from the spacecraft. *Where are you?*

Then, suddenly, she thought she saw several figures appear on the railed platform on the west side of the service structure—the side where the escape baskets were located. But the distance of the video cameras from the pad, and the obscuring effect of the smoke, made it hard to be immediately certain.

Annie watched and waited, her eyes still narrowed on the screen, locked undeviatingly on the screen.

She had no sooner grown convinced that she had, in fact, spotted *Orion*'s crew, or at least some of its crew members, than the first explosion rocked the service structure with a force that was powerful enough to rattle the LCC's viewing window. Annie seemed to feel rather than hear that sound, feel it as a sickening, awful percussion in her bones, feel it in the deepest part of her soul as a huge blast of fire ripped from the tail of the shuttle, leaping upward, engulfing the lower half of the stack.

She snapped forward in her seat, mouthing a prayer to any God that would listen, watching the tiny human shapes on the tower scramble into the rescue baskets as the flames rose behind them in a solid shaft. She couldn't distinguish one from another, nor even be certain how many of the astronauts were on the platform. From her perspective they were barely larger than insects.

The rainbirds above the pad had activated, flooding it with water. For a long, excruciating moment Annie could see nothing through rising clouds of steam and smoke . . . nothing except the hideous glare of the fire raging, unquenched, around the shuttle.

And then one of the baskets was released. It arced toward the ground with tremendous speed, moving away from the tower just as a ragged tendril of a flame shot through its metal framework, lashing greedily at the platform. Horrified, Annie could still see members of the team on that platform, their bodies outlined against the flaring edges of the blaze. And then a second basket was released, descending the slide-wire ten or fifteen seconds behind the other—a delay that would have been unacceptable during practice aborts. Annie wondered about it briefly, but pushed her thoughts aside before they had a chance to fully form.

Yet she had seen what she had seen . . . and would later reflect that the thoughts you tried *not* to let into your head sometimes turned out to be the ones that took deepest hold, lingering with the tenacity of restless ghosts.

The next few minutes were sheer torment. Along with everyone around her, she had been unable to do anything but wait for the astronauts to resume communications from the bunker. Wait, and stare at the monitor, and try not to surrender to the madness of what she'd been witnessing.

There was silence. And more silence.

Annie gnawed at her bottom lip.

Finally she heard an excited voice in her headset.

"Launch Control, this is Everett. Second basket's down and I think we're all—"

He abruptly broke contact.

Annie sat without moving, her heart slamming in her chest. She didn't know what was going on, didn't even know what she was feeling. The relief she'd experienced upon hearing Lee's voice had gotten all tangled up with profound despair. Why had he ceased to respond?

Control was hailing him now. "Lee? Lee, we're reading you, what is it?"

Another unbearable measure of silence. Then Everett again, his tone distraught, almost frantic: *"Oh, God, God . . . where's Jim? Where's Jim? Where's . . . ?"*

Annie would remember little about the moments that followed besides a sense of foundering helplessness, of the world closing in around her, seeming to suck her into an airless, shrinking hole.

And there was one other thing that would stand out in her memory.

At some point, she had glanced over at Roger Gordian. His face pale, his posture somehow crumpled, he appeared to have been violently thrown back into his seat. And the empty, blown-away look in his eyes after hearing Lee's anguished question—

It was a look that told Annie he knew its answer as well as she did, knew it as well as anyone else in the room.

Colonel Jim Rowland . . .

Jim . . .

Jim was gone.

15

TWO

5:00 P.M. Eastern Daylight Time

THEY HAD LEFT PORTLAND INTERNATIONAL JETPORT in a rented Chevy that had seen better days, taking the Maine Turnpike north for over a hundred miles to the Gardiner terminus, where it merged with the interstate leading by turns northwest and northeast past Bangor to the Canadian border. Now the traffic, sparse since the Bath-Brunswick exits, had entirely dissipated, leaving theirs the only car on a road flanked by a profusion of evergreens and a variety of hardwoods denuded by the long, sedentary New England winter.

The toll stop was unmanned, with no barricade or surveillance cameras, and an exact-change basket that took the requested fifty cents or whatever the driver's conscience decided was adequate.

Pete Nimec fished two coins out of his pocket and tossed them in.

"Quarters?" Megan Breen said from the passenger seat. They were the first words she'd spoken in almost an hour. "Never knew you were such a choirboy."

He regarded her through his dark sunglasses, his foot resting lightly on the brake.

"You should've looked closer," he said. "They were Canadian coins some toll clerk stuck me with on my last trip to this state. Been waiting to return the favor ever since."

"How long ago was that?"

"A year," he said. "Or so."

Nimec drove on through. About fifteen miles beyond the toll he turned right at the Augusta exit, stopped for gas, then continued past some worn-looking strip malls and a couple of traffic circles onto Route 3, a hilly stretch of two-lane blacktop rolling eastward toward the coast.

Beside him, Megan looked out her window and fell back into preoccupied silence. The sky was a drab gray sheet of clouds, the wind becoming increasingly aggressive as they neared the coast. It sheered off the sides of the car, skirling into the interior through invisible spaces between its doors and frame, blowing across the dashboard in chill currents that slowly brought the heater into submission. In between long unvaried stretches of woods there were filling stations and junk dealers, and more filling stations and more junk dealers, few with any customers, the scenery rambling on with a kind of lowering, stagnant monotony that seemed endless. Meg could have easily believed the haphazard piles of reclaimed sinks and bicycles and Formica tabletops and dishes and garden rakes and knickknacks being hawked out of shacks or trailers along the road had been accumulating for decades and never went anywhere at all.

Shivering, she sank her chin deeper into her collar. She was wearing a black leather jacket, blue jeans, and black ankle boots. Her thick auburn hair was pulled back in a ponytail under a duckbilled Army field cap.

Nimec thought she looked uncharacteristically tired around the eyes.

"Wonder who'd buy those old throwaways," she said.

"I don't know," he said. "You've got to keep in mind that everything in this part of the country has an afterlife, including inanimate objects."

"Sounds unholy."

He shrugged. "Some might call it Yankee frugality."

She gave him a wan smile, leaned forward, and turned on the radio, but the Boston all-news station she'd been able to pick up earlier in the ride had grown unintelligibly faint. After almost a minute of listening to static drift, she pushed the "Off" button and sat back.

"Nothing," she said.

"Probably better for you."

She glanced over at him. "What's that supposed to mean?"

"We saw the newspaper headlines at the airport, heard the updates on the radio driving out of Portland," Nimec said. "I'm no less anxious to hear about the *Orion* investigation than you or anyone else. But it gets to where you know there won't be any developments for a while and are just letting the media beat you over the head with information that's already been reported a thousand times over."

"I'm not prone to self-abuse, Pete."

"That wasn't my meaning. But I can't help thinking it might've been better for you to postpone this trip—"

"We had an agreement. You show me yours, I show you mine."

"Nice way of putting it," he said. "Still, you've had a rough couple of days."

Megan shook her head.

"Rough is what happened to those shuttle astronauts. To Jim Rowland and his family. I just want to know the reason it happened," she said. "I never understood, at least not fully, not *viscerally,* why it almost always becomes important for the loved ones of plane crash victims to learn the minute details of what went wrong with the aircraft . . . whether it was engine failure, structural problems, pilot error, whatever. I thought sometimes that knowing wouldn't change anything for them, wouldn't bring anyone back. That it might be better if they were encouraged to try moving on and letting the investigators do their work." She shook her head again. "What bothers me now is that I could've been so damned thick."

He sat very straight behind the wheel, his eyes on the road. "That won't get you anywhere. It's hard to put yourself in people's shoes when such extreme circumstances are involved."

She didn't say anything. Outside, the repetitive sequence of gas stations and ramshackle shops had been interrupted as they came up on Lake St. George State Park, its wooded campgrounds extending up the rugged granite hillside on their left, the smooth gray opacity of the lake spreading out to the right. Wet and heavy with snowmelt, the carpet of fallen leaves along its near bank seemed lasting and immovable, wholly resistant to the wind's attempts to sweep it apart.

"You obviously consider our appointment worth keeping," she said finally. "Enough so you didn't rush off to Florida."

He shrugged. "The FAA and a half-dozen other federal agencies are already on-site, and that's not counting NASA's in-house people. Gord's also pushing his agency contacts to let UpLink send in a group of its own technical personnel as observers. But a launchpad accident is altogether outside my area of expertise. At the Cape I'd just be in the way. Here I can get something accomplished. We—"

Nimec suddenly paused, clearing his throat. He had been about to say, *We need to find a replacement for*

Max, and was grateful he'd caught himself before the words slipped out.

Before his recent death, Max Blackburn had been Nimec's second in command in UpLink's security division, a role that had evolved into his becoming the designated troubleshooter at their international facilities, particularly in hot spots where his covert skills sometimes became indispensable. But there was a high price to be paid for Max's eagerness—even overeagerness—to put himself at personal risk. Max had not died peacefully in his sleep. Far from it, he had gotten killed long before his time, killed in a way Nimec still found difficult to accept or even think about. And in his efforts to avoid thinking about it *today,* he'd almost forgotten the rumors that Blackburn and Megan had been briefly involved in an intimate relationship.

Perhaps, then, the shuttle accident—terrible as it had been—wasn't the only reason for her moodiness. No matter how delicately he tried to frame it, how convenient it was that neither of them had mentioned Blackburn's name at any point on the way here, there was no hiding the fact that finding someone to take his place was the reason they had traveled to Maine. If Colonel Rowland's shadow had been hanging over them since they'd left San Jose that morning, then so too had Max Blackburn's.

"We need to shore up our end of things," Nimec resumed, choosing his words with care. "Those new robot sentries we're using at the Brazilian ISS plant are fine and dandy, but well-trained manpower's the foundation of any security operation. We need to beef up our force strength and tighten the organizational structure there. And that really ought to go double for the Russians in Kazakhstan." He paused. "I only wish Starinov wasn't under parliamentary heat to keep us out of the loop. You'd expect our saving his skin a few years ago would help on that front, but it's actually worked against us. Seems his government has made proving it can look out for itself a point of nationalistic pride. Typical paranoid Russkie thinking, you ask me. Give them another two centuries and they still won't have gotten over Napoleon taking Moscow."

"As if we'll ever forget it was one of *their* politicians who ordered Times Square leveled at the turn of the millennium."

"Not to be compared. Pedachenko was a rogue and a traitor to his own country. And last I heard, Napoleon wasn't an American—"

Megan raised her hand. "Wait, Pete. We can get into all that later if you want. But there's something you said a second ago . . . were you implying that you suspect the shuttle explosion wasn't an *accident*?"

"No," he said. "Nor do I see any cause to be suspicious. But I like to be ready."

"And you honestly feel Tom Ricci's the best person to get things in shape?"

Nimec paused again, no stranger to her skepticism in connection with Ricci.

"I appreciate your reservations and agree he's a long shot," he said. "But you ought to keep an open mind. At least meet the guy before ruling him out as a candidate for the job."

She frowned. "Pete, I'm sure Ricci's a good man, and if I wasn't willing to give him a fair shake I wouldn't be here. But if we've learned anything from Russia and Malaysia, it's that UpLink's global enterprises can put us smack in the middle of some incredibly volatile political situations. You and Vince Scull have both insisted we need to raise our security force to a higher level of performance so we can adequately respond next time we're caught in the cross fire. I'm just agreeing with you, and proposing that someone with a less, shall we say, *checkered* background would be best qualified to implement the changes that have to be made."

Nimec furrowed his brow. He'd heard her argument before, and certainly acknowledged that it had a degree of merit. But . . .

But what? Was he simply being mulish insisting that Ricci had what it took to help restructure a world-spanning organization that was, as Megan had suggested, increasingly coming to resemble the military in style and scope?

Surprised by his own doubts, Nimec gave the matter a rest and concentrated on his driving. The lake area behind him now, he made a left turn off Route 3 in the town of Belfast and got onto U.S.1 northbound, crossing the bridge that spanned the harbor inlet, then heading on along the coast. Here the roadside junk dealers were shuffled in with restaurants and summer resorts and had obvious upscale pretensions, their deliberately quaint shop fronts geared toward tourists rather than hard-scrabble locals. Most had the word ANTIQUES hand-painted across their windows in ornate lettering. Many were closed for the winter. The motels, inns, and cottages were also battened down for the dregs of the season, their lawn signs wishing patrons a happy and joyful Christmas and inviting them back after Memorial Day.

They continued north on the coastal highway, talking very little for some miles, catching frequent glimpses of Penobscot Bay behind and between the tourist traps on the right side of the road—its shoreline extending in belts of jumbled stone and harsh wind-carved ledges, giving intimations of a primal wildness that seemed dormant rather than lost, capable of hostile reassertion. There was a constant sense of nearness to the sea, the sky swirling with gulls, the water refracting enough pale sunlight to lift some of the cloud cover's gravid heaviness.

"It's much different here from inland, isn't it?" Megan said at length. "Still sort of forlorn, but, I don't know . . ."

"Beautifully forlorn," Nimec said.

"Something like that," she said. "There's a disconnection from the rest of the world that makes me understand why Ricci chose this place to hide out. If you'll pardon my choice of words."

"Nothing wrong with it," Nimec said. "That's exactly what he's been doing for the last eighteen months."

Nimec nodded toward a green and white road sign ahead of them that read:

ROUTE 175—BLUE HILL, DEER ISLE, STONINGTON

"Looks like we're coming up to our turn," he said. "Another forty minutes or so and you'll be meeting my friend and former colleague for yourself."

As it happened, he was right about the turn but wrong about the length of time remaining on their trip, for only ten minutes later Megan Breen got her introduction to Tom Ricci . . . as well as two local law-enforcement officers.

It was by no means a pleasant encounter for any of them.

Nor was it one Megan would soon forget.

2:00 P.M. Pacific Daylight Time

It always struck Nordstrum as fascinating that Roger Gordian, who had made opening up and changing the world through telecommunications a crusade, rarely opened *himself* up to the world, and possessed the most contained and *un*changing nature of anyone he knew. But that sort of contradiction seemed a familiar story with men of towering accomplishment, as if by directing vast amounts of energy outward to achieve their broad public goals, they drained off reserves that most ordinary people applied to their private lives.

Or maybe I'm getting carried away and Gord just likes his furniture, Nordstrum thought as he entered Gordian's office.

He paused inside the doorway, giving the room a bemused visual audit, comparing the way it looked now to how it had looked a decade ago, a year ago, or the previous autumn, when he'd last been inside it. Not to his surprise, everything was precisely the same—and in the same condition—as always. The place was a testament to careful upkeep, a paradigm of maintenance and preservation. Over the years, Gord's desk had been refinished, his chair reupholstered, the pens on his blotter refilled, but heaven forbid that any of them ever might be replaced.

"Alex, thanks for coming." Gordian got up from behind his desk. "It's been too long."

"Gord and Nord, together again for one outstanding SRO performance," he said. "How are Ashley and the kids?"

"Pretty good," Gordian said. He hesitated. "Julia's moved back home for a while. Personal reasons."

Nordstrum gave him a meaningful look.

"Husband with her?"

Gordian shook his head.

"The dogs?"

"Probably napping on my sofa as we speak," Gordian said, and then motioned Nordstrum toward a chair.

Slam, Nordstrum thought. *End of subject.*

They sat facing each other across the desk. There was, to be sure, an aura of bedrock consistency and dependability here that Nordstrum, who had left his Czech homeland, a White House cabinet appointment, a D.C.

town house, possessions, lovers, and most recently his multifaceted career behind with a lightness of foot equal to Fred Astaire sliding across a dance floor, found impressive and reassuring. It wasn't as if time was standing still—Gord's hair was a little grayer and thinner than it used to be, his once-petite secretary had filled out around the hips, and on the positive side, both had managed to stay reasonably in line with current fashions. But through tide and tempest, Gord's office was Gord's office.

"So," Gordian said. "How's temporary retirement agreeing with you?"

Nordstrum raised his eyebrows. "Temporary? You need to check your sources."

"Spoken like a true journalist," Gordian said. "Alex, you're under fifty and one of the most competent and knowledgeable men I know. I'd just guessed you would eventually want to get back to work."

"I won't reject the compliments," he said. "Fact is, though, that after the crypto brawl, and almost being hijacked aboard a nuclear submarine, and getting frozen so far out of the White House that its gardening staff fends me off with hedge clippers if I get too close, I don't feel the urge to be anything but a couch potato."

Gordian sat there without comment for several moments, Mount Hamilton visible through the window behind him, thrusting high above San Jose's urban development, extending the atmosphere of benign yet unassailable permanence beyond the confines of the room.

"I know you were at the Cape for the shuttle launch," Nordstrum said. "I'd tuned in to watch it on CNN." He shook his head. "A god-awful tragedy."

Gordian nodded.

"Not something I'll ever forget," he said. "The sense

of loss . . . of personal grief in that control room can't be described."

Nordstrum looked at him. "I've been assuming," he said, "that *Orion*'s why you got in touch."

Gordian met his gaze and slowly nodded again. "I was conflicted about it," he said. "While I respect your wish to stay free of involvement, I could use your advice. A great deal."

"Every time I think I'm out of it they pull me back in," Nordstrum said.

Gordian gave him a thin smile. "Thanks for sparing me the full Pacino impression."

"Don't mention it."

There was another pause. Gordian steepled his fingers on the desk, looked down at them, then looked up at Nordstrum.

"You wrote an analysis of the *Challenger* disaster for *Time* magazine back in the eighties, before we knew each other," he said. "I never forgot it."

"And I never knew you read it," Nordstrum said. His brow creased. "That was my first major piece. If recollection serves, we met a month or two after its publication."

"At a Washington cocktail party thrown by one of our mutual acquaintances," Gordian said.

"Coincidence?"

Nordstrum waited.

Gordian didn't respond.

Nordstrum sighed, giving up.

"After *Challenger* went down, the media struck up the tune that NASA and the space program were finished," he said. "I remember hearing this constant rattle about how an entire generation of children had suffered permanent emotional scarring from having viewed the explosion on television, and innumerable comparisons between that event and JFK's assassination, and predic-

tions that we would never be able to recover or muster
the will to go into space again."

"You very strongly attacked that notion."

"Yes, for a whole list of reasons," Nordstrum said. "It
allows a terrible accident to be packaged as a neat blend
of pop psyche and sensationalism for the nightly news
and the Oprah show. It completely discounts human re-
siliency and says we're compelled to act as we do by
external forces that are beyond our control. Maybe worst
of all, it assumes failure to be a given, and then relieves
us of responsibility by promoting a linear fiction, a sim-
plistic cause-and-effect explanation for that failure.
'Don't blame me, blame my psychological deficits.' In
my opinion, nothing could be more misleading and de-
moralizing."

Gordian looked at him. "You see why I miss having
you around, Alex," he said.

Nordstrum smiled a little.

"Lay a soapbox at my feet and that's what you get,"
he said after a moment. "At any rate, the central point
of my article was that blaming *Challenger* for the loss
of public confidence in NASA was getting causes and
symptoms totally mixed up. We all grieved for the astronauts who died aboard that spacecraft, but the
agency's tarnished reputation after the accident didn't
result from a national trauma. It was a consequence of
institutional problems that had been developing and
compounding for quite a while, and the ugly blame
game that erupted when the Rogers Commission, and
later the Augustine Report, brought them to light."

"Concluding that NASA's internal bureaucracy had
gotten so large there was a total disintegration of authority and decision-making procedures," Gordian said.
"Each manager had become lord of his own kingdom,
and their feuding had broken down vital lines of communication."

"That's the short version, yes. But it misses too much that's really disturbing. Information about the O-ring weakness and other potential launch hazards was suppressed—consciously, actively suppressed—because those managers were looking out for their own competitive interests to the exclusion of everything else. Funding needs, political pressures, and production deadlines drove agency officials to lower the bar on safety practices. A lot of people were worried about the launch, yet nobody wanted to be the one to stand up and make the decision to scrub. It wasn't that they intended to put the astronauts at increased risk, it was that they'd succumbed to a kind of organizational group-think that conditioned them to see the risks as being less serious than they clearly were. With every launch, they became more like problem gamblers, telling themselves their luck would hold and everything would work out okay. They made their mistakes with their eyes wide open."

Gordian had been watching Nordstrum quietly as he spoke. Now he crossed his arms on the desktop and leaned forward over them.

"Alex, it isn't the same with *Orion*," he said. "The space agency is a different entity these days. More cohesive and goal-oriented. More transparent in its internal operations. Its standards have been restored. I never would've committed UpLink's resources to ISS if that hadn't been demonstrated to me."

Nordstrum looked thoughtful.

"Gord, you may be sold," he said. "But the currency of trust NASA built up with the public during its *Mercury* and *Apollo* years is almost depleted. Selling *them* is going to be a problem."

"You aren't sounding very sanguine."

Norstrum expelled a breath. "The accident creates uncertainty even for those of us who believe in space research. And long before *Orion*, a great many taxpayers, maybe a majority, considered the program a wasteful frittering away of their money. For its critics, a forty-billion-dollar international space station, with hundreds of millions going to bail out the Russians—who couldn't pay for their end despite Starinov's pledges to the contrary—is emblematic of that waste. They haven't seen any practical value in it and nobody's done an adequate job of making them feel otherwise. And now, with the death of Colonel Rowland . . ." He spread his hands. "I wish I could be more optimistic."

Gordian leaned further across the desk.

"Okay," he said. "What do we do?"

Nordstrum sat quietly for several moments before answering.

"I'm not your paid consultant anymore. Not a newspaper columnist. I can only speak to you now as someone who sees the workings of government and big industry as countless other people in this country do, from the outside through shaded windows, and maybe that's a good place to come at this from, maybe it makes it easier to be their voice." He paused. "Convince them, convince *me,* that the *Orion* investigation is going to be completely aboveboard. I don't want to hear about its progress from some evasive media spokesman who believes his primary responsibilities are to spin the facts and keep me mollified while those in the know go about their work in secrecy. I'm sick of those types and am going to hit the clicker the instant they show their faces on my TV screen. When something surfaces that hurts, let it hurt. For once, just *once,* I want the truth straight up. And I want it from someone I can trust."

He fell silent, studying the brawny shoulder of Mount Hamilton through the window.

The silence lasted awhile.

At last Gordian unfolded his arms, lifted them off the desk, and reclined in his chair so slowly Nordstrum could hear every creak of its burnished leather as a separate and distinct sound.

"Anything else?" he asked.

"As a matter of fact, yes." Nordstrum checked his watch. "Don't let another news cycle go by without a statement to the media. There's still time to put one out before the end of the business day. And before the six-thirty network broadcasts."

Gordian smiled a little.

"Hell of a mouthful," he said. "Just like the old days."

"The sole difference being," Nordstrum said, "that in the old days I got handsomely compensated."

Their insertion technique highly modern, their means of delivery an airborne relic, the twelve HAHO jumpers vaulted from a blacked-out DC-3 that had carried Allied troops on missions of liberation during World War II.

This was a very different sort of mission, plotted by men with very different objectives.

The propeller-driven transport had flown from a hidden airstrip in the Pantanal, a sprawling wetlands in central Brazil, to within a dozen miles of their drop zone outside the frontier city of Cuiabá. While a traditional parachute jump might have occurred at an altitude of three thousand feet, they were ten times that distance from the ground when they exited the plane. It was a height at which the atmosphere was too thin to support human life and where, even in the tropics, the extreme cold could damage the flesh and freeze the eyelids shut.

Survival for the high-altitude-high-opening team therefore hinged upon specialized equipment. Oxygen canisters rigged to their jumpsuits made it possible for them to breathe. Protective goggles allowed them to keep their eyes open in the frigid, lashing wind. Pullover face masks and thermal gloves offered insulation against the worst effects of exposure.

Free fall through the moonlit sky was brief. Their

airfoil-shaped chutes released moments after they jumped, unfolding front to back, then from the middle out to the stabilizer edges—a sequence that checked their deployment until they were just below the backwash of the props, reducing the opening shock.

Their canopies filled with air, hands on their steering toggles, the jumpers descended at an initial rate of about eighteen feet per second, passing through a high layer of cirrocumulus clouds composed of supercooled water and ice. Fastened to their harness saddles, the bags containing their assault weapons doubled as seats that helped distribute their weight and compensate for drag.

The lead jumper was a man who had gone by many names in the past, and presently chose to be called Manuel. He snatched a glance down at the altimeter atop his reserve chute, checked his GPS chest pack unit for his current position, and then signaled the HAHO team to form up in a crescent around him. He wore a small, glowing blue phosphorous marker on his back, as did three of the other jumpers. Another four had orange markers, the remaining four yellow ones. The colored markers would allow them to maintain close formation as they glided through the inky darkness, and provide easy identification when they broke off into separate groups on the ground.

For now, however, it was vital that they stay together through their long cross-country flight, silently riding the night wind, sweeping down and down toward their target like winged, malicious angels of death.

THREE

FROM AN ASSOCIATED PRESS BULLETIN:

Space Agency and UpLink International Pledge to Keep ISS on Track Despite Shuttle Disaster

Kennedy Space Center, Cape Canaveral—In a joint statement released late this afternoon through NASA press spokesman Craig Yarborough, agency officials and Roger Gordian, whose firm, UpLink International, is chief contractor of the ISS project, have declared their undivided commitment to resuming assembly of the orbital station as soon as possible. "We will reach beyond loss and grief," Yarborough said in his opening remarks, and then went on to

announce the formation of an investigative task force to determine the
cause of the blast, which has re-
awakened grim memories of the 1986
Challenger accident that claimed the
lives of seven astronauts and nearly
crippled America's space program.

Asked about the composition
of this fact-finding team—and apparently mindful of the widespread
criticisms leveled upon NASA in the
wake of *Challenger*—Yarborough
replied that it would include personnel
from both inside and outside the
organization, and promised more
specific information about its makeup
within days.

According to the prepared text of
the statement, Mr. Gordian will take
a "personal role in the probe," and
"see that it includes a top-to-bottom
review of safety procedures at his ISS
production site in Brazil," where
the station's components are being
manufactured under UpLink's overall
management.

Gordian's assurance is viewed as a
sign that he intends to avoid the
divisive, public finger-pointing in
which NASA and its contractors
engaged after *Challenger*'s ill-fated
launch fifteen years ago. . . .

When Nimec and Megan spotted the police cruiser, it
was parked at the gravel shoulder of the road, about a
car length behind a red Toyota pickup, its roof racks
throwing off circus strobes of light.

The two officers, who had obviously arrived at the

scene in it, were scuffling with a third man outside the pickup.

One of the lawmen was fortyish and burly and wore a Hancock County deputy's uniform and badge. The other was perhaps twenty years younger and forty pounds leaner and wore a State of Maine warden's uniform and badge. The civilian, a tall, dark-haired man in a green chamois shirt, tan goose-down vest, jeans, and hiking boots, was standing out on the road with his back pressed up against the driver's door of his truck. The warden was jammed halfway inside the door, his head under the steering column, his body bent across the front seat, his backside sticking almost comically out of the cab. The deputy had the pickup driver's collar bunched in his fist and was attempting to wrestle him away from the door, but he was putting up a hard fight, shoving the deputy back with one hand, throwing punches at his face and neck with the other. The cop had an open cut below his right eye. A pair of mirrored sunglasses lay on the blacktop near his feet, one lens popped out of the wire frame. He was shouting furiously in the pickup driver's face, but neither Pete nor Megan could make out what he was saying through the windows of their Chevy.

"What in the world's going on up there?" she asked, peering out her side of the windshield.

Nimec breathed deeply and slowed the car.

"I don't know," he said. "But you see the guy in the green shirt?"

She glanced over at him, reading his face. "Pete, don't tell me."

Nimec breathed again.

"Tom Ricci," he said.

She looked outside again, rolling down her window to try and hear what the shouting was about.

Unable to pry him away from the truck, the thickset

deputy had switched tactics and moved in on Ricci, throwing his greater weight against him, getting him in a clinch. Standing his ground, Ricci caught him on the cheek with two quick overhand punches, then followed through with a right uppercut to the jaw. The deputy rocked backward on his heels, breaking his hold, his Smokey the Bear hat sailing off his head to the ground, where it flipped over once and then landed beside the broken sunglasses.

"You crazy son of a *flatlander bitch!*" he shouted, spitting blood. "I'm tellin' you, move away from that door or you're gonna be in deeper shit than you already are!"

Ricci stood there looking at him, hands balled into fists. The warden he'd pinned in the door squirmed a little, and Ricci kicked him in the back of the shin with his heel. A string of curses gushed from inside the cab.

Ricci seemed to pay no attention to them. Nor were any of the men yet paying attention to the Chevrolet that had eased to a halt some ten yards down the road.

"I already explained how it has to work," Ricci told the deputy. "I get to keep my product, your boy Cobbs gets to pull his ass out of the air. Otherwise we can all stick around here from now till Saint Swithen's Day."

The deputy wiped his mouth, glanced at the red-flecked saliva on his hand, and spat again.

"You got balls," he said, glaring. "Givin' me orders, expectin' me to believe some *concoction* about—"

"The catch is legit, Phipps."

"Says *you*. As Cobbs tells it, you 'n' your crackpot tender were way out past your zone."

"We can talk about Dex later. You and Cobbs saw my license."

"But I didn't see where your boat was, or where you was divin', or where you come up, and besides, that's all *his* area of respons'bility." Phipps poked his chin out at the pickup. "You let Cobbs be 'n' leave us the totes without any more carryin' on, maybe I let you slide for assaultin' an officer."

"Two officers! Don't you let the wicked fuck forget about me, Phipps!" Cobbs shouted from inside the cab. His head was still wedged beneath the steering wheel. *"Don't you goddamn let him—"*

Ricci kicked Cobbs with the heel of his boot again and his sentence ended in a yelp of pain.

Phipps released a heavy sigh.

"Two officers," he said.

"Two *crooked* officers."

Phipps frowned indignantly.

"That's it, no more crap from you," he said, dropping his hand to his holster and bringing out his side arm, a .45 Colt automatic.

In the Chevy, Megan turned to Nimec.

"Uh-oh," she said. "Looks like trouble."

He nodded and reached for his door handle.

"Sit tight," he said.

"Pete, you sure it's wise to—"

"No," he said. "I'm not."

And then shouldered open the door, exited the car, and walked toward the pickup over the narrow country road.

That was when Sheriff's Deputy Phipps seemed to take notice of him—belatedly and for the first time. He cast a quick glance at Nimec, then past him at the parked Chevy, keeping the pistol trained on Ricci . . . who had also partially turned in Nimec's direction.

"You *blind,* mister?" Phipps said. One eye on him, the other on Ricci. "Or did you just happen to miss what's going on here?"

Nimec shrugged.

"Tourist," he said. "We've been waiting awhile."

The deputy said nothing. He looked at the Chevy

again, this time suspiciously checking out its front tag.

"It's a rental," Nimec said. Stalling, trying to cook up some kind of plan that would extricate Ricci, not to mention himself, from the situation.

Whatever the hell the situation was.

"Wife and I are headed for Stonington," he said. "Figured I'd ask when we might be able to pass."

Phipps stared at him, vexed and confused.

"You see," Nimec said, "we've got reservations at an inn that they'll only hold for another half hour. And being that we just drove all the way up from Portland on Route 1—"

"Which is what you're gonna have to swing back around onto," Phipps interrupted. "Right this minute."

Nimec shook his head.

"Sorry," he said. "Can't do that."

Phipps looked incredulous. "*What* did you say?"

"Can't do that," Nimec repeated, knowing he'd really stepped into it now. "There aren't any other inns open. Being that this is the off-season."

Phipps flushed. Though he was still pointing his gun at Ricci, his attention had turned fully to Nimec.

"Another fuckin' *flatlander,* why the fuck we let them people into the fuckin' state of Maine?" Cobb screamed from inside the truck, his voice only slightly muffled. "You better arrest the whole queer bunch of them, Phipps, 'cause my back's gonna snap like a *twig* I stay stooped over like this!"

Phipps eyed Nimec with a kind of hostile exasperation, unconsciously wagging his head, looking uncertain about what to do next.

An instant later Ricci made the decision for him. Taking advantage of Phipps's distraction, he suddenly stepped away from the door of the pickup, caught hold of his outstretched gun hand at the wrist, and bent it sharply backward, simultaneously turning sideways and snatching the pistol with his free hand.

Phipps released a cry of pain and surprise as the pistol was torn from his grasp. He was still gaping in disbelief when Ricci's leg snapped forward and up in a powerful front kick, the ball of his foot striking him in the broad, chunky stretch of his stomach. The air whoofing out of him, he stumbled backward and landed hard on his bottom, his legs wishboned in front of him.

Cobbs, meanwhile, had pulled his head out of the pickup's open door and come charging at Ricci from behind. But before he had gotten more than a couple of feet, Ricci spun in a smooth circle on his left leg, his right leg swinging parallel to the ground and thrusting out at the knee, catching Cobbs in the groin with a roundhouse kick. He flew back against the side of the car and doubled over, groaning, his hands between his thighs.

Ricci ejected the Colt's magazine and tossed it into the spindling roadside brush, then shoved the gun into his vest pocket. Nodding at him, Nimec rushed over to Cobb and took his pistol from its holster. Its clip joined the one that was already in the bushes.

Ricci knelt over Phipps and patted down the bottom of his trouser legs.

"Nothing there to say peekaboo?" he said.

Phipps glared and shook his head.

"Okay," Ricci told him, stepping back. "Here's how it goes. We're all driving off, me with my catch, you two without your guns, our friendly tourist with his nice wife and rental car. You forget about this thing, maybe I don't report the little scam you and Cobbs tried running on me to Fish and Game or the attorney general's office down in Augusta. You *really* behave yourselves, maybe I won't tell anybody in town how I kicked both your asses and disarmed you barehanded. In two seconds flat."

Phipps continued glaring at him in baleful silence for another moment, then slowly nodded.

"Good," Ricci said. "Stay right where you are until I'm gone. Ground needs thawing anyway."

Phipps snorted, hawked over his shoulder, and looked back up at him. "How the hell am I supposed to explain losing my gun?"

Ricci shrugged.

"Your problem," he said.

Behind them, Cobbs was still leaning against the pickup, moaning and clutching himself. Ricci turned, strode over to him, grabbed his shoulder, and shoved him roughly away from the truck. Cobbs tripped and fell on his side, drawing his knees toward his chest.

Ricci looked at Nimec, then moved up close to him.

"Poor bastard should've kept his hands off my ignition keys," he said in a voice too low for the others to hear. "Welcome to Vacationland, Pete. Better get back in your car and follow along behind me. I'll explain everything once we're at my place."

They had come in from the rugged plateau country of Chapada dos Guimarães, a convoy of four dusty jeeps bumping along the unpaved track in the deepening dusk, traversing the seventy kilometers to their destination with arduous slowness. After many long hours of riding shotgun in the forward car, Kuhl had finally seen the compound through a break in the overhanging foliage, and then ordered their headlights dimmed and their vehicles pulled off the road.

Once under cover of the trees, he turned to his driver. *"Que horas são?"*

The driver showed him the luminous dial of his wristwatch.

Kuhl studied it a moment without comment. Then he glanced over his seat rest and nodded to the man behind him.

"Vaya aqui, Antonio."

Antonio returned the nod. He was dressed entirely in black and had a Barrett M82A1 sniper's rifle across his lap. Accurate to a range exceeding a mile, it utilized the same self-loading, armor-piercing .50-caliber ammunition normally fired by heavy machine guns—bullets capable of pounding through an inch or more of solid steel armor. The weapon's incredible firepower and semiautomatic action were its notable advantages over other sniper guns. On the negative side, it was weighty, long-barreled, and would kick back with a recoil matching its destructive performance. But Antonio's targets would be shielded, and he would need to penetrate that shield at a considerable distance.

Slinging the Barrett over his shoulder, he opened his door and slipped from the jeep into the darkness.

Kuhl settled back and looked out the windshield. His team was right on schedule despite the wearisome inconveniences of their ride. There was nothing to do now except wait for Antonio to complete his work, and then for the others to arrive and give their signal. Perhaps he would even be able to glimpse them coming over the treetops.

They sat in absolute silence, hard, lean men in black combat outfits, their faces daubed from chin to forehead with camouflage paint. All but the sniper who'd gone on ahead carried French FAMAS assault rifles fitted with modular high-explosive munition launchers and day/night target-tracking systems.

Still undergoing field trials by the French military, these adaptations of the standard FAMAS guns represented the state of the art in small arms, and were not slated for mass production or issuance to general infantry troops until 2003—two full years in the future.

Kuhl always made it a point to stay ahead of the game. It cost money, true, but unless one was willing to accept failure, the expense was more than acceptable. And he himself was paid handsomely enough that he didn't mind spreading the wealth.

Impatient, he raised his night-vision goggles to his eyes, swung them from the compound's checkpoint gate to the pair of men occupying its sentry booth, then studied the irregular outline of the buildings that lay beyond. He wanted nothing more than to get moving. While his team might be outside the observable range of the compound's guards, he had seen enough in his mercenary career to know that only a fool or an amateur neglected to consider the unpredictable, and that each passing second brought an increased risk of discovery. It mattered little how well they formulated their plans, or how careful they were in bringing about their execution.

Secrecy, he thought. It was an essential requirement of his profession, and yet the very idea paradoxically seemed a joke. In an age when satellites could photograph a mole on your chin from somewhere up in space, there were no true blind spots, and nobody was ever out of sight for long. The best one could wish for was temporary concealment. If his men failed at that, if they were noticed too soon, all their elaborate precautions would be worthless.

Kuhl sat, watched, and waited. In his taut silence, he could almost feel that gigantic, damnable eye overhead, looking down, *pressing* down. Seeing what it wanted to see, peering through every shadow, its relentless gaze scouring the world. . . .

Yes, Kuhl felt it up there, he did, and was only hoping it would once again blink as he went about the lucrative business of destruction.

●　　●　　●

"There's smoke in the cabin. Elevated CA 19-9 and CA 125 levels. LH2 pressure's dropping. Terra nos respuet."

Annie feels her book about to slip off her lap, catches it just in the nick of time. She blinks once or twice, completely out of sorts, guessing she'd sunk into a light sleep while reading on her sofa.

She *had* been reading, hadn't she?

She readjusts the book and glances up at the man standing in front of her, the man whose voice startled her from her doze. In his midfifties, he has reddish-brown hair, a full mustache, and is wearing a white doctor's frock. Phil Lieberman, she thinks. The oncologist who has taken over her husband's case, not exactly the type to make house calls. She wonders what he's doing in her living room, wonders whether one of the kids might have let him in the door . . . but then suddenly realizes that this isn't her living room after all, isn't even part of her home, and that the children are nowhere around her.

She straightens, blinks again, rubs her eyes.

The chair on which she is sitting is contoured plastic. The air has a recycled quality and carries commingled antiseptic and medicinal smells. The walls are an institutional noncolor.

It abruptly dawns on her that she is in the hospital.

In the hospital, in the third-floor waiting room that has become so numbingly familiar over these past few months, and where she must have dropped off like a stone with an open book on her lap. The hospital, of course. However strange it might ordinarily seem for her to have forgotten, these are far from ordinary days, and her brief disorientation is understandable in view of what's been happening in her life. She has gone for weeks with precious little rest, rushing from her husband's bedside to her training sessions at the Center and back again, trying not to neglect the kids amid her com-

pounding pressures. It would not be the first time lately that the effort of keeping everything together has caught up to her without warning.

Looking at the doctor, she begins fidgeting nervously with the edges of the book—actually, she sees now, it is a magazine, a dog-eared copy of Newsweek *with a featured piece about upcoming space shuttle launches connected with the ISS program—the magazine, then, that is spread across her thighs. The doctor's expression is unrevealing, his voice without intonation, but there is a sobriety in his eyes that sends a cold, silent shiver running through her.*

"Like the old Titan rockets," he says. "Third stage fires, you're up and out."

"What?" she says. "What was it you—"

"Mark's latest tests, we need to discuss their results," he interrupts with the kind of patronizing abruptness medical professionals seem to take as their right, an exalted privilege bestowed on them the moment they recite the Hippocratic Oath. It is as though even the ones capable of showing some compassion—and Annie acknowledges that Lieberman has, by and large, been decent with her—must insist on reminding you they have other patients, other cases, more urgent demands than having to explain their findings.

"Laparoscopic exam revealed metastic tumors in the liver and gallbladder," he says rapidly. "Statistically common once the disease has spread from the intestine to so many of its associated lymph nodes. Would have had a better chance with three lymphomas, but five is quite a bad crop. Very, very unfortunate."

Annie sits very still as she listens, but can feel herself crumbling from the inside out, truly crumbling, as if her soul is made of brittle, hundred-year-old plaster. She gives him a decimated look.

"He'll be gone in five months," she says, the absolute

certainty behind those words filling her with horror and bewilderment. She feels weirdly detached from the sound of her own voice, almost as if she hasn't really spoken at all, but is listening to a tape recording of herself, or maybe even some flawless impersonation issuing from a concealed intercom.

Dr. Lieberman regards her a moment in that serious yet matter-of-fact way of his. Then he shrugs his sleeve back from his wristwatch, glances down at it, and holds it out to her, turning his arm to display the dial.

"Yes, five months, three days, to be precise," he says. "We're on the fast track now. Time runs by until there's none left."

Perplexed by his comment, Annie looks at the watch.

Her eyes quickly grow enormous.

Its face is a blank white circle. Perfectly featureless, without digits, hands, or markings of any kind.

She feels another chunk of herself give way.

Blank.

The face of the watch is blank.

"Stay calm, Annie, it tends to run a bit ahead," Lieberman says. "There's still a chance for you to say good-bye."

Annie suddenly finds herself out of her chair, and this time makes no attempt to catch her magazine as it spills off her thighs, landing on the floor at her feet. From the corner of her eye, she sees that the cover, which has partially folded under one of the interior pages, consists of a photo of a shuttle and launch tower consumed by a roiling ball of flame. Its bold red copy—also less than altogether visible from where she stands—screams something about an explosion involving Orion, *one of the mid-schedule ISS assembly flights.*

Confusion churns within her. How can this be? Orion's *mission is still a couple of years off, and besides, the article had been an overview of the ISS program . . . at least she'd* thought *it had . . .*

All at once Annie isn't sure she remembers, just as she'd initially been unable to remember being at the hospital. Her memory seems a flat, slippery surface without depth or width.

"Your husband is in Room 377. But you already know that, you've been there before," Dr. Lieberman is saying. He gestures toward the far end of the corridor. "Not often enough, perhaps, although I'm no one to talk. We're both busy professionals."

Annie watches Lieberman turn in the opposite direction, her eyes following him as he starts up the hall. While his voice had remained neutral, that last remark had been superloaded with accusation, and she is unwilling to let it pass. He might think it is his God-given prerogative to relate his test results without climbing down off his perch to tell her what he means to do about them, but if there is some criticism he wants to level at her, then he damn well ought to be saying it in plain English.

She starts to call out to him, but before she can utter a sound, Lieberman pauses and looks back at her, giving her a thumbs-up.

"Turnips first and always," he says, and grins. "I'd advise you to hurry."

Then he tips her a little salute and hustles up the hall, dwindling in perspective like a motion picture character about to vanish over the horizon.

I'd advise you to hurry.

Her heart stroking in her chest, she forgets about Lieberman and whirls toward the room in which her husband lies dying.

In instant later Annie is standing at its door. Breathless, she feels like she's come running over to it at full tilt, yet has no sense of her legs having carried her from *the waiting room, of physically moving from point A to point B, of* transition. *It is as if she'd been staring at Lieberman's back one moment, and found herself here in front of the door the next, trying to stop herself from falling to pieces in spite of the death sentence that has been pronounced upon her husband.*

For his sake, trying to hold up.

She takes a deep gulp of air, another. Then she reaches for the doorknob, turns it, and steps through into the room.

The light inside is all wrong.

Odd as it may be for her to register this before anything else, it is nevertheless what happens. The light is wrong. Not exactly dim, but diffuse enough to severely limit her vision. Although she can see the foot of her husband's bed without any problem, things start to blur immediately beyond it. As if through a layer of gauze, she sees the tubes, fluid drains, and monitor wires that run to the bed, sees the outline of Mark's legs under the blankets, sees that he is resting on his back, but his face . . .

She thinks suddenly of those televised news reports in which someone's features are concealed to protect his or her anonymity, the sort that might involve use of a hidden camera, or show crime suspects being led toward their arraignments by the police. Pictures in which it almost looks as if Vaseline has been dabbed over the part of the frame in which the person's face ought to appear.

That is how Annie sees her husband from the doorway of Room 377 in the hospital where he will die of cancer in five months and three days. Five months, three days that have somehow collapsed into a dreadful and inexplicable now.

"Annie?"

Mark's voice is a hoarse whisper. Its weakness shakes

47

Annie, and for an instant she thinks she is going to burst into tears. She covers her trembling lips with her palm.

"Annie, that you?"

She stands there, trying to regain her composure, the room silent except for the quiet beeping of the instruments at Mark's bedside. The fuzziness of the light makes her feel strangely lost and isolated, like a small boat adrift in fog.

Finally she lowers her hand from her mouth.

"Yes," she says. "It's me, hon. I'm here."

He slips his right arm partially out from under his blankets and beckons her with a feeble wave. His face is still a blur, but she has no difficulty seeing the gesture.

Her eyes fall briefly on the sleeve of his pajama.

"Come over here, Annie," he says. "Hard to talk when you're standing there by the door."

She steps forward into the room. His sleeve. Something about it isn't right, something about the color of it—

"Come on, what are you waiting for?" he says. Pulling his arm further out from underneath his blankets and tapping the safety rail of his bed. "You belong with me."

There is a harshness in Mark's voice, an anger that has become huge within him in recent days—but although Annie often brushes up against its sharp outer edges, she is aware that the cancer is its real target. In the beginning it had flared up from beneath the surface only on occasion, but its progression has matched that of the disease, consuming him, ravaging his personality. He is resentful of his loss of independence, resentful of his inability to care for himself, resentful of his neediness . . . and beyond all else resentful of having his future stolen from him by something as insipid and indiscriminate as an uncontrollable growth of cells. Annie has come to accept those feelings as constants that she is helpless to relieve, and can only hope to skirt past on delicate tiptoes.

She wades through the filmy light toward her husband. His IV stand and the wall of beeping instruments are on the left side of the bed, so she walks around its foot to the right and rolls back his plastic hospital tray in order to approach him.

Suddenly his hand reaches over the safety rail and clutches her wrist.

"Give it to us, Annie," he says. "Let's hear how sorry you are."

She stands there in shock as his fingers press into her with impossible strength.

"We trusted you," he says.

His fingers are digging deeper into the soft white flesh under her wrist, hurting her now. Though Annie knows they will leave bruises, she does not attempt to pull away. She looks at Mark across the bed, wishing she could see his face, mystified by his words. Their hostility is more intense, more cuttingly directed at her than at any time in the past, but she can't understand why.

"Mark, please, tell me what you mean—"

"My girl," he breaks in. "Always in a hurry, rushing from one place to another without a look back."

She winces as his grip tightens.

Us. We.

Who can he be talking about? Himself and the kids? Annie can scarcely guess.

No, that isn't the truth. Not really.

The simple, inescapable truth is that she's afraid to guess.

His grip tightens.

She wishes she could see his face.

"You were supposed to be responsible. Supposed to look out for us," he says.

Annie still doesn't pull away, absolutely refuses to

pull away. Instead she moves closer to him, pressing up against the bed rail, thinking if she could just see his face, if they could just see each other eye-to-eye, he would stop this nonsense about her leaving him—

The thought is abruptly clipped short as her eyes once again fall on his sleeve. The color, yes, the color, how had she failed to identify it right away? She doesn't know the answer, but realizes now that what he's wearing isn't a pajama, its carrot-red color and heavy padded fabric marking it as, of all things, all impossible things under the sun, a NASA flight/reentry suit. At the same instant this occurs to her, the quiet beep of the instruments measuring her husband's vital functions pitches up to a shrill alarm, an earsplitting sound she recognizes from some other place, some other when.

It is a sound that makes her gasp with horror.

The faceless man in the bed is shouting at her at the top of his voice: "H2 pressure's dropping! Look for yourself! Check the readings!"

On impulse, Annie shoots her gaze over to the right side of the bed, recognizes the forward consoles of a space shuttle where she had seen hospital instruments only moments before. For some reason this causes her little surprise. She takes in the various panels with a series of hurried glances, her eyes leaping from the master alarm lights to the smoke-detection indicators on the left-hand panel of the commander's console, and then over to the main engine status displays below the center CRT.

Again, what she sees is not unexpected.

"Stay calm, Annie, we're on the fast track now! Better reach for that ejection lever or nobody's making it home!" *the man in the bed practically howls, and then wrenches her arm with such violence that she stumbles off balance and crashes forward against the rail. She flies across it, whimpering, throwing out her free hand to check her fall. It lands on the mattress beside him, preventing her from sprawling clear across his chest.*

"The world spits us up and out, so where's our goddamned parachute?"

He keeps holding onto her right arm, keeps shouting at Annie as she braces herself up over him with her left. Though their faces are just inches apart, his features are still too distorted for her to make them out.

Then, suddenly, the sense of disconnection she had experienced in the waiting room recurs for a fleeting moment, only now it is as if she's been split in two, part of her watching the scene from high above while the other struggles with the man on the bed. And with this feeling comes the whole and certain knowledge that his face would not belong to her husband if she could see it; no, not her husband, but someone else she has loved in a very different way, loved and lost. Annie doesn't understand how she knows, but she does, she does, and the knowledge terrifies her, seeming to rise on the crest of a building hysteria.

"Where's our goddamned parachute?" *he shouts again, and yanks hard at her wrist, pulling her down onto himself. As she finally tries to break away, Annie catches another glimpse of his clutching fingers . . . and sees for the first time that they are horribly burned, the fingernails gone, the outer layer of skin sloughing off the knuckles, baring raw, strawberry-red flesh underneath.*

She wants to scream, tells herself she must *scream, thinking . . . still without knowing why . . . that it might somehow bring her ordeal to an end. But it refuses to come, it is trapped in her throat, and all she can do is produce a small cry of anguish that is torn to shreds by her vocal cords even as she wrings it out of them—*

Annie awakened with a jolt, her heart knocking in her chest, the trailing edge of a moan on her mouth. She had broken out in a cold sweat, her T-shirt plastered to her body.

She looked around, taking a series of deep breaths, shaking her head as if to cast off the lacy remnants of her dream.

She was home. In Houston, in her living room, on her sofa. From the TV in the kids' room she could hear the *Teletubbies* carrying on with manic effervescence. On the carpet at her feet, her newspaper was still folded to the article she'd been reading when she'd fallen into an exhausted sleep. Its headline read: "AFTERMATH OF TRAGEDY." Above the columns of text was a photo of *Orion* in its catastrophic final moments.

Annie bent her head and covered her stinging eyes with her palm.

She'd flown back from the Center after having been there since very early that morning and attended meeting after meeting in which the participants—NASA executives, government officials, and representatives of the various shuttle and ISS contractors—had ostensibly been trying to sift through what they knew about the accident and lay out a preliminary framework for an investigation into its causes. Instead, they had spent the majority of the time staring at one another in dazed silence.

Perhaps, Annie thought, it had been a mistake to expect anything more constructive so soon after the explosion. At any rate, she had felt nothing but a sense of leaden futility by the end of the final session, and been grateful for the chance to go home.

Home sweet home, where she could take her mind off what had happened, enjoy some light reading and a refreshing nap before getting started on dinner.

Her hand still clapped over her eyes, she felt a small, bleak smile touch her lips.

An instant later the tears began streaming between her fingers.

• • •

The Barrett rifle against his shoulder, his cheek to its stock, Antonio aligned his target in the crosshairs of its high-magnification sight.

Moments after leaving Kuhl's vehicle, he had scurried up a tree that afforded a direct line of fire with the guard station, and was now half-sitting, half-squatting in the fork of its trunk, his feet braced on two strong branches. The thirty-pound weapon ordinarily required a bipod for support, but here on his treetop perch he'd been able to rest its barrel over his upraised knees.

He inhaled, exhaled, gathering his concentration. A series of dry trigger pulls had helped him find a comfortable body position and make minor adjustments to his aim. He would be shooting across a distance of over nine hundred yards, and could not afford to be even slightly off balance.

There were two guards inside the booth. One stood at a coffeemaker, pouring from its glass pot into a cup. The other sat over some papers at a small metal desk. He would be the second kill. The man on his feet would have greater mobility, and a mobile target always had the best chance of escape, requiring that it be the first to be taken out.

Antonio took another inhalation, held it. The guard at the coffee machine had filled his cup and was putting the pot back on its warming pad. He raised the coffee to his lips, but would never get a chance to drink it. In a practical sense he was already dead. The booth's bullet-resistant window would be easily penetrated by the tungston-carbide SLAP rounds chambered in Antonio's weapon, doing the men behind it no good at all.

"Mi mano, su vida," he whispered, releasing his breath. As always before a kill, he felt very close to God.

He pulled smoothly on the trigger of his weapon, his eye and forefinger welded in seamless action.

His gun bucked. A bullet split the air. The window shattered. The guard spun where he stood and went down, the coffee cup flying from his hand.

Antonio breathed again, took aim again.

Still behind his desk, the second guard barely had the time to turn toward his crumpled partner before another bullet whistled in from the night and caught him in the left temple, tearing through his skull and snapping him up and out of his seat.

The sniper remained in position a short while longer, wanting to be thorough, watchful of any hint of movement in the sentry booth. Nothing stirred in the pale yellow light spilling from its blown-out window. Satisfied he'd gotten two clean kills, he shouldered the rifle, and was about to slip from the tree when a fluttering sound overhead gave him momentary pause.

A glance up through the foliage revealed that he'd been none too hasty in executing his task.

The jump team had arrived and was descending from the darkness.

FOUR

CLEARING THE PERIMETER FENCE BY A HUNDRED ME-
ters, Manuel dropped his gear bag on a tether and continued his descent into the compound. He was aware of
his teammates floating in behind him, aware of the
ground rushing up.

Now he pulled his left toggle to turn into the slight
westerly wind, trimmed more altitude, waited until he
felt the bag land below him with a thump, and hit the
quick-release snap to disengage it. An instant later, he
drew both toggles evenly down to his waist to flare the
chute. It collapsed in on itself, spilling air.

He landed softly on the balls of his feet.

His chin low to his chest, Manuel let himself move
forward in a kind of loose-legged trot, remaining up-
right, checking his momentum as he separated himself
from the canopy. The others, meanwhile, had come rus-
tling to the ground on either side of him. Most of them
were also on their feet, but one or two had dropped a
little harder, tumbling onto their backs and sides in fluid
parachute landing falls.

And then they were up and slipping free of their harnesses. They hurried to recover their bags and collect the equipment inside them—grenades, plastic explosive charges, and upgraded FAMAS rifles like those that would be used by the extraction team. Exchanging their jump helmets and goggles for combat helmets with optical display units, they donned dark special-purpose visors, coupled the electronic gunsights on their rifles to the helmet-mounted displays, lowered their monocular eyepieces, and then stealthily moved out at their leader's command, splitting into three groups of four.

If the information they had obtained was correct, it would only be seconds, at most minutes, before their presence was detected.

Along with other things of vital interest to their employer, that information would be well tested as the night ran its course.

The employees at the facility mostly called them "hedgehogs."

Rollie Thibodeau, who headed the night security detail, preferred the term "li'l bastards," grumbling that the way they responded to certain situations resembled human behavior a bit too closely for comfort. But Rollie was technophobic to an extreme degree, and being a Louisiana Cajun, felt an inborn obligation to be both voluble and contrary.

Still, when he was in a generous mood, he would acknowledge their value by adding that they were *"smart* li'l bastards."

In fact, the mobile security robots weren't very bright at all, possessing the approximate intelligence of the beetles and other insects that hedgehogs of the living, mammalian variety preferred to dine upon. And while they could function as surrogates for human beings in performing a host of physical tasks, scientific experts of an Asimovean bent would have contended it was improper, or at the very least imprecise, to even define them as robots, since they were incapable of autonomous thought and action, slaved to remote computers, and ultimately monitored and controlled by human guards.

True robots, these experts might assert, would have the ability to make independent decisions and act upon them without any help from their creators, and were perhaps twenty or thirty years from actual development. What existed now, and what laymen wrongly considered to be robots, were actually robot*like* machines.

These conflicting definitions aside, the hedgehogs were versatile, sophisticated gadgets that had been put to effective use patrolling the four-thousand-acre ISS manufacturing compound in Mato Grosso do Sul. Through a rather complicated agreement with the Brazilian government and a half-dozen other countries involved in the space station's construction, UpLink International had managed to win administrative and managerial control of the plant, simultaneously assuming blanket responsibility for its protection—something the Brazilian negotiators had been finagled into thinking was an expensive concession on UpLink's part, but which had actually pleased Roger Gordian and his security chief, Pete Nimec, to no end. If their experience operating in transitional and politically unstable nations had taught them anything, it was that nobody could look out for them as well as they could look out for themselves.

The hedgehogs unarguably made looking out for themselves easier. "R2D2 on steroids" is how Thibodeau described them, and in its own way that was an apt representation. Their omnidirectional color video cameras were encased in rounded turrets atop vertical racks or "necks," giving them a vaguely anthropomorphic appearance that many female staffers found cute—as did quite a few of the plant's male employees, though rarely by open admission. Mounted on tracked 6x6 drive platforms, they were quick, quiet, and capable of maneuvering across everything from narrow corridors and stairwells to rugged, heavily obstacled outdoor terrain. Products of UpLink's own R&D, they boasted a wide range of proprietary hardware-and-software-based systems. Their hazard/intruder detection array included broad-spectrum gas, smoke, temperature, optical flame, microwave radar, vehicular sonar, passive infrared, seismic, and ambient light sensors. Their clawed, retractable gripper arms were strong enough to lift twenty-five-pound objects and precise enough to pick the smallest coins up off the ground.

Nor were the hedgehogs limited to merely sounding the alarm should they find something amiss. They were, rather, midnight riders and first-wave militia rolled into one, ready to neutralize threats ranging from chemical fires to trespassers on command. Packed aboard their chassis were fluid cannons that could unleash high-pressure jets of water, polymer superglues, and anti-traction superlubricants; 12-gauge sidewinder shotguns loaded with disabling aerosol cartridges; laser-dazzler and visual stimulus and illusion banks; and other fruits of UpLink's ambitious nonlethal weapons program.

There were a total of six hedgehogs at the Brazilian compound, four posted near the borders of its approximately rectangular grounds, an additional pair safeguarding its central buildings. Each of the ground patrols encompassed an entire perimeter line and a parallel sector reaching inward for one hundred meters, and each mechanical sentry on that beat had been given a nickname whose first initial corresponded with the first letter of the direction it covered: Ned toured the northern perimeter, Sammy the compound's south side, Ed its eastern margin, Wally its western. The two indoor sentries were Felix and Oscar, assigned to the factory and office complexes respectively. On average, a hedgehog would patrol for eight to ten hours at a stretch before having to recharge its nickel-cadmium batteries at one of the docking stations along its route, with more frequent pauses in the event of an increased task load.

And so they went about their rounds, smooth-running and tireless, responding to an anomalous motion here, an unusual variation in temperature there, investigating whatever seemed not to belong, relaying a stream of environmental data to monitoring stations attended by their human supervisors, and alerting them to any sign of danger or unauthorized entry along the fenced-in margins of the compound.

An invasion from above, however, was another matter altogether.

The hedgehog was midway through its third tour of the facility's western quadrant when its infrared sensors picked up a wavelength reading of twelve to fourteen microns—the distinctive heat signature of a human being—some fifty yards in front of it.

The robot paused, tracking the emission source, but it had quickly backed out of sensor range.

Its computers triangulating the object's line of movement to project its likely path of retreat, the hedgehog gave chase, slinging across the rocky soil on its all-terrain carrier.

Suddenly another source of human IR emissions appeared, this one behind the hedgehog.

Then a third on its right, and a fourth on the left.

The robot stopped again, boxed in. Its various turret sensors needed just an instant to perform a sweep extending for fifty meters in a full circle. At the same time, its infrared illuminator was casting a light field that enabled its night video equipment to scan for images in the pitch darkness.

Again the four anomalous radiation sources dashed into and out of range, still surrounding the robot, their pattern of motion keeping them roughly equidistant from it.

Its logical systems correlating the input from its probes, the hedgehog had definitively classified the circling objects as human entities and potential threats. But very much by design, its programming did not include any options for dealing with them.

Instead, it was transmitting the processed data to its monitoring site via an encrypted radio channel, leaving its flesh-and-blood handlers to decide what to do next.

"What's up with Wally?" Jezoirski said. "You see how he's sniffing around?"

"Yeah," Delure replied with concern. "And I don't like it a bit."

Beside them, Cody, the senior man in the room, leaned pensively over his surveillance monitors and said nothing.

At their monitoring station in the bowels of the Brazilian ISS compound, the guards were studying a complex bank of dials, controls, and electronic displays that placed them at the informational heart of its security network. All three wore the indigo uniforms and newly issued shoulder patches—these depicting a broadsword surrounded by stylized satellite bandwidth lines—of UpLink's global intelligence and threat countermeasure force, dubbed Sword as a reference to the legend of the Gordian knot, which Alexander the Great was supposed to have undone with a swift and decisive stroke of his blade. It was a method analogous to Roger Gordian's no-nonsense approach to crisis management, making for some interesting word play, and forming the direct basis of the section name.

Jezoirski slid forward in his chair, his features limned by the pale green radiance of an infrared video display, his eyes on the IR meter directly beneath it.

"Shit," he said. "Look at that heat emission. Somebody's definitely out th—"

Jezoirski broke off midsentence as a warning indicator lit up on the panel. He glanced over at Delure, who took hurried note of this development and then pointed back at the video screen.

Green-on-green images flashed across the monitor— a group of human figures moving around the security robot, alternately closing in and backing away.

Cody thought of bloodhounds harrying their prey. But why would those sons of bitches play tag with the 'hog? The robots' main effectiveness lay in their early alert and standoff capabilities against a perimeter attack. Their purpose was to buy time until human reinforcements arrived, to repel or delay an intrusion attempt while it was in progress. Their purpose was *not* to engage in close skirmishing once the grounds were already compromised. At that stage getting past them would be easy, and crippling or taking them out just slightly more difficult.

His forehead crunched with tension, he scanned the radar imagery in front of him. On screen, the hedgehog and the men surrounding it showed up as color-coded shapes positioned against a set of grid lines and numerical coordinates.

"This doesn't make any sense," Jezoirski said. "There's nothing to show the outer fence was breached—"

"We can worry about that later." Cody was already reaching for the phone as he broke his silence. "Key the 'hogs for full gamut intruder suppression. I'm getting Thibodeau on the horn."

• • •

On Jezoirski's radioed command, Wally hit them with a barrage of light and sound.

Its first optical counterstrike was a burst from the neodymium-YAG laser projector on its turret. To the four men around the robot, it seemed almost as if a small nova had ignited at ground level, momentarily filling the night with diamond-edged brilliance.

They scattered rapidly, fanning out over several yards—but the flash was something for which they had come prepared. They had known that a laser pulse could temporarily impair the vision or burn out the retina, dazzle or blind, depending on its power, intensity, and length. They had also known that the weapons used by Sword's robotic defenders were calibrated to produce no lasting damage. And they had worn dark filters on their visors to shield them from the brightness, correctly betting this would make its effects tolerable.

The hedgehog's sensory assault, however, was about to kick into overdrive. The laser flash had barely faded in the air when a group of red-and-blue halogen lights on Wally's main equipment case began to strobe in a preprogrammed sequence, its pattern and frequency closely matching that of normal human brain waves. At precisely the same instant, the robot's acoustic generator had begun transmitting 100-decibel *sound*waves at a controlled rate of ten cycles per second. It was a resonance the invaders seemed to feel more than actually hear, a sour, abrasive humming that remained just below the level of audibility, working its way deep into their bodies, swelling thickly in their stomachs and intestines.

Each directed-energy weapon worked on the same principle, targeting specific areas within the human body, coupling the spectrum of its emission to characteristic waveforms within those areas, and manipulating them by hyperstimulation. The flashing lights attacked the visual receptors of the hindbrain, triggering a storm of electrical activity akin to the sort that occurred during a sudden attack of epilepsy. The acoustic generator had multiple targets—the inner ear, where abnormal vibrations of the fluid within its semicircular canals would throw the sense of balance into upheaval, and the soft organs of the abdomen, where similar vibrations would lead to convulsions of pain and nausea.

The combined effect of these measures overtook the invaders at once, scrambling their senses and motor functions, confusing and sickening them, provoking a hallucinatory and physically wrenching disconnection from their surroundings. Shaking, gagging, and retching, they staggered in confused, purposeless circles. One of them dropped onto his back, his bladder releasing, grotesque herky-jerky spasms running through his limbs. Another sank to his knees, clutched his heaving stomach, and vomited.

Partially overcome, Manuel knew he had bare moments in which to act. Forcing his legs to remain steady underneath him, he turned in what he thought was the hedgehog's direction, clenched his eyes against its strobing lights, raised his FAMAS rifle, and pumped a 20mm HE round from its grenade launcher attachment. It was a crude, inaccurate use of an extraordinarily refined weapon, but it achieved its desired results. The shell struck the 'hog's carrier scant yards from where he stood, detonating with an explosive flash.

Manuel dove to the ground as the concussion swept over him, waited a second or two, then got back to his feet and dusted himself off. A quick look around revealed that one member of his band had been killed in the blast, his flesh and clothing shredded by flying shrapnel. He himself had an open gash above the elbow. But the robot was wreckage. It leaned sideways on the burning remains of a rubber track, smoke and flames spitting from its mangled carrier. He could smell the odor of its fused wiring.

Wreckage.

He saw his remaining teammates struggling to regain their equilibrium, allowed them a few moments to recover, then hurried to gather them to his side. There was no time to linger over their single casualty.

"Vaya aqui!" he hissed. "Come on, we still have work to do."

Much as Rollie Thibodeau loved his job at UpLink, much as he felt it was an *important* job, he hated how its hours screwed up his biological clock, turned his daily routine inside out, and cramped his lifestyle in more ways than he could have stated.

Take sex, or the lack of it, for one thing. Where would he find a woman who'd be in amorous sync with his schedule, falling into bed with the sunrise, emerging after sunset like a vampire? Take sleep for another. This was Brazil, land of bronzed bodies and the *fio dental*. How could he get any rest with the tropical daylight pressing against his window blinds, tantalizing him with its warmth, reminding him of the long, gorgeously romantic afternoons dancing past? Take, for a third example, something as important to a man as eating. Could cheerfulness truly be expected of him when his meals were fouled up beyond description? It was rotten enough being a hundred miles from the nearest city and having to subsist on the bland, unseasoned fare they served in the commissary. Rotten even when those tasteless dishes were hot out of the kitchen. But consuming them after they'd sat in a refrigerator for half a day, and then been warmed over in a microwave, was a gross indignity. And the hours at which one was forced to eat when working the night shift, *calous ve,* the hours were nothing short of unspeakable!

Thibodeau sat in his small but tidy office in a sublevel of the ISS compound's main headquarters building, staring down at the plate of overcooked beef and watery, reconstituted mashed potatoes on his desk with a kind of savage contempt. It was slightly past eight P.M., and a new kid on his shift by the name of McFarlane had just strolled in with the meal, holding a dish for himself as well, looking as if he could hardly wait to get back to his post and dig into it . . . something that had so annoyed Thibodeau, he'd been unable to even feign appreciation as he dismissed the youngster, which left him feeling still worse for having rudely punished the messenger for the message.

Well, he would just have to make it up to him later. Explain that even the most upbeat person in the world could have his disposition ruined by two years of eating lunch at eight o'clock at night, and a repulsive approximation of dinner between midnight and three in the morning. Breakfast alone provided a modicum of satisfaction, and only because the prep cooks would arrive for work around six o'clock, giving him an opportunity to send for some fresh eggs or waffles before the end of his shift, and thus eat at least one relatively decent meal at a relatively sane hour.

"Lord, thank you for our fuckin' daily slop," Thibodeau muttered in his thick Cajun accent.

His features glum, he was about to reach for his knife and fork when the phone at his elbow shrilled. He glanced over at it, saw the redline light blinking, and promptly snatched up the handset.

Other than for training drills, the extension had never been used during his term at the facility.

"Yes?" he said.

The man on the line was Cody from the monitoring station.

"Sir, there's been a penetration."

"Where?" Thibodeau sat up straight, his culinary woes forgotten.

"The western quadrant." Cody's voice was edged with tension. "Wally detected several intruders. Thing I don't understand, we aren't seeing any damage along the fence. No sign perimeter integrity's been violated."

"You sic the li'l bastard on 'em?"

"Affirmative. We actuated its VSI banks and acoustic cannon, but . . ." A hesitant pause. "Sir, Wally's gone off-line. It doesn't look good."

Thibodeau breathed. He'd insisted a thousand times that the 'hogs couldn't be trusted. The hell of it was, he'd never *once* wanted to be proven right.

"You hear from Henderson and Travers at the gate?"

"We've been trying to radio them and there's been no response."

"Christ," Thibodeau said. "Send some men out right away. I also want a full detail around the plant and warehouse buildings. Seal 'em up tight, hear me?"

"Yes, sir."

Thibodeau paused to collect his thoughts, gripping the receiver in his fist. He was anxious to get into the monitoring room and see what was happening for himself. But first he wanted to be sure he was covering all his bases.

"We better have us some air support ready," he said after a moment. *"Laissez les bons temps rouler."*

"What was that, sir?"

Thibodeau rose from his seat. "Tell the chopper pilots to fasten their goddamn seat belts, out."

Manuel crouched behind the gate, his arm throbbing, the sleeve of his jumpsuit warm and moist where he'd been injured. His rapid movement had worsened the bleeding, but the sentry robot's destruction was certain to draw security personnel to the area, and any holdup would increase the risk of capture. He'd have to attend to the wound later.

Making an effort to ignore his pain, he took a triangular slice of C4 explosive from his gear bag, peeled off its outer foil, and molded it carefully around the bottom of the gatepost. Next he extracted a twelve-inch segment of Primadet cord, one end of which was connected to an aluminum blasting cap, the other to a battery-powered timer about the size and shape of a marker pen. He inserted the end with the blasting cap into the saddle charge and set the timer's simple dial mechanism for a five-minute delay. When he pulled the safety pin holding it in place, the arrow on the dial would start to turn, initiating the detonation sequence—but he couldn't do that until his teammates finished wiring together the charges they had already planted on supports along the fence. The thin orange detonating cord would set off the linked charges almost instantaneously, and he intended to be well away from the area before that happened.

He settled down to wait. Several yards to his left a light shone in the guard booth's broken window. The single wall he could see from his position was spattered with blood. A limp, upflung arm rested against it above the spot where one of the lifeless guards had fallen.

Manuel looked away from the booth, moving his gaze out along the perimeter fence to where the others were at their tasks, dark blurs against the deeper darkness. Blowing a gap in the fence hadn't been his own idea. The watchmen on duty would have known the gate's electronic access codes, and he'd proposed they be captured and made to unlock it at gunpoint. But Kuhl had formulated a minute-by-minute plan and wanted them killed before the jump team's arrival. With the robot and guards in the compound's western sector eliminated, he had reasoned there would be a surveillance lapse until backup security units could arrive. This would give Manuel's group an opening to set their explosives while Teams Orange and Yellow carried out their end of the plan.

Manuel hadn't argued. It was Kuhl's role to make the final calls, and his to carry them out.

Now Manuel saw one of the other jumpers come scurrying up toward the gate, a length of 'det cord winding out behind him. Not a moment too soon, he thought. His wound was large and ugly, the torn flesh imbedded with sharp fragments of metal. He would need to take care of it soon.

He inhaled to clear his head, then took the cord from his teammate and inserted it into the charge he'd just primed.

"Bueno, Juan," he said. "Where is Marco?"

"Coming," Juan said. He gestured toward Manuel's arm. "You all right?"

Manuel looked at him.

"Yes, all right," he said. He willed himself not to stumble as he rose to his feet. "Radio Tomas and the others. Let them know we're through here. Then I pull the pin."

In the center of the compound, three levels underground, Thibodeau rushed through the monitor room's entrance to find Jezoirski, Cody, and Delure agitatedly studying their displays.

"What the hell's goin' on?" he said, noting their flustered expressions.

Delure swiveled his chair around to look at him.

"Sir, it's Ned . . . the 'hog's detected a group of intruders in its sector. Could be the same ones we saw at the western perimeter, there's no way to tell."

Thibodeau eyed the screen and made a low, apprehensive sound in his throat. He cared less about whether these were the same trespassers Wally had encountered than how they had gotten into the compound without initiating any perimeter alarms, and what the purpose of their intrusion might be. A man who relied heavily on instinct, he saw a pattern and tempo to their movements that took him back to his days as a Long Range Recon Patrolman with the 101st Air Cav in Southeast Asia, awakening suspicions that were almost too crazy to share.

But he could not ignore the guideposts of his own experience, and commanding a LRRP unit out of Camp Eagle had taught him plenty. Outrageous as it seemed at first blush, what was happening had all the earmarks of an airborne insertion. That would account for the intruders' seeming ability to materialize out of nowhere, and also explain their otherwise mystifying cat-and-mouse game with Wally. They hadn't taken on the 'hog because they needed to, but because they'd *wanted* to, as if their aim was to put the goddamned contraption through its paces.

Thibodeau pictured the confused expressions he'd seen on the faces of the men around him when he'd come bolting into the room—expressions that must have perfectly mirrored his own. He felt sure those looks would have given tremendous pleasure to the unwanted visitors rushing around out there at the installation's margins. Certainly he'd have enjoyed that sort of thing on his runs through the jungle between 1969 and 1970. The slicks would swing down low over the trees wherever they saw pockets of North Vietnamese and quickly insert their LRRP teams, who would plunge into the brush seeking out targets of opportunity, causing disruption and confusion for the enemy. *Faire la chasse.*

"Can you give me a better fix on those bastards?" he said.

Delure fingered a button on his console to superimpose a digitized map over the radar image they'd been viewing.

"How's that?"

"Good, good, now bring it in closer."

Delure hit another button and zoomed the image. Thibodeau saw geographical features of the compound's western grounds enlarge and clarify around the blips of light indicating the intruders' position.

"*À non.*" He pointed at a curving blue line on-screen. "Take a look at where they are."

Delure gaped up at him. "Near the west drive. That's the quickest route from our motor vehicle pool to the perimeter."

Thibodeau nodded.

"Get the 'hog on their asses, an' this time hit 'em with something stronger than fancy lights," he said. "Our chase cars gon' be on that road any minute!"

The anti-vehicular mines they had set were simply but cleverly camouflaged, wrapped in tar paper to blend in with the pavement. By day they would have been difficult for a driver to spot. At night they would be completely invisible.

Moments after they left the access road to rejoin their teammates, Tomas and Raul heard a low whirring sound close by to the right. They were turning to investigate, their FAMAS rifles at the ready, when the security robot sped nimbly up on them, a tubular apparatus on its side swiveling in their direction, liquid issuing from its nozzle in a pressurized stream.

Neither man got to trigger his weapon before the polymer superlubricant fanned over them, drenching them at first, and then abruptly solidifying in a thin layer over their skin, combat garb, and the ground under their boots.

Raul's immediate thought was that they had been

sprayed with a disabling foam, but he quickly realized this substance was something very different—more like dry ice in the way it hardened, except scarcely cooler than the air around him. Indeed, it was almost as if the fluid had altered *his* physical state rather than its own, as if every part of him that it touched had meta- morphosed into smooth, slick glass. All at once he couldn't hold onto his rifle. The more he tried, the more slippery his grip became. His eyes widening in alarm and incomprehension, he watched the weapon leap from his hands, snapping out the cable that joined it to his helmet display like a hooked fish at the end of a line, then dangling almost ludicrously from his helmet. He snatched at it, his fingers making wild grabs at its stock and barrel, but it slid out from between them and dropped near his feet.

He was bending to recover it when the soles of his boots lost their traction and his legs went skating out from under him.

The ground came up hard against his back, knocking the wind from his lungs. He attempted to scramble up- right, and only flopped onto his side. Tried again and slid back down. The grass beneath him was stiff and slippery. His clothes were as unbending as molded plas- tic. His skin was brittle and much too tight. Out of the corner of his eye he saw Tomas skidding about on his stomach in the same helpless, flailing manner that he was, looking weirdly like a man trying to swim across solid ice.

He screamed then, his mind hurtling over the edge of fear to full-blown panic, screamed at the top of his lungs, and was still crying out when the security cars dis- patched by Thibodeau came racing up the access road behind them.

The same road where, moments ago, the two invaders had planted their mines.

• • •

The three dark-blue quick-response cars beat their air support out of the gate by several minutes—partly because their drivers had been closer to the motor pool than the chopper pilots were to the helipad, and partly because the Skyhawk copters had longer crank times than the armored Mercedes 300 SE sedans, which sprang to life with the turn of an ignition key.

The drivers knew going into their pursuit that the lag would be a problem. Their chopper-automobile teams were equipped with integrated thermal tracking systems that allowed them to accurately pinpoint the location of their quarry, accomplishing this by means of a microwave video link between the Skyhawks' pod-mounted surveillance equipment and receivers on the chase cars' dashboards. But without the aerial transmissions from the helicopters, the men in the cars were relying on nothing more sophisticated than their headlights to spot the intruders.

Tragically, they also lost any chance of being forewarned about the concealed mines awaiting them on the access road.

There were two men in the first car besides the driver, one seated next to him, another in the rear. Neither passenger ever knew what hit him. The driver did see an almost unnoticeable dark patch on the roadway about three yards before the mine came up on him, and thinking it was a bump or pothole, tried to swing around it. But the high speed at which he was traveling made that almost impossible.

The mine went off with a booming explosion as the edge of his left tire rolled over it. The Mercedes shot up into air, its front end bucking higher than the rear. While its armor-plated chassis had been designed to withstand a direct and sustained small-arms assault, its undercarriage was vulnerable to the blast of orange flame that went tearing into it, instantly killing all three of its occupants. A second later the vehicle came down on its right side and rolled crazily forward on two wheels before tumbling onto its roof, fire jetting from its shattered windshield.

His eyes large with shock and horror, the driver of the second vehicle pumped his brake furiously, swerved sideways, and went shooting past the ruined vehicle, coming close enough to see the charred, blistered remains of a face amid the flames in its rear window. Then his tires tripped a second mine and there was another roaring explosion. The last thing he heard as his vehicle was blown apart was the sound of his terrified scream mingling with those of his passengers.

Scarcely a dozen yards behind him, the third car's driver succeeded where the others hadn't. Chunks of metal and blasted pavement raking his hood, he wrenched his steering wheel sharply to the left, jolting off the road and onto the bordering lawn, his tires spinning up clots of soil and grass. With precious extra seconds to react, the man at the wheel of the last car veered in the opposite direction, also screeching to a halt in time to avoid sudden death.

In the darkness beyond the road, two members of Orange Team lay in silent hiding. Both intruders had moved off slightly ahead of their companions after sowing the road with mines, managing to outpace the northern perimeter's security robot and stay well beyond its surveillance range.

They lingered where they were for several moments, peering at the conflagration through their night-vision glasses, watching the dazed survivors of the ambush stagger from their cars. Then a fresh explosion shook the compound to the west, sending a ragged wedge of fire into the sky.

Blue Team's success violently confirmed, the two

men retreated into the shadows. Their trap had been sprung, but they were not yet finished here tonight.

The final stage of the operation was about to get under way.

Kuhl stared ahead into the explosion's glare and imagined its shock waves sending ripples through the hearts of his opposition. He had planned tonight's mission carefully, overseen its every detail, and his preparation was bringing its dividends in results.

Now he heard a tearing metallic sound like some inhuman cry of agony, and saw a crumpled section of the perimeter fence launch into the air and then plunge earthward in a shower of sparks and debris.

It was time.

Kuhl turned to his driver and instructed him to give the signal to mobilize. He nodded in response, and flicked his headlights and taillights on and off once.

The driver at his rear did the same, and then the driver behind *him,* the signal rapidly making its way down the line of jeeps.

Their engines coming to life, they began rolling toward the fire and thunder of the blasts, the way into the installation open before them.

His face chalk-white, Thibodeau passed the radio headset back to Delure with an unsteady hand. Even underground, the detonations around the compound had been audible as muffled thuds, the last and most powerful of them shaking the walls as if there had been an earthquake. But it was not until after they'd heard from the ambushed quick-response team—or what was left of it, God help those poor boys—that *he* had started to tremble. Now, in the ominous silence that had followed the blasts, he realized only a supreme effort of will would make that trembling stop.

Thus far they, whoever *they* might be, had outmaneuvered and outthought him. Been ahead of him at every stage. And that couldn't be allowed to continue.

He meshed his hands behind his back and paced the room, his teeth clenched, struggling to exert control over himself.

What was happening out there? And what was he going to do about it?

He figured the best way to start answering those questions, or trying to answer them, was by reviewing what he already knew—bad as it all was. The west gate was down, the most direct route there blocked by the fiery wreckage of his own chase vehicles. A group of heavily armed, well-trained men had penetrated the installation and were now rampant within its borders. And they had proven themselves capable of ruthless murder as well as sabotage.

He didn't yet know the size of their force. Nor could he know their ultimate goal. But it was a sure thing their plans extended beyond scattered attacks at the periphery of the compound.

No matter what they wanted, it would be in the core manufacturing and storage areas. Possibly even the living quarters—there were some very important members of the ISS scientific team on the facility. He had already ordered these areas sealed up tight, but did he have the manpower to maintain that seal against a concentrated strike?

Thibodeau stopped pacing and laid a hand on Delure's shoulder.

"How many people we got protecting the buildings?" he asked.

"Fifteen, twenty, sir."

"That'd be our full day and night details. Am I right?"

"Yes, sir. With the exception of the men in the cars and choppers. And whoever's off base."

Thibodeau nodded. A handful of Sword operatives and other staffers preferred the long daily commute from Cuiabá to the isolation of living on the compound.

He was silent a moment, his jaw tight. *Ahead of me all'a way, those devils, while I been dancing like a turkey on hot coals.*

He suddenly released Delure's arm, strode over to a steel supply cabinet across the room, and extracted a Zylon ballistic vest from inside it.

"You boys hold the fort down here," he said, and slipped into the vest. "I'm goin' topside."

The jeeps stopped briefly about ten meters after passing through the gap in the fence. Little blazing islands of debris were spread over the grass around them, casting dashes of light and shadow across the faces of their occupants.

The remnants of Blue Team and Orange Team were waiting there as arranged. They scurried into the vehicles.

Manuel climbed into Kuhl's jeep without assistance, but not without difficulty. He could hear droplets of his own blood splashing the rear seat as he settled into it beside Antonio.

"You performed well," Kuhl said. He sat perfectly still in front.

Manuel leaned against the backrest, breathing hard. It felt as if a thousand white-hot needles had been jabbed into his arm. "Marco was killed. Two men from Orange Team had to be left behind."

Kuhl remained motionless.

"Losses must be expected," he said tonelessly.

Then he sliced his hand in the air and the jeep started to move again, the others following in close procession.

•　•　•

The first thing Ed Graham thought when he spotted the jeeps from his Skyhawk chopper was that the sight reminded him of his many years as an LAPD pilot. His second thought was that the *first* thought was an odd and scary comment on modern American society, given how once upon a time it would have been the Hollywood sign and Mann's Chinese Theater that were symbolic of Los Angeles, not maybe twenty men riding around in full combat gear.

His third thought, which followed within a heartbeat, was that he had better *stop* thinking and start acting toot-sweet, because he was right now looking down at a major shitload of trouble.

"Christ, we got us a helluva situation," said the man seated at his right, almost yelling to be heard above the loud whop of the rotors. He reached for his communications handset. "Better radio for an assist and then shine the welcome light on our guests."

Ed nodded, his hands working the sticks. Mitch Winter was the best copilot on the installation. They thought alike and got along well, which made partnering together easy.

He took the bird down lower as Mitch sent his message out to base and the rest of their fleet. A hundred feet beneath them, the jeeps had come to an abrupt halt, their drivers and passengers craning their heads back, staring directly up at the Skyhawk.

Peering out his bubble window, Ed briefly released the cyclic and hit the chopper's Starburst SX-5 searchlight. At the same time Mitch touched a button on his comm unit to shift from radio to public-address mode.

The searchlight's 15-million candlepower beam washed over the men in the convoy, its stark illumination transfixing them, turning night into brilliant noonday.

Ed glanced at Mitch. "Okay, all yours."

Mitch nodded and raised the control mike to his lips. "Stay where you are and—"

"—drop your weapons!"

Bathed in merciless light from above, Kuhl thrust his head out his open window and looked back down his row of jeeps, shielding his eyes with one hand. The command booming from the helicopter's PA had been unequivocal. His response would be equally straightforward.

"Open fire," he shouted. *"Ahora!"*

The four members of Yellow Team had approached to within a few yards of the building, darting from one position of concealment to the next like specters in the night. Their probings had led them to conclude that their primary objective was too heavily guarded to be achieved, but they had been prepared with flexible alternatives and the one ahead of them looked much more vulnerable.

Pausing behind a maintenance shed to check their weapons, they heard the burp of automatic gunfire from off near the west gate, and then the overlying sounds of cars and helicopters converging on the area.

It might for all intents and purposes have been a pre-arranged cue.

Moving as one, they slipped toward their target.

Bullets rattling against his underfuselage, Graham shoved forward on the cyclic and added collective to pull pitch. The cockpit's lightweight boron shielding had literally saved his ass, but he wasn't about to press his luck by taking any more direct hits. Not without being able to return fire owing to Brazilian restrictions against Sword's fixed- and rotary-wing aircraft being fitted for attack capabilities. *Muito obrigado* to whoever came up with that one.

As the Skyhawk banked into a steep climb, he glanced out his windscreen and quickly noted the firepower his attackers were bringing to bear. Neither the rifles nor the HMDs to which they were connected looked like anything he'd ever seen before.

"I'm sticking around till you get a shot of those lunatics out to the chase teams, Mitch," he shouted, nodding toward the television screen on their console. "I don't want anybody being surprised by their hardware."

Mitch returned his nod and reached for the video controls. Gripping the sticks hard, Graham figure-eighted back toward the jeeps to get his nose pod aligned for a good camera angle—and then some of the gunmen abruptly jumped from their vehicles and began darting for cover.

There was, he observed, a considerable amount available to them, mainly crawler cranes, bulldozers, excavators, wheeled compactors, and other heavy equipment that had been rolled into the area for construction of some new buildings. They were big and stationary, their sheer size making them ideal places to hide behind.

Graham continued to orbit the scene in a weaving pattern. Out beyond the bulking machinery he saw the radial web of access routes that led in toward the installation's hub, and turning his gaze northward, spotted the burning ruins of two chase cars on the main roadway from the motor pool. An emergency rescue vehicle and additional cars had pulled up nearby. A number of security men were walking up and down the road with long-handled mine sweepers, while others milled around the wreckage in a desperate attempt to extinguish the flames and locate survivors.

Then he saw what had sent the invaders scrambling. Their roof lights flashing, two quick-response squads were speeding toward them on secondary access roads, one on the left, the other on the right, each three-car

group escorted by a Skyhawk. They would be on top of
the jeep convoy within seconds.

"We sending down pictures yet?" he asked, glancing
at Mitch.

Mitch nodded again and gestured at the television
screen. It showed a detailed IR image of the gunmen in
one of the jeeps.

"Nice shot, real nice," Graham said. "Now let's pray
the guys on the ground are seeing them clear as we are."

The pictures were just fine, coming through on the monitors of the chase cars and helicopters exactly as they
appeared to Graham and Winter in the air. Moreover,
the information relayed by those pictures proved invaluable to the QR squads, giving them an instantaneous
heads-up on the number of invaders they would be
facing, the positions they held, and the type of weapons
they were carrying.

The guns in particular looked formidable, but the men
in the cars took some comfort from their own specially
modified firearms. The Variable Velocity Rifle System,
or VVRS, was an M16 chambered for 5.56mm dual-
purpose sabot rounds and fitted with a vented barrel and
rotating hand guard. A twist of the hand guard would
widen or narrow the vents, increasing or decreasing the
amount of blowback gas within the barrel, and thus the
velocity at which the rounds were discharged. At a low
velocity, the padded plastic sabots would remain around
the bullets and cushion their deadly impact. At a high
velocity, they would peel apart like shed cocoons, and
the bruiser ammunition would turn lethal.

There was little question about whether to use deadly
force in the mind of QR squad leader Dan Carlysle as
he came up on the convoy's left flank. The men scrambling from the jeeps had killed without hesitation. Their
weapons presented an obvious mortal threat. It had to

be met with a willingness to respond in kind.

Still, Carlysle wanted explicit authorization if at all possible. Some political elements in Brazil were already upset by UpLink's powerful security presence, and would be further incited by a small war occurring on their soil. While Carlysle was ready to make an on-the-spot decision, he was aware of the diplomatic mess that might follow and preferred getting a nod from his immediate higher-up.

Tearing along in the forward chase car, he reached for his dash microphone and hailed Thibodeau on the radio.

"You do what you gotta, Dan, hear me? We catch heat from the locals, *soit,* we'll deal with that later."

"Yes, sir. Over."

Thibodeau clipped his radio back onto his belt, lit up a cigarette, and smoked in silence. Far out at the western edge of the compound he could hear a percussive exchange of gunfire, tires screeching, and more overlapping volleys punctuated by loud explosions. Christ, the whole thing was insane. He had not in his wildest imaginings expected to find himself in an engagement of this magnitude outside of the military. Nor did he relish giving orders and instructions from a distance, sending others into action rather than participating in it himself. But tonight the full responsibility of command had fallen upon his shoulders.

Still, he wished he didn't have to hear that hellish clamor.

He dragged on his cigarette, standing outside a cluster of five low-rise concrete buildings that housed the installation's key personnel and their families—each four stories high with between eight and ten apartments per floor, lodging a combined total of 237 men, women, and children. Thibodeau had concentrated his manpower around them in the likelihood the invaders had kidnaping or hostage taking as their goal . . . which was not to say there weren't other probabilities to consider. Theft of the multimillion-dollar ISS components on base—or their design blueprints—might be an equally powerful motive for the raid, but safeguarding human lives was his foremost concern regardless.

He stood there and thought, tobacco smoke streaming slowly out his nose. Caught shorthanded, he was trying his best to manage the situation and make optimum use of his resources. Toward these ends, all non-security personnel had been restricted to their apartments for the duration of the crisis. Over two thirds of his available operatives had assembled around the residential complex, enclosing it in a defensive ring. He could see them on patrol now, and was confident they would hang tough against any attack.

However, it worried him deeply that bolstering his strength here had required shifting people away from the industrial section of the compound. The detail charged with its protection was too small in number, too thinly dispersed around a large area—a weakness that could be easily exploited by determined raiders with surprise on their side. He continued to know almost nothing about them, but what might *they* know about the layout of the installation? The strength, tactics, and priorities of his force? From the time they'd first appeared, his opposition had led the dance while he'd reeled and stumbled trying to keep up.

What might they know? Considering the damage they'd already inflicted, it seemed the answer was *too much.* Could they have used that knowledge to manipulate his decisions?

Thibodeau thought about that a moment, his heart pounding. *Mon Dieu,* were they dancing him right into quicksand?

His inspection of the scene suddenly concluded, he

snapped his half-finished cigarette to the ground and started off toward the warehouse and factory buildings.

Taking cover behind a jeep, Antonio balanced his Barrett .50 across its hood and aimed down its reticulated scope at the lead chase car. With the car coming straight at him, he had made a split-second decision to shoot for one of its front tires, thinking it would be an easier target than the driver, whose head was ducked low behind the windshield.

He pulled the trigger. There was a crack as the gun stock recoiled against his shoulder, then a popping outrush of air as the tire exploded in a storm of flying rubber. The car's front end bounced down, then up, then down. But although it slowed a little, it barely veered off course—to Antonio's utter surprise.

Its wheels holding to the middle of the road, the car kept moving dead-on toward the convoy of jeeps.

Carlysle was racing up on the jeep pulled crosswise ahead of him when he saw the twinkle of partially suppressed muzzle flash above its hood, heard a gunshot, and then was jolted hard in his seat as a bullet blew his right front tire to shreds.

Clenching the steering wheel, he resisted the impulse to slam on his brakes, and instead tapped the pedal lightly and repeatedly with his toe. The car bounced another couple of times and tried slewing toward the right, but he held on tightly and kept it under control. In a moment he got the feel of the runflat roller that had been emplaced within the tire and was now in contact with the road, ragged bits of rubber flapping around it, its shock-absorbent elastomer surface preventing the wheel rim from being damaged, stabilizing the car, and allowing him to keep moving almost as if the shot had never been fired and his tire was still intact.

As the invaders opened up on them, the QR squads reacted according to well-rehearsed tactical procedures.
Carlysle's trio of cars broke sharply to the left and
stopped aslant the road, their wheels turned outward.
The other group cut to the right shoulder of the access-
way on which they were approaching and halted with
their tires at a similarly extreme angle. Then the men in
both squads poured out the sides of their cars, using their
open doors and outturned wheels for protection.

Carlysle had no sooner gotten into a crouch behind
his door than bullets came ripping into it from several
different directions at once. The man who'd been riding
shotgun with him, a recent transfer from the Malaysian
ground station named Ron Newell, returned fire, aiming
toward the spot where he'd seen the slender outline of
a rifle angling out from behind a mobile crane, and then
flattening against the car just as more gunfire studded its
armored surface.

Squatting beside him, Carlysle thrust the barrel of his
VVRS weapon around his door and squeezed out a long
volley. He couldn't help but wonder when their remote
corner of Brazil had turned into Dodge City.

He looked over at Newell, saw that he hadn't been
hit, and gave him a thumbs-up to indicate he was also
doing okay. Then there was another burst of incoming,
followed by a bright flash in the darkness, and a whis-
tling noise that rapidly got closer and louder. An instant
later some kind of explosive projectile smashed into the
chase car to Carlysle's right, detonating with a bright
rush of flame, crunching in the flank of the Mercedes as
if it were the side of a tin box.

Carlysle stayed put, his ears ringing from the blast.
The situation had to change, and change ASAP. He
would not let his men remain pinned down behind their
vehicles, where they were sitting ducks for whatever was

being hurled at them by an enemy that could draw an accurate bead without breaking cover.

His right hand around his pistol grip, he reached into the car with his left and snatched his dashboard microphone off its hook, pressing one of the mike's control buttons as he eyed the video screen above it. The invaders' advanced night-vision equipment was formidable, but he and his men had something else going in their favor. Something that could prove even more advantageous if used to its best capacity.

They had the Skyhawks.

In the copilot's seat of his circling chopper, Winter lowered his handset and turned toward Graham. Carlysle had just broken contact after sending up his request over a ground-to-air channel.

"We need to peel the blankets back from over those fuckers' heads, give our guys downstairs a better fix on where they're shooting from," he said above the roar of the blades.

Graham gave him a look. "If we go any lower, it'll be hard to avoid the ground fire."

Winter made a face that said he knew.

Graham shrugged.

"Okay," he said. Then: "Here's how I want it done."

How Graham wanted it done was for his chopper and one of the others at the scene to pull in tight over the invaders and provide closeups of their positions, while the third aircraft continued making passes from a greater height, beaming down wide-angle images. The picture-in-picture options on the QR cars' monitors would enable all three video feeds to be seen simultaneously, giving the chase squads a composite view of the fire zone.

It was, as Graham and Winter had acknowledged, a

risky plan. Submachine guns burst up at the two Sky-hawks the instant they dropped in altitude. Steeling himself, Graham slipped between two huge earthmoving vehicles where some of the invaders had taken cover. Bullets sprayed his fuselage as he swept over them, rattling against it like gravel.

Graham steadied the bird and hovered. To his right, he saw the second descending Skyhawk come under heavy fire. Never a religious man, he was surprised to find himself muttering a silent prayer on behalf of its crew.

His fingers moist around the sticks, Graham hung over the attackers for several more seconds, his camera transmitting its information to the mobile receivers. Then he throttled into high gear and leapfrogged off toward another group of invaders, hoping he'd given the ground units what they needed.

The guard was sprawled on his stomach, his face turned sideways so one cheek was in the dirt. His name tag read BRYCE. He had been stabbed from behind, the knife driven in below the shoulder blades and then upward and across into the soft organs. There were tiny bubbles of blood and saliva in the corner of his mouth, and they glistened in the revealing output of Thibodeau's flashlight.

Thibodeau knelt beside him and touched the pulse points on his wrist and neck, but felt nothing. Dead. Like the two other guards he had discovered around the corner of the building. In their case a gun, or guns, had been used. Probably, Thibodeau thought, the shots had attracted Bryce's attention. His position suggested he had been rounding the side of the building to investigate when his killer came up and sank the knife into his back.

Thibodeau turned his flash onto the warehouse's loading dock, and was not surprised to find its door half raised. Countless dollars had been spent on providing security for the installation—the 'hogs alone cost hundreds of thousands—but their placement had been largely intended to detect outside intruders, and in any event, no system was without gaps. While this section of the warehouse complex held important spare parts for the ISS's laboratory racks, it was not among the handful of restricted storage or R&D areas. The level of security clearance needed to gain access was minimal. An employee swipe card taken off one of the dead guards would have been all it took.

Rising from the body, Thibodeau stepped over to the partially open door. He would need to call for assistance, but it would take at least five minutes for the nearest men to arrive, possibly as long as ten. If he waited, what sort of damage might the intruders do in the meantime?

Hesitant, a sick taste in his mouth, Thibodeau glanced again at the corpse on the ground. Bryce. He had a smooth, clean-shaven face and hair the color of wheat, and was maybe twenty-five years old. Barely more than a kid. He'd been new on the job and Thibodeau hadn't known him too well. Never would now.

Thibodeau stood there outside the warehouse entrance and looked at him. The foam of oxygenated blood on his lips was the kind that came brewing up from the lungs with a deep stab wound. His scrubbed features were still contorted with the agony of his final moments. The killer had been savage and pitiless.

Frowning unconsciously, Thibodeau shined his flashlight through the partially open door, pushed it further up, and stepped into the darkened space beyond.

"We've got ten, twelve of them behind that big half-track crane on the near left, about half as many using the 'dozers for cover, a couple more—"

Momentarily releasing the "talk" button of his radio,

Carlysle held his breath as a stream of ammunition babbled noisily in his direction, striking the outer flank of his car. Thus far his plan was working, the chase squads' aerial support providing a visual lock on their opponents' positions. Those chopper pilots, opening themselves up to direct fire, putting their lives in jeopardy . . . if he hadn't been busy trying to keep his own skin from acquiring any unwanted holes, he'd have been singing their praises to the sun, moon, and stars. But maybe there would be a chance to express his gratitude later.

He lifted the radio back up to his mouth, taking advantage of a lull in the fire to get his orders out.

"—a couple more scattered behind that mound of dug-up soil over to the left. The rest are still clustered between the jeeps," he shouted. "My squad's the shortest distance from that crane, and I think we can swing around back of it pretty quick. I'm going to need Squads Two and Three to go up on the bulldozers. Stick to the right of the road . . ."

Less than thirty seconds later, his instructions completed, Carlysle signed off and led his team from the protection of their chase car, running hard toward his self-assigned target.

Thibodeau hastened through the dimness of the corridor, rifle across his chest, eyes moving alertly from side to side. His old jungle recon instincts had kicked in like voltage, heightening every sense.

Seconds ago he had called for backup, sending the message out wide so it would be squawked by his ground patrols as well as Cody's team in the monitoring station. Then he'd moved on ahead without waiting for a reply. It might be somebody would be available to help, it might be they wouldn't, but there was no way he could wait around to find out.

He'd made his need clear; the rest was out of his hands.

He turned a bend in the corridor, another, a third, and then stopped abruptly where it forked off in opposite directions. There was still no sign of the men he was trailing. But the path he'd followed had been the only one running from the loading dock. Up until this point. The hallway on the right would take him onto the main floor of the storage bay, the one on his left to a freight elevator that, as he recalled, rose to a catwalk that spanned the bay about halfway up toward its ceiling.

Which would the invaders have taken? A little while back he'd have figured it was fifty-fifty they'd have gone either way. But the evidence was that they had not stumbled upon this place by chance, that they'd known in advance how to gain access and had a specific goal in mind. And if they were familiar with the building's layout, it stood to reason they would head straight for the storage bay, where ISS elements were actually kept and maintained.

Okay, then, he thought. Odds were they had gone down the right-hand corridor. But did that mean he ought to do the same? He was one against several ... exactly how many he didn't know. It would be suicidal to plunge headlong into the thick of things. The principles of engagement ought to be the same here as in any battle. While they had numbers in their favor, the edge would go to whoever held the high ground.

Thibodeau stood there another second or two, feeling constricted in the narrow sterility of the corridor. Then he hefted his weapon, his mind made up.

Turning left, he rushed toward the elevator.

Carlysle had approached the mobile crane from its left side and gotten within about three yards of it, the rest of the squad close at his heels, when he thrust his hand out and signaled them to stop behind a pile of bulldozed earth and pebbles. He wanted to take one last look at the invaders before commencing his attack.

The high-intensity lights from the choppers showed a half-dozen of them spread out behind the crawler's ringer, a sort of metal apron used to balance its weight when the boom was telescoped upward. This huge configuration was like a circular wall that gave the invaders excellent cover—but the flip side was that it also impeded their field of view and hampered their ability to follow the chase squad's movements. Even the electronic imaging devices on their weapons were of little use unless the guns were pointed directly over or around the ringer's edge. The instant one of them lowered his weapon he was blind, whereas the chase squads had their helicopters in continuous radio contact, reporting on the raiding party's positions, tracking them minute by minute.

Carlysle had made the most of the opposition's handicap, leading his team across exposed stretches of ground in short, rapid sprints. But their job was to take the invaders, and to accomplish that they would have to break from hiding and open themselves up to fire. There was no way to avoid it.

Now he waved his hand briskly in the air to get his men moving again. They raised their weapons and buttonhooked around to where the invaders were huddled behind the ringer.

By the time the invaders realized they were under attack Carlysle's men were almost on top of them, dashing up from behind, their VVRS rifles chattering in their hands. Two of the invaders went down instantly, surprised expressions on their faces. Then the remaining four returned fire with their own guns. Carlysle saw Newell fall to his right, his leg covered in blood. Pivoting toward the shooter, he squeezed a burst from his weapon that knocked him backward off his feet. Another invader swung his rifle up at Carlysle in retaliation, but was hit by one of Carlysle's men before he could trigger a shot. Moaning and clutching his bloody middle, he rolled onto his side and drew himself into a tight ball.

The remaining two tried making a run for it. Carlysle swung his weapon in their direction and tilted its muzzle toward the ground and fired a short burst at their heels.

"Hold it!" he shouted in Spanish. That was a tongue they were certain to understand regardless of where on the continent they were from, the *lingua franca* all regional Sword ops were instructed to use when addressing an unidentified hostile. "Both of you, drop your guns and get down on your bellies!"

They stopped running but stayed on their feet, holding onto the rifles.

Carlysle fired into the ground behind them again, spraying up dirt.

"On your bellies, you sons of bitches!" he said. "Now!"

This time they listened and went down, hands behind their helmets. A moment later Carlysle and his men kicked their guns aside, twisted their arms behind their backs, and got them flex-cuffed.

Carlysle ran over to Newell and crouched to check out his leg wound.

"Lay still," he said. "You'll be okay."

Newell looked up at him, managed a nod.

Carlysle took a breath.

It felt as if it was the first one he'd had in a while.

The payload storage bay was an enormous space enclosing three elevated work platforms of sizable dimensions, as well as an interconnected assembly of catwalks, bridge cranes, and other types of metal rigging designed to ease the movement and transfer of equipment between these platforms. Rows of large office windows looked down upon the vaulting room on two sides. A beehive of corridors, elevator shafts, tunnels, and stairwells not only linked it to the rest of the warehouse and manufacturing complex, but also to different buildings within the ISS compound.

After eliminating the guards outside the warehouse—stealing up on them had been simplicity itself—Yellow Team had entered through its loading dock, raced through several winding passageways, and finally pushed through a set of double doors that gave into the storage bay, where the team's designated leader, Heitor, planned to drop their satchel charges. Each of the two black canvas bags contained fifteen pounds of TNT, enough high explosive to bring down the steel beam supports underneath the work platforms, the space station hardware on top of them, and quite possibly the walls of the room around them.

It was much more than the saboteurs had thought they would be able to accomplish. Surely not even Kuhl had expected them to get this far into the compound, Heitor mused.

Now he hastened to one of the platforms, slipped a satchel charge off his shoulder, and placed it at the foot of a tall support post. Both timer pencils he was using had been preset to a ten-minute delay, an acceptable opening in which to get out before the blast. Silent and vigilant, their weapons held ready across their bodies, his teammates stood watch behind him in the central aisle. The vast room around them was dark except for the few widely spaced fluorescents normally left on after the close of daily operations.

Crouching at the foot of the support, Heitor removed the timer pin to initiate the detonation sequence. Then he quickly went to the next platform and dropped his other charge.

It was just as he pulled the second pin that Thibodeau stepped from an elevator onto one of the flying catwalks and, looking out over the expansive floor of the storage bay, was shocked to discover what was happening below.

"Thibodeau's backup is on the way," Delure said. "I pulled four men from the office complex, another six off other details."

"How long before they reach him?" Cody asked from his station.

"Could be as long as ten minutes for some of them."

"Not good enough," Cody said. He produced a harsh sigh and turned to Jezoirski. "What about Felix? How fast can we bring him to Thibodeau?"

"Give me a sec to call up a floor plan of the building." Jezoirski tapped his keyboard, scanned the screen in front of him. " 'Hog's in the Level 5 propulsion lab—"

"How *fast*?"

Jezoirski studied the schematic, then lifted his face. "There's a connecting walkway between the research and warehouse complexes. We can move him straight along this corridor right here to the elevator, then down three levels to the walkway," he said, plotting a course across the screen with his finger. "From there it might need a minute, maybe a minute and a half to reach the warehouse, another couple to get down to the payload storage bay."

"That's at least six minutes."

Jezoirski nodded. "Best we can do."

"Suppose we'll have to live with it then," Cody said. Sweat glistened in the furrow above his lip. "All right, let's hurry up and get the 'hog rolling."

The earthmovers were parked near a ditch they had scooped out of the ground, and had offered solid cover to the invaders until the helicopters marked their positions. As they came under intense fire from a chase squad now, the group of invaders scurried down into the ditch, where they pressed up against its sides and began shooting over its stony rim.

The Skyhawks stuck to them like the predatory birds that were their namesakes, one nailing the tracked vehicles with its SX-5 searchlight, the other shining its light directly into the trench.

"Nest's ready to be cleaned out," the chopper pilot above the ditch radioed the ground team.

"Roger, we're on it," its leader replied.

He turned the barrel vents of his rifle to their closed setting and ordered his squad to move.

The chopper pilot stayed on the horn to guide their advance, and continue reporting on the position of the invaders. As he hovered over the bowl-shaped ditch, the incandescent brilliance and swirling gun smoke inside it gave the eerie illusion that he was peering down into a lava pit filled with almost a dozen trapped human beings.

But the situation below was such that the distance between illusion and reality rapidly closed. The chase squad attacked in a flanking rush, looping around the dozers and front-end loaders to hose the ditch with their guns. Although return fire was heavy, they had the cold confidence of men who had stolen the offensive and gained a maneuverability their opposition had lost. Surrounded, their FAMAS weapons' targeting systems overloaded by the unsparing glare of the searchlights, the invaders had in fact run themselves into a trap.

One of them tumbled down the side of the trench, soil and pebbles spitting up around him. A second rose to trigger an explosive round, but was slammed off his feet by a blaze of fire.

A third sprang up and looked briefly as if he might attempt a suicidal charge over the rim . . . but then he backed off, tossed his weapon aside, and dropped face-down onto the bottom of the ditch in surrender, his hands stretched above his head.

The chopper pilot watched another invader follow suit and disarm, then another, then the rest seemingly all at once. A moment later the chase squad's leader gave the hand signal to suspend fire, followed by a thumbs-up to the pilot.

He smiled and returned the gesture. His searchlight would make it impossible for those on the ground to see it, but what the hell.

Disengaging his auto-hover control, he skipped off to another spot where he might be needed, the other chopper close behind.

Thibodeau would never know what caught the attention of the invader standing lookout on the warehouse floor—the slight movement of his fingers when he raised the gas pressure in his rifle barrel, the click of the hand guard as it locked into its new setting, or maybe something else completely.

In the end the only thing that mattered was the invader's bullet, and the damage it did to him.

For Thibodeau, it all happened in what his combat buddies used to call *slow time*. There was the surprising realization that he'd been spotted as the invader's weapon angled up in his direction. There was a spark of alarm inside him, cold and bright, like winter sunlight glinting off ice. Then he felt his reflexes kick in, felt himself reacting, and was sure his reaction was quick enough . . . should have been quick enough anyway. But as he ducked down below the rail the very air seemed to gain thickness and density, to *resist* him. It was as if he was sinking through jelly.

And then there was a loud crack from below, and something walloped him on the right side, and he felt heat spread through his stomach and went crumpling onto the floor of the catwalk as time resumed its normal speed like a train jolting from the station.

Thibodeau tried to get up, but his body was all dead-weight, somehow apart from him. He lay half on his belly, looked down at himself, and saw that his vest hadn't been penetrated, that the hit was nothing but a fluke, the trajectory of the bullet having carried it up into the space between the bottom of the vest and his stomach, some goddamned nasty bit of *gris-gris*. And now here he was, blood draining out of him to the floor's treaded runner, filling the spaces between the treads, flowing down along them in thin scarlet streams—when had *he* ever stepped on Satan's tail to earn this one?

He heard the crash of footfalls, managed to lift his cheek off the floor so he could see more than the blood and the railing in front of him.

The man who'd shot him was clambering up the metal risers to the catwalk, a second invader right behind him. The two of them coming to finish him off.

Furiously wishing to God that he knew where he'd dropped his rifle, Thibodeau turned his head downward and saw to his amazement that was it still in his right hand, his fingers clutched around the grip, its barrel jacket pressed almost vertically against his side.

He dropped his cheek to the floor again, dropped it into a pool of his own blood, no longer able to keep it up. He was funneling all his willpower into getting the hand to move. He told it to move, begged it to move, and when it failed to respond silently began cursing it, demanding that it quit giving him bullshit, insisting angrily that it could fuck with him later on, could fall right off his shoulder if that was how it had to be, but that right now it was going to obey him and raise the god-damned rifle.

Thibodeau heard himself take a racking breath. He

could see the invaders in their black helmets and uniforms, getting closer, pounding up the stairs.

Come on, you bastard, he thought. *Come on.*

And then suddenly his arm was coming up, dragging the gun with it, dragging it through his spilled blood, getting its barrel under the railing and pointed down at the stairs.

He triggered the rifle and felt it rattle against his body, spraying the stairs with rounds. The invaders almost collided with each other as they halted in their tracks and shot back with their own weapons. Bullets whizzed over Thibodeau's head, tocking like hailstones against the projecting edge of the catwalk and the wall behind him. Recovered from their surprise at being fired upon, seeing that Thibodeau was badly wounded, the two invaders were coming at him once again, crouching, their guns stuttering as they began climbing the stairs. A third man, meanwhile, had opened fire from the aisle below.

Thibodeau pumped out another burst, but knew he was weakening, knew his clip would be empty soon, knew he was nearly finished.

Laissez les bons temps rouler—wasn't that what he'd told Cody earlier? Let the good times roll, roll on to the very last, take me rolling down nice and easy, amen, God, amen, he thought half deliriously.

And fired again at the invaders with the remainder of his strength and ammunition, braced for what he was certain would be the final moments of his life.

"Thibodeau's down," Delure said. "Christ, we've got to *do* something."

"Give me the 'hog's position," Cody replied. He was staring at pictures being sent by ceiling-mounted surveillance cameras in the payload storage bay. Now under the remote control of the monitoring room, their feeds normally appeared on a television screen every ten minutes in a rotational sequence that included feeds from other medium- and high-security buildings, and that should have been automatically overridden in the event of a trespass, with the system tripping an alarm and locking its visuals upon the area that had been breached. But the cameras' regular transmissions had been neglected as the attack at the compound's periphery gathered momentum, and the invaders had apparently gained entry to the warehouse through authorized means, defeating the override.

It was a lapse whose consequences had become terribly clear to Cody's team in the past several minutes.

Jezoirski was looking closely at the hedgehog's video transmissions. "Felix is at the warehouse . . . about thirty feet down the corridor it'll bear left, take another elevator down to the storage bay. . . ."

"You said that means, what, another minute until it's actually on that catwalk?"

Jezoirski nodded. "That's my estimate, yeah."

"Thibodeau might not last that long," Delure said. "I'm telling you, Cody, he needs our help right now."

"Our orders are to sit tight."

"But we can't just sit here and watch them *kill* him."

"Listen to me, goddamn it!" Cody snapped. He was sweating profusely now, the moisture dripping down over his lips. "We'd never make it to the warehouse before the 'hog and the backup team. You want to help Thibodeau, keep your eyes on those screens, and be ready to tell that robot what to do when it reaches him!"

Kuhl crouched behind his vehicle, the sounds of gunfire surrounding him, helicopters whirring overhead. His expression was rigid with thought, almost brooding, as if he were oblivious to it all.

In fact he was keenly attuned to his situation, his mind distilling and evaluating its every aspect. Up until now the mission had been a success. His men had met almost every objective set out for them, and in some cases done better than expected. But the stage at which events could be orchestrated was past, and sustaining further losses was unacceptable. It was necessary to recognize that the balance had shifted toward his opposition. If he continued, his force might be so badly weakened it would be unable to retreat. And he was not one to bait chance.

He turned to his driver, who was huddled beside him.

"We're pulling out," he said, and motioned toward the jeep. "Radio the others to let them know."

Manuel was sitting on the ground nearby, leaning back against the door of the vehicle. His untreated wound had sapped him and he was breathing in short, labored gasps.

"We can't." He nodded toward the interior of the compound. "Yellow Team is still in there."

"They knew the risks," Kuhl said. "We've waited as long as we can."

Manuel slid himself up along the side of the door, wincing with the effort.

"They haven't had enough time," he croaked.

"I've given my order. You can stay behind, if you wish." There was anger in Kuhl's eyes. "Decide quickly."

Manuel looked at him for a long moment, bent his head to stare at the ground, then slowly looked back at him with resignation.

"I'll need some help getting into the jeep," he said at last.

Outside the warehouse complex, a group of ten Sword ops raced on foot toward the service door through which Thibodeau had pursued the invaders. The team was composed of men who had been pulled from dispositions around the compound's residential and office buildings.

They came to where the murdered guard lay on the ground, stopped, gazed down at him. The knife wound in his back was still bleeding out.

One of them mouthed an oath, his right hand making the sign of the cross on his forehead and chest.

"Bryce," he said. "Ah, shit, poor guy."

Another member of the ad hoc team grabbed his arm.

"No use standing here," he said.

The two of them looked at each other. The first man started to say something in response, but then simply cleared his throat and nodded.

Turning from the body, they ran into the open service door, the rest of the team pouring into the warehouse behind them.

Thibodeau could feel the world slipping away. He was trying to hold onto it, trying desperately, but it was loose and runny around the edges, made of soft taffy, and out beyond where it waned off into formlessness, he could sense a black mass waiting to swallow it all up. He knew what was happening to him, no brain flash needed on that score. It was blood loss, it was traumatic shock, it was how it felt to be dying from a large-caliber bullet hole in your gut. The world was slipping away, and though he would have preferred it didn't, the choice didn't seem to be within his making.

Thibodeau breathed hard through his mouth, coughed. It was a thick, liquidy sound that admittedly frightened him a little, and the air felt cold entering his lungs, but there wasn't much pain, and things seemed to get more distinct afterward. He saw the two invaders who'd been shooting at him emerge from the blurred corners of his vision, one behind the other, hurrying up the stairs to the catwalk. He had held them off as long as he could, firing his gun until its magazine was exhausted. Now he wasn't even sure whether or not the weapon was still in his hand.

The invader who had led the way up was standing over him, pointing his rifle straight down at his head.

Thibodeau took another breath, managed to lift his cheek off the catwalk's bloody runner. Its grooves had marked his cheek with smears of his own blood.

"Get it done," he said weakly.

The invader stood over him. If he had any expression beneath his face mask, Thibodeau had no way of knowing what it might be.

"Come on," Thibodeau said. "Get it done."

And still standing there looking down at him, the invader lowered the rifle's bore to his temple.

Felix rolled out onto the catwalk from the same elevator Thibodeau had taken minutes earlier.

High above the payload storage bay, the 'hog went swiftly toward him, its navigational sonar mapping its surroundings in layered echo patterns.

This was a built-in redundancy to prevent accidental collision, for Jezoirski now wielded full command of its operation from the monitoring room. Having donned virtual-reality glasses, he could see three-dimensional graphic representations of everything the 'hog "saw" with its optical array. At the same time, the joystick controls on his console were now directing its robotic mobility systems, allowing him to guide and determine its every turn and action.

Biting his lips, Jezoirski rushed the 'hog over the catwalk. Like a sorcerer possessing an entity from afar— using technology instead of talismans, and algorithms instead of incantations—he had extended himself into the hedgehog's physical space and was, in effect, in two locations at once.

Felix glided around a curve, its wheels whispering softly, the immense room's recessed fluorescents reflecting twinkles of pale blue light off the poker-chip sensors on its turret.

Then, all at once, it came to a halt.

Was *brought* to a halt.

Panic sweeping through him like a whiteout blizzard, wiping all his training from his mind, Jezoirski had frozen at the remote controls. A hundred feet above him in another building, yet right in front of his eyes, Rollie Thibodeau was about to die.

And Jezoirski suddenly didn't know what to do about it.

"What's wrong?" Cody asked.

Jezoirski's heart bumped in his chest. His eyes were wide under the VR wraparounds.

He gripped Felix's controls, blinded by indecision, knowing his slightest error or miscalculation would mean Thibodeau's end.

"I asked what the hell's *wrong with you*!" Cody repeated beside him. His voice trembled with stress.

Jezoirski inhaled, felt his muscles unclamp. Cody's demanding, excited tone had jolted him from his momentary paralysis.

"I'm okay, I'm okay," he muttered quickly, as much to himself as his superior.

Taking another breath through gritted teeth, he resumed working the controls.

Thibodeau's glazed eyes widened with surprise as Felix came speeding toward him from the right, its wheels swishing over the catwalk's runner, its gripper arm extending straight out in front of it.

Startled by the sound of its advance, the invader standing over Thibodeau whirled toward the 'hog, bringing his rifle up from Thibodeau's head. But the 'hog's side-mounted shotgun discharged with a belch of smoke and flame while he was still bringing the rifle around to fire at it.

The invader spun back against rail of the catwalk, his rifle flying from his hands. The advancing robot tracked his movement, angled its gun, and fired another shot at nearly point-blank range, hitting him hard enough to lift him off his feet. Shrieking and clutching at the air, the invader went sailing over the guardrail and plummeted to the floor of the storage bay, his body landing with a heavy crash.

The roar of its shotgun still echoing in the air, Felix hurtled toward the second invader, who triggered his own weapon, spraying the 'hog with a short burst of automatic fire. But he'd been unable to recover from his surprise in time to position himself for his shots, and only one or two nicked Felix's carrier, the rest going completely astray, ricocheting off the wall and catwalk.

He did not get a chance to unleash another volley. The hog's gripper claw shot out just as he was taking aim, snatched his leg below the knee, and clamped down with several hundred pounds of force.

His trouser leg suddenly wet with blood, the invader screamed and tried to twist away, but Felix's hold was unyielding. Screaming in pain, his rifle clattering from his hands, he bent and wrapped his fingers around the robotic arm, struggling in vain to tear it loose.

Watching blearily from inches away, Thibodeau saw him sink onto one knee, then heard the bones of his opposite leg splinter with a sickening crunch under the relentless pressure of the gripper claw. His screams growing in shrillness, the invader continued to pull at the arm as the robot resumed its advance, shoving him implacably backward, out of reach of his fallen weapon.

Sonsabitchin' contraption's good for somethin' after

all, Thibodeau thought, then let his head slump to the floor again, no longer able to keep it up.

His field of vision contracting to a small, fuzzy circle, he lay there motionless, the side of his face against the floor. He was vaguely aware of footsteps far below him, a lot of them. Someone shouted—first in Spanish, then English. He heard a fusillade of gunfire.

Before he even had time to wonder what any of it meant, Thibodeau's eyes rolled back under their lids, and he ceased to be aware of anything at all.

As the Sword ops bolted into the payload storage bay, they heard two reverberating shotgun blasts over their heads, and then saw a man in a black cammo suit fall from one of the catwalks, screaming and flailing as he dropped to the floor to their left, slamming down with a hard thud, then neither screaming nor moving anymore. An instant later there was a chop of automatic fire in the air high above them. Looking up, they spotted another dark form on the catwalk, this one suddenly folding to his knees as a hedgehog launched at him across the catwalk, its gripper arm rapidly whipping out to snatch him like the foreleg of a preying mantis. Several of the ops saw a third man sprawled on the catwalk behind the 'hog, and noticing his Sword uniform, realized instantly it must be Thibodeau.

But before they could react to this sight, a third figure in black sprang from a crouch below a towering work platform up ahead, leaving an object behind on the floor near one of its supports. All of them were experienced enough to know it was a satchel charge—and they could see two more in plain view below other platforms.

"Stay right where you are!" one of the ops shouted, raising his weapon.

The man wasn't inclined to listen to his warning, regardless of the language. He raised his gun and swung it toward the group of Sword ops.

The response from the Sword op who had called out to him was immediate and conclusive. Bullets spurted from his gun, cutting the invader down before he could fire a single round.

Lowering his barrel, the op sprinted past the invader to the platform support, knelt over the satchel charge, and rapidly assessed its threat. He was no demolitions expert, but it looked like it was on a simple timer pencil and fuze configuration . . . although looks could be deceptive. There could, he knew, be internal wiring that would detonate the explosives if he tried yanking out the fuze, or other types of booby traps totally unfamiliar to him. Yet the timer's pin was nowhere in sight, and it only had a couple of minutes left on it, leaving him with no chance to move the bomb or call for help—

He hesitated briefly, feeling his body tighten. Then, gritting his teeth, he pinched the fuze between his thumb and forefinger and gave it a hard pull.

A moment later he took a deep breath, and then another, thanking God that the bomb hadn't gone off in his hands, that he and everyone around him were still there, still there and not blown to bits.

Which did not yet mean they were in the clear, he quickly reminded himself.

"This one's out of commission, we better get on to the others!" he shouted. "Let's hurry!"

Back in the driver's seat of his chase car, Carlysle looked out his windshield at the fleeing group of invaders and swore aloud. Less than a minute ago, their jeep had sped through the gap in the perimeter fence and he had followed on their tail.

The problem was that he wasn't at all certain he ought to be doing that.

He tried to think it through even while gunning his engine, pushing to close the distance between them.

Having sent Newell for medical treatment and dispatched their prisoners to a holding area with one of the other units, his squad had been returning to their car when they saw the invaders hasten back into their own vehicle, pull it around in a screeching circle, and whip toward the fence. As the men who by chance were closest to them, Carlysle's team had launched off in pursuit . . . but the jeep had been passing through the fence before Carlysle even got behind the wheel, giving it a good head start.

What troubled him was a simple question of authority. UpLink's host government had sanctioned the emplacement of an independent security force on the ISS compound, period. It was not prepared to have that force move about at will, engaging in what amounted to a small war. Carlysle was sensitive to that, and because he was a disciplined professional, could not close his eyes to the boundaries of his license to operate. If there had been no prisoners taken on the compound to hopefully yield information about the motives and objectives behind their raid, he might have been inclined to push those bounds and carry on the pursuit, calling in the Skyhawks for aerial support. But there were, and it was hard to justify going forward knowing the repercussions that might be expected as a consequence.

He gripped the wheel, his eyes on the taillights ahead of him. Stop or go, what was it going to be? With Thibodeau not answering his radio, the decision was his to make.

Producing another string of curses, he shifted his foot to his brake pedal and eased it down. The chase car lurched to a halt over the bumpy road.

"Never mind that bunch, we're going back," he said to the man beside him. "There's a whole lot of pieces that need picking up at the facility, and nobody but us to do it."

Its engine throbbing, Kuhl's jeep shot through the gap in the fence at full horsepower, reversing the path it had taken into the compound.

Kuhl turned in the front passenger seat and saw the twin points of headlights in the darkness behind him. But they were a good distance away, and that distance seemed to be growing. Still, he wanted to keep his eyes on them.

The jeep plunged ahead into the jungle, bouncing over the road, vines and branches lashing its windshield, leaving behind long, drippy swipes of moisture. Soon the unbroken tunnel of vegetation around it was screening out the sky.

Kuhl watched the headlights steadily, convinced they were indeed becoming further off. Why might that be so? he asked himself. Certainly their position beside the jeep had given Kuhl and his three companions a jump on the security teams, who had dispersed from their own vehicles during the firefight. But that only accounted for his head start, not the absence of any concerted and determined pursuit. And what of the helicopters? Why hadn't they been sent after him?

A faint smile touched his lips. Even flight had its lessons, and it struck him that he'd just gained another bit of understanding about UpLink's vulnerabilities, limitations, and the dynamics of its relationship with the Brazilians.

It was knowledge he would have to carefully digest along with the rest of what he'd learned tonight.

Knowledge that was bound to be very useful as the next phase of the game commenced.

FIVE

THE BALD EAGLE LAUNCHED FROM THE TALL TREES downhill to their right, soaring above the old pilings at the marshy tidal band, its long outspread wings a serrate outline against the sky, the untinged whiteness of its head and tail feathers contrasting so strikingly with its blackish body they seemed almost like luminous, painted-on accents to guide the eye across its perfect form.

Megan watched it circle the pilings twice, rise gracefully on an updraft, and then swing out across the shiny waters of the bay. The shore below her was silent. Nothing moved amid the rushes. Nor was there any motion in the tangled scrub sloping off from the deck where she sat with Nimec and Ricci, a cup of strong black coffee on the table in front of her.

"It'll generally stay quiet for five, ten minutes after she's gone. Then you'll see the gulls, terns, and ducks come back, sometimes a few at a time, sometimes hundreds of them at once, like there's been an all-clear," Ricci said. "The eagles prefer eating fish to anything else, but when they're really hungry or nursing a brood, they'll make a meal out of whatever they can sink their talons into. Smaller birds, rodents, even house cats that stray too far from their backyards."

Megan reluctantly dropped her gaze from the eagle's path. Its sudden appearance had given her a thrill of excitement, but Ricci had promised an explanation for the ugly scene on the road, and she was more than ready to hear it.

She shot a glance across the table at him. "How about urchins?"

Ricci smiled a little. "Them too," he said.

She kept looking at him pointedly.

"I think Megan was offering you a neat little segue there," Nimec said from the chair beside her. "Might not be a bad idea to take it."

Ricci paused a moment, then nodded.

"You two want to go inside first?" He gestured toward the sliding door leading back into his house. "It's getting pretty brisk out here."

Nimec's shoulders rose and fell. "I'm okay."

"Same," Megan said. "I can use the fresh air after all the *schlepping* around we've done. To use an Irish word."

Ricci sat there, his face showing not one iota of concern about the headaches he'd caused them. That irritated Megan, and she hoped the expression on *her* face made it abundantly clear to him. The *schlep* she'd mentioned had included following his pickup for nearly an hour as he'd led them to a fish-smelling wholesale seafood market on a wharf at the foot of the peninsula, where they'd had to wait while he'd spent another hour hustling back and forth between one saltbox shed and another, haggling with buyers over the value of several large plastic trays he'd been carrying in the flatbed of the truck . . . or more accurately the layers of spiny, tennis-ball-sized green sea urchins inside those trays, what he'd earlier referred to as his catch. And all that after she and Nimec had traveled three thousand miles across the country by air and ground, and the unexpected confrontation with the warden and deputy sheriff.

"I suppose," Ricci said at length, "you'd like me to tell you why those uniformed humps were on my case."

Megan watched him coolly over the rim of her cup.

"That would be nice," she said.

Ricci lifted his own coffee to his mouth, sipped, and then set it down on the circular tabletop.

"Either of you know anything about urchin diving?"

Megan shook her head.

"Pete?" Ricci said.

"Only that urchins are a specialty item in foreign seafood markets. I'd assume they can bring good money."

Ricci nodded.

"Actually it's the roe that's valuable. Or can be, anyway. You ever been to a sushi bar, it's what they call *uni* on the menu. The bulk of it gets shipped out to Japan, the rest to Japanese communities in this country and Canada," he said. "Its price depends on availability, the percentage of roe in comparison to its total weight, and the quality of the roe, which has to be a bronzy gold color—kind of like a tangerine—if you want to fetch a premium. Those trays I unloaded had about two and a half bushels of urchins each and were worth almost a grand to me."

Megan looked at him. "If somebody had told me that when I was ten, I'd be worth millions today. My big brother and I would walk along the beach and collect them off the jetties in our plastic buckets. Then we'd fill the buckets with ocean water and try to convince our parents to let us bring them home as pets. My dad would tell us to get those damned sea porcupines out of the house."

Ricci smiled faintly.

"People have different nicknames for them around here, but they shared your father's sentiments till recently, when everybody heard about the Asian demand and got a yen for the yen," he said. "Before that, they were just considered nuisances. Most of the old-time lobstermen still refer to them as whore's eggs because they mess up their traps. Clog the vents, eat the bait, even chew through the headings and lathe to get at the bait. The nasty little buggers have some sharp teeth to go with their spines."

"You gather the urchins yourself?"

"Harvesting's done in teams of at least one scuba diver and a tender, who waits above in the boat," Ricci said. "I like to do the underwater work alone. Take a big mesh tote below with me and pick the best-looking urchins. When a bag's full, I send up a float line so my tender, this guy named Dexter, can spot it and hoist it aboard."

"Tender?" Megan said. "Define, please."

"It's the diver's equivalent of a golf caddy. He's supposed to maintain the scuba equipment, look out for the diver's safety, make sure the catch doesn't freeze, and if time allows, cull the urchins. Something goes wrong, how he reacts can be critical." He paused. "That's why the profits get split down the middle."

Nimec raised an eyebrow. "I heard you mention a Dex when you were facing off with the deputy. . . ."

"That's him," Ricci said.

"Didn't sound like your partnership's exactly rock solid."

Ricci shrugged.

"Maybe, maybe not," he said. "I'll get to that."

Megan watched him, warming her hands around her cup. "Is it always your job to bring the catch to market?"

He leaned back slightly in his chair.

"I'm getting around to that too," he said, and drank

more coffee. "The urchins are found in colonies, usually in subtidal kelp beds. Once upon a time they practically carpeted the bottom of the Penobscot from the shoreline on out, so you could scoop them up without dunking your head." He paused. "Past few years have been slim pickings. Overharvesting's driven the value of the catch up into the stratosphere, and made people so protective of their zones they're baring their teeth and beating their chests if you come anywhere close to them."

"These zones . . . I presume they're demarcated by law."

Ricci nodded.

"There's a license that costs almost three hundred bucks, and with the conservation restrictions nowadays you have to wait your turn in a lottery to get one. When applying for it, you have to choose the area and season you want to dive in. Wardens inspect it very carefully. Tells them whether you're legal in black and white."

"Your trays were packed full," Nimec said. "Seems to me you're doing okay."

Ricci nodded again.

"Also seems to me that would get noticed fast during a period of decline in the overall yield. By other divers, buyers, and the warden if he's got his eyes open."

Ricci looked straight at him and nodded a third time. "You won't find a whole lot of guys who like going out as far, or down as deep as I do . . . especially not this time of year, when the water temperature can still drop near freezing and the currents are rough. But there are hundreds of tiny islets in the bay, a few of them within my diving area, and I hit on one that's got a deepwater cove where the urchin count's wild and wonderful."

Nimec looked thoughtful.

"Word got around," he said.

"Uh-huh," Ricci said. "When you're talking about a stake that's worth serious cash, and men who are having a hard time feeding their families, it's a volatile combination. There are resentments toward people from away that go back a long, long time and are maybe even a little justified. Back around the turn of the century, rich out-of-towners started buying up acres and acres of bay-front land around their summer mansions as privacy buffers against the fishermen and clam diggers they thought of as white trash. Stuck 'No Trespassing' signs up everywhere, restricting their access to the water that was their livelihood."

"Somebody twist the locals' arms to sell?" Megan said.

Ricci gave her a sharp look.

"Either you've never been poor, or you've forgotten what that can be like," he said brusquely. "Watch your kids starve through a Maine winter, and you won't need any other kind of arm-twisting."

She sat there in the brittle silence that followed, wondering if his reaction had made her feel guiltier about her remark than she should have.

"Dex and the warden cut some kind of deal?" Nimec said. The last thing he wanted was to get sidetracked.

Ricci turned his coffee cup in his hands, seeming to concentrate on the steam wisping up from it.

"Let's get back to whether it's usually me who drives the catch to market," he said at last. "I've been working with Dex for over a year and never went there without him before today. Guy likes wheeling and dealing, likes to get the wholesalers bidding. The whole thing from soup to nuts, you know?" He paused. "He also looks forward to having his cash in hand. But this morning he tells me something about needing to rush home to watch his kids after school. Said his wife had to work late and there was nobody else. The minute we pull the boat in, he's up and away."

"Happens when you're a parent," Nimec said, think-

ing he could have cited any number of comparable situations from when his own children were young and his
wife was not yet his *ex*-wife.

Ricci shook his head.

"You don't know Dex," he said. "Ask him to rec-
ommend a local bar, he'll rattle off the names of two
dozen watering holes from here to New Brunswick and
tell you every kind of beer they have on tap. Ask him
his kids' birthdays, he'd be stumped."

"So you think he arranged for you to be driving by
yourself when you got stopped," Nimec said.

Ricci turned his coffee cup but said nothing.

Nimec sighed. "Was it the warden who pulled you
over?"

"Yeah. Cobbs is one of those down-easters I told you
about resents outsiders . . . and just about everybody and
everything else besides, but that's just his endearing personality. I move here from Boston, earn a decent buck,
it's like I'm taking something away from him. Add that
I'm a cop . . . an ex-cop . . . and he gets even more both-
ered."

"He feels intimidated and threatened by you, and that
translates into a sort of competitive hostility," Nimec
said. "Common equation in places where they don't get
much new blood. Especially when it's coming from the
big city."

Ricci shrugged.

"There's all that, and with Cobbs it goes even further," he said. "He's a weasel and he's dirty. I'd heard
stories about him from divers as well as lobstermen.
Give him a skim of your profits, he'll let you operate
without a license or outside your zone, even look the
other way if you row out at night and raid somebody's
lobster traps. Up until now, you didn't play along, he'd
hassle you for the slightest infraction of the rules, but
wouldn't actually squeeze anybody outright. The stunt

he tried to pull on me takes him to a new level."

"Claiming he'd seen you dive outside your zone so he could confiscate your entire catch," Nimec said. "That it?"

Ricci snapped his pointer finger out at him and nodded.

"Like you said, times are rough," Nimec said. He exhaled, deciding to take another stab at a question Ricci had already angled past twice. "I want to try this with you again . . . you think Dex and Cobbs have something going?"

Ricci stared at his cup, still turning and turning it in his hands. It was no longer steaming.

"Been trying to work that out in my own mind," he said in a hesitant tone. "Cobbs and his deputy dog were waiting for me on the road, and I doubt it's a coincidence that they knew exactly when I'd be driving out to the market, and what route I'd take. Also bothers me that the day they chose to pull me over happened to be the one and only day Dex wasn't around to keep me company."

"Wouldn't it have been better for him if he came along for the ride?" Nimec said. "To act surprised, I mean. The way it went down just makes him look suspicious."

Ricci moved his shoulders. "Dex is no genius. Assuming the worst about him, could be that he was only worried having to look me in the eye when I drove into their little setup. Or maybe he doesn't care what I suspect. Maybe with Cobbs he gets a better than even slice of the action, and all that matters to him is running me out of it."

"And out of town in the process," Nimec said.

Ricci nodded. "Like I said, assuming the worst-case scenario. But right now that's all just for argument's sake."

They sat in silence for a while. Megan watched them, feeling strangely like an observer. She sensed the easy intersection of their thoughts, the unspoken communication of men who had done police work for much of their lives, and all at once thought she had an inkling why Nimec wanted Ricci for Max's position.

"Let's stick to Cobbs for the moment," Nimec said finally. "He's not going to just leave things as they are. You know his type. The way you embarrassed him, he'll be twisting like a corkscrew until he can get back at you. And that's probably going to happen sooner than later. He'll lick his wounds, convince himself you got lucky today."

"I know," Ricci said.

"Being hooked into the sheriff's office, he'll think he can get away with whatever he wants. Your warning about getting in touch with outside agencies won't stop him. Far as he's concerned, they're a world away."

"I know."

Nimec looked at him.

"What are you planning to do?" he said.

Ricci grunted indeterminately. He took a drink of coffee, frowned, and set the cup down on the table.

"Flat," he said, and pushed it away from him.

More silence.

Megan's gaze wandered briefly down to the bay. The sunlight was fading, and white patches of sea smoke had begun rising from the water as dusk's cold breezes slipped over its warmer surface. The birds had returned with the eagle's departure, bearing out Ricci's prediction. She could see rafts of ducks near the shoreline almost straight below, and further off, gulls descending through the mist to alight on shoals exposed by the receding tide. Broad-chested and gray-patched, they seemed instantly to enter a state of repose, puffing out their feathers against the dropping temperature.

Suddenly it seemed very late in the day.

"We should talk about why Pete and I came to see you," she said. "You still haven't given us your feelings about it."

Ricci looked at her. "Now that you mention it, why *did* the two of you come?"

Megan blinked.

"You don't know," she said. It was a statement rather than a question.

He shook his head.

She turned to Nimec. "You didn't tell him?"

Nimec shook his head. "I thought we'd wait until we got here," he said without explanation. "Discuss it face-to-face."

She rubbed her eyebrows with her thumb and forefinger, shook her head a little, and sighed resignedly.

"We'd better go inside after all," she said. "Seems this is going to take longer than I expected."

A little past five-thirty in the afternoon P.D.T., two urgent calls were placed from the Brazilian space station facility to UpLink's corporate headquarters in San Jose.

The first was to Roger Gordian.

Standing near his office window, looking out at the rain that had just started pouring down on Rosita Avenue, Gordian was about to leave for the day when his desk phone chirruped. He stared at it a moment, tempted to let it remain on the hook, one arm halfway inside his trench coat. Whoever it was could leave a message.

Chree-eep!

Ignore it, he urged himself. Ashley. Dinner. Home.

The phone rang a third time. On the fourth, the caller would be automatically transferred to Gordian's voice mail.

Shrugging out of his coat, he frowned in acquiescence and grabbed the receiver.

"Yes?" he said.

The man at the other end identified himself as Mason Cody from the Sword operational center, Mato Grasso do Sul. His voice seemed to come out of an odd, tunneling silence that put Gordian in mind of what it was like holding a conch shell up against his ear—listening to the ocean, they'd called it when he was young.

He sat behind his desk, realizing immediately that he was on a secure digital line. And that the call was therefore anything but routine.

"Sir, there's been an incident," Cody said in a tone that made his back stiffen.

Gordian listened quietly as the violent events at the ISS compound were outlined for him in a rapid but collected manner, his hand tensing around the receiver at the news of injuries and fatalities.

"The wounded men," he said. "How are they doing?"

"They've all been medevaced from the scene," Cody said. "Most are in fair shape or better."

"What about Rollie Thibodeau? You said he'd been pretty badly hurt."

"He's still in surgery." A pause. "No word on his condition."

Gordian willed himself to be calm.

"Has Pete Nimec been told about this?" he asked.

"My feeling was that I should brief you first, Mr. Gordian. I plan to call him the moment we sign off."

Gordian rotated his chair toward the window, thinking about what he'd just been told. It was all so difficult to absorb.

"Is there anything else?" he said. "Any idea who was behind the raid?"

"I wish I could tell you we know, sir," Cody said. "Maybe we'll get something out of the prisoners, though right now I'm not even sure how long we can hold onto them."

Gordian inhaled, exhaled. Cody's meaning was clear. As members of a private security force that operated internationally, Sword personnel were obliged to abide by stringent rules of conduct, some of them preconditions set by host governments, some internal guidelines, occasionally complicated formulations premised on the simple reality that they were guests on foreign soil. While adjustments for different cultural and political circumstances were built into their procedural framework, it would be pushing beyond acceptable bounds to interrogate the captured attackers even if the on-site capabilities to detain them existed—which was doubtful. Moreover, an incident on the scale he'd been told about would have to be reported to the Brazilians, assuming they hadn't already learned of it through their own domestic intelligence apparatus. Once the prisoners were in their custody, it was impossible to guess whether Brazilian law enforcement would share any information obtained from them. The politics of the situation were going to be touchy, and the last thing Gordian wanted was to start stepping on toes.

"Have you been in contact with the local authorities?"

"Not yet," Cody said. "Thought I ought to hold off, see how you wanted that handled. Hope that was the right thing."

"It was exactly right," Gordian said. "I suspect they'll be showing up without word from us, but notify them as soon as possible anyway. Tell them that we mean to provide our absolute cooperation in terms of whatever questions they have. And that we're confident they'll reciprocate. It's in our common interest to get to the bottom of this." *I assume,* he thought, but did not add. "You have my home telephone number on file?"

Gordian heard the tapping of computer keys.

"Yes, it's right up in front of me."

"Okay. Keep me posted on any developments. Doesn't matter what hour it is."

"Understood," Cody said.

Gordian took another breath.

"I suppose that's it," he said. "Hang tight, I know you've got hell on your hands."

"We're doing our best, Mr. Gordian," Cody said.

His voice dropped into that hermetic tunnel of silence again.

Gordian cradled the receiver and sat looking out his window in sober contemplation. Rainwater splashed against the glass, washing down its surface in long rippling streams. From his angle, he could see nothing of the street below, no pedestrians scurrying through puddles for someplace dry, no cars crawling along with their windshield wipers on. Mount Hamilton too seemed beyond the reach of his vision, rendered a gray, featureless blur by the heavy curtains of moisture blowing across the sky.

It was, he thought, as if the world was made of rain. Only rain.

As Gordian had been assured, Cody's next call was to Pete Nimec. He was not in his office, and the recorded greeting on his voice mail said he would be away overnight and checking his incoming messages regularly. His cell phone number was given for emergencies.

Cody quickly terminated the connection and dialed it.

"So you want me to be your, what, eyes and ears around the world," Ricci said. He crouched and put a log into the woodstove opposite the comfortable leather sofa where his visitors were seated. "That about it, Pete?"

"Not quite, if I may interject a point or two," Megan said, glancing at Nimec.

He gave her a shrug. They were in Ricci's spacious

living room, a mid-1980's rear addition to a Colonial home built a century earlier, with natural wood plank walls and glass sliding doors that gave onto the water-front deck where they'd been talking until a few minutes ago.

"The person we select will be responsible for implementing and coordinating security functions at UpLink's various international and domestic sites," she said. "He or she will be second in authority only to Pete. But I want to stress that we're primarily here so you and I can get acquainted, and to gauge your interest in us."

"And yours in me," Ricci said, facing her.

They exchanged looks.

"Yes," she said. "It's a unique and demanding job. We naturally want to see if you've got what it takes to meet its challenges."

Ricci considered that a second, then nodded.

"Fair enough," he said. "You still assembling your candidate list?"

"The only other person whose qualifications we're presently weighing is a current member of our Brazilian team named Roland Thibodeau. And to be frank, his interest in the position hasn't yet been determined. I plan on speaking to Rollie sometime within the next couple of days."

Ricci turned to Nimec. "How come you wouldn't tell me anything about the reason for this visit over the phone?" he said.

"If I'd tried, I would have heard a click in the receiver before the words were finished leaving my mouth. Figured it would be best to come and talk. See how you felt about it face-to-face."

Ricci silently took three sheets of newspaper from a shallow wine crate beside him, crumpled them, and pushed them underneath the grille of the stove. Then he struck a match and held it to the newspapers to start them burning. Flames crackled up and licked at the bottom of the log.

When the log had caught, he carefully shut the glass-paneled door of the stove and looked at Megan again.

"I figure you've heard the long sad story of how I lost my badge," he said.

"Pete gave me his take on it," she said. "I'd already gotten another from the papers."

"You can see why I like using them as tinder then," he said.

She smiled a little.

"The thought had occurred to me," she said. "In light of today's events, it also strikes me that you have a knack for making enemies in the wrong places."

Ricci hesitated for the barest moment. "You read the version where they say I'm an uncontrollable maverick, or the one where I'm called an outright disgrace to the Boston police department?"

"Both, actually, but I tend to ignore the descriptive nouns and home in on the bare facts," she said. "A kid falls to his death from an Ivy League campus rooftop. The group of frat boys who were up there with him claim it's a terrible hazing accident. Too many beers, reckless behavior. As the city's chief homicide detective, you head what everyone expects to be a perfunctory investigation, until the coroner's report reveals there was no alcohol in the deceased's bloodstream. You start digging around, find out the boys who were on that roof are heavily into dealing drugs and other unsavory after-school projects, then find out there's been some bad blood between the group leader and the kid who was killed. The alpha gets charged with first-degree murder; his friends deal down in exchange for their cooperation as state's witnesses. There's a trial and he's found guilty, which should mean a mandatory twenty-five-to-life sentence. But the jury's verdict is overturned by the judge

123

and he walks on a technicality. Something about an error in how certain evidence was processed by the medical examiner's office." She paused. "How am I doing so far?"

Ricci's eyes held to her firmly.

"You don't mind, I'll wait for the next part before rating you," he said.

Megan nodded. The log in the woodstove popped and spat sap, flames flaring brightly around it.

"Next you do a spate of media interviews repudiating the judge, arguing that the error shouldn't have been enough to get the case into Appellate Court, let alone warrant nullification from the bench," she said. "Even more seriously, you allege that the judge was bought and paid for by the killer's father. They go on television with their counterclaims, say you have some kind of personal ax to grind. A number of details from your departmental records are leaked to the press, including information that you'd received counseling for problem drinking and depression while on the force. There are stories that you have a bad attitude. When it's all over, the kid is still free and you've turned in your badge. The general impression is that you were given the choice of either resigning or being discharged without pension."

She sat quietly again, watching him.

"That's not bad, far as it goes," Ricci said. "But there's also what you left out."

"I didn't want to sit here giving a recitation," she said. "It might be better to hear the rest from you. If you care to tell it."

Ricci nodded.

"Sure," he said. "In the interest of good public relations."

She waited without comment.

"The murdering little prince's father was a Beacon Hill millionaire," he said. "I learned during the trial that the judge belonged to the same A-list country club as Dad, which in my opinion ought to have been enough to have him removed from the case. Prosecution could've taken it up in district court, but didn't, and since it's their call I couldn't let myself worry about it. After the trial's over, though, I hear from a couple of staffers at the club that there were three separate meetings between Dad, the judge, and the oak wainscoting while the jury was in deliberation. One of them's the manager, a solid guy who's been working there forty years and has no reason to be spinning tall tales. Came forward out of feeling guilty, like the other two." He shrugged. "They denied it later on, when I went public."

"Somebody cured their guilt," Megan said. "Money and power being the prescribed remedy. If I'm to believe your version."

Dead silence. Ricci looked hard at her, the fire tossing shadows across his angular features.

"What is it exactly that bothers you about me?" he said at last.

His blue eyes level and probing.

She opened her mouth as if to reply, closed it, and merely stared back at him without saying anything.

"I believe it," Nimec said, breaking into the silence. "His account, that is."

Ricci turned to Nimec, leaving Megan surprised by her own relief at being out from under his steady gaze.

"I don't need an advocate," Ricci said.

"Your credibility shouldn't be at issue here."

Ricci's features beamed with sudden intensity. "I told you I don't need to be defended. Not by you or anybody else."

Megan raised her hand in a curtailing gesture.

"Wait," she said. "I'm not trying to be antagonistic, and apologize if that's how I came across. It's been a wearing day."

Ricci looked at her in silence, those penetrating eyes back on her face.

"I think we should take a step back," she said. "Concentrate on your feelings about the job with UpLink."

Ricci looked at her a while longer. At last he exhaled audibly.

"I don't know," he said. "To be straight, I'm not sure it's something I'd want any part of, or even that I've got the background for. This is big stuff. Seems to me you ought to be looking at heavy artillery, not a Police Special."

Nimec leaned forward, his hands clasped on his lap.

"Except that the background you're so quick to dismiss includes four years with SEAL Team Six, an elite within an elite created for antiterrorist operations," he said. "And that's just for openers."

"Pete—"

Nimec cut him short. "After leaving the military in '94 you joined the Boston police, earned your first-class detective shield in record time. Worked deep cover with the Organized Crime Task Force, an assignment for which you were particularly well-suited because of your experiences with ST 6, where one of your special areas of expertise was infiltration techniques. Upon conclusion of a major racketeering investigation you requested a transfer to the Homicide Division and stuck with it until the bad affair we've been talking about."

Ricci knelt there by the stove, looking across the room at him.

"Running down my stats doesn't change how I feel," he said. "There are ten years between me and the service. That's a long time."

Nimec shook his head.

"I don't get you, Tom," he said. "Nobody's twisting arms, but this isn't a take-it-or-leave-it proposition. It deserves fair consideration. By all of us. We should at least agree to—"

He abruptly broke off. Set to its vibration mode, the palm phone in his shirt pocket had silently indicated he was receiving a call.

"One second," he said, holding up his pointer finger.

He took out the phone, flipped open the mouthpiece, and answered.

His features showed surprise, then sharp attention, then a mixture of both.

It was Cody from Mato Grasso.

Speaking in the same tone of controlled urgency he had used with Roger Gordian, Cody ran down the situation in Brazil for the second time in less than ten minutes, his voice routed via that nation's conventional landlines to an UpLink satellite gateway in northern Argentina, transmitted to a low-earth-orbit communications satellite, electronically amplified, retransmitted to a tracking antenna operated by a local cellular service in coastal Maine, and sent on to Nimec's handset all virtually instantaneously.

Nimec asked something in a hushed voice, listened, whispered into the phone again, and ended the call.

"Pete, what is it?" Megan said, reading the deep concern on his face.

He kept the phone open in his hand.

"Trouble," he said. "A level-one in Brazil."

She looked at him knowingly. His use of the code meant a crisis of the gravest nature had occurred, and that he did not want to go into details about it in Ricci's presence.

"Roger been informed?" she asked.

He nodded.

"We'd better check in with him," he said. "Got a feeling he's going to want us back in San Jose right away."

•   •   •

The doctors knew they had their job cut out the moment he was brought into the emergency room.

It would have been clear even to an untrained observer that he was in terrible shape; clear from his near-comatose state; clear from all the blood that had soaked from the gaping hole in his belly through his clothing, the thin blankets covering him, and the uniforms of the technicians who had delivered him on the stretcher; clear from the blue cast of his skin and the weak, irregular rhythm of his breath.

To the expert eye, these physiological signs pointed toward specific life-threatening complications that would have to be assessed and treated without losing an instant. The severe hemorrhaging alone would have led them to evaluate him for shock, but his lividity left scant doubt of its onset, and the blood pressure cuffs placed on his arm as his stretcher was rolled in had given systolic and diastolic readings of zero over less than zero, indicating a near-cessation of his circulatory processes. His thready breathing also suggested that a tension pneumothorax—in laymen's terms, an air pocket between the lungs and their surrounding tissues developing as a *result* of shock—was putting pressure on the lungs and causing them to fully or partially collapse.

The condition would lead to respiratory failure and certain death unless relieved by external means.

Managing a medical crisis requires a constantly unfolding and frequently accelerating series of prioritizations. In this case the priority was to stabilize his vital functions even before the injuries to his internal organs could be determined by Xrays and exploratory abdominal surgery. Only then would it be known with certainty how many times he'd been shot, or what path the bullet, bullets, or bullet fragments had taken.

With the clock ticking, the surgeon in charge at once

began giving directions to his assistants in a rapid and assertive manner.

"I want MASTs . . ."

This being an acronym for medical shock trousers, which could be slipped onto the patient and inflated with air to force blood up from his lower extremities to his heart and brain.

". . . seven units of packed RBCs . . ."

Shorthand for red blood cells, the hemoglobin-rich component of blood that provides life-giving oxygen to body tissues. In a typical situation requiring transfusion, the patients's serum is cross-matched for compatibility with a sample of the blood product to be administered, but because he was an employee of UpLink, this man's type was already on file on the doctors' computer database, eliminating that step and conserving precious minutes.

". . . a big line . . ."

A wide intravenous catheter used to get the RBCs into his system by quick, massive transfusion.

". . . and a needle aspirator in him *stat*!"

The needle aspirator being a large syringe used to drain the air out of the pneumothorax, inflate the lungs, and restore normal breathing; stat, medical jargon for *I need it done five seconds ago,* a word derived and abbreviated from the original Latin *statim,* meaning immediately.

While the image of medical professionals working in conditions of ordered, clockwork sterility is a common one, nothing will dispel it faster than a glimpse inside a trauma room, where the battle to save lives is a close, tense, chaotic, messy, sweaty affair. Jabbing a 14-gauge big-bore needle into the chest of a powerfully built two-hundred-pound man, clenching the attached syringe in your fist and unsuccessfully attempting to insert it between hard slabs of pectoral muscle once, twice, and again before finally making a clean entry, then drawing out the plunger and getting a rush of warm, moist air in your face as the pocket that had formed around the lungs decompressed, was nobody's idea of a picnic—as the young doctor who had been hastily summoned on duty tonight, and who was now toiling away over Rollie Thibodeau here in the ISS facility's critical-care unit, trying to prevent him from dying before he made it onto an operating table, would have attested if he'd had the time. But he was too busy following the instructions called out by the chief physician, himself standing over the patient, working to get the big line and saline IVs connected to him in a hurry.

With the syringe in place and the air suctioned from the pneumothorax, it was essential to prevent its recurrence and keep the patient breathing. This meant going ahead with a full closed-tube thorascostomy.

The first step was to create an airtight seal around the tube. Barely registering the frantic activity around him, the young doctor lifted a scalpel from an instrument tray and sliced into the flesh between the ribs, making a horizontal incision. Then he took a Kelly clamp off the tray and pushed it into the incision, holding it by the shaft, expanding it to spread the soft tissue and create a tunnel for his finger. Blood splashed up around the clamp as he removed it from the opening and pressed his gloved finger between the lips of the cut, going in as deep as his knuckle, carefully feeling for the lung and diaphragm. After assuring himself that he had penetrated through to the intrapleural area—the space between the lungs and ribs where the air pocket had formed—he asked a scrub nurse for the chest tube and carefully guided it into the opening.

He paused, studied the patient, and exhaled a sigh of relief. The patient's breathing was stronger and more regular, his skin color vastly improved. A water collection system at the opposite end of the chest tube would keep the air draining from the patient's chest while insuring that no air was drawn back into it. To complete the procedure, the young doctor would suture the skin around the tube to preserve the seal.

A very long night still lay ahead, but Thibodeau would have something like a fighting chance as the doctors hustled him into the OR, opened him up, and got a look at the extent of the damage that had been done inside him.

SIX

A LOOK OF QUIET GRATIFICATION ON HIS FACE, HARlan DeVane watched the line of three flatbed trucks roll along the hardpack at the eastern border of his ranch as they approached the airstrip and the waiting Beech Bonanza in a cloud of dust. Now, before midday, the sun was a firebrand hanging above the battered old *camiones* and the wide, flat pasture closer by, where he could see his cattle, prime heifers imported from Argentina, grazing indolently in the heat. There was no wind, and the ash and smoke from the forest fires seemed an inert smear above the horizon. Once the afternoon breezes stirred, however, it would rise and spread into a blanketing gray haze, dimming the sun so that one could look directly up into it with the unprotected eye. It was a price of development that DeVane found regrettable, but he was a man who dealt with realities as they presented themselves. The loggers bulldozed new roads, and the opportunistic peasant farmers and ranchers who came here to settle followed along those roads, and because the soil was quickly depleted in the Amazon basin—good for no more than three years' growing of crops—they would clear previously untouched tracts of forest as their fields dried up and grew fallow. The cycle was implacable yet unavoidable. Nothing in life came free of charge, and most often you paid as you went.

"It appears the plane soon will be on its way, Harlan," Rojas said, taking a sip of his chilled *guapuru*.

DeVane looked at him from under the brim of his white Panama hat. His skin was tightly stretched over his cheeks and almost colorless. His eyes were a frozen shade of blue set deep in their sockets. He wore a white double-breasted suit that had been custom-tailored from some lightweight fabric, probably in Europe. The collar points of his blue silk shirt were neatly buttoned down under blue-and-yellow pinstriped suspenders. Unbothered by the torrid weather, he seemed to occupy his own still pocket of space, putting Rojas in mind of the lionfish that floated in the waters of the Carribean—so illusively delicate in appearance, so serenely poisonous.

"And you, Francisco?" he said, speaking Portuguese although Rojas was proficient in English. "Will you be leaving with it? Or can I assume you've made other arrangements?"

"You know it is my habit let the *perico* fly on separately," Rojas said. "As a precaution."

DeVane was inwardly amused by his choice of words. The cocaine made you manic and talkative. Like a parrot, *perico* in Spanish. It was a term of low slang he might have expected from some street-level dealer in San Borja, not a Brazilian police official of considerable rank. But Rojas was of a type. A gutless, corrupt, lazy little south-of-the-equator bureaucrat trying to affect the manner of an outlaw. Light a firecracker outside his office window and he would hide quailing under his desk.

"I'll have my driver take you back to the airport in Rurrenabaque when we're finished," he said. "You're entitled to feel safe."

Rojas heard the note of derision in DeVane's voice and held his hands apart.

"Things happen," he said. "I expect no problems, but as always will be relieved when the shipment reaches its destination."

In fact, Rojas thought, his relief would begin the moment he was out from under the hard eyes of DeVane's bodyguards. And away from Kuhl. Kuhl seemed less a human being than a cold precision weapon . . . and how dangerous it was for such a murderous instrument to be controlled by someone with a boundless appetite for wealth and power. Kuhl had acquired a forbidding reputation on his own, but there was no doubt that his association with DeVane had enhanced his innate capacity for violence and given it a chance for its fullest, bloodiest expression.

Yes, it would be good to be elsewhere.

Rojas reached for his glass again and took a long drink. This was not the first time he had met with these men, and by now he ought to be able to curb his uneasiness. The trick was to steer his attention away from Kuhl and the armed guards. Concentrate on his physical surroundings. He would try, and be satisfied if he were halfway successful. Certainly the scenery was pleasant. They were at a table shaded by a flowering mimosa in the foreyard of DeVane's impressive ranch house, a place of rambling sunbaked walls and a tiled roof that might have been built for a Spanish Don—some descendent of the Conquistadores perhaps—with only the swimming pools and tennis court on its desultory grounds betraying its far more recent vintage. Quite grand indeed, and just one of many lavish homes DeVane kept around the world, traveling continuously between them as he oversaw his far-reaching business empire.

Out across the grassland, the *camiones* had reached

the tarmac and lumbered to a halt in the shadow of the waiting plane. Rojas watched as their ragtag Quechua drivers began to unload the backs of the trucks and carry their bundles toward the Beech's cargo bay.

"Your ability to keep the Indians loyal is extraordinary, Harlan," he said. "I'd never ever have expected it."

DeVane studied his face.

"How so?" he said. "They've traded with Americans before."

Rojas tried to make his shrug look casual. "Yes, but not on the terms you have set. It is a singularly unusual arrangement. Buying from the Peruvians, employing the local *cocaderos* only for refining and distribution . . ."

He let the sentence fade.

DeVane kept his eyes on him.

"Go on," he said. "Please."

Rojas hesitated, then said, "The laborers are poor and the Chapare crop is their main resource. A hundred kilos might bring three million dollars in greenbacks if they handled production from beginning to end. Instead, they must either find other buyers for their plants or have them rot in the field."

Devane smiled, his small, even white teeth showing suddenly and briefly. "Give your people too little and they resent you. Too much and they no longer need you. The secret of holding onto their loyalty is to let them have just enough, Francisco."

"I would still think that your dealing with outside growers would cause resentment," Rojas said, his curiosity momentarily overbalancing his caution. "And that the Sendero Luminoso would have its own reasons to balk. They have long had their own processing system in place, and are adamant about protecting their interests."

"No more so than I am, and they know it," DeVane

said. "I have my reasons for keeping the leftist rebels part of the operation. And they have their unprecedented earnings to make them happy."

Rojas decided to back off, feeling vaguely as if he'd been maneuvered.

"As I say, you have my admiration," he said. "It is a dance of devils that I could never manage."

DeVane didn't seem inclined to end the conversation. "The devil can be the best of partners once you know his steps," he said. "You are aware, I'm sure, that the nickname he has been given by the tin miners in the southern mountains is *El Tio*. The Uncle. On Sunday mornings they attend church with their families, make their genuflections, and sing the praises of Jesus and his saints. But before going down into the mine shafts, they pause at their entrances to leave offerings before statues of *El Tio*—alcohol, cigarettes, and coca leaves."

Rojas's discomfort was escalating again.

"Appropriate gifts for the Lord of Hell," he commented.

"Precisely." DeVane flashed his quick, icy grin again. "Their reasoning is wonderfully pragmatic. If you're going to work where it's dark and hot, you must learn how to get by. And appease the gods whose bounty you seek."

There was a long period of silence. The sun had climbed into the center of the sky and hammered the livestock across the field into immobility. Rojas glanced around at the young guards standing near the table with their Kalashnikovs in plain view, then turned his attention back toward the airstrip and the workmen moving heavily between their trucks and the plane. He felt tired and depleted, and once more wished he were somewhere else.

DeVane took a small sip from his glass, then placed it carefully down on the table.

"I'd like your assistance with something, Francisco,"

he said. "A matter of considerable importance."

Rojas had been waiting for this moment. In most instances he would have sent a courier along with payment for a shipment of product, but when DeVane had insisted on his presence today he'd obliged without asking for an explanation—aware the American wouldn't offer one until he was good and ready.

"If it concerns the Guzman fiasco, then you may be pleased to know I've gone ahead and intervened," he said. "Give me another day and I'll have him out of his prison cell and back across the border."

"I appreciate that and will provide whatever funds are necessary to secure his release," DeVane said. "But this has nothing to do with him."

Rojas lifted his eyebrows. Eduardo Guzman was a bottom runner in DeVane's organization, an errand boy whose arrest on suspicion of narcotics and weapons trafficking had resulted from his involvement with a prostitute who was cooperating with the anti-drug police. In ordinary circumstances he would have been beneath DeVane's notice, a scrap to be thrown to the wolves, but because it was widely known that his uncle was one of DeVane's major executives in Sao Paulo, Rojas had assumed the American would want him pulled out of his own shit, and made discreet overtures to the prosecutors getting ready to arraign him on formal charges. Little to his surprise, nearly all of them had hinted they might be influenced into changing their minds for a price.

However, DeVane had just made it very clear that he did not want to talk about Guzman. Leaving what he did want to talk about a mystery.

"Forgive my confusion," Rojas said. "I'd thought—"

"There was an incident last night in the Mato Grasso, a break-in of sorts at an American industrial site," Kuhl interrupted. It was the first time he'd spoken since Rojas's arrival. "Did you hear anything about it before starting out this morning?"

"I don't think so," Rojas said. In fact, he knew that he hadn't. But as a rule, it paid to stay out of the water until you knew which way it was flowing.

"Rest assured, you will before too long," Kuhl said. "What you should know is that a number of the intruders were captured or killed by this facility's private security force. I can't tell you how many survived, or even if they've been turned over to the gendarmerie. But that is certain to occur. When it does, you must see that these men are never interrogated. I don't care whether they are freed or executed or simply disappear. My sole interest is making sure that they do not talk to their captors."

Rojas looked at him, trying to think of a response. Eight months ago his relationship with DeVane had begun with a straightforward purchase of cocaine, but almost before he knew what was happening, it had grown into a complicated tangle of affairs. He had helped DeVane to cloak transactions that might otherwise have attracted the unwanted interest of the Brazilian government. He had been a conduit to political and law-enforcement circles. He had been a small link in a very long chain, a tiny drop of oil in an immense machine, and he'd been handsomely rewarded for it. There had been money and women, stays in extravagant hotel suites, and trips to foreign countries.

Only in recent weeks had Rojas awakened to how deeply he was enmeshed in DeVane's affairs. The things he was being asked to do were becoming riskier, and the pressure to carry them out increasingly direct. But there were limits. There had to be limits. And it sounded as if the problem he was being asked to fix went beyond any he could have imagined.

"I don't know," he said. "The Mato Grasso is outside

my jurisdiction. I could ask some questions. Find out the status of the prisoners without too much difficulty. But if the regional authorities want to conduct an interrogation, I can't think of how to stop them."

Kuhl was staring at him.

"You'll cope with it," he said. "There is no other choice."

Rojas looked into his eyes and was quiet for close to a full minute. The sun seemed suddenly hotter. His palms and underarms were moist with sweat. It had been mad to believe he could link himself to DeVane without losing his independence. Completely mad. He had been bought and paid for in regular installments, and was now expected to obediently jump to his master's wishes.

At last he turned to DeVane and said, "You understand that I don't want to make promises I can't keep."

"Nor would we want that, obviously," DeVane said. "All we expect is that you give it your best."

Rojas raised his drink to his lips and drained it. The mimosa's shade had dwindled, making the heat almost intolerable. For an irrational moment he pictured himself spontaneously erupting into flames while DeVane and Kuhl looked on without expression.

"Is anything wrong, Francisco?" DeVane said. "You seem disconcerted."

Rojas shook his head. He heard the noisy rumble of the Beech's engine starting up, and looked out toward the head of the airstrip. The *cocaderos* had emptied their trucks and were moving them back onto the dirt road as the plane prepared for takeoff. His general practice of never traveling with a shipment aside, he almost would have preferred to be on board. He did not think his nerves could stand the company of these men much longer.

"I should be leaving," he said. "There are very few flights out of the country and their schedules are erratic."

DeVane nodded, then signaled to one of his body-guards with a wave of his fingertips. The guard nodded slightly and spoke into a handheld radio.

"Your car is on its way," he said. "We wouldn't want you to be stranded here."

Rojas manufactured a smile.

"Muito obrigado, you are most kind," he said, sickened by his own toadying subservience, and thinking with disgust that the example of the tin miners was one he had followed for some time without allowing himself to acknowledge it.

Like them, he had ventured into a place where it was hot and dark, and learned all too well how to appease its gods.

SEVEN

THE THING WAS, SHE NEVER PLAYED MUSIC BEFORE having her morning coffee, and that puzzled him.

In the veranda of his Palo Alto home after many long hours on the telephone, Roger Gordian sat with an untouched plate of scrambled eggs and toast on the table in front of him, a steaming cup of coffee near his right hand, and his cordless within fast reach of his left. Making decisions was for him an adaptive reflex, a coping mechanism that pressure only honed and energized, and he'd reacted to the news from Brazil as he would to any emergency, gathering whatever information was available, then digesting as much of it as circumstances allowed before settling upon a logical and systematic plan of action.

In this instance, the information-gathering process had kept him in his study all night. There had been a string of updates from Cody, interspersed with his own calls to advisors and political contacts, including one to a high-placed official in the Department of State, and a subsequent late-night conversation with his close friend Dan Parker, who had been the congressman from California's 14th District until his recently lost reelection bid, and was somebody whose opinion Gordian never failed to solicit in times of crisis.

With each of them pursuing intelligence about the Brazilian situation through his own respective channels, Gordian's next order of business had been to contact Charles Dorset, the top executive at NASA. The call had had two purposes. The first was to inform Dorset of events at the ISS compound before news reached him from other, unpredictable sources whose accuracy might be questionable—the media being foremost on Gordian's mind. The second involved a slew of matters relevant to the *Orion* investigation, which Gordian was continuing to view as a separate affair for the present, although the close timing of the episodes in Florida and Brazil, and the fact that both would have damaging repercussions for the ISS program, made it impossible to avoid the possibility of some connection between them. While he was not about to jump to conclusions, he was also unwilling to push such thoughts aside. Distressful as they might be, the Machiavellian conspiracy to bring UpLink down the year before had been a costly and agonizing reminder that they were never to be ignored.

Thus, his final call of the morning had been made to Yuri Petrov, Dorset's counterpart at the Russian Space Agency, through a Sword translator, its purpose having been to keep him abreast of unfolding developments and strongly advise that security around the Baikonur Cosmodrome in Kazakhstan—and other RKS complexes in his directorate—be placed on heightened alert.

Right now, however, his phone had gone silent, giving him a chance to poke his head out of his study and sample the morning. Dorset had promised to get back to him within the next hour with word on an especially important issue, and Gordian had delayed heading out to the office until then, wanting to be certain he was absolutely free to take the call.

He looked over his plate, shifted around a forkful of eggs without raising it to his mouth, then decided to wait for Ashley's return before getting started on breakfast.

He sat back, noting that his daughter Julia had fared just slightly better than himself in working up an appetite. Across from him were the vestiges of her own half-eaten meal—a picked-apart blueberry muffin and a cold and mostly full cup of coffee. Tied up in knots, she'd rushed off for her first painful meeting with a divorce attorney just as he'd stepped into the sunlight, leaving her dishes where they were, and her grayhounds in his and Ashley's care. Actually, Gordian's exclusive care at the moment, since his wife had sprung up from the table and gone into the house to put a CD into the stereo, something that he could not for the life of him recall her doing in over twenty-five years of marriage, and which was particularly baffling because of the abruptness with which she'd abandoned him, her muffin, and her coffee to do it.

Wondering what had gotten into her, wishing he could clear his mind of distractions and relax, Gordian glanced to one side of him, then the other, and frowned at the utter impossibility of it. The dogs tended to favor him at mealtime, and were flanking his chair like bookends, staring up at him with their bright, brown, pleading eyes.

He reached for a wedge of his toast, broke it in half, and gave each of the dogs a piece. As usual Jack, a brindle male and the larger of the two, sucked his down whole and went back to staring at him. Considerably more high-strung, Jill excitedly sprang onto all fours and spun in a full circle while gobbling her portion, slamming her backside into the legs of the table.

Gordian's breakfast settings rattled and bounced, coffee sloshing over the rim of his cup and flooding the saucer underneath it.

He released an aggravated breath.

"That's how you always get yourself in trouble, you know."

Gordian turned, and saw Ashley reappear from inside the house to the recorded accompaniment of Fats Waller's stride piano.

"Hmmph," he said, dabbing up the spilled coffee with a paper napkin. "What do you mean?"

"I mean feeding the dogs off the table," she said. "Besides being against Julia's orders, it's sure to cause a disaster."

He frowned.

"You know how these poor dogs were treated at the track? Before Julia got them from the placement center? They were literally running for their lives."

"Yes, I do know, but that's not the point—" she said.

"Grayhounds are given six chances to either win, place, or show before being 'retired.' Which is generally a euphemism that means they're put down, unless the rescue people can get hold of them first."

"Roger, that's still beside the—"

"They spend all their days penned up in something like a three-by-three-foot crate, except for when they're turned out to eat or relieve themselves. Wind up with pressure sores, swellings on their joints, bald spots from rubbing against the walls of the crates, not to mention—"

"Roger—"

"And besides, I've seen Julia break her own 'no table scrap' rule at least a dozen times this week."

Ashley gave him a long-suffering smile and sat in the chair to his right.

"She's their mother," she said. "Which makes that her prerogative."

146

Gordian watched as she reached for the thermal pitcher on the table, and freshened her coffee. She was wearing an open blue denim shirt over a peach-colored T-shirt, jeans, and white tennis sneakers. The smart angular cut of her light brown hair was the latest fashion collaboration between herself and Adrian, her stylist, accenting her high cheekbones and sea-blue eyes in a way that seemed like nature's consummate design.

"I wouldn't feed them off the table if they didn't beg," he said.

"And they wouldn't be begging if you didn't feed them. Or haven't you noticed that they never park themselves anywhere near *me* while we're eating."

He looked back down at the dogs. They had resumed their positions on either side of his chair, Jill sitting barely at rest and shifting her weight from one front paw to the other, Jack staring at him in rigid and unblinking expectation, his snout tilted upward.

"It's a vicious circle," he said.

"Or maybe just you being a pushover for any creature in need." She picked up her muffin and nodded her chin at his plate. "You ought to have some of that food yourself."

He turned toward his dish and ate without enthusiasm, still unable to muster an appetite. On the stereo, Waller had launched into "Cash for Your Trash," his left hand swinging between octaves to lay down rhythmic bass and chord patterns, his right hand running up the scale with a bright introductory melody line.

Gordian found himself listening to the opening vocals.

"Haven't heard this one for ages," Ashley said, waiting until midway through the song to comment.

He nodded, took a bite of his eggs.

"I believe," she said, "that no other performer has ever been quite so up about being down. If you catch my meaning."

Gordian turned and looked at her.

"I do," he said. "When you consider that he was a black man in a time of obscene racial inequality, then take into account everything his generation lived through . . . the first World War, the Depression, World War II. If memory serves, he made his final recordings just as we were about to send our boys to Europe."

"Stormy weather," she said.

He nodded.

"His music's all about surviving bad times with a kind of resolute good humor," she said. "About having confidence that just being here, and alive, gives us the chance to see better times ahead . . . trite as that may sound."

He nodded again.

"Yes," he said.

"To the trite part, or the other?"

"Both," he said. "But mostly the other."

They ate quietly and listened to the personnel on the various recordings—Benny Carter, Slam Stewart, Bunny Berigan, and others, in addition to Waller himself—roll through driving versions of "Lulu's Back in Town" and "I Ain't Got Nobody" and "Gonna Sit Right Down and Write Myself a Letter."

Ashley watched him awhile, then gestured toward the phone on the table.

"So," she asked. "Care to tell me what's going on?"

"I'm expecting to hear from Dorset at NASA," Gordian said. "We've been working to get the *Orion* inquiry up and running. I've given a lot of attention to its procedural mechanisms, but Alex Nordstrum talked to me yesterday about another aspect of the probe that ought not be neglected."

"Alex?" Her eyebrows rose with surprise. "I thought he was busy stroking off on the fairway."

Gordian gave her a thin smile.

"I think you mean teeing off," he said. "Anyway, I asked him to come to the office as a favor and he did." He shrugged. "You know."

She looked at him.

"No, I don't, but I'm assuming it's a male thing that you can explain to me later," she said. "Tell me what the two of you discussed."

"In a nutshell, he reminded me that we need to earn the confidence of the American people rather than sit back and take it as a given. I've got some very definite ideas about how to accomplish that based upon his suggestions, and don't intend to let this turn into anything resembling the debacle where an outside commission appointed by the White House went head-to-head against the space agency because of skepticism about its in-house probe."

"Well-deserved skepticism, as I recall," Ashley said.

"Yes," he said. "There are going to be doubts about the credibility of this investigation's findings no matter how thorough a job is done. But if we can't manage to cut them down to size, I don't think the program will ever recover."

She swallowed some of her muffin. "How's Dorset feel about your input? People get territorial."

"Thus far, we're in synch. Chuck is a reasonable man and has the best interests of NASA at heart." He turned to face her. "Also, he's got very little choice but to be receptive to my suggestions. Without UpLink's technology and access to foreign governments there's no ISS. Period."

She smiled at him.

"Hard to imagine *anyone* trying to ignore you when you get that steely look in your eyes," she said.

He cleared his throat, lowering his head to study his plate, a boyish sign of embarrassment that Ashley pretended not to notice.

She decided to wait a few seconds, then asked, "Which of your specific recommendations is Dorset supposed to call about this morning?"

"I told him who I'd like to head up the investigative task force. Unequivocally."

"And?"

"And his only real problem—or concern, I should say—was that he didn't want anybody in his organization to feel resentful about being bypassed for the job."

"Understandable," Ashley said. "Turf again. You know how it can be."

"I do, Ash. But there's no time to worry about NASA's bureaucratic harmony right now. The faster we get things done, the better. There's the Russian launch at the end of the month, and I want to see it come off without postponement. Because I *am* concerned about what'll happen if my old blowhard friend Senator Delacroix, or somebody equally good at being on the wrong side of every issue, starts calling the entire cooperative effort into question on the talk shows."

"Delacroix," she said. "He the one you saw wrestle that big stuffed bear in the hammer-and-sickle trunks?"

"On the Senate floor." He exhaled slowly. "Anyway, Dorset's going to let me know if the person I want is even interested in the appointment. If this pans out the way I'm hoping it will, we'll have taken a huge step toward gaining the public trust. And it'll be a deserved step."

"Any reason you haven't named your pick to me?"

He shrugged, looking slightly awkward.

"Pure superstition. Another mark of an old flier," he said. "I'll tell you if you insist, but—"

She held up her hand. "Far be it from me to lay on the jinx. Being an old flier's wife, I know how to sit back and keep my fingers crossed until you're ready. Just don't forget that I'm waiting for the dish."

They were silent for a bit, eating their breakfasts, Jack and Jill watching Gordian's fork with undeviating involvement. On the stereo, Fats Waller belted out a line about someone's pedaling extremities being obnoxious. Gordian smiled almost imperceptibly and ate with increasing relish.

All at once, Ashley wanted to reach over and hold him tightly in her arms. But she refrained, just as she had chosen not to ask him any questions about what had occurred in Brazil. She would not do that, not yet, though what little she already knew made her suspect it represented an impending threat to her husband's safety that, like others he'd had to face in the past, would keep her tossing restlessly in bed tonight and for many nights to come, fearing it might take him from her forever.

Their breakfasts finished now, they sat listening to the stereo in the fresh grass-scented air and sunshine pouring through the veranda's open louvers. His plate cleaned off except for a single wedge of toast, Gordian glanced down at each of the dogs and then gave Ashley a questioning glance.

"I don't think you should," she said. "But if you go ahead and do it, there'd better be no complaints about the rotten, hungry hounds to me or Julia afterward."

He lifted the toast from his plate and portioned it out between the dogs—Jack consuming his half with what appeared to be a single inhalation, Jill accepting hers somewhat more demurely, and then licking Gordian's fingers as if to make up to him for having bashed the table.

"Such salivating adoration," Ashley said.

He wiped his hand on his pants and looked at her.

"Mind if I ask *you* something now?" he said.

"Sure."

"I was wondering why you put on the stereo."

Their eyes met.

"Easy," she said with a shrug. "I suddenly remembered that Fats Waller's always been one of your favorites."

He kept looking at her.

"Well, that explains your choice of music," he said. "Not your uncharacteristic timing. Since you always say you enjoy your morning peace and quiet."

She smiled.

"Surely you've guessed," she said.

"No," he said honestly. "I don't have a clue."

She moved closer beside him.

"It's a female thing," she said, leaning her head against his shoulder. "Now be still, dear husband, and maybe I'll explain it to you later."

EIGHT

AS THE GROANING, RUST-SPOTTED CITROEN NEARED the rendezvous point on the high Balkan pass some thirty miles outside Tirana, Sergei Ilkanovitch considered his two fellow Russians in the car, and suddenly and unexpectedly remembered his father's oft-repeated maxim that one could always judge a man by the shoes he wore. Rich or poor, it made no difference, he had insisted. A vagrant in rags would take pains to keep his shoes in the best possible condition if he had any character at all, while the most elevated member of the Presidium would be oblivious to their scuff and wear if he were of an inferior caliber.

The person he'd frequently pointed to as an example of the latter had been Khrushchev, someone he'd held in the lowest esteem, calling him a simpleton who was overly impressed with American capitalism, a coward for yielding to Kennedy's bluff during the Cuban missile standoff, and an economic and political bungler responsible for the Black Sea uprising of 1963 and America's early lead in the arms race. When he'd theatrically banged his shoe on the desk before the United Nations

General Assembly, it was clearly seen to be shabby and run-down at the heel, providing a repellent insight into his character, and demeaning his country before the eyes of the entire world. In his boyhood, Sergei had heard his father complain endlessly about the Premier's supposed *faux pas* and had no idea what to make of it. He had seen the grainy black and white news footage of the event and been able to tell nothing of the shoe's condition. Nor had he known what it could have signified about Khrushchev or anything else.

But Sergei had soon given up trying to extract any wisdom from his father's observations, and remembered him now as a gruff, strident little man who might have been comical for his endless diatribes had he not been so full of anger and sulky frustration. An inspector in a state-operated automotive plant on the Volga, he had been incapable of relaxing after a day's work without his vodka. Consequently, Sergei's lasting image of the elder Ilkanovitch was one of him lying passed out drunk on the couch in their austere one-bedroom worker's flat.

Sergei had been twelve when his father died of a heart attack in 1969, the youngest of four boys left to be supported by their mother's earnings as a seamstress and woefully inadequate government maintenance. Six months later, he had been sent to live with an uncle who was a mathematician with the government think tank in Akademgorodoc, the Western Siberian township for the intelligentsia that had been presumptuously known as Science City back in the days when the Communists still held romantic notions about leading the world into some futuristic paradise.

When he'd asked his mother why he had been chosen to go rather than one of his siblings, she had explained it was because he'd always excelled in school and had the greatest chance of benefitting from his uncle's tutelage. But despite her stated reasons Sergei had felt discarded, cast off like an undesirable sentenced to the Gulag, and suspected she had been more concerned with the wages his working-age brothers could bring into the household than his academic prospects. In the end, however, he had come to be grateful for her decision. Whatever he knew about life and living he had learned on his own, but to his uncle he credited the scientific curiosity that had led to his becoming a physicist.

Now the Citroen took a sharp curve in the road, flinging Sergei sideways so that he was bumped against the right passenger door. He peered out his window, where the switchback skirted the very edge of the mountainside, a dizzying sight that knotted his stomach with tension. Yet his driver had only accelerated as he took the turn, as if never pausing to consider that a single lapse would plunge them over the dropoff into some nameless chasm. How odd, then, for Sergei to still find himself thinking about an absurd paternal injunction to always take notice of men's shoes—but perhaps it was just a distraction to keep his panic at bay.

What, he wondered, would his father make of the pair of men who had been his guards and traveling companions for the past several days? Both had on Western-style boots of finely tooled leather, yet both were also adorned with tattoos that literally stamped them as hardened career criminals. The burly, thick-featured one on his left, Molkov, had a cross on each knuckle of his right hand, indicating the number of times he had been imprisoned. The "seal" of the ring tattoo on his middle finger, a dagger entwined in a fanged serpent, denoted a murder conviction. The signet on his index finger resembling an inverted spade on a playing card labeled him as a gangster who had been jailed for a violent offense such as assault or armed robbery. The larger gladiator tattoo on his right arm—its bottom half discernible below the rolled-up sleeve of his khaki shirt—was perhaps the most malign of all, identifying him as an executioner with a passion for inflicting sadistic deaths upon his victims.

Alexandre, the thin, bony Georgian seated in front of Sergei, wore a similar résumé of offenses on his flesh—the knuckle crosses, the symbols boasting of myriad felonies. But there was another that Sergei found of particular interest, a signet-ring tattoo rendered in careful detail, depicting the sun rising above a horizon that was patterned like a checkerboard. This, he knew, was a testament to Alexandre's criminal ancestry, a proud declaration that he was upholding a familial tradition of lawlessness.

Sergei could not help but linger another moment on droll thoughts of his father, who presumably would have considered Molkov and Alexandre exemplary human beings from a glance at their feet, overlooking everything else about them. He, Sergei, appreciated irony the way some men did fine wine, caviar, or Cuban cigars, and there was one of most exquisite flavor to be found in these reflections—for he was also wearing shoes that were scrupulously cared for. Always wore the very *best* of shoes, in fact. It was a personal compulsion that, not unlike the tattoos of his companions, was a lasting mark of his own upbringing, although imprinted on his psyche rather than his body. But had his father been alive to know the moral threshold he was about to irrevocably cross, it might have been enough to make him rethink his singular method of gauging a man's worth.

Preoccupied with these thoughts, Sergei took several moments to realize that the car was finally slowing to a halt, its overstressed motor clanking and knocking as the driver guided it toward the sheer mountain wall rising to some great height on the left. He looked down at the hard-shelled suitcase between his feet and gripped its handle, a sense of unreality washing over him.

"Is this the place?" he said, leaning toward the man behind the wheel.

A dark-skinned ethnic Gheg with a black scruff of beard on his cheeks and a knitted white skullcap of the sort favored by his nation's Moslem majority, the driver shook his head—an affirmative gesture in Albania—his look in the rearview mirror intended to make Sergei feel foolish for having asked an unnecessary question. He possessed the unmistakable scorn of the zealot toward one whose motives were seen to be venal and selfish, although that hadn't seemed an obstacle to the procurement of the deadly technology Sergei had offered up for sale. There were, he thought, endless degrees of hypocrisy bridging the gap between world and want.

Sergei studied the heavy brush on the slope as the driver came to a full stop alongside it, pulling close enough for the tangled outgrowth of leaves and stems to rake across the Citroen's flank. The wait that followed prompted another attack of nerves. Sergei knew the car's approach would have been observed, and his inability to detect any sign of his hidden watchers made him feel uneasy and vulnerable. Still, he fought to take hold of himself. The Albanian guerrillas had every reason to be cautious. Furthermore, his two comrades were adequate insurance against deceit, and imposing reminders of his own linkage to the *organizatsiya,* a force whose enmity it would be madness to provoke.

He had waited for nearly five minutes when his eye caught a slight shuffle of movement in the brush above him. Then, at last, the guerrillas came threading down the slope, scurrying from the foliage one and two at a time and descending onto the pass just yards in front of the car.

There were a half dozen of them altogether, coarse, rugged men that shared many of the driver's dark tribal features. They had assault rifles slung over their shoulders—Kalashnikovs, Berettas, MP5's. Their clothing was grimy from long wear, and ranged from combat fatigues to the name-brand American denims, athletic jackets, and sneakers that had become status symbols in the Asian and Eastern European nations where they were often cheaply manufactured before being shipped to the States, given an inflated value, then exported to the very countries in which they had been made to be sold at an astronomical profit. It was another of the delicious ironies that had occurred to Sergei today, bringing to mind an image of the legendary serpent devouring its own tail.

But he had no time now to mull these things. The apparent leader of the group, a taut, sharp-nosed man in fatigues with a long diagonal scar on his right cheek, was moving up closer to the car, two of his clansmen several paces behind him. He held in his right hand a worn leather satchel, and would be no less eager than Sergei to complete their business.

When he reached the Citroen's front grille, Sergei lifted his own case off the floor and turned to the stocky guard beside him.

"Let's go," he said.

Molkov nodded. A short-barreled Micro-Uzi hung outside his shirt. Weighing under five pounds and just ten inches long with its tubular metal stock folded, the compact submachine gun was scarcely larger than a pistol. In front, Alexandre displayed an identical SMG, as well as a shoulder-holstered Glock 9mm, with equal impunity. They had driven out of Tirana with the weapons stashed beneath their seats, but now were too far from any policed area to worry about having to conceal them. The control of the outlaw bands that occupied these mountains was based on ancient clan ties and validated by strength of arms. Brandishing the guns in open view was as much a matter of earning their respect as it was of physical protection.

Leaving the Albanian behind the wheel, the three of them got out of the car and walked around its front grille. As they did, Sergei's companions fell in on either side of him, Molkov to his right, Alexandre to his left. The guerrillas stood very still on the road and eyed them warily. There was no sound except for a brief ripple of birdsong that seemed to be sucked into the vast and hollow silence of the chasm below like a brightly colored ribbon caught in a vacuum.

Sergei approached the man with the scar on his face, a cord of tension once again twisting in his stomach. On the surface, the transaction he was about to conclude seemed almost routine—an exchange of money for black-market goods on some remote alpine pass in a country that was known for its illicit trading, and that amounted to nothing more than a parenthesis on the European continent. He did not know exactly where he was, would not be able to find this forsaken place on the map once he left it behind.

But it was here, in what were appropriately called the Mountains of the Damned, that he was about to commit treason on a scale previously unheard of, perhaps even expand the very definition of the word to new conceptual bounds. Indeed, if he were to contemplate it, he imagined he might feel like a swimmer who had gone out farther from shore than ever before, each stroke fueled by a little inner dare, his confidence sustained with occasional backward glances to reassure himself he was still within sight of land, until at one point he turned and saw nothing but ocean ahead, ocean behind him, ocean stretching off infinitely in every direction, and suddenly realized that some trick of the tide had swept him off in an eyeblink, carrying him beyond the point of no return.

But enough, he admonished himself. Enough of that. He had made his choices and there was a deal to be done.

He and the guerrilla leader looked each other over with obligatory nods of acknowledgment. Then Sergei set his suitcase down on the hood of the car, thumbed open its combination latches, and raised the lid.

The guerrilla leader glanced down into the case.

"Yes," he said in Russian, something like wonder on his features. "Yes, yes."

"It's all inside," Sergei said. "The component, of course, as well as detailed instructions and schematics for its placement within the larger device. And a little something extra that you may tell the purchaser is both a test and a taste." Ah, yes, a taste. Like caviar. Or a vintage cigar. "Everything that will be needed in Kazakhstan."

"You are certain the information is reliable?"

"Absolutely. I've provided it in duplicate, both on disk and paper." Sergei gave the guerrilla another moment to study the contents of the briefcase, then closed its lid. "Now the payment."

A thin smile touching his lips, the guerrilla nodded, then presented his satchel to Sergei.

Sergei felt a spark of excitement at the weight of its contents. Suddenly his fingers were trembling. Holding it by the strap with one hand, he lifted its flap with the other and looked inside.

It took him a moment to react, and when he did it was with shock and icy disbelief. He paled, all the blood in his body seeming to flush to his feet.

The satchel was filled with thick packs of blank white paper cut to the approximate size of American banknotes and bound together with rubber bands.

He snapped his eyes up at the guerrilla leader, saw that his smile had tightened at its corners, then turned quickly to Molkov.

"These bastards have dared to cheat us," he said.

Molkov was staring at him without expression.

"Did you hear me?" Sergei's voice was furious as he upended the satchel, letting the rectangular bundles of paper spill to the ground. *"There's no money!"*

Molkov kept staring at him.

Gaping with bewilderment, Sergei spun toward Alexandre.

The Glock was in his hand, raised level with Sergei's chest. Its silenced barrel spat twice, and Sergei reeled backward and dropped to the road, killed instantly, his jacket stained red where both shots had penetrated his heart. A look of confusion and betrayal was frozen on his face.

Molkov glanced down at the corpse a moment, nodded approvingly, then turned to the guerrilla leader.

"Now," he said, holding out his hand. "Let's have the payment."

The outlaw gestured briskly toward one of his men, who stepped forward to pass him a leather satchel much like the one Sergei had been given. He opened the bag himself, then angled it so both Russians could easily see inside. This time it was stuffed with authentic packs of U.S. bills.

"It's all here. Send our regards and goodwill to your *bochya,* Vostov," he said, using the Russian slang term for godfather as he handed the satchel over to Molkov with a little bow.

Molkov removed one of the banded packs at random and riffled its edges with his thumb, holding it close to his eyes. Satisfied, he put it back inside, closed the bag, and slung it over his shoulder.

"Okay," he said to Alexandre. "Let's go."

They turned back toward the waiting Citroen, careful to avoid stepping in the blood that had pooled around Sergei's body.

It was Alexandre, chancing to glance through the windshield, who noticed that their driver was no longer in the car, his door flung wide open. Instantly realizing what that meant, he jerked his head toward Molkov.

But by the time he opened his mouth to warn him, it was too late for either of them.

Even as the Citroen had arrived and their leader and comrades-in-arms broke cover to meet it, a dozen other members of the Albanian *fis,* or outlaw clan, had remained concealed amid the vegetation uphill, their attention and weapons trained on the road.

Everything had gone wholly according to plan. When the Russian physicist was shot by his supposed bodyguard, the Citroen's driver had taken advantage of the momentary distraction to exit the car unnoticed and plunge into the roadside brush, putting himself safely out of harm's way and leaving his brethren with a clear field of fire.

They had watched their leader hand the second satchel to the larger of the Russian gangsters. Watched him open it and inspect its contents—again, exactly as anticipated. As soon as he had confirmed receipt of their actual payment to the second Russian, the men lying in wait had readied themselves, their guns angled downward, their targets in steady view. To insure that the Russians would not be alerted to the deception in time to use their own weapons on their clansmen below, they had held their fire until the *mafiyasi* started back toward the car, turning away from the guerrillas.

In the moment before the trap was sprung, it appeared the wiry Russian had recognized the deception and turned to alert his partner.

He hadn't had the chance. The gunmen on the slope opened up on the Russians, cutting both down where they stood. The volleys continued for several seconds, spraying the dead bodies, riddling the left side of the car, near which they had fallen, with bullet holes, dissolving its windshield in an avalanche of jagged glass shards.

At last the shooting ceased, its echoes rapidly swallowed by the engulfing silence of the defile. Bits of leaves and branches that had been trimmed by the gunfire fluttered to the road.

Down below, the guerrilla leader waved approvingly to the men behind the screen of foliage, then strode over to Molkov's bullet-riddled corpse and knelt to retrieve the satchel of money that was still slung over his shoulder.

Their mission had been easily accomplished.

Now all that remained was to inform Harlan DeVane.

NINE

THE LYNDON B. JOHNSON SPACE CENTER, A CLUSTER of one hundred buildings located off Interstate 45 midway between downtown Houston and the Galveston Island beaches some twenty-five miles southward, is the primary administrative, testing, and astronaut training facility for NASA's manned space exploration program. Its Mission Control Center (Building 30), a windowless, bunkerlike structure at the core of the 1,620-acre complex, has been the locus of ground support and monitoring operations for American space flights since the *Gemini 4* launch in June 1965, and contains two Flight Control Rooms—or *fickers*—manned round the clock by large teams of flight controllers for the duration of any given mission. For the thousands of scientific researchers, engineers, and management officials who have dedicated their lives to "the expansion of human knowledge of phenomena in the atmosphere and space"—the agency's mandate as defined in its Eisenhower-era charter—the JSC is where that goal has been advanced through imagination, intelligence, audacity, ingenuity, and irrepressible perseverance. For the far smaller hand-

ful of candidates who apply and qualify for the astronaut
program, it is something even beyond that, a kind of Oz
where they are bestowed the magical ruby slippers that
will transport them to their hearts' most wished for destination . . . only not the familiar terrestrial landscapes of
home, as was the case with Dorothy, but the beckoning,
mysterious heavens.

"Just click your heels together three times and say
there's no place like Betelgeuse," Annie Caulfield muttered dryly to herself, aware she was about to make one
of the most crucial decisions of her life. Immersed in
thought, she sat looking out her office window at the
tram that was moving across the JSC's landscaped
grounds as it delivered personnel and visitors to its various installations. Then she rotated her swivel chair and
began absently studying the three framed photos on her
otherwise bare desk. By chance the first one her eye fell
upon was of her parents, Edward and Maureen, an 8 x
10 taken five years ago at a party to celebrate their for-
tieth wedding anniversary.

Annie smiled a little. Their preferred travel itineraries
aside, she'd had a thing or two in common with Dorothy
in her formative years, being an only child whose be-
ginnings had been in rural Kansas. Her father had operated a one-man air transport service, and their family
had lived so close to the airfield where he'd hangared
his rattletrap Cessna that Annie could observe his take-
offs and landings from her second-floor bedroom window.

Perhaps that had been what eventually led to her interest in sky-watching, she didn't know, but when she
was coming up on her eighth birthday Annie had asked
for and received an inexpensive 60mm Meade refraction
telescope for her gift, along with a Carl Sagan *Cosmos-
phere* that she had used to locate the planets, constella-
tions, and galaxies from her porch on countless spring

and summer evenings, Dad helping her level and rotate
the tube on its tripod until she was old enough to manage
it by herself. Seven years later he'd helped her accomplish another of her goals in the same attentive, patient
way and given her flying lessons. By the time she was
eighteen Annie had earned her license and was making
air runs for him during breaks from school.

It seemed a sure thing in hindsight that her obsessions
with astronomy and flying would converge into a desire
to become an astronaut, though her decision to start her
career by joining the Air Force had come as a total surprise to her mother and father. It had also been a source
of great anxiety to them given the potential risks of warfare, risks that seemed particularly high in an age of
limited regional conflicts for which the military relied
heavily, and often exclusively, upon airpower to achieve
their precision objectives. But her proficiency in the
cockpit during her years of active duty had convinced
her she could cut it with NASA, and Annie had submitted her application to its Astronaut Selection Office
long before her F-16 Fighting Falcon was reduced to
burning scrap metal while on a surveillance mission over
northern Bosnia.

After her rescue, she had been reassigned stateside by
her C.O. in keeping with standard Air Force policy to
shunt pilots who had been downed in combat away from
the theater of operations, regardless of their eagerness or
apparent fitness to get back in the air—the understandable concern being that they might have suffered some
hidden trauma that would cause them to blink for a split
second when they needed to act, or conversely, *overreact* to a perceived threat, not a good idea either way
when you were roaring over enemy territory at speeds
upwards of five hundred miles per hour. Whatever inclination she'd had to argue the matter had been offset
by her concern for her parents, whose fears for her safety

had been borne out by events. For nearly a week before NATO searchers picked up the signal from her emergency locator beacon, it had been thought likely she had perished in the crash of her plane, and she hadn't wanted to put them through that kind of gut-wrenching ordeal again.

She had been elated after getting contacted for an initial NASA interview within weeks of her transfer, but then had come the long, tortuous screening process of reference checks, *re*-interviews, and physical examinations prior to her qualifying for finalist status, to be followed by another series of prelims, and then the nail-biting wait for a conclusive yea or nay.

When Annie was notified that her candidacy had been accepted, her excitement had been so intense she had felt as if she might soar beyond the bonds of gravity without benefit of a spacecraft, knowing full well that there was still no guarantee she would ultimately be sent into space. Before that would come two rigorous years of basic astronaut training during which her skills would be developed and subject to constant evaluation. But she had attained the high ground and was, as Tom Wolfe had put it in *The Right Stuff,* within sight of Olympus. Nothing would stop her from going the rest of the distance.

Driven by her lifelong ambition, and aided by an innate self-discipline and passion to excel that her parents had always reinforced, she'd applied herself to the challenges of training with a kind of fierce, single-minded dedication, come through at the top of her class—right up there with Jim Rowland—and been selected for formal mission training immediately upon graduation.

Annie and Jim had flown their first shuttle mission together in 1997, he as commander, she as pilot.

Now she rapped her fingers on her desk, her eyes leaving the photo of her parents on the left end of the row for the one on the far right, an official NASA group shot of the crew on the flight that had "put her on the bronco's hump and broken her cherry," to quote not a famous writer this time, but rather the ever tactful Colonel Rowland. Of the seven men and women on that shuttle, two had been Turnips besides Jim and herself— mission specialists Walter Pratt and Gail Klass. It had been the multitalented, multilingual Gail, a computer scientist and electrical engineer by trade, who had designed their unique crew patch and translated the motto she and Jim had concocted into Latin . . . to give it class and authenticity, she had explained.

Ah, Jimmy, how I wish you were here with some dumb wisecrack, preferably one built around an obscenity . . . as if you knew any other kind, Annie thought. Sorrow infiltrating her smile, she studied his face as it appeared in the starch official public-relations shot. Somehow his prankish sense of humor had managed to show through the stiffly formal pose their photographer had elicited from him.

She expelled a long, sighing breath and shifted her attention to the middle picture frame, having bypassed it a few seconds earlier, precisely because she had known it would make her struggle to keep her emotions under control unwinnable.

Behind the frame's nonreflective glass panel was a montage she had painstakingly composed from photo clippings of Mark, her children, and herself, using dozens of snapshots taken over the years, the images overlapping like the recollections they stirred within Annie. She was no Gail Klass in the creativity department, and most of her choices had been of the typical doting-mother, loving-wife sort that would have drawn afflicted little smiles had they been shown to friends or coworkers, boring them to death like nothing else besides home videos of birthday parties and backyard barbecues. Here

was Mark proudly displaying a flounder he'd hooked
from a fishing pier on Sanibel Island; here Linda on a
playground seesaw; here the kids on a Christmas morning three years ago, still in their pajamas, wading into
the presents under the tree; here the entire family at
Disney World photographed by a roving six-foot-tall
Mickey Mouse. And in the center . . .

Annie stared at the picture, transported back in
thought to the night it was taken.

She and Mark had toured the British Isles for their
honeymoon, a trip that had lasted almost a full month
and led them from London to Edinburgh to the coastline
of South Wales, with stops in a dozen villages and twice
as many old castles along the way. It was at a small pub
and guest house in the Scottish Highlands, where they
had envisaged getting a good night's rest before heading
on to the Orkneys, that they'd wound up tossing back
far too much single-malt whisky and dancing to Celtic
folk music with the riotous locals, kicking up sawdust
until the caller had finally lost his voice around day-
break. When they had left their room late the next afternoon after sleeping off murderous hangovers—and
missing their ferry out of town—the innkeeper had
handed them a sixty-second Polaroid some anonymous
fellow reveler had taken of them doing their eightsome
reel in tweed caps that they hadn't recalled putting on,
and had never made it back to their room with them.

The combination of their goofy, plastered expressions
and the cockeyed angles of the caps on their heads had
made them chuckle every time they pored through their
photo album, but somehow it had done more than capture a delightful memory, a rare uninhibited moment for
two people who had built their lives around ceaseless
discipline and hard work; it had exemplified the easy
consonance between them, a lightness and looseness that
neither ever had been able to share with anyone else,

and was so much the essence of their marital union that she had felt the picture naturally belonged at the center of her little cut-and-paste.

Annie began tapping the desktop more rapidly, her eyes clouding up. Eight years, that was all they'd had together. Eight years before the cancer took Mark from her, making him suffer a thousand monstrous indignities as it consumed him.

But she could not allow herself to dwell on that, not now, and instead turned her thoughts to the meeting she'd had with Charles Dorset just a half hour ago. No sooner had she arrived that morning than he had summoned her to his office and, virtually without preamble, asked whether she would be interested in directing the *Orion* probe. The prospect had caught her completely off guard, and she had sat before his desk in silence for several moments, as if there was something about his question she wasn't quite getting.

"Mr. Dorset, there's a long list of people I'd supposed might be appointed to the position, and I really hadn't imagined myself being on it," she had said at length.

"Why is that?" He had watched her over a steaming coffee mug in his hands. "What would make anyone more eligible than you?"

Annie had shaken her head, still at a bit of a loss. "Seniority. Technical expertise. I'm not sure I would know how to begin managing such a huge responsibility."

His broad, florid face was very serious.

"I have always believed NASA's greatest investment is in the men and women we send into space, not the technology that carries them there. The *human* element," he said. "And you have proven yourself good enough to handle the training of our astronaut corps for the past three years."

Annie paused a moment, then said, "I'm flattered by

171

your confidence, but it frankly doesn't eliminate my concerns. My background isn't in technical science. Every one of *Orion*'s electronic and structural systems will have to be analyzed to find out what went wrong—"

"You've operated a shuttle and taught others to do so, which makes you intimately acquainted with its workings. But that's almost beside the point. Of course no one is expecting you to do it all. I'm talking about leadership. You would have wide discretion in handpicking a team of professionals from both inside and outside the agency."

She looked at him. "I'd expect a few ranking members of the organization to be very unhappy about being passed over for consideration."

"Leave that to me," he said with a dismissive sweep of his hand. "If their feelings get hurt, they can come in here and I'll hand out Kleenex, scold them, compliment their hairdos or neckties, whatever it takes to settle them down. Ninety percent of what I do, day in and day out, is play conciliator between massive egos. I can butter a bun as well as any diplomat."

A thought suddenly crossed Annie's mind as she listened to him.

"I have to ask you right out," she said. "Is this whole thing about trotting me out before the television cameras again? Using me as a figurehead?"

"Fair question," he said. "And I won't tell you the esteem with which you are held by the public hasn't been taken into account. They need to believe in the findings of our task force, and truth from government is a hard sell. But the fact that you go down well with television viewers is only part of it." He paused, his eyes meeting Annie's. "I hope I've already made clear that the high regard for your ability and integrity extends into this office. And you also should know that Roger Gordian is pushing like hell for you."

The revelation left her nonplussed again. "You've consulted with him?"

"We were on the telephone earlier this morning." Dorset's lips hinted at a smile. "And I can assure you, he left no room for confusion about his preference."

Annie felt an unaccountable twitch of nervousness as that sank in.

"I don't know what to say," she told him. "There are other issues. The shuttle will have to be reconstructed piece by piece, and the Vehicle Assembly Building at Canaveral's the only facility we have that's large enough to hold it. I'd have to be in Florida to constantly oversee things, stay on top of the progress that's being made. It would mean uprooting my family. . . ."

"Housing won't be a problem. We have excellent condominiums where you can sit on your balcony under a sun umbrella and watch the manatees and dolphins swim by."

"It isn't just that. The children are both in school—"

"Gordian's offered to arrange for them to attend the best private school on the coast and pay their full tuition indefinitely. He will also take care of any day care and tutorial needs that may arise from the transition."

"Sir—" She paused, overwhelmed. "I appreciate your offer. And Mr. Gordian's generosity. But I need to think about this."

"I understand." He gulped down some coffee. "Take half an hour."

She looked at him, speechless, wondering for a stunned moment if he might have been joking. The unchanged sobriety of his expression told her he wasn't.

"I'd been hoping for somewhat more time," she said. "A day or two—"

"And you ought to have at least that long. Unfortunately, though, the media leeches have turned up the rheostat. You know the atmosphere they've created.

People expect everything from civil wars to natural disasters to be paced like hour dramas, their storylines concluded in time for the eleven o'clock news, and when reality conflicts with that expectation, sentiments can turn ugly. I promise that you won't be pressured into rushing the investigation, but we need to demonstrate that we're moving quickly to get the ball rolling. The Kazakhstan launch *can't* be held up."

Annie shook her head a little. "I'm not quite sure I see the connection. Apart from coordinating our schedules, the Russian mission was intentionally planned to be independent of *Orion,* and ought not be affected."

"I know that, and you know that, but they've gotten cold feet before. Citing technical problems for every delay, when all it's ever boiled down to is their unwillingness—or inability, I want to be fair—to pay for their own ticket to the show. As Gordian reminded me, they are quite capable of bumping their launch if they get jittery about the United States backing away from its financial commitments."

Even before Dorset was finished talking, Annie had realized she couldn't argue that with him on that count. He was right. Absolutely right.

She had nodded in agreement and risen from her seat. "I'll be in my office," she had said.

"And get back to me in thirty?"

"In thirty," she'd assured him.

And here she was, here she was, the clock ticking down, leaving her with less than five minutes to give him her answer.

Her fingers drummed the desk. Why was she having such trouble making a decision? Dorset's offer should have been irresistible. The kids would love Florida, especially knowing they would return home to their regular gaggle of friends once the investigation was concluded. With Orlando and all its razzle-dazzle tourist attractions less than an hour's drive away, she could arrange her schedule so that every weekend would be a visit to paradise for them. And for her it would mean the chance to make certain no effort was spared in determining what had made *Orion* go up in flames, why Jim Rowland had died in such a horrible way . . . and to see that no other astronaut was ever threatened by a similar malfunction.

Annie probed her mind for the basis of her hesitation. Could it be she was afraid of failing to discover the cause of the fire, and thus failing Jim as well? Or was there some other underlying reason she was holding back, a failure of a different sort that had kept her chained and manacled in a dungeon of self-reproach since the night Mark died. Maybe, just maybe, she was like a prisoner acclimated to captivity who shrinks from her cell door as it is opened in an offer of release, looking directly out into freedom, and feeling a sudden terror that she no longer knows how to live with it.

Unconsciously at first, then with growing awareness, she studied the picture of Mark and herself in Scotland again, two people exulting in the moment, and welcoming a future that was by its very definition uncertain. Studied the picture, and all at once knew what her response to Dorset would be.

What it *had* to be.

Taking a deep breath, she reached for the telephone and punched in Dorset's extension.

His receptionist put her through to him immediately.

"Yes?" he said, taut anticipation in his voice.

"Sir, I'd like to thank you for your offer," she said. "And also ask if I may have Roger Gordian's phone number, so I can express my appreciation for his support. And personally inform him of my acceptance."

• • • •

An instant after reading Gordian's number off the display of his pocket computer, Dorset congratulated Annie Caulfield on her decision, hung up the phone, then rose from behind his desk and went over to the coffee machine on its small stand across the office. This would be his fourth—or was it his fifth?—mug of the morning and he'd only gotten in a bit over an hour ago. But what the hell, who was counting—he had enough to occupy his mind without keeping a tally.

He lifted the pot from its warming plate, filled his mug almost to the brim, and took a drink of the strong black brew while still standing at the machine. He began to feel calmer right away. How was it he always needed to be sipping a beverage loaded with caffeine, a *stimulant,* to relax? Though one could, of course, ask the same thing about chain smokers, nicotine being another notorious hyper-upper. Perhaps it was simply an oral fixation, as with overeaters. After all, what inherent calmative properties might there be in a sausage pizza, a Subway sandwich, or a cheeseburger with a side of batter-fried onion rings?

Dorset sipped the coffee down to a level where he could carry it without spilling any on his hand, then returned to his desk and sat. The affirmative answer from Caulfield was excellent news, especially in light of her initial reluctance to take on the job. An understandable reluctance too. She'd been through a lot in the past year. Her husband's cancer, and then her not making it to his bedside the night he'd passed on. That part of the tragedy—not being there at the end—had devastated her, and for a time afterward Dorset had privately braced for her resignation.

Yet she had rebounded somehow. The woman kicked ass, no two ways about it. Dorset presumed the demands of getting a crew trained and ready for the *Orion* mission must have helped keep her going. But now, to have lost

Jim Rowland, who had been like a brother to her . . . ass-kicker or not, there was only so much weight a person could carry. She had every reason to want to distance herself from the investigation, never mind refuse its leadership responsibilities. Which was a major reason *he* hadn't seriously considered her for the position until Roger Gordian's phone call.

Dorset raised the steaming mug to his lips and drank. Annie's acceptance had given him a lift, but he wondered why it hadn't proven greater than it was. He had no reservations about her being able to tackle the job, and indeed, felt her talents could not be overestimated. Maybe, then, the flatness of his mood had to do with Gordian exercising his clout. Not that he'd been heavy-handed. On the contrary, if there was a gentle way to remind someone you were holding him by the balls, Gordian had the touch. But from the moment he had suggested that Annie Caulfield head the *Orion* task force, Gordian had made it crystal clear his wishes were to supersede any other considerations Dorset might have about making the appointment. And also that, barring an outright refusal from Annie, he wouldn't take "no" for an answer.

Yes, Dorset thought with a swallow of coffee, it was largely his resentment over Gordian's intervention that had robbed some of the moment's luster. But that wasn't all of it. Not if he wanted to be honest with himself. There was also the troubling news about Brazil, and his deliberately having kept it from Annie when he ought to have done the opposite. The attack on the base might very well turn out to be unrelated to *Orion*. He was certainly hoping and praying it would—why assume the worst? But she'd had a right to know about it. To know what she was getting into prior to making her choice. Because once word of the incident leaked to the press, she would be barraged with a shitstorm of wild speculation, and any misstatement from her, however innocent, would be enough to raise suspicions of a cover-up from some of her questioners. Annie needed to be informed, to be *prepared,* and he would do it within the next hour . . . but he had withheld the information earlier so that she couldn't factor it into her decision, wanting to stack the deck in favor of a positive response.

Wanting to make sure Roger Gordian was accommodated, Dorset thought with a mixture of irritation and guilt. *And who's going to butter my goddamned bun?*

He sighed. *Orion,* Brazil, the Kazakhstan launch . . . he had the sense that events were moving too fast, getting too far ahead of him. It was as if he was Charlie Chaplin or Buster Keaton in an old silent comedy film, working the pump of a handcar while clownishly trying to catch up with a chugging, whistle-blowing locomotive. Funny. Hysterical even. If you happened to be in the audience, and not sweating it on the rails.

Now he reached for his mug again, and was amazed to discover that it was almost empty. Christ. What kind of abuse must he be heaping upon his stomach? His nervous system?

Dorset stared down at the remainder of his coffee and frowned. Really, he ought to reduce his consumption. Fifty-eight years old, heart palpitations, elevated triglycerides, a grab bag of other chronic health problems—you had to watch out. Get on a treadmill once in a while, take one of those stress-management courses, anything besides brewing pot after pot after pot. On the other hand, there were worse addictions. Italian roast couldn't be more harmful than cigarettes, booze, or prescription sedatives. He'd even heard some people got hooked on nasal sprays—what kind of habit was that? What the *hell,* right?

Expelling another breath, he pushed his chair back from his desk and went to pour himself a fresh cup.

TEN

QUIJARRO, BOLIVIA
APRIL 19, 2001

EDUARDO GUZMAN HAD BEEN JUST A BIT SURPRISED when the Land Rover in which he was driven across the border from Brazil had turned into the dreary village of Quijarro instead of swinging onto the highway heading west toward the Chapare region, but as they had wound through the town's mud-splashed, tumbledown streets, his driver had explained that he wanted to buy something to drink from one of the vending stalls near the railway station. Had Eduardo known of his intention to stop for a refreshment, he might have suggested doing so before they passed through the customs post in Corumba, where there had been many decent places to eat along the river promenade. Though a long ride and many miles of open country lay ahead, the filthy conditions outside their vehicle had squelched any hunger or thirst he might have worked up in the last few hours.

Still, he needed only to consider what he had left behind in order to cheer himself. There had been his betrayal by that damnable whore who had been working in league with the national police even as she worked his cock, performing brilliantly on both counts, tricking him into selling thirty kilos of cocaine to some "associates" of hers who turned out to be undercover agents. After his arrest, Eduardo had spent three days in lockup with piss-smelling thieves and drunks, sweating out the days and nights trying to remember everything he'd foolishly told the woman of his activities and waiting to see what charges would be pressed against him.

Thank God, someone in the organization—it was unclear to Eduardo whether this had been his uncle Vicente, or Harlan DeVane himself—had reached out to a government functionary and secured his release. Before dawn that morning, only hours before his scheduled arraignment, two plainclothes officers had appeared outside his detention cell, quietly removed him, and accompanied him into an unmarked sedan parked in front of the Sao Paulo jailhouse. They had taken him as far as the Corumba border crossing, exchanged some private words with the customs guards, and transferred him to the Land Rover in which his current driver, a barrel-chested man named Ramon, had been waiting near the checkpoint.

Once Eduardo had climbed into the front passenger seat and they were under way, Ramon had explained that they would be traveling to DeVane's ranch outside San Borja to meet with him and Vicente. This had caused a knot of apprehension in Eduardo's stomach, but speaking with the air of fraternal confidentiality common to rank-and-file members of any organization when discussing their superiors, Ramon had told him that a substantial payoff had been needed to compel the authorities to drop their case against him, and that the two bosses merely wanted to be shown proper appreciation for having interceded on his behalf.

After all that he'd endured, Eduardo had replied, he was prepared to demonstrate his gratitude and contrition with relish, even if it meant getting down on his knees to kiss their bare bottoms.

"Everything in life is easier to get into than out of," the driver had commented with a chuckle.

Now the Rover slowed as he guided it up a side street lined with grimy, leaning hovels that seemed on the verge of collapse, took a series of turns along nearly identical streets, then guided it onto a narrow gravel lane running between a stretch of empty lots. Eduardo, who had been paying little attention to their dismal course through town, suddenly furrowed his brow in puzzlement. A glance through the windshield showed that they were heading toward a dead end, their way blocked up ahead by a sentry gate, beyond which was a low, gray, flat-roofed structure with six or eight tractor-trailer trucks parked on either side of its cinder-block walls—presumably a warehouse of some kind.

"Perdoname, donde esta la estacion?" he said in Spanish. Asking where the railway station was.

The driver smiled and motioned to the right.

"Sólo al norte de aqui," he said, slowing as he approached the sentry gate. "It's just north of here."

Eduardo glanced in that direction, and saw nothing but the wide, muddy lot. Then he heard Ramon's push-button window roll down, jerked his eyes back toward him, and saw him reach out the window to swipe an identification card through a gatepost security scanner.

Eduardo felt a cold spark of alarm as it swung open to admit them and Ramon pulled to a halt several yards in front of the building.

"Qué es esto?" he blurted. "I don—"

Its movement a blur, Ramon's hand had shot beneath the dash and come back into sight gripping a pistol that must have been clipped to the dash's underside.

"Open your door and get out," he said, brandishing the gun at Eduardo. "Slowly."

Eduardo swallowed thickly, dumbfounded. One look at the weapon had told him it was a Sig Pro .40 semi-automatic—a standard-issue DEA sidearm. The thought that he'd fallen for another anti-drug squad setup flashed through his mind, and was quickly dismissed. What sense did that make? He had not escaped from confinement, but been willingly freed by his jailers. Nor had he uttered a peep about his business dealings to his driver or the plainclothes men who had escorted him to the border crossing.

He decided that Ramon, if that was his real name, must indeed be with DeVane—but the suddenly aggressive look in the man's eyes, the deft speed with which he'd produced his concealed weapon, and the particular model of gun he was using were all indications that he was no mere chauffeur. While conducting anti-drug operations in Bolivia and elsewhere in South America, DEA and U.S. Special Forces units had recruited and trained in-country field commandos who knew the territory and were able to speak the language. After completing their mandatory one-year tours of duty these natives—many of whom had blood ties to the coca farmers and distributors—would often put their skills and inside knowledge of narco police tactics up for sale to the cartels they had once sworn to oppose.

Eduardo cursed himself for a fool. His uncle was a respected lieutenant in the DeVane organization, and he had assumed it was Vicente, acting out of familial loyalty, who had brought about his release. But it could have been DeVane who'd engineered it. Must have been. And for reasons that, it seemed, were far from benign.

His face paling, Eduardo did as he had been instructed. Almost before he had exited the vehicle, Ramon was out his own door. He hurried around to Eduardo's side, grabbed him roughly by the arm with one hand, and shoved him along toward the building's corrugated metal door, the Sig pistol jammed against the back of his head.

There was an intercom beside the entrance. Ramon leaned toward it, pushed a button under the speaker, and announced himself, his gun held steady. An instant later the door rose clankily on its metal tracks.

Ramon prodded Eduardo through the entrance with the Sig and followed him inside. Then the door rattled down behind them, shutting out the daylight. Eduardo found himself thrown into sudden gloom. The air was stale and warm. Incandescent lightbulbs on the ceiling, covered by simple metal grills, seemed to propagate rather than dispel the interior shadows.

Ramon forced him to keep moving. As his pupils adjusted to the dimness, Eduardo glanced from side to side, and noticed the shipping crates on wooden pallets stacked all around him. Just as he had suspected, a warehouse. He guessed it was a hundred feet deep and twice as wide.

Then he looked straight ahead of him, saw the group of men waiting in the cleared-out space at the end of the aisle, and felt a sharp jab of fear. Only two were seated, the backs of their chairs against the bare unpainted walls. Vicente was one of them. Although Eduardo had never met him in person, he knew the slightly built American in the incongruous white suit seated to his uncle's right was Harlan DeVane. On either side of them stood a pair of guards holding short-barreled Micro Uzi assault rifles.

The tall, muscular man standing rigidly in front of the others, his chiseled face impassive, was DeVane's chief lieutenant, Siegfried Kuhl.

"Eduardo," DeVane said, his voice carrying softly across the room. "How do you do?"

Eduardo tried to think of something to say, but thought was impossible, swept from his head in the whipping gale of terror generated from the group of men before him and the pressure of Ramon's gun against the base of his skull.

DeVane steepled his hands on his lap. His legs were crossed, his right thigh hanging loosely over his left knee.

"You look frightened," he said. "Are you?"

Eduardo still could not wring any sound from his throat. He felt a choking, breathless nausea.

"Tell me if you are afraid," DeVane said.

Eduardo opened his mouth in another unsuccessful attempt at speech, then closed it and simply nodded. The tiny projection of the Sig's front sight ruffled his neck hairs as his head moved up and down.

DeVane sighed.

"You know, my boy, I am as loath to be here as yourself," he said in his smooth, quiet voice. "I preside over a great many enterprises, and generally a small complication such as you have caused would be the sort of thing I let others handle. I cannot be everywhere at once. A leader must have confidence in those who work for him." His hand left his lap and fluttered toward Vicente. "Solid, honorable men like your uncle."

Eduardo glanced over at Vicente. A rail-thin man in his mid-sixties with a sweep of white hair over a high forehead, Vicente looked back at him for only a second, his wrinkled face grim. Then he dropped his eyes.

Eduardo's legs weakened underneath him. It was the expression on the old man's face. The way he had avoided his gaze.

"This isn't to say your situation hasn't been of interest to me, or that I feel it is inconsequential," DeVane went on. "The problem isn't your arrest. That happens. In any competition there are errors and setbacks. Times when the best of plays are outdone by your opponent. Do you understand me so far?"

Eduardo nodded.

"Good," DeVane said. "And since you've admitted to your own fear, I'll tell you what scares me." He leaned slightly forward in his chair. "I fear the stupid and the weak, because history illustrates that their actions can bring down the most powerful. When someone like you is gullible enough to be duped by a common street-walker, letting her convince you to deal with men you do not know, men you do not bother checking out, there is no telling what information might slip to the other side. It doesn't matter how much or how little you have to offer, because one thing leads to another, and that to another, and so forth.

"For example, by contacting Vicente to bail you out of trouble, you put him in a position of having to ask a favor of me. Out of respect for your uncle, I then felt obliged to offer bribe money to a petty government bureaucrat, some of which filtered down to the magistrate in charge of your case, with smaller amounts trickling in dribs and drabs to a federal prosecutor, and then, I suppose, to a police clerk in an evidence control room who conveniently made the proof of your transaction disappear. These are markers, my boy. And they may lead an astute and determined opponent from you to Vicente, from Vicente up to me, from me down to a lackey officer, and then finally back to you—a connective loop that could theoretically cause me trouble without end."

He paused a moment. "Are you still following, Eduardo?"

Eduardo nodded agitatedly again.

DeVane's eyes bored into him with such awful, palpable force he thought his knees would finally give out.

"Open your mouth and answer me," he said. His expression was brittle. "Find that much strength."

Sick, dizzy, Eduardo again struggled to speak. He knew that he was standing at the brink of Hell, and if his silence were perceived as defiance, he was finished.

"Yes," he said in a faint, cracked voice. "I—I understand."

DeVane sat back in his chair and put his fingers together in a steeple again, resuming the relaxed, self-assured posture in which Eduardo had first seen him.

"Good," he said. "Then you should finally understand something else. I am here, now, as a gesture of respect for Vicente, for whom I know your punishment will be difficult. Were it not for him, it would have been unworthy of my attendance. I would have ordered it done from the comfort of my home, and devoted no more thought to it than I do to blinking my eyes."

With that, he looked at Kuhl, who had turned partially in his direction. There was an unspoken interaction between them—a brief meeting of their gazes, barely perceptible nods.

Then Kuhl reached back around his right hip and pulled something from his wide leather belt. Squinting in the semidarkness, Eduardo could see that it was some sort of wooden club or nightstick.

He looked beseechingly at DeVane, but he was staring at his own hands as if contemplating some unrelated matter. Beside him, Vicente sat with his head still lowered.

Kuhl stepped toward him, his hand gripping the stick.

"Please," Eduardo said. He cowered backward, came up against Ramon's solid body and the unyielding gunmetal pressed to his neck. *"Please."*

Kuhl was on him an instant later. Even as Eduardo raised his hands in defense, Kuhl struck a sharp, precise blow to his right arm with the end of the stick. His wrist bone broke free of the long bones of his forearm with a clean and audible snap. Kuhl swiftly brought the stick to the right and down again between Eduardo's neck and collarbone, then swung it across his middle. Eduardo simultaneously crumpled to his knees and vomited on himself.

Kuhl hit him three more times with the stick, smashing his nose with one blow, then striking him twice in the head. Eduardo collapsed further, curling his knees up into his chest. Blood gushed from his pulverized nose onto the rough concrete floor.

His eyes rolled blearily upward. He could see Kuhl standing above him, holding the stick in a vertical position, pulling at its upper end. And then the stick's handle detached and the long length of a knife blade slid from inside its bottom segment.

Kuhl stood there without expression, the knife in his right hand and the remaining portion of the stick in his left, looking as if he were about to plunge the blade into Eduardo's body. But instead he turned and passed it to someone who had come up beside him.

Eduardo shifted his head as far as he could, saw the man standing next to Kuhl, through a haze of pain, and released a low, tormented groan.

Vicente stared down at his nephew a moment, his eyes solemn, the lines around his mouth deepening. Then he knelt over him with the knife and sliced its edge across his throat to deliver the *coup de grace*.

Eduardo jerked, made a gurgling noise, and expired.

Rising, the old man gave the weapon back to Kuhl, turned toward DeVane, and bowed his head a little.

"I am sorry for your loss, dear friend," DeVane said gently.

Vicente nodded again but remained where he stood.

DeVane rose from his chair as Kuhl approached him, the knife dripping in his hand.

"Have Vicente driven out of here so the others can scrape that garbage off the floor," he said. "The Albanians have come through for us, and you and I have matters of vital importance to discuss."

ELEVEN

SAN JOSE, CALIFORNIA
APRIL 19, 2001

"ANY WORD ON THIBODEAU?" GORDIAN ASKED.

"He's still in ICU, but his condition's been upgraded from critical to serious," Nimec said. "The doctors are encouraged. They say he's alert. Also told me he's already getting on their nerves."

"How so?"

"Asking a lot of questions."

"Good sign."

"*And* demanding they find him a Stetson."

"Even better."

"Exactly my thought."

"Either of you care to explain?" Megan said. "About the Stetson, I mean."

Gordian looked at her. "Thibodeau was Air Cav in Vietnam. It was their tradition to wear Stetsons as part of their military wardrobe when they received awards and decorations. Still is, I think."

"Ah," Megan said. "So he's presumably of a mind that there's something to celebrate."

Gordian nodded.

They were in a sub-basement meeting room at Up-

Link's corporate HQ that looked much like any other in the building—beige carpet, oval conference table, recessed fluorescents—but differed from them in many important respects. The most apparent to the handful of top-tier executives permitted access were the electronic security panels outside the door incorporating voice-activated key-code software and retina-fingerprint scans, and the total absence of windows once they got inside.

The most substantive differences involved the interstitial matrix of comint technology that had been subtly worked into the room's design and construction. Layers of two-foot-thick concrete and acoustical paneling soundproofed its walls to human ears. Steel reinforcements, white-noise generators, and other counter-surveillance systems had been imbedded within them to block the tapping of conversations and electronic communications. Adding to security were twice-weekly sweeps for bugs, and spectrum and X-ray scans of all electronic equipment coming into or out of the room. While continual advancements in eavesdropping technology made it unrealistic to guarantee that any space on earth was strongboxed against *droops*—a word meaning "dirty rotten snoops" coined by UpLink's risk-assessment man, Vince Scull—its occupants could feel a comfortable degree of assurance in the inviolability of their discussions.

These occupants presently being limited to Gordian, Nimec, and Megan Breen, who had convened in this high-tech sanctum sanctorum to see what they could make of Brazil.

"Thibodeau's doctors mention the *sort* of questions he's been asking?" Gordian said now.

"No, but Cody did. He's the guy Rollie insisted on talking to," Nimec said. "It's pretty much as you'd expect. Who, what, why. And how the invaders knew as much about our perimeter security and grounds plan as they did."

"The answer to the last part seems painfully obvious."

"A mole," Megan said.

"Or *moles,*" Nimec added.

"Anybody look good for it?" Gordian asked.

"Not yet, and I expect it'll take a while before we find solid pointers," Nimec said. "There's no evidence our internal defenses were compromised in the sense of systems shutdowns or restricted databases being hacked. The reconnaissance that was gathered wouldn't have required a high level of clearance, just a familiarity with the complex and the time and incentive to do a thorough job of mapping it out. My guess is there are over a thousand administrative, R&D, production, building construction, medical, maintenance, and even kitchen staffers who could've provided the information."

"Nor can we rule out Sword personnel," Megan said.

Nimec looked at her. "That's right," he said. "We can't."

Gordian glanced from one to the other. "Impressions?"

"The invasion force was well organized and armed to the teeth," Nimec said. "It had land and air elements that performed with exceptional tactical coordination and were equipped with a French integrated weapon/helmet-mounted targeting package that gave them the equivalent of our country's Land Warrior system—ordnance that's technically still in field trials. The airborne teams that we think took out the robots made their insertion using high-altitude-high-opening para techniques. Again, we're looking at skills, experience, and equipment generally associated with elite commando units. They made the terrorists who hit us in Russia a couple years back look like toy soldiers."

"I assume none of the men we captured gave up information about who sent them?"

"There hardly would have been a chance if they'd *wanted* to," Megan said. "Brazilian federal police scooped them out of our hands within an hour after we notified them of the strike."

"Which is pretty much what I expected. Have we made official inquiries of the gendarmes since then?"

"Several, but they haven't exactly been eager to respond. Nobody we've contacted even seems sure where the prisoners are being detained."

"And I'd be willing to bet they're never seen or heard from again." Nimec rubbed his thumb over his fingers. "Whoever could launch an operation of the kind we saw the other night has got to have plenty of grease. The hinky bastards that pass for lawmen down there would be just the ones to soak it up. Mark my words, Gord, we'll get zero disclosure from them."

"We have our own intelligence resources. The ground units would have needed to stage from positions somewhere relatively close to the plant."

"The key word being 'relatively,' " Nimec said. "There are hundreds of miles of wilderness in the Mato Grasso. Territory where you could hide a fair-sized encampment if you have the know-how. As those people clearly would."

Gordian rubbed the back of his neck.

"They've got concealment and cover, we've got the Hawkeye," he said. "Let's put our new bird through its paces and see who wins the Kewpie."

"What I was just about to suggest," Nimec said. "I'll order the satellite jogged into position soon as I get to Brazil."

Gordian shook his head. "You can do that from a ground station right here in the states, Pete."

"Sure, but my point is that with Rollie's situation uncertain, we need somebody in charge down there—"

"I agree," Gordian said. "However, right now I'd prefer to have you in Florida as our liaison and advisor to the *Orion* investigation."

Nimec looked at him. "I thought you'd wrangled it so that Annie Caulfield was chosen to head the probe."

"I did. And I have complete confidence in her leadership."

"Yet you still want *me* to keep an eye on things?"

"To keep me abreast of developments," Gordian said. "Furthermore, there are some people at NASA who may be in a snit about Annie's accession, so to speak, and I'd like to have someone in place to backstop her should she run into difficulties."

"Right off the top of my head, I'm able to name at least a dozen people in our organization who can do the job as well as I can," Nimec said.

"Only if we disregard your experience in identifying the characteristics of sabotage," Gordian said. "I hope it doesn't become essential, but we have to be ready just in case. Which is my third reason for wanting you at the Cape."

Nimec sat there for a moment of dead silence. Gordian's fixed expression told him it wouldn't do any good to contest his decision, that things would have to go his way whether Nimec liked it or not. Besides, he could present no logical argument; everything Gordian had said made perfect sense.

In spite of the logic and sense, though, all Nimec could think was that he was finally getting his due for Malaysia. That Gordian was expressing his concern about a replay of the cowboys-and-Indians scenario that had grown out of Nimec's tolerance of Max Blackburn's unauthorized investigation into Monolith Technologies a year ago. He could still remember Gordian's words when he'd found out about it. At that point it had been evident that Blackburn was in trouble. No one had yet guessed how serious it would turn out to be, but Max had disappeared, and Nimec had finally had to ask his employer's permission to go looking for him.

Yes, he could remember Gord's exact words.

"It's beyond me how you could have been part of something this reckless, Pete. Completely beyond me . . . the two of you launched a caper that could have sunk us in quicksand. And very likely has . . ."

Nimec breathed. Maybe it hadn't sunk them, but Max was dead, and he owned a share of the blame. Maybe, too, he deserved to be making reparations.

"Who you plan on sending to Mato Grasso?" he asked.

Another dead moment.

Megan shifted in her chair.

"Gord's asked me to go," she said.

Nimec looked at her.

"I apologize." She averted her eyes for the briefest instant. "I probably should have told you sooner."

He was quiet.

"Pete, one more thing," Gordian said, breaking into the silence at what he thought was an opportune moment. "Have you heard from Tom Ricci? We can't afford to get hung up as far as the Sword position."

"He left a message on my voice mail this morning. I plan to return the call as soon as I get back to my office."

"No indication yet about how he's leaning?"

Nimec shook his head.

"He'd want to talk to me directly."

Gordian nodded. "I can see that."

Megan smoothed her skirt over her legs.

"Must be a guy thing," she half-muttered.

Gordian looked at her, raising his eyebrows.

"You haven't spoken to my wife lately, have you?"

"No," she said. "Why do you ask?"

Gordian looked at her another moment.

"Never mind," he said, and scratched behind his ear. "It's nothing important."

TWELVE

ANNIE CAULFIELD HAD BEEN THRUST INTO THE ROLE of NASA spokeswoman often enough to have grown philosophical about it. See it as a burden and it would become one, and when it became one it would start to show on camera, and when it started showing on camera you'd be perceived as touchy and evasive, i.e., having something to hide, and the press corps would pound you without mercy. See it as a sort of friendly jousting match with reporters and interviewers, get too cute, and you would come off as one of the gang, an egotistical, overly glib insider who was enjoying the limelight, cozying up to your questioners for personal advancement—perhaps in anticipation of joining their ranks as a pundit, or expert consultant as it was formally called—and had very likely gotten into cahoots with them to put one over on the average citizen. See it as a means of serving the public's legitimate right to know while doing your best to shape a positive perception of the agency, be honest about the facts you disclosed and equally aboveboard explaining instances when you *couldn't* make certain information available, and you'd be solidly on Annie's preferred course. Yes, it was always part performance and part ritual . . . but a performance could be either sincere or insincere, a ritual of light or shadow, and she tried her earnest best to stay on the side of the angels.

It was a tough balancing act that often put her resilience and composure to the extreme test.

The day after she accepted the assignment of *Orion* task force leader, her face was all over the televised landscape. In addition to being the subject of pieces on virtually every national and local newscast, she made appearances on two of the three morning coffee klatch shows via satellite, conducted the first of what would be a series of regular afternoon media briefings at the Cape, and was the leadoff guest on cable TV's highest-rated prime-time interview program, again via remote feed.

Her first booking was a five-minute spot with the same Gary Somebody-or-other who'd snared her for the cameras just before the shuttle launch was to have taken place. A genial man in his thirties, his plain-vanilla good looks and honey-voiced manner contributed to his talent for reducing conversations about wars, disasters, and the latest showbiz buzz alike into a homogeneous puree that washed down smoothly with breakfast and made him a consistent Nielsen winner. While Gary was certainly opportunistic, Annie had to admit that she sort of liked him, finding him to be further removed from a Gila monster than many of his peers, and a whole lot sharper than his soft and fuzzy veneer let on.

"We appreciate your taking the time to join us, Ms. Caulfield," he began in a tone of gentle empathy. "On behalf of this broadcast's staff and viewers, I'd like to extend my condolences to NASA and the family of James Rowland. Our thoughts go out to all of you."

"Thank you, Gary. The support we've gotten from the public obviously means a great deal to us, and has been a particular comfort to Jim's wife and daughter."

"Can you tell us what sort of impact the tragedy has had on you personally? I know that you and Colonel Rowland were close friends as well as colleagues."

Don't choke up, she thought. *Answer him, give him his follow-up, and maybe then he'll drop it.*

"Well . . . like anybody who suffers the loss of someone dear, I find it hard to put all my feelings into words. Jim's death has been devastating for everyone who knew him. He had a huge, warm personality, and it's hard to believe he's gone. He'll be terribly missed and remembered always."

"You flew several missions into space with Colonel Rowland, didn't you?"

One word. Don't choke.

"Yes."

"As crewmates on several missions, did the two of you ever discuss the possibility of being harmed in what is, after all, a highly dangerous occupation?"

Please, let's move on.

"I don't recall that we ever did. I think every astronaut feels a sense of privilege about being chosen to go into space. We're always aware things can go wrong and try to prepare for these eventualities in training, and I'm convinced it's because of this training that the rest of *Orion*'s crew escaped the shuttle unharmed. But we really can't afford to dwell on the risks of our job any more than a firefighter or police officer can worry about them when he starts out each day."

"Of course, I understand, and believe it's one of the main reasons that astronauts have come to epitomize an almost mythic spirit of heroism to those of us who've only been able to see the stars from the ground, and *dreamed* of seeing the ground from the stars."

Whatever that means, as long as you please, please move on, she thought with an interim smile, having no idea how to respond.

"On the subject of your present duties as *Orion* task force leader, how do you intend to proceed with your efforts to determine the cause of last Tuesday's terrible calamity at the launchpad?"

Thank you. I think.

"Speaking in general terms, and that's the best I can do at this juncture, we'll assemble a team that will look at what happened and search for clues to help us isolate the factors leading up to it. Any forensic probe is largely a process of elimination, and it's going to require a painstaking examination of *Orion*'s remains."

"May we assume your investigative team is to be composed of NASA personnel?"

"As we expressed in our initial statement to the press, we're quite firmly committed to using experts from inside *and* outside the space agency—"

"When you say outside experts, I find myself wondering where they'd be drawn from, this being an occurrence that's had few historic parallels. Other than *Challenger,* and *Apollo 10* before that, nothing else gratefully comes to mind . . . and I do want to emphasize the word *gratefully.*"

"I understand the basis of your question, Gary. But we've learned a great deal from the accidents you mention, and many of the people who helped determine what occurred in those instances are available for consultation—or even active participation—in our investigation. Also, while it's true that the shuttle is a unique and advanced spacecraft, many of its systems and subsystems share a common baseline with the technologies used in other modern flying machines. Consequently, there's a wide pool of authorities from government and civil aviation who can be of tremendous assistance to us."

"Does that mean the FAA and National Transportation and Safety Board will be involved?"

Name the two agencies that nobody but nobody *trusts,*

why don't you? Might as well ask about the possible inclusion of former KGB operatives, or maybe Nixon's White House plumbers while you're at it.

"We'll be working alongside those groups to get to the bottom of what happened, and may very well include representatives from both as part of our team's composition. However, we've already had many specialists from the aerospace industry and other parts of the private sector volunteer their expertise, and we will certainly be taking full advantage of it. What matters to me is that the job gets done, and I'm inclined to engage anyone who can have constructive input, regardless of his or her professional affiliation."

Gary Somebody-or-other paused a beat. Though Annie was looking directly into the bland eye of a television camera and had no video monitor with which to see him long distance, she suspected he was getting instructions from the control room.

A moment later her suspicion was confirmed.

"I'm being told we're short on time, so some final questions," he said. "We've heard from various sources that there's been a break-in at an UpLink International facility in Brazil, where critical elements of the International Space Station are being manufactured. Several accounts indicate that a military-style assault force was involved. Can you tell us anything about this?"

Have to get back to you on that one. Soon as somebody gives me more than the Cliff Notes version of what's going on over there. Which may eventually happen if I'm lucky.

"To be frank, I've spoken with Roger Gordian just once since my appointment as head of the probe, and didn't have a chance to discuss the matter at length—"

"Can you confirm that there indeed *was* an attack on the plant?"

"Apparently a break-in, to use your characterization

of the incident, did take place and was contained by UpLink security forces. That's all I've gotten up to this point, but I plan to be in further touch with Mr. Gordian sometime today or tomorrow, and will hopefully have additional information to share with you afterward."

"Any idea about the size of the attack force, what they were after, or who might have been sponsoring them?"

"No, none. I really *do* wish I could tell you more right now, Gary, but everyone needs to try and be patient."

"Still, I must ask you—given the nearly simultaneous timing of the two incidents, and knowing that *Orion*'s primary cargo was a lab element of ISS—has a connection between what happened in Brazil and the shuttle blaze been considered?"

"I have no knowledge that would lead me to believe that, and don't think we should go too far with that kind of speculation. NASA maintains a very close relationship with UpLink, and we'll be keeping track of any developments in Mato Grasso that could impact on the program. I intend to be absolutely forthcoming to the press about whatever we learn, bearing in mind that we need to be careful about any details that might jeopardize the safety of UpLink personnel abroad."

"So you're not concerned about Roger Gordian suspending operations at the plant? If the stories coming out of Brazil turn out to be true?"

Huh? Suspending operations? Where'd that come from? Feel free to whip something up out of thin air, why don't you, Gary?

"No, I've heard nothing at all to indicate that's being contemplated."

Another pause.

"Unfortunately, I'm being signaled that we're coming up on our daily 'Keep Your Lawn Lean and Green' segment. Please accept our prayers and best wishes as you move forward with your investigation. I hope you'll return to give us an update."

"Thank you, Gary, I'm sure that I will," Annie said. *Onward,* she thought.

It was at her afternoon press conference that Annie detected an emerging thread to the coverage, one that was being gradually twisted through a journalistic hook with sales figures and ratings points as the intended catch.

She'd scarcely taken a breath after having completed her opening statements when an Associated Press reporter opened the Q&A by shooting his hand into the air and jumping from his seat in front of the podium like a kindergartner desperate for his teacher's permission to visit the potty.

"In your appearance on a national television broadcast earlier today, you discussed Roger Gordian closing down his International Space Station plant in Brazil due to an attack on its grounds by armed militants," he said. "Can you elaborate on that situation for us?"

"As I stated before, I've heard nothing whatsoever about any such closing, and have to point out that your categorization of the intruders as *militants* is incredibly premature—"

"But you confirmed that a break-in took place, am I correct?"

"Yes, though *break-in* was the interviewer's phrase, not mine," she said. "My purview is the *Orion* probe and that's where I wish to keep my focus. In my prepared comments a moment ago, I explained that the shuttle's remains are being transported from the launch site to the Vehicle Assembly Building for reconstruction, a procedure I've been busy coordinating throughout the day. The remainder of my time has been spent working out procedural guidelines for the investigation, selecting members of our team, and doing everything I can to let the press know what we're up to."

Annie motioned to another print man, Allen Murdock, a staff reporter with the *Washington Post*.

"To stay with the issue my colleague from AP just raised," Murdock said, "when asked on television whether the events in Brazil could have been linked to *Orion,* you stated you had no knowledge of it—quote, unquote—but refrained from dismissing the possibility outright. Does that mean there *may* be signs that they're related acts of sabotage? And if so, who do you believe might have been responsible for them?"

"Allen, I don't think it serves me any purpose to parse words. 'No knowledge' means precisely that—"

"But it's well known that Roger Gordian has been a steady proponent and financial backer of ISS for many years. *If* the reports of his company closing up shop in Brazil *were* to prove accurate, *wouldn't it be reasonable* to conclude that the decision was precipitated by a serious threat to his employees?"

That makes, what, three qualifiers in a single sentence?

"You're asking several questions at once, all of them hypothetical, and I'd rather stick to the facts. Again, I'm not sure how this notion about UpLink abandoning the program originated, though it seems to me it's based on a supposition drawn from a misrepresentation of some remarks that were made on the air earlier, which I think everyone here would agree can really get things in a tangle."

Next!

She pointed to a fresh face. A young woman swimming amid a school of combative males. *Sisterly kinship. Feminine rapport.* Her press pass identified her as Martha Eumans from CNBC.

Martha stood. "Should UpLink decide to withdraw its

support of ISS, *whatever* the reason, how seriously would it impact upon the space station's future prospects . . . ?"

And so it went for another very, very trying half hour.

"Annie, I realize these are difficult times, but gotta say you're looking magnificent."

"That's very kind of you, Mac."

"Mac" was McCauley Stokes, the sixtysomething cable talk show moderator popularly known for his folksy interviewing style, ever-present ten-gallon hat, and gold clasped string tie, as well as his string of *twentysomething* silicon-enhanced wives—all of which served as trademark reminders of his virile, high-in-the-saddle Texas cowboy heritage. The rough-rider routine, however, was as ersatz as his current bride's outrageous bustline. For while Stokes *had* been born in Texas, it was to parents who had been the third-generation beneficiaries of an oil family fortune, migrated to the exclusive blue blood community of Greenwich, Connecticut, when he was four years old, and raised and educated him in an atmosphere of pampered gentility, where the closest he'd ever gotten to a horse had been the viewing stands of the local polo grounds.

"Hey, I'm not just being polite, Annie, you really *are* something else. A woman to be admired in every way." He tipped his hat. "We're gonna cover a lot of ground with you tonight, a whole lot, I say . . ."

My God, he's doing Foghorn Leghorn.

". . . but before we get to *Orion,* let's play catch-up, hear how you been holding up on the home front. Last time you were a guest, you'd just returned from six weeks in space, remember? That was back in, what, late '99?"

"I believe so, Mac. It was after my third and final mission."

"And since then we know you've suffered the loss of your husband, Mark."

She inhaled, looking at Stokes in the monitor that, in this particular instance, had been provided to her by the studio technicians.

"Yes, that's true. Mark died just over a year ago."

"A woman like yourself—two children, high-octane career—it must be tough trying to lead an active social life. Have you dated anyone since Mark passed?"

Deep, deep breath.

"My professional and maternal responsibilities are very fulfilling, Mac. And about all I care to handle right now."

"But a lady with your beauty, smarts, and class, with all your *verve,* catch me, has gotta have scores of young bucks locking antlers—"

Bucks? I don't believe this.

"Mac, forgive me for interrupting, but I'm sure my personal affairs are of less interest to your viewers than the progress we at NASA are making with regard to the *Orion* investigation."

"Then I just better put my tongue in a tooth corral and let you do some talking. But first, how about the lowdown how NASA's gonna convince Roger Gordian to change his mind about bailing out of Brazil . . . ?"

The place where *Orion* had been delivered into the world had become its morgue.

At nine-thirty P.M., an hour after her appearance on *McCauley Stokes Live*—which had concluded with a leering wink from the host, and was, blessedly, her final media engagement of the day—Annie Caulfield stood alone inside the Vehicle Assembly Building at the KSC, a structure that spanned eight acres at the north end of the Cape and rose 525 feet into the air, proportions that made the VAB the only indoor facility in America able to house the space shuttle's orbiter, solid rocket boosters, and external fuel tank both before and after they were mated into a vertical stack.

About a month ago, one of the center's two crawler-transporters had borne *Orion* across the three and a half miles from the VAB to Launch Pad 39A, its engines guzzling 150 gallons of diesel fuel per minute for the entire five hours it took to reach the pad. Earlier today, that same tracked vehicle had conveyed the spacecraft's remains back to the building before the solemn eyes of NASA personnel like a funeral wagon for a slain Colossus. And now the charred and twisted segments of *Orion* lay spread across the floor of High Bay 1, smelling of smoke, burned fuel, and melted plastics—the acrid, resinous odor seeping into the processed air of the facility so that it stung the inside of Annie's nose and made the lining of her throat feel swollen and irritated.

Why had she driven here tonight in her UpLink-leased Saab, making a detour to the Cape before heading back to her condo from the television studio, calling ahead to let her kids' nursemaid—flown in from Houston with her family, also courtesy of Roger Gordian—know she'd be an hour late getting home? She scarcely needed to be reminded that her trip to Florida was no all-expenses-paid dream vacation won after a bouncy performance on *The Price Is Right,* or a knock on the door by someone from Publisher's Clearinghouse. She had been here at Canaveral only the week before, when the scorched wreckage in the aisles around her was still a commanding, majestic vessel about to pierce the upper limit of the atmosphere. When Jim Rowland had pointed to the Turnip patch on his chest, mouthing their old training class motto to her, flashing his crooked little grin before entering the silver bus that had carried him to his death. When *Orion* had been something other than a name that would be forever synonymous with tragedy and irrevocable loss.

Terra nos respuet.

No, she did not need any reminders about the reason she was in Florida.

Annie looked around the vast floor of the room, her brows drawn into a contemplative M above her eyes, deep grooves bracketing the corners of her mouth. If the explosion had occurred even seconds after *Orion* began its ascent, the debris would have been scattered across the bottom of the Atlantic, which would have made its reclamation a prolonged and arduous task requiring a flotilla of recovery ships and scores of divers. But because the fire had taken place prior to liftoff, almost every part of the craft—from the smallest, still-unidentified scraps of scorched metal, to the gigantic bolts that had held the stack together, to large sections of the Orbiter's delta wings and fuselage—had been salvaged from the launchpad area, then brought here to be tagged and audited like bodily remains awaiting a coroner's exam. What word could she use to describe her feelings about that? Encouraged? Thankful? It seemed obscene to use either in a context of such utter grimness and heartache.

The segments of the craft and equipment numbered in the hundreds, a few of them relatively unscathed, most damaged by flames and smoke. Tomorrow she would run herd over the first group of forensic specialists to inspect these parts that could never again add up to a whole . . . no, not even if every last screw and inch of wiring had been recovered. There would be a fresh round of interviews with newspeople, mountains of paperwork, a long list of phone calls—including Roger Gordian's promised briefing on the Brazilian incident. She needed some rest. A shower, a peek in at the kids, then bed.

So why on earth *hadn't* she gone directly home instead of coming to view this terrible, oppressive scene after everyone but the uniformed men in the gatehouse had left for the night?

Annie frowned, trying to think of an answer to her own question—and then suddenly realized that her need to do some thinking might very well *be* the answer. Or most of it anyway.

If she'd been asked to grade her own first-day-on-the-job media performance, Annie believed she might at best find herself deserving of a C minus. The coverage had veered in a direction she had not meant for it to take . . . and worse yet, had been torn from her grasp by the newshounds and begun to feed off their intentional and unintentional distortions. What had originated with Gary HoneyVanilla's offhand question about the *possibility* of Roger Gordian withdrawing from Brazil had led several media outlets to assert there were "rumors"—*plural*—of an UpLink pullout by midday, a word that hardened into "reports" at her afternoon press conference—thank you, Allen Murdock—giving the story a false legitimacy, and inciting fervid debate about its ramifications for ISS on *Crossfire* and kindred early evening shout fests some hours later.

Insofar as Annie could continue tracing its genesis, the next permutation of the story occurred when one of the early evening network news broadcasts blended an *analysis* of the day's speculation into its overall coverage, creating an ambiguous muddle of fact and fiction that was later used as source material by yet *another* national news program. It had all culminated with the rootin'-tootin' McCauley Stokes asking Annie how NASA meant to *stop* UpLink's pullout as if it were an actuality rather than something that had sprung from Gary HoneyVanilla's imagination.

Hence, the story had incredibly gone through *seven* distinct stages over the course of a single news cycle, and Annie had needed to spend most of her air time with Stokes addressing the compounded inaccuracies rather than getting out the information *she'd* wanted to present. And despite her repeated clarifications, dismissals, and denials, it was now almost certain that tomorrow would kick off with a swarm of Stokes-derived headlines about the UpLink retreat—adding more quick-to-solidify layers of nonsense to the story, while increasing the self-perpetuating momentum that had allowed it to snowball over the last twenty-four hours.

And it's going to keep rolling over me unless I start being a lot more careful choosing my words, Annie told herself. *This isn't like anything I've dealt with before, and I need to get real about the sort of media glare I'm under.*

Perhaps subconsciously, then, another reason she'd come here was to *let* the reality of the task confronting her fully sink in. Perhaps her initial awkwardness—and occasional defensiveness—in publicly dealing with the aftermath of *Orion* stemmed from a reluctance to entirely acknowledge what had happened in her own mind. She had assumed a responsibility that would not permit her the shock or denial that were the normal early stages of grief, and had compelled her to take a wrenching shortcut to acceptance. No sense condemning herself for that, but her future effectiveness demanded that she understand and confront her mistakes.

She walked slowly around the room, working her way between the mutilated fragments of what once had been *Orion*. On this side of her were some cracked thermal tiles, on that side a skeletal mound of aluminum ribs and spars from its airframe, over there an almost unrecognizable chunk of the pilot's console with a thatch of fused cables dangling from its blown-out rear panel. At her feet, she could see an elevon that must have become detached from the edge of a wing in one of the explosions that had rocked the firing room where she had been a hapless witness to the disaster.

Here, in this place, acceptance was inescapable, and that was also largely what had steered her along past home, the kids, and the chance to get some much needed sleep. And there was one final motivation for this self-guided tour of Hell, one last thing she'd needed to contemplate in absolute solitude . . . one last thing, while she'd known she would be willing and able to lay herself open to the worst of possibilities.

Amid all the noise pollution that had bombarded her throughout the day, all the half-baked theories she'd heard and tried to deflect, all the *craziness,* there had been a single burr of speculation that had attached itself to her thoughts and defied her persistent attempts to brush it off. It had first been put to her by the sharper-than-he-seemed Gary HoneyVanilla near the end of their interview.

"*. . . given the nearly simultaneous timing of the two incidents, and knowing that* Orion's *primary cargo was a lab element of ISS, has a connection between what happened in Brazil and the shuttle blaze been considered?*"

Not by her, not until that moment. But she had been considering it on one level or another ever since.

What if there were proven to be a link between *Orion* and Brazil?

What if someone had intentionally caused the disaster?

What if Jim Rowland had not perished because of some accidental failure of construction or technology, but a willful, murderous act of destruction by someone who wanted badly enough to keep the launch from taking place?

She stood there in the mortuary silence of the bay, her hands laced behind her back, the crescent-shaped lines around her mouth deepening and deepening as these questions proceeded along their dark, ceaseless orbit through her mind.

What if?

THIRTEEN

SOUTHEASTERN BRAZIL
APRIL 21, 2001

IN THE MONTHS AFTER THE CATASTROPHIC DERAIL-
ment of the Sao Paulo–Rio de Janeiro night train that
left 194 passengers dead or seriously injured, there
would be many separate investigations with respect to
its surrounding conditions and circumstances. To no
one's particular surprise, their findings proved contra-
dictory and disputatious, and led to a prolonged blizzard
of litigation. The railroad line and its insurers would
blame the company from which it leased the track, citing
as factors a plethora of signaling, switching, and maintenance problems. The track owner and its insurers
would point *their* fingers right back at the rail line, al-
leging a laxity of safety precautions overall, and specifically accusing the engineer, Julio Salles, of job dere-
liction. Attorneys for the victims and victims' families
would side with the track owner following a computer
analysis by accident-reconstruction experts who were
hired in support of their class action lawsuit.

Upon Salles's suspension without pay pending settle-
ment of the various torts, his personal lawyers argued
that he was being scapegoated by the rail line *and* the

track owner for their own negligence, while also dragging the corporation that had designed the train's new electro-pneumatic braking system and Doppler speedometer into the legal cross fire with claims that both systems had malfunctioned in the moments preceding the wreck.

The Brazilian government commission charged with reviewing the incident would take eighteen months and three thousand pages to tamely state their opinion that the facts were inconclusive and endorse an arbitrated agreement between the host of plaintiffs and defendants. With issuance of this white paper report as impetus, deals were cut between nearly all the opposing camps—the sole holdout being Julio Salles, who remained adamant that he was without culpability and insisted his reputation had been irreparably sullied by the allegations leveled against him. Yielding to advice from counsel, he eventually accepted an offer of retirement with full pension and back pay in exchange for a halt to court proceedings and public contention, but would privately continue to feel embittered toward the company to which he had given thirty years of his life, and sink into a deep depression.

Two years to the day after the disaster, Salles would mark that tragic anniversary with a lethal, self-inflicted gunshot wound to his head in the one-bedroom Sao Paulo flat he shared with his wife, making him in a very real sense its 195th human casualty.

In the end, what happened to the train in the hilly darkness along the line between Barra Funda station and its intended destination would remain a mystery.

It was 11:00 P.M. when the plain gray van pulled onto the roadside embankment a quarter of a kilometer west of where the railway track took a sharp bend along the steeply descending valley wall. The driver immediately cut the ignition and headlamps, then sat behind the wheel studying the rail bed. Although the night was moonless and starless, its darkness untinctured by village lights here in the sparsely populated hill country east of Taubate, he could see the signal post up the tracks through the lenses of his NVGs.

He briefly lowered his goggles and turned toward the rear of the van to give the order. A pair of men dressed in black, balaclava masks over their faces, emerged from the vehicle's side door. They untied the fastening cords of the tarpaulin that bedecked its roof, then pulled the tarp to the ground to expose a twelve-inch-diameter dish antenna mounted atop the van.

They folded and stowed the tarp, climbed back inside, and made some final calibrations. The dish rotated ninety degrees to the east and spotted on the automatic railway signal. Behind them in the van's cargo area, a small mobile generator hummed faintly in the dead quiet.

Facing front, the driver put the NVGs up to his eyes again and glanced to his left, westward, the direction from which the train would come rolling down the hillside. Then he shifted his attention to the signal post. When the moment came, the dish would bathe it with a wideband pulse lasting several hundred nanoseconds— less time than it took to blink—then turn on its axis and emit another short, pulsed beam as the train entered its line of sight. According to the Russian, Ilkanovitch, that was all that would be required.

What was the clever little message he had asked the Albanian to deliver with the rest of the material?

A test and a taste.

Soon Kuhl would see for himself whether either was to his pleasure.

At five before midnight he heard the rumble of the train in the distance. While he knew the open acoustics of the valley would make the train sound closer than it actually was, Kuhl's teeth came together with an eager click. It would appear within minutes, chugging along at close to seventy miles an hour on the straight downhill gradient.

He watched the signal, which was now displaying a yellow "slow" aspect.

The clank and rumble of the train grew louder.

Closer.

Kuhl watched the signal. He thought he perceived a rise in the generator's hum, a crackle in the air around him, but doubted it was anything more than his gaining anticipation.

The first pulse was initiated.

Kuhl watched.

The yellow light fluttered off, on, off. Then *stayed* off.

A breath hissed through his teeth. His jaw muscles tight, he whipped his head to the left and saw the approaching locomotive's lights splash across the ties. Then it nosed into sight below him, the figure of the engineer visible through the windows of its raised cab, a long, streamlined set of passenger cars hugging the slope behind it.

The dish rotated silently on the roof of the van and released its second pulse.

She was tall, tan, young, lovely, and from Ipanema, just like the girl in the old song. Christina from Ipanema, could you believe even her *name* rhymed with the title?

Darvin had met her in a bar at Barra Funda station, where he had stopped for a martini while waiting for his train. He'd been sitting there sipping from his glass, thinking about the big-money deal he'd clinched for his company in New York—well, his father-in-law's company, if you wanted to nitpick—when she came walking along, just *like* in the song, strutting right past the bar in this light, scoop-backed, flowery cotton shift—diamond earrings, black pearl necklace, chic *mehndi* lotus tattoo on her bare shoulder, her hips swaying to the rhythmic Afro-samba music blasting from the P.A. system, her hands loaded with shopping bags from the expensive boutiques downtown. Christina from Ipanema.

Darvin had scarcely been able to believe it when he'd found himself leaning off his stool to ask her if she wanted to join him for a drink, first because he was a married man—it had been six months since he'd tied the knot, not at all coincidentally the same length of time he'd been employed as a salesman for Rinas International Hotel Supplies—and second because he hadn't had a pot to piss in before that, when he'd been hawking costume jewelry door-to-door at thirty bucks a ring and thirty-five a necklace for some Israeli *gonif* who had his office on 10th Avenue, getting a ten-percent commission on each piece of soon-to-discolor crap he unloaded, his assigned route running from 125th Street in Harlem to Washington Heights—try to earn a living wage *that* way, bro.

Back then, before he got hitched, before his wife's father consequently became his boss and handed him the company's plum Brazilian accounts, Darvin wouldn't have had the cash or confidence to so much as dream of picking up a woman in Christina's league, which was kind of funny if you thought about it, like something you'd expect to read in *Penthouse Forum*. Maybe he ought to send in an article, use one of those dumb pen names to protect his identity: *Marrying to Score Babes, by Lucky Strike.*

At this very moment, in fact, streaking through the inky South American night toward Rio and Darvin's room at the Ritz Carlton, snuggled close together in the dimly lit coach of the express train—the fifth of six cars coupled to the locomotive—they were engaged in an activity that would itself make for a great opening teaser. Ten minutes earlier they had asked the attendant for an afghan and thrown it over their laps, not because either of them was cold, but because Christina from Ipanema, who had herself been waiting for the train after an afternoon shopping spree in Sao Paulo with a girlfriend—or so she said—had put her mouth to his ear and whispered a suggestion or two about how they might while away the long hours of the ride, provided they could keep from being noticed by prying eyes.

This being a luxury line, they'd *already* had a nice amount of privacy. Their high-backed, buttery leather chairs blocked the view of them from behind. The wall-to-wall carpeting muted most of the sounds around them and, more importantly, most sounds they might make. The fluorescent lights over the central aisle had been switched off for the benefit of passengers wanting to catch some shuteye, and many of those who weren't asleep were in the buffet car having cocktails and canapes. Small incandescent lamps with rose-colored shades mounted between the windows gave off a subdued glow that was enough to read by, or whatever, and was also kind of romantic. The afghan, therefore, had niftily finalized yet another major deal for Darvin, giving them all the added cover they'd needed.

Now Darvin looked over at her and gasped. She looked back at him, her lips curling upward, and produced a soft, furry moan. Their faces were almost touching, their breaths mingling in moist little puffs. Their hands roved beneath the blanket like a couple of warm, burrowing animals, hers delving industriously into his unzipped and unbelted pants, his digging deep under the hem of her dress.

Darvin was about to reach the unquestionable high point of his journey—or this leg of it, at any rate—when the fluorescents running over the middle aisle abruptly flickered on, flooding the train with their stark radiance. Startled from her rapture, Christina from Ipanema straightened beside him, her hand becoming frustratingly still under the afghan, then slipping all the way out of his pants. She looked around in distracted confusion. Most of the dozing riders had been awakened by the sudden surge of light and were doing the same. Though Darvin remained dug in under her dress, figuring he'd stay there until explicitly asked to leave, he likewise found himself glancing about the coach. It wasn't just that the lights were on. It was that they were buzzing loudly and seemed much too *bright,* as if their wattage had been turned up to a hot, glaring level. And the attendant, who was staring up at the ceiling of the car, looked as bewildered as everyone else.

"O que e isto?" a guy behind him asked loudly in Portuguese. *"Tudo bem?"*

What is this? Is everything okay?

Seconds later, the speeding train jolted on the track and the emergency horn in the locomotive burst into clamorous, ear-splitting sound, making it clear that everything was very definitely *not* okay.

Minutes after that, Darvin, the woman who called herself Christina, and twenty-five other passengers aboard the car were dead.

When they were young and struggling to meet the rent in the Baltimore rowhouse apartment where they'd raised their four children, Al and Mary Montelione had played a silly little game with each other virtually every time they went to the supermarket. It had started soon after their next-to-youngest, Sofia, was born. Because they'd been living exclusively off his modest postman's salary and had needed to cut corners wherever possible, they would very carefully compare prices on grocery items, household supplies, really anything and everything they purchased.

One Fourth of July weekend during a particularly lean spell, they'd decided to treat the family to some ice cream, but standing at the dairy freezer, had suddenly realized they could scarcely afford even that meager indulgence, given that they'd had not a cent in the bank and about ten dollars cash between them to stretch over the holiday. Seeing the crestfallen look on Al's face as he'd read the price labels, Mary had grabbed him by the elbow and exclaimed: "Come on, mister, go for it! Whoever finds the cheapest quart *wins a free trip to Rio*!" It was one of those situations when you either had to laugh or cry, and her mock announcer's voice had pushed Al's precarious emotional balance toward the former. Cracking up hysterically, he'd plunged into the freezer as if he actually *had* been a contestant on a game show, all at once a whole lot less depressed than he'd been a moment before—which, of course, had been Mary's intent. Though she'd outscrounged him by twenty-two cents that evening, they had bought the ice cream for the family and he'd come home feeling like a winner for a change. From then on, the "trip to Rio" bit had become a standard tactic they'd used to relieve the strain of their constant financial woes. After a while even the kids had gotten in on it.

Four decades later, living simply but quite comfortably on Al's postal supervisor's retirement pension—things had gone well for them after his promotion, except for a health scare three years earlier, when he'd developed a severe cardiac arrhythmia that required normalization with an artificial pacemaker—Al and Mary were celebrating their Golden Anniversary with a *real* trip to Rio as well as other sight-seeing locales in Brazil, the travel and hotel reservations fully paid for by their now grown and married children, who had cooked up the idea as a surprise gift. Thus far the vacation had been spectacular. They'd spent five days in Copacabana, taken an air shuttle to Brasilia for a tour of the country's western region that included a breathtaking hot-air balloon ride over a wildlife preserve in the Pantanal, then flown back east, making a two-day stopover in Sao Paulo before boarding the night coach back to Rio, where they planned to spend the final weekend of their vacation.

After sampling the buffet in the dining car about three hours into the ride, they had taken their seats in the middle of the train, Mary pulling a Danielle Steele novel out of her travel bag, Al settling in for a snooze beside her, when the fluorescent overheads flashed on and started buzzing like a nest of wasps.

Quizzically scrunching her eyebrows, Mary looked up from her paperback, then turned to her husband.

Her expression at once became frightened.

Al had awakened with a start and had both hands on his chest his face pale, his mouth wide open and pulling in shallow snatches of air.

"Al what is it?" she said, her book dropping from her fingers as she reached over and took hold of his shoulder. "Al, honey, *Al,* are you *sick?*"

He nodded, too short of breath to answer.

Terrified now, oblivious to the murmurs that had arisen throughout the car over the lights going on, Mary frantically looked around for an attendant.

"We need a doctor over here!" she cried. *"Please, someone help us!"*

But no one responded. A sudden, violent jolting of the train, followed by the loud blare of the emergency horn, had thrown the other occupants of the car into their own constricted spheres of panic. Mary heard cries of alarm all around her. Heard metal wheels grind over the tracks as the train's jarring, bumping, swaying movement worsened, threatening to fling her off of her seat.

Beside her, Al was gagging, his hands still clutching his chest directly over the spot where the pacemaker was implanted. Acting on impulse, not knowing what else to do, she threw herself protectively over him, put her arms around him, and held him to her.

It was in this position that their bloody, broken bodies were found the next day when the search teams recovered them from the wreckage.

In the second car of the train, Enzio Favas was proudly showing off his UpLink Telecommunications pager/wristwatch to Alyssa, one of the Australian runway models he'd hired to showcase his upcoming beachwear line at the fashion designers' convention in Rio the following week.

"It send and receive E-mail, do you know? *E-mail!*" He pointed to the bottom of the readout display. "You touch screen and words appear right here!"

Alyssa glanced over at him. She'd been studying an unsightly calcium deposit under her fingernail and wishing there were a manicurist aboard.

"Uh-huh," she said.

"And it adjust to different *time zone*! *Automateeek!*" he enthused in thickly accented English. "Fly from New York City to Los Angeles, Paris to Tokyo, time never off by a minute! It all done by satellite, do you know?"

"Uh-huh." A little girl giggled several rows back and Alyssa frowned. "You think those brats behind us are ever going to shut up and go to sleep?"

Enzio shrugged. The "brats" were actually three very adorable sisters who were being shepherded cross-country by their nanny. Enzio had chatted briefly with the woman earlier in the ride and gotten the entire story: Parents divorced, mother living in Sao Paulo, father in Rio, joint custody arrangement, the poor babies constantly bouncing between them like Ping-Pong balls. Enzio, himself the product of a broken home, sympathized. How could Alyssa be so icy? So vain and self-absorbed? And besides that, how could she not have *any* interest in his watch?

"It has twenty different kind of tone, some of them music! And—what it is called?—GPS feature!" he said, thinking that last would be certain to impress her. "Get lost anyplace, *anyplace in whole world,* you send message to UpLink operator. He send message back, tell you where you are! Do you know?"

Alyssa ran her tongue around the inside of her lips, trying to curb her annoyance. If Enzio's rambling about the watch didn't drive her bonkers, his verbal tics absolutely would. And those giggly kids, Jesus.

"Uh-huh," she said, beginning to regret that she hadn't sat across the aisle with Thandie, one of the other models . . . although all *she* ever talked about was how she could eat as much rich, high-calorie food as she wanted and stay thin, let's not *mention* the diet pills and the fingers down her throat as her meals went straight into the toilet.

Beside Alyssa, Enzio decided to make a last-ditch attempt at awing her with his expensive new toy. He thrust his wrist out in front of her, the watch's dial so close to her face it almost clipped the tip of her nose.

"You enter names, phone numbers, addresses! *Up to one thousand people!* Mark appointments on calendar! Download *informacion* to PC! Do you—?"

The fluorescents above them suddenly blinked on. Alyssa had no idea why—maybe one of the pint-sized monsters behind her had gotten up and fiddled with the switch. In which case, she was thinking she really ought to be grateful, since it had at least shut Enzio up for the moment.

The thing she didn't get, though, was why the lights

were so bright. And what was that weird *humming* noise they were making?

She glanced over her shoulder and saw that the three girls were all in their seats, looking this way and that in surprise along with the rest of the car's passengers.

Well, almost all of us, she thought, noticing that Enzio was still staring adoringly at his goddamned cook-your-dinner-screw-your-significant-other-for-you Dick Tracy Superwatch, seemingly oblivious to everything around him.

"Enzio," she said. "Do *you* know what's going on—"

"Shhh!" he said. "Not now!"

Surprised by his unusual curtness—Enzio might be a royal pain in the ass, but he was always a polite one—Alyssa looked at him and realized that he was no longer *admiring* the watch, but frowning at it. Whatever he saw on its face was making him upset. *Very* upset actually.

She leaned over to check it out for herself, then raised her eyebrows, the reason for his distress becoming evident.

The display no longer showed the time, but was covered with rows of tiny, blinking ones and zeroes. Also, the watch's alert tones all seemed to be sounding at once. Chirps, beeps, blips, trilly fragments of simple melody. She supposed she might have noticed it right away if her attention hadn't been diverted by the buzzing lights and the confused, edgy vibe running through the car.

Even before the first jarring bump, she got the feeling that something was about to go terribly wrong.

Then the train seemed to bounce off the track and she clutched her seat for support.

"Enz—?"

She stopped herself. He was just staring at the watch, shaking his head dolefully, concerned with nothing *but* the watch. Looking like his best friend in the world had just had a fatal stroke right in front of him.

The train was shaking and rattling now, swinging wildly back and forth on the track, the air horn emitting deafening blasts. A few people were screaming, the little girls behind her starting to cry, asking the woman who was sitting with them what was happening.

Allysa's last coherent thought before the front of the car behind her smashed into the rear of the one she was sitting in, ramming it *forward* into the locomotive, crunching it between them like a wad of aluminum foil in an angry fist, was that those brats, those poor little helpless brats, were going to get hurt.

In the proverbial perfect world filled with perfect human beings, Julio Salles *might* have been able to reduce the loss of life that occurred that night. Though the fifty-five miles per hour that Salles was doing while still nearly two miles from the disabled "slow" signal fell within the limit of his authorized speed, it did so just barely, and slower would have been wiser on a downhill grade. Though he had been alert at his post and looking out for the signal, and had no reason to suspect anything might be *wrong* with the signal, it would have been an intelligent precaution to use geographic landmarks as he neared the place where the track looped around the hillside in the unlikely event that it *did* fail.

But there can be such a thing as overfamiliarity with a route, particularly in country where the terrain rolls along with a dulling sameness, one stretch of track bleeding into the next. Anybody who regularly drives to work in a rural area knows this; after taking the same roads day in and day out for several months or years, you begin to ignore the scenery and depend on a general sense of your bearings rather than its specific features, until coming to a sign or stoplight that marks a necessary turn. The building, brook, farmyard, radio tower, or cherry '63 Mustang in someone's driveway that once caught the eye on every trip will be passed unnoticed along the way. You feel free to straddle the speed limit, and perhaps even slightly exceed it without risking a traffic stop, knowing the police will in most instances tolerate a person going, say, sixty-eight or seventy in a sixty-five-mile-per-hour speed zone.

Salles had been driving railroad trains for three decades, and made the Sao Paulo-Rio run over five hundred times in the two years since it had been assigned to him. Never in his career had he come close to having a mishap. The night of the derailment, he was watching in anticipation of a signal that had ceased to function, and relying on equipment that no one had thought to harden against the sort of destructive black technology with which it was targeted. He was performing his job in compliance with the rules, and his response to the first indications of a problem was rapid. If blame had been apportioned by a judge possessing complete, objective knowledge of the facts, Salles's slice of it would have been truly inappreciable. Moreover, his public and courtroom accounts of the incident were, from his available perspective, a hundred percent candid and faithful to the truth.

This is how he recalled it in deposition:

His train was proceeding normally along a series of climbs and dips in the large, undulating hills that are crossed by the Sao-Paulo-to-Rio intercity railway. The forested countryside east of Taubate being exceptionally dark and repetitive in its features, Salles had always relied on his instruments and track signals rather than terrain landmarks as visual aids. On his descent along the slope where the derailment took place, he had approximated that he was about five miles west of a blind curve that required the train to slow to between eight and ten miles per hour, his discretional latitude based upon factors such as weather conditions or the presence of another train on the opposing track. His usual practice was to begin gradually applying his brakes *two* miles west of the curve, where the continuously lighted yellow "slow" signal came into view, and he had been keeping his eyes open for it since starting along the decline. But Salles's estimate of his position was off by three miles. He had already *passed* the signal without knowing it—and without being *able* to know it because its light had given out.

In the pitch darkness, the curve seemed to come up out of nowhere. Salles had spotted it in the arc of his headlamps from a distance of perhaps thirty yards and immediately glanced at his Doppler indicator for a speed check, but its digital readout was flashing double zeros and an error code. This first sign of a problem with the electronic systems whose reliability Salles would later challenge was accompanied by a peripheral awareness of the lights in his cab brightening as if with a sudden flood of voltage. Forced to guess his speed, Salles decided he was moving at about fifty-five miles per hour, and immediately took emergency measures to decelerate and warn any oncoming train of his approach, sounding the air horn and attempting to initiate his brakes. But the high-tech braking system—which used a network of sensors and microprocessors to emulate the function of conventional pneumatic control valves, and had been retrofitted into the train a year earlier—didn't engage. Like the Doppler speedometer, the flat-screen display of its head-end control unit was flashing an error condition.

Salles was not only racing toward the curve at breakneck speed, but nearing it with his electronic brakes out of commission.

He knew right away that things were going to be very bad. The fail-safe mechanism designed to automatically vent the brake cylinder in the event of a power loss or hardware crash would deprive him of any ability to graduate the release of air pressure and smooth the stop. And at his accelerated rate of motion, descending from the summit of a large and rugged hill on a sharp bend, the hard, shaky jerks that would result from the train coming to a dead stop would make derailment a certainty. It was the worst circumstance imaginable and he was helpless to avert it. He was at the helm of a runaway train that was about to turn into a slaughterhouse.

It was just as Salles was reaching for the public-address switch to warn his passengers of the impending derailment that the train reached the curve. The fail-safe penalty stop initiated at that same instant. Before his hand could find the switch there was a sudden, rough jolt that threw him off his seat. He slammed into the window in front of him like a projectile fired from a giant slingshot. His last memory of what happened that night was his painful impact with that window, and the sound of glass shattering around him.

Upon regaining consciousness some hours afterward, Salles would learn the forward momentum that had propelled him into the window was also what had saved his life, for it had been powerful enough to plunge him *through* the window and onto the brow of the hill, with relatively minor physical injuries as the result—a concussion, a fractured wrist, a patchwork of bruises and lacerations. These would be easily detected and treated by his doctors.

Not so, however, the psychological wounds that would drive him to suicide two years later.

The rest of the crew and passengers were less fortunate than Salles. As their wheels locked up and derailed, the cars in which they were riding smashed into each other in a pileup that turned three of them into compacted wreckage even before they plunged off the tracks to go tumbling end-over-end into the valley hundreds of feet below. One of the coaches broke apart into several sections that were strewn across the slope to intermingle with a grisly litter of human bodies and body parts. Bursting into flame as its fuel lines ruptured and ignited, the locomotive slammed into the dining car to engulf it in an explosion that incinerated every living soul aboard.

Other than Salles, only two of the 194 people who had been riding the train survived the catastrophe—an attendant named Maria Lunes, who suffered a severed spine and was left paralyzed from the neck down, and a ten-year-old girl, Daniella Costas, whose two sisters and nanny perished in the tragedy, and was herself found miraculously unharmed, wrapped in the arms of a young Australian fashion model identified as Alyssa Harding.

According to the child's subsequent testimony, Harding had sprung from her seat two rows in front of the girl moments after the train hurtled from the track, and shielded Daniella from the collapsing roof of their car with her own body as it rolled down the hillside.

It was an act of selfless, spontaneous heroism that had eliminated any chance Harding would have had at survival.

FOURTEEN

THE OPEN FIBERGLASS SKIFF LEFT THE PIER JUST BE-
fore 7:00 A.M., Ricci amidship on the bench, Dex at the
stern after having started up the Mercury outboard with
a couple of hard pulls. The oxygen tanks and portable
compressor were in the well near his feet.

"Gonna be a honey of a day, looks like to me," he
said, and yawned. His eyes were slightly puffed. "We
ought to do all right, don't you think?"

Ricci was gazing out past the bow, his gear bags on
the deck in front of him.

"Depends whether we get lucky," he said.

Dex worked the tiller handle, guiding the boat into
the channel. A tall, rangy man in his mid-thirties with a
full reddish-blond beard, he wore a navy blue watch cap
over his shoulder-length hair, a plaid mackinaw, heavy
dungarees, and rubber waders. He had a fair complexion
that was typical of his French-Canadian bloodstock, and
the parts of his face and neck not covered by the beard
were chafed from repeated exposure to the biting salt
air.

"Don't see what luck's got to do with it," he said.

"You told me yourself there were plenty of urchins left down deep after that last haul, and it ain't as if they do anythin' but stick to whatever they're stuck to till somebody comes along and plucks 'em off." He made a chuckling sound. "Regular as you are about where an' when you dive, the buggers should have you figured by now. Plan on movin' to a safer neighborhood, or leastways makin' themselves scarce between seven an' three every other day."

Ricci shrugged. "Can't figure anything unless you've got brains to speak of," he said, glancing over at him. "And they don't."

He turned back toward the front of the boat and stared straight ahead, hands in the pockets of his hooded pullover jacket. Despite the stiff breeze, it was indeed a decent spring morning, with a flood of five or six knots and plenty of sunshine in the mackerel sky. The vapor was thin enough for Ricci to easily read the numbers on the nuns and cans as the channel widened out and Dex goosed the throttle to get them moving faster against the tide.

The light sixteen-footer accelerated with a roar, its props churning up a fine, cold spray. Ricci estimated the water temperature would be about forty degrees, and was wearing a black-and-silver neoprene dry suit and Thinsulate undergarment to retain body heat during his dive.

Soon they were well beyond the channel buoys and red-and-black markers indicating the spot where the shoal at the harbor entrance presented a concealed hazard to low-slung craft, lurking just below the waterline at high tide. All along the surface of the bay Ricci could see patches resembling rippled glass insets on an otherwise smooth mirror, signs that the gusty, variable wind had stirred up circular eddies where salt water and unsettled bottom sediment had mixed with the lighter freshwater flow. He made a mental note to be careful of them later on. As a rule, the current's westward drift became gentler at the lower fathoms, but the upswellings could exert a strong, sudden pull on a diver, and the phytoplankton that tended to generate in them could severely reduce underwater visibility.

The two men buzzed across the water in their skiff, neither of them speaking above the engine noise for the half hour it took to reach the island where Ricci had found his urchin colony. Not quite an acre in size, it was shaped like a cloven hoof, the split on its northeastern side forming a cove that plunged to a depth of at least a hundred fathoms and was densely forested with eelgrass along its inshore ledges.

Dex simultaneously shifted to port and throttled down as they came in close, then steered them around toward the cove. Ricci sat near the starboard gunwale, scanning the cobbled edge of the shore and the parallel band of trees and brush just yards further inland.

Seconds before Dex maneuvered the skiff into the cove, Ricci thought he noticed a twinkle of reflected sunlight in the shrubbery near a large granite outcropping. He momentarily focused his eyes on that spot, saw the starry glint of light again, and committed the features of the little slice of beach to memory. As an added reference, he glanced at his wrist-mounted diving compass for its coordinates. The reflection could have been from some shards of glass that had washed ashore, or a beer can or bottle discarded by a fisherman who had stopped on the island for a solitary lunch. But just in case it wasn't, the big hunk of rock made as perfect a landmark as he could have wanted.

After lowering anchor, and paying out rope until it was fast and the skiff was head to wind, Dex yawned, stretched, then reached into the well for his thermos.

"Guess the kids must've worn you out," Ricci said. He was staring out across the bow again.

"Huh?" Dex unscrewed the thermos lid. "What do you mean?"

Ricci turned to face him.

"Way you've been trying to catch flies with your mouth all morning," he said. "I figured it was from filling in for your wife after school the other day. Either that or you haven't been getting enough sleep."

Dex looked down, pouring himself some coffee.

"Been sleeping fine," he said, and sipped. "But it's true the brats wouldn't stay off my back for a second."

Ricci watched him.

"Nancy climbed into bed that night feelin' randy as a catamount under a full moon, and it's me was holdin' out the red flag for a change," Dex said. "Don't know if it was the boys got me down, so to speak, or thinkin' about that awful shit Phipps an' Cobbs pulled on you while I was playin' nursemaid." He scrubbed a hand down over his beard. "Suppose it was mostly the second. I mean, them tryin' to make off with our *catch*. Talk about luck, me not bein' there with you was a bad piece, hey?"

"Don't sweat it," Ricci said, still watching him. "They got what they had coming."

"Should've been around to help you give it to 'em, is all I'm sayin'." Dex drank a little more coffee from the thermos lid, then held it out to him. "Want some a' this mud the ol' lady brewed?"

Ricci shook his head.

"Thanks, but no thanks," he said, then shrugged out of his pullover. "I want to get started while the water's still halfway calm."

Dex nodded, set down the lid, and went to work. He hoisted the metal dive flag, then reached down into the well for one of the scuba tanks, rose from the cockpit, and put the tank overboard on a rope line.

Meanwhile, Ricci bent over one of his gear bags, unzipped it, and began to extract his scuba apparatus and arrange it on the deck in front of him. He put on his diving hood, then slid his arms into his vestlike buoyancy compensator—the double bladders of which would draw their air from his tank—and fastened the quick-release buckles of its cummerbund around his waist. He had four twelve-pound weights evenly arranged on his nylon-webbing weight belt, and an additional two pounds each on ankle bands to help keep him balanced and relieve tension on his spine. Although the total fifty-two pounds would be excessive under average diving conditions, Ricci had often found that he needed it to remain at the depths inhabited by the urchins in the powerful, spiraling undercurrents.

After donning the belt, Ricci put on his mask, gloves, and fins, then reached into the bag again for his two dive knives and their harnesses. His chisel-tipped urchin knife went into a scabbard secured to his thigh, a pointed titanium backup blade into a similar rig on his left inner arm. Finally he used an elasticized lanyard to hang an underwater halogen light from his wrist.

Once suited up, he opened his second gear bag and extracted three nylon mesh totes, all of which had been packed in long, neat rolls that were held snug with bungee cords. He clipped their float lines to snaplinks on his buoyancy compensator, then raised himself onto the gunwale and sat with his back to the water.

"Don't forget your spare O2," Dex said. He took from the well an aluminum canister/snorkel assembly about the size of a bicycle pump, put it into a waterproof satchel, and carried it over to Ricci.

Ricci hung the satchel around his shoulders.

"Okay," he said. "Ready to go."

Dex cocked a thumb into the air.

"If you can't send me up some whore's pussy, I'll settle for the eggs she been droppin'," he said, and grinned as if he'd gotten off a sharp witticism.

Ricci went over the side with a backward roll, swam over to his floating tank, slipped it on, and attached the BC's narrow low-pressure inflator tube, which would draw air from the tank through a twist valve within reach of his hand. For backup—and lesser, more incremental adjustments in buoyancy than this method easily allowed—his BC also had over its right shoulder strap an oral-inflation assembly consisting of a large-diameter air hose much like that of a vacuum cleaner or automobile carburetor, with a mouthpiece that could be actuated at the touch of a simple button-and-spring mechanism.

The last thing Ricci did before going under was check the submersible instrument console attached to a port atop his scuba tank by yet another rubber hose. On the console were two gauges—a digital readout for measuring depth and temperature, and an analog PSI air gauge below it. The air gauge showed the tank to be at its max-rated 4,000-psi working pressure, with the standard ten-percent safety overfill.

Glancing topside, he saw Dex lean forward over the rail, still grinning and poking his thumb skyward.

Ricci kicked away from the hull of the skiff, dumped air from his BC, and submerged.

Dex's smile lasted only as long as it took for Ricci's outline to disappear underwater. Then it, too, vanished. His eyes narrow, his mouth a thin line of tension, he stood at the gunwale watching the bubbles from Ricci's exhalations reach the surface, the words they'd exchanged earlier that morning suddenly echoing in his mind.

"Regular as you are 'bout where an' when you dive, buggers ought to have you figured by now," he'd said

to Ricci, before going on with some nonsense about the urchins moving out of town or some such. Just kind of wanting to break the silence between them.

"Can't figure anything unless you have brains to speak of," Ricci had answered. *"And they don't."*

Well, Dex thought, maybe the urchins didn't have brains bigger than tiny specks of sand in their heads, didn't even have *heads* that Dex could see, but he had smarts enough to do some figurin' of his own. Not that God had made him a genius; if that was the case he wouldn't have to be tendin' boat every winter season, when the bitter mornin' cold was like to shrivel your balls up into your stomach an' turn the drip from your nose to icicles. But he knew for sure that Ricci would be thinkin' about what happened with Cobbs an' Phipps, and gettin' to wonder about him bein' in on the shakedown too. Was maybe even holdin' onto some suspicions about that already, to guess from how he'd been quieter than usual this mornin'—not that he was any kind of chatterbox in what you might call his sunniest moods.

Still, Dex couldn't afford to wait for Ricci to go the distance from bein' suspicious of him to reachin' any right conclusions, short a hop as that was. Maybe he didn't run off at the mouth about himself like so many flatlanders did, telling you everythin' about their lives from A through Z within five minutes of makin' your acquaintance, but once in a while Ricci would mention something about when he was a police detective down in Beantown, an' furthermore, Dex's buddy Hugh Temple, whose girlfriend's sister Alice worked at the real estate office in town, said she'd heard from her boyfriend worked at the Key Bank that Ricci used to be in some hotshit military outfit like the Rangers or Navy SEALs or maybe the Boy Commandos—whatever the fuck—before his cops-and-robbers days. That particular bit a' scuttlebutt hadn't surprised Dex, 'cause there was times when all you had to do was look in his eyes to see that he could be one dangerous son of a bitch to anybody who got on his wrong side.

Dex shook a cigarette from the pack in the breast pocket of his mackinaw, shoved it between his lips, and cupped a hand over its tip as he fired up his Bic lighter. He stood there smoking at the gunwale, his eyes following Ricci's stream of bubbles. Truth was, he'd got on okay with Ricci, who always gave him an even shake as far as business went, and never treated anybody as if he was their better, the way a lot of folks from out of town did as a matter of course, especially the summer people with their kayaks, canoes, an' mountain bikes on the roof racks of their whale-sized, showroom-new 4 x 4 wagons.

Those people, they'd stand around the middle of town in bunches of five, six, an' more, wearin' white shorts an' sneakers that matched their perfect white teeth, never movin' aside to let you pass, talkin' so loud you'd think every one of 'em was deaf as a board. Cloggin' the sidewalk as if they owned it, an' couldn't damn well see themselves sharin' the street with anybody, like they was on some kinda movie set that was laid out just for them on Memorial Day, an' got packed away into storage after they headed south come September, gatherin' dust an' cobwebs until the next summer of fun rolled round.

No, Dex hadn't held any ill feelings for Ricci, not the other day when he'd taken off on him with that bullshit story about havin' to mind the kids, not even now, after havin' done his bit of tinkerin' with Ricci's air gauge last night, an' preparin' to leave him for a goner. But what choice did he have? Way he felt, it was kinda like goin' to war an' bein' forced to shoot somebody you bore no personal grudge against, somebody you might even think was an okay fella if you got to know him over a frosty glass of suds, all because of circumstances that you could no more control than the turnin' of the world. Havin' been a soldier, Ricci would prob'ly understand that.

What Ricci could *never* understand, though, comin' from away, was the kind of pressure he, Dex, had been under to cut a separate deal with Cobbs. How could he have refused that prick without jammin' himself up bigtime? Cobbs was in so tight with the sheriff an' town managers, he'd see to it that Dex got cited for some kinda safety violation whenever he turned on the heat in his double-wide, an' was pulled over, breathalyzed, an' tossed in the drunk tank every time he drove his pickup home after havin' put down one or two at the bar.

Ricci, on the other hand, didn't have any such worries. He'd arrived in town with money enough to buy that nice house on the water, an' likely had himself a hefty pension from the police force, not to mention military benefits that covered his meds an' checkups at the V.A. hospital in Togas, plus Lord knows what other cookies the government might've tossed him. Ricci was a loner with no wife or kids, an' it was a sure thing that sooner or later he'd be on his way to greener pastures.

Dex frowned, his brow creased in thought. What the fuck was he supposed to do? He had to make a *livin'* here, year in, year out, or see his family starve from hunger. Had to be able to walk down the street without lookin' over his shoulder for Phipps or some other asshole deputy followin' behind in a sheriff-mobile, ready to bust balls for any lame excuse could be concocted on the spur of the moment.

He took a drag of his cigarette and puffed a swirl of smoke and steam from his breath into the brisk salt air, his comments to Ricci as they'd left the wharf once again recurring to him.

"Regular as you are 'bout where an' when you dive, buggers ought to have you figured. . . ."

An' regular as clockwork he was. Lining his gear up on the deck the same exact way every mornin' they went out, puttin' it all on in the same order every time, an' then divin' to his normal spots, takin' no longer'n half an hour to fill his first couple totes with what he found on the underwater ledges at the head of the cove. Soon as their markers came to the surface, Dex would haul the bags aboard, knowin' Ricci was on his way down into the thickest part of the eelgrass forest, where he'd drift with the current 'stead of *against* it like divers usually did, so they'd be swept back toward the boat rather than away from it if they lost their bearin's. Drift divin', as it was called, was risky business, but by lettin' the current carry him along, Ricci could cover the most amount a' bottom area in the least amount a' time—and it was at the bottom where he'd find the best, plumpest urchins.

Dex, meanwhile, was supposed to lift anchor, throw the outboard into reverse, an' keep his eyes peeled for Ricci's bubbles while backin' up slow an' easy to tag along behind him. Some divers clipped a float line to themselves so the tender could stay on the lookout for the bright-colored marker rather'n have to keep his eyes peeled for bubbles, which were a helluva lot harder to spot. But in these waters there was so damn much eelgrass that the line would just get tangled up in it.

Dex glanced at his wristwatch. Just a few minutes to go 'fore Ricci was down maybe five, six fathoms. Too far to make it back up without air, an' right when his air *supply* would run out. Dex would wait a little while longer, then throttle up the engine in forward, haulin' ass away from there as fast as he could, knowin' his partner was drownin' to death somewhere below, his

lungs swellin' in his chest till they burst like balloons
got stuck with a pin.

Yeah, Dex thought, he'd sold Ricci out, no puttin' it
any different. Sold him out, and now good as killed him.
But what was there to say?

He'd had no choice, he thought. No choice at all.

Things were as they were, an' there was really nothin'
more to say about it than that.

Ricci had been at his bottom depth for nearly half an
hour when he hit the jackpot.

Having filled two of his three totes with smallish urchins from the upper levels of the slope, he'd sent their
floatlines to the surface, left them for Dex to recover,
and then descended below the eelgrass canopy. The going proved rough much of the way down. As he had
noticed leaving the harbor channel, the changeable
winds had produced fairly strong turbidity currents, forcing him to waste a lot of energy fighting the drag, and
stirring up so much sand and detritus that he'd been
unable to see further than five or six feet in any direction
at some points during the dive. Although conditions improved once he neared the floor of the cove and began
to go with the drift, his outer field of vision had remained limited to about a dozen yards, making him
wonder if he'd have to cut his dive short without bag-
ging any first-rate specimens.

Then the recess had revealed itself to him through
pure chance. Hidden from above by a wide ledge of
rock, its entrance sheeted over with eelgrass, it would
have gone unnoticed had the current not disturbed the
fronds just as he'd been swimming past.

He glided closer to investigate, sweeping the area with
his flashlight, using his free hand to part the long, ser-
pentine strands of kelp ribboning up to the surface.
Schools of silvery herring and other tiny fish Ricci

couldn't name bulleted in and out of the light as he shone it into the opening.

The penetrating high-intensity beam revealed the hollow to be quite small, cutting no more than twelve or fifteen feet into the slope of the ridge, its entrance barely wide enough to admit Ricci in his scuba outfit and tank—a tight squeeze. Still, he felt a surge of excitement over his find. The interior of the cavity was filled with mature, whoppingly big urchins. Urchins galore, clinging three and four deep to every vertical and horizontal surface. The incredible concentration would allow him to stuff his goodie bag to the top just by gathering those nearest the entrance, leaving the rest of the spiny creatures to do whatever they did when they weren't intruded upon by foraging predators, human or otherwise.

He reached down to his thigh and pulled his urchining knife from its scabbard.

Before getting started, Ricci checked his watch and gauge console, then did some quick mental computations based on the scuba instruction he'd received in the Navy. Though his psi dial showed an ample reserve of air, he was already edging beyond a no-decompression profile and would need to make a decompression stop on ascent. Not atypical for him, but very definitely something to remember.

He swam into the recess, his legs scissoring behind him, taking pains not to scrape his air tanks on the ceiling. Given his imminent plans to kiss his urchin-hunting career good-bye, he found his excitement over the score puzzling, and maybe even a little bit funny. *Me in a nutshell,* he thought. Never a natural at anything, but bent on giving the job his dogged best to the end. It was the old blue-collar ethic Ricci guessed he'd inherited from his steelworker father, and often wished he could wring from himself once and for all, having learned the hard way that a job well done could just as soon bring on problems as any sort of credit or reward—and worse, that you occasionally wound up getting screwed for your diligence.

Ricci went at his newfound bounty, the tote in his left hand, the knife in his right. The urchins crawling slowly over the backs of those on the rocks were easy pickings, and so plentiful that it took him just a few minutes to fill the mesh bag to a third of its capacity. Pleased with his rapid progress, he got down to collecting the others, sliding the flattened tip of the knife under the suction discs at the tips of their tubular feet, then carefully working them loose from the surfaces to which they were anchored. A slower task than the first, it needed to be performed with some delicacy if he was to avoid cracking their shells—which would be an unfortunate waste, since they were worth zilch to him unless brought up alive.

Ricci had been absorbed in his task for about twenty minutes when his thoughts wandered back to the twinkle of brightness he'd noticed from the skiff. Might have been from something left behind by an ecologically challenged sailor, or a bit of shiny flotsam tossed up onto the island by the surf. Might have. But he couldn't shake the idea that it also could have been the sun glancing off the lens of a pair of binoculars—or a telescopic gunsight. Maybe his long years of soldiering and police work had lent undue weight to what ought to have seemed an overly imaginative notion, but why discount it offhand?

And it wasn't just *his* experience that had to be considered. Pete Nimec, after all, had nailed Cobbs's personality type right on the head. Ricci had humiliated him, shaken up his confined little world as if it were one of those snow globes people bought at souvenir shops, and Cobbs would be stewing in his own juices until he regained some of his pride. Word spread fast in a small town, and he'd want to be sure he got even with Ricci before the tale of his ass-kicking found its way into local folklore. It might be that he'd take some time to plot out his reprisal, but Cobbs was a hothead, and sort of crazy. The far greater likelihood was that he'd act while he was still worked up—and try something as extreme as it would be rash.

Ricci dropped an urchin into the tote, pried at another with his knife. Okay, he and Pete had Cobbs's number, but what exactly did that have to do with the sparkle of light on the beach? If he assumed Cobbs was out to take him down, that one was obvious. As shellfish warden, Cobbs was authorized to carry firearms, and had access to a speedboat for patrolling the bay compliments of Hancock County. He also knew where Ricci did his diving. He could pull the boat aground or moor it on the far side of the island, then conceal himself in the brush until he was ready for whatever move he intended to make.

In the water, Ricci was a highly vulnerable target. Cobbs could wait until he was surfacing, then zoom up in his motorboat and clip him like a duck in a shooting gallery. Or if he were good enough with a rifle and had a high-powered scope, he might be able to do it from shore, without ever having to break cover. And Ricci would simply disappear into the vast waters of the Penobscot. Urchin diving was filled with inherent hazards that had claimed several lives in recent years, with the diver's body having gone unrecovered in two or three of those instances. Between the circulating currents, profuse eelgrass, and marine scavengers, it was a rough environment in which to dredge for a corpse.

After four days and nights of mulling all this over, Ricci had grown convinced Cobbs would be looking to come at him when he was out on a dive. If not this time, then certainly the next. Which had left him to determine where Dex might fit into the picture. Ricci could see how his partner might have gotten drawn into an attempt to scam him out of his percentage of the catch money, and, in fact, had been left with no doubts about Dex's guilt on that score when the subject of his supposed baby-sitting was raised on the boat. It had been evident in all of his mannerisms—the way he'd nervously rattled on about how lousy he felt because of what happened to Ricci in his absence, expressing a bit too much regret and dismay, fidgeting around and tugging at his beard while never looking him in the eye.

These were textbook signs of deception Ricci had recognized from the countless suspect interrogations he'd conducted during his years as a detective. But there were betrayals, and then again there were betrayals. Ricci didn't believe Dex had it in him to take an active hand in helping Cobbs settle his grudge. Unless, of course, he didn't know Cobbs had anything too drastic in mind. Or felt pressed into it. Dex led a difficult, hand-to-mouth existence, and Cobbs and his buddies in badly soiled blue could make it even more difficult for him if they wanted to. Whether suckered or squeezed, Dex *could be* persuaded to stay mum about anything he witnessed.

At last, Ricci had seen only two options—he could either back away from the situation, or hang tough and go back to his usual routine, keeping his eyes as wide open as possible. He had opted for the latter, and was still confident he'd made the right decision. If it proved absolutely conclusive that Dex had turned on him, was perhaps even willing to let Cobbs get away with *killing* him, his motivations were ultimately of little consequence. Ricci's ingrained sense of accountability demanded that there would have to be a reckoning for his breach of trust. And as for Cobbs . . .

Cobbs would have to be dealt with too. Dealt with very severely.

Now Ricci heard the throb of a motor somewhere above him, and paused for a second to listen. It seemed diffuse, coming from all sides at once—which was how the human ear perceived most lower-frequency sounds underwater—but was recognizable to him as the skiff's engine being cranked. Nothing out of the ordinary, he thought. Depending on the windage up top, Dex would occasionally open the throttle to keep apace with his drift.

Ricci glanced at his instruments again, noted that he had plenty of air left in his cylinder, and went back to filling the tote, in no particular hurry to get done.

He'd chosen to play a game of *Wait and See,* and intended to stick it out. Whatever the hell that meant for him.

Dex had planned to wait until Ricci's exhaust stopped bubbling at the surface before turning the skiff hard about—no more bubbles equaling no more breathing and a dead man underwater. But it had got to where the tenseness in him was making his stomach hurt as if he'd swallowed a handful of thumbtacks, and he just couldn't stand there watching anymore.

Besides, what did it matter? he thought. He'd fixed the needle of Ricci's air gauge to read like his tank was filled higher than it really was—higher by more'n a thousand psi, a *quarter* of its total hold—then figured the outside time Ricci could stay at the bottom an' make it back up alive, bein' generous about the amount of air he'd have used by now under the best dive conditions, which was anythin' but what the water was offerin' today, given them funnels an' crosscurrents Dex had been seein' from the get-go. Takin' things combined, Ricci didn't stand a chance. Was pitiful thinkin' how he was gonna check out, his insides goin' all to jelly. Goddamn pitiful. But there was nothin' to do about it, an' Dex guessed that by havin' kept from gettin' the shakes, he could count himself as holdin' together okay. *Better* than okay, under the circumstances. That standin' an' watchin', though. The waitin' for no more bubbles on the top . . . Jesus, that was too much.

His hand clenched tightly around the stick, his long hair whipping back from under his knit cap, Dex kept on at full throttle, as if by doing so he could leave his guilt behind him, washed away in the white wake of foam trailing the skiff as it planed upwind toward his meeting point with Cobbs.

His binoculars raised to his eyes, Cobbs squatted in the weeds and bushes behind the strand and watched the skiff approach from his right, northward, Dex driving the little boat so hard that it almost seemed it would take off into the air like a rocket.

He took a deep breath of ocean-and-pine-scented air, wanting to remember the moment in detail, to impress its every sight and sound upon his brain so that he could call them up at whim even when he was old and fee-bleminded and unable to recall his own name. For several minutes before the skiff had appeared, Cobbs had heard the loud revving of its engine from out on the water, but had tried to curb his expectation until he'd actually spotted it through his lenses. And when he did, when he'd seen Dex was alone, well, Cobbs had felt almost like he was going to lift off into the stratosphere himself. Only at that moment, when the suspense had finally ended, had he realized the true fervor with which he'd hated Ricci. Only then too had he learned the whole of his capacity for murder without remorse or fear of punishment, without anything in his heart but gleeful satisfaction.

Now the skiff veered to starboard and came on dead ahead toward shore, its bow riding up high over the chop, the roar of its engine reaching a crescendo that appropriately matched the joy swelling up inside Cobbs as he imagined how Tom Ricci must have suffered in his last, struggling moments of life.

Within seconds after Ricci got his first hint that something might be wrong with his air supply, it became apparent that he had a serious problem. Before a full minute had passed, that problem escalated to a full-blown crisis.

The breath that triggered the warning seemed slightly harder to draw from his regulator than normal, and while it could have been attributable to minor overexertion—he'd been working steadily against strong currents for over an hour—a skeptical voice in his head dispelled that idea outright. He was an experienced diver, and pacing himself underwater was second nature.

He took another inhalation, another. Each came with greater effort than the last, and gave that inner voice an edge of added urgency.

Ricci snapped a glance down at his psi gauge. Its dial told him the cylinder had over 1,000 psi left in it—a full twenty-five percent of its capacity—but his mind and body were telling him something else. Although he had stopped all movement, put himself at rest in the water, his tank was barely complying with his demand for oxygen.

The dial was wrong.

The dial was lying to him.

Ricci cast aside his questions about how that could be, and bore in on his essential predicament. He was running out of air. Running out, and would very possibly exhaust what the tank had left in it within moments.

His heart pounded. He felt panic hatching inside him, and chased it off. He had to hang on and stay calm, take things one small step at a time. If he couldn't think straight, it was time to get somebody to blow taps, because he was good as dead.

He pulled the regulator away from his mouth and reached into the satchel that contained his reserve canister, making sure to exhale into the water as he did so. At his present depth he'd be under almost four atmospheres of pressure, and with the scant volume of air in his lungs, would put far too much squeeze on them by holding his breath.

Quickly placing the flange of its snorkel mouthpiece between his lips and gums, he twisted open the valve and breathed.

Nothing flowed from it.

Somehow he was not at all surprised.

Hang on. Small steps. One at a time.

The thing he needed to do now was to get outside the hollow. No, wait, check that. *First* he had to get rid of whatever encumbrances he didn't absolutely need to be carrying.

Ricci released his bulging tote and, given the extremity of his circumstances, was surprised by the keen pang of regret he felt over having to part with his unprecedented take. He almost tossed the spare oxygen tank as well, but caught himself at the last instant, pulled off its J-shaped snorkel attachment, and put it back into his satchel before letting go of the useless canister. Then he put both hands on the rocky floor of the hollow—an area he had just moments ago picked clean of urchins—and thrust backward and out through its entrance.

He tried to wring more air from his primary tank as he emerged into the eelgrass, but could scarcely get enough to fill his chest. It was like trying to inhale through a gag, or a smothering hand clapped over his mouth. Two labored inhalations later, the unit was depleted.

Ricci again felt desperation skittering around the

edges of his thoughts. And again he blocked it out, like someone slamming the shutters against a cold December wind.

Exhale, he told himself. *Nice and slow.*

If he'd learned anything from his underwater survival training with the SEALs, it was that diving was all about balancing pressure. Internal and external, mental and physical. When you ran into trouble in the water, your immediate impulse was to focus solely on getting air into your lungs. It was what made a drowning person climb on the back of a would-be rescuer and inadvertently push him under. And it was usually a fatal error. Unless you were born with gills, you had to learn to modify your instincts. Concentrate on the balance, and the skills you'd acquired for maintaining it through controlled breathing, to maximize any available oxygen resource.

Assuming you had one.

His mind raced back to one of the early lessons he'd been taught by his drill instructor, a former UDT man named Rackel who'd seemingly been born in a frog suit. The last-ditch technique for surfacing with no obtainable oxygen was a free ascent. You shed your weights and let your own positive buoyancy take you up, breathing out through your mouth to release air from the lungs, while spread-eagling your body to increase friction between yourself and the water—and slow your upward motion. Air compressed as you dove, expanded as you rose, and there was always some contained in your lungs, however starved for it they might be. Ascend any faster than sixty feet a minute *without* exhaling, and you risked having them literally inflate until they ruptured.

The impossible hurdle for Ricci was that he was ninety feet down, and had *already* been emptying his lungs for several seconds. Seconds that felt like an infinity, and were about all he could tolerate. Regardless of how fast he allowed himself to rise, he would have gone past the limit of his ability to exhale long before reaching the surface. Nor could he make his decompression stop . . . and that might lead to the bends, a condition with the potential to cause severe brain and nerve damage or even death.

Never mind that for now. One small step at a time, remember? Get to the surface alive, and then you can worry about what might *happen afterward.*

He needed an air source. One that could sustain him for at least part of the ascent.

And maybe he had one.

The bladders of his BC were almost entirely deflated, but the physical stresses upon them were identical to those upon his lungs. They too would have retained some compressed oxygen that would expand as he got closer to the surface and the atmospheric pressure on them decreased. And just as the air in his lungs would seek its outlet via the passages leading to his nose, throat, and mouth, so would the air in his BC try to escape through its artificial equivalent—the oral-inflator hose. A thirty- or forty-second supply would bring him up to a level of sixty feet, from which he *might be* able to exhale the rest of the distance. A long shot, but it was either that or call out the bugler and honor guard. Or *dis*honor guard, considering how his police career had finished out.

Abruptly turning faceup in the water, Ricci rolled his body to the left, away from the hose, to bring it up off his shoulder, puffing what little breath he had left into its mouthpiece to clear it of water. The safest way to rise would be on his back with one hand raised, so he could see and deflect himself away from any potential obstacles—and also so the hose would be above his head, allowing the water pressure to bear down upon it, and promote the free flow of air *from* it.

But there was no time to lose. His brain reeling, the veins in his neck and temples throbbing, close to suffocating, Ricci placed the mouthpiece over his lips, pushed the button to open its valve, and inhaled greedily as he held it down.

A thin stream of air entered his lungs. Hardly enough to sate his aching need, but nonetheless precious beyond description.

He exhaled into the mouthpiece, then breathed from it again, more slowly and evenly this time. The oxygen cleared his head a little.

Time to lift off.

Ricci unfastened his weight belt and ankle straps, and they went tumbling down and down into the eelgrass.

Then the water ripped him away from the bottom and cast him upward in a dizzying rush.

FIFTEEN

"COMMENT ÇA VA, ROLLIE?"

"Beautiful woman walks through the door speakin' French, come all'a way from the States to see me, I gotta be doin' awright."

Megan smiled at Thibodeau and entered the room. He was in a semi-sitting position, the backrest of his hospital bed elevated to help support his weight. She could see a fluid drain in his abdomen, and an IV drip running to his arm from a stand beside the bed's steel frame.

He nodded his chin at her brown paper shopping bag as she sat in the chair to his right.

"Tell me you got some Mardi Gras King Cake in there, or maybe some 'gator sauce piquant, I swear I'm gonna ask you to marry me."

"There honestly such a thing as 'gator sauce?"

"I could eat it every day a' the week."

"Ugh." She set the bag on the floor next to her chair. "You Cajuns must have iron stomachs."

"Darlin', I'd probably be dead wasn't for that," Thibodeau said. "Accordin' to the docs, slug that hit me would've gone straight *through* my stomach an' into my aorta if it hadn't got detoured by my abs. Instead it only cost me part a' my large intestine an' my spleen."

"Only, huh?" she said.

He gave her a weak shrug. "You gonna get gut-shot, you catch your breaks where you can."

"There much pain?"

"Could be worse," he said. "White coats say the biggest problem for me could be infection. Say the spleen helps fight off bacteria in the blood. Say the liver an' my other organs gonna take over for it, but not for a while."

Rollie paused, shifted on his pillow. Megan could see that he was trying not to wince.

"C'mon, now, enough a' the gory details," he said, settling back. "How 'bout we get to what's in the bag an' my offer of marriage? Contingent, as I mentioned, on that sauce."

Megan smiled again.

"Both of them in a minute, I promise." She leaned closer, extending her hand over the rail to touch his arm. "Doctors treating you okay?"

"I guess," he said. "Except for their pokin' and proddin'."

"Which is what they get paid to do," she said. "You've had one hell of a week, Rol."

"Least I'm still alive." His face became serious. "Not everybody here been that lucky."

"No, not everyone," she said. "I'm very sorry for the men you lost."

Thibodeau was silent a moment. Then he nodded slowly.

"Like you said, helluva week, an' not just for us on this base." He moistened his lips with his tongue. "You hear 'bout that train wreck near the coast?"

"It's been on the news, yes," she said. "A horrible accident."

"Blood's been spillin' everywhere round these parts lately," he said. "All I'm waitin' for now's the frogs, gnats, boils, an' whatever else gonna come down."

She shook her head.

"I'm not religious," she said. "But the things we're talking about, I can't believe they're caused by the finger of God."

Rollie gave her a neutral sort of shrug.

" 'Less maybe it's His way a' *givin'* us the finger," he said. "Them reports you heard mention how that li'l girl's doin'? You know the kid I mean. . . ."

"Daniella Costas," Megan said. "Latest is that she's fine. With one of her parents, I think."

"Bon," he said. "I was her father, I'd wait till the engineer's all recuperated, then kill him with my bare hands."

"He claims it wasn't his fault."

"Who's he blamin'?"

"Not who, *what,*" she said. "Mechanical failure."

Rollie looked thoughtful a moment, then shrugged again.

"Anyways," he said. "Ain't that I could ever mind a visit from you, but I been wonderin' what this one's about since they told me you were on your way."

"Roger thought I could help out until you're back on your feet," Megan said. "But I had my own reasons for wanting to come see you in person, Rollie. And one of them was to give you what's in this bag."

"You sayin' I really *do* rate a get-well present?"

She nodded. "A very special one. Something I know you'd really appreciate."

He looked at her in silence. A nurse in a white uniform dress and crepe-soled shoes swished up to the door, poked her head briefly into the room, then continued on down the hall.

Megan waited until she was gone, then reached into the shopping bag.

"Pete Nimec told me you've been wanting your Stetson," she said. "And that the doctors won't let you wear it yet."

His shoulders became slightly more erect.

"You bring it here to me from my quarters?" he said.

She shook her head.

"I'd never go against hospital rules." She pulled an object in loose wrapping tissue out of the bag and gently placed it on his lap.

"Whatever it is, it sure's *shaped* like a hat," he said, glancing down at it.

"Well, they didn't mention any brand of headware besides a Stetson *per se*," she said, and smiled. "Why don't you go ahead and see if this makes a decent substitute."

His brows furrowing, he removed the tissue paper.

And audibly gasped.

The acorn-ended campaign hat was old and battered almost to shapelessness, its gray felt balding in spots, its black leather chin strap scuffed and gnarled. But its gold-and-black intertwined-braid hat cord and the silk ribbon around its crown were almost perfectly intact—as were the crossed gold cavalry sabers pinned to the side of its upturned brim.

He looked up at her. "Don' let me make a fool a' myself by sayin' what I *think* it is an' bein' wrong."

"You wouldn't be," she said. "It belonged to my great-grandfather. He was one of Teddy Roosevelt's First Volunteer Cavalry."

"Mon Dieu." He ran his fingers over the outside of the hat with open awe. "The Rough Riders."

She nodded. " 'Far better it is to dare mighty things, to win glorious triumphs, even though checkered by failure, than to rank with those poor spirits who neither suffer much nor enjoy much—"

"—'cause they live in the gray twilight that knows neither victory nor defeat,' " Thibodeau finished. "I don' know what to say about this, Megan. I truly don't."

She smiled.

"Taylor Breen went from holding a racket on the tennis court to a rifle on Kettle Hill in the space of six months. Joined the unit at TD's personal request, took a leave of absence of his professorship at Yale to go to war against Spain." She paused a moment, quietly watching him. "Rollie . . . I've got my own request goes along with the hat. I won't pressure you to agree to it. But I'd like your decision now."

He met her eyes with his own.

"This have to do with me fillin' Max Blackburn's old job?"

She gave him another nod.

"When we discussed the issue a few weeks back, you told me that you needed to think about it, that you weren't sure you wanted to tackle the responsibility—"

"Or that Pete Nimec wanted me to," he said. "My dope was that he had someone else in mind, an' the two of you were buttin' heads about it."

"He did, and we were, but things have changed. Part of it's what happened here the other night. How well you handled it."

"Nimec feel the same way?"

"He and I had a talk before I left for Brazil," she said. "And have reached a tentative agreement."

"Sounds to me like there's a catch hid somewhere in this proposition."

Megan laughed a little.

"I *am* a woman."

"As I did say, I'd noticed." He looked at her. "The catch . . . you gonna mention what it is?"

"Yes," she said. "After you tell me whether you'll accept the promotion."

Thibodeau looked at her a moment, looked down at the campaign hat. Then he lifted it off his lap and placed it carefully on his head.

"Fit okay?" he asked.

"Perfect."

"Will you marry me?"

"No."

He shrugged.

"Might as well accept *your* offer just the same, if only 'cause it'll get me off the night shift."

Megan put her hand over the back of his and gave it a fond squeeze.

"Congratulations," she said.

"And?"

She smiled at him.

"And," she said, "here's the catch. . . ."

SIXTEEN

COASTAL MAINE
APRIL 22, 2001

"YOU LOOKED TO MAKE SURE?" COBBS SAID. HE WAS
chewing on a thick wad of gum. "I mean, you were
watching, right?"

Dex plucked an imaginary lint ball off his mackinaw.
It had been maybe ten minutes since he'd tied up the
boat and Cobbs had already asked the question half a
dozen times in one form or another.

"I told you, it's done," he said. "What more you want
me to say?"

The look Cobbs gave him felt like a shove. He was
wearing his Smokey hat and warden's uniform, and held
a Remington 870 pump gun with 20-gauge chambering
and a collapsible stock. His binoculars hung from a strap
around his neck.

"I want you to tell me what you saw," he said bluntly.

Dex licked his lips. He heard something scrabble
across the limb of a tree in the nearby woods and
glanced distractedly toward the sound. Perched on the
budding maple, a squirrel twitched its bushy tail as it
nibbled on whatever morsel of food was in its forepaws,

the bright black beads of its eyes warily studying the two humans below.

He turned back to Cobbs.

"Important thing's what me an' you *ain't* seen," he said.

"Meaning what?"

"Meanin' I didn't see no bubbles from my boat, an' you didn't see Ricci's head bobbin' up out the water through them binocs of yours," Dex said.

Cobbs stared at him and chewed his gum. They were in the shade behind the prominent slab of rock that marked their meeting spot on the beach.

"Let's sum this fucking thing up once more, just to help me picture it right in my mind," he said.

Dex expelled a deep, tired breath and nodded with resignation.

"You waited while the bubbles was still comin' up," Cobbs said.

Dex nodded wearily again.

"And when there *wasn't* any more you turned back here."

Dex nodded a third time.

"So in other words," Cobbs said, and hefted his Remington, "I won't need to get in the motorboat and use this shotgun to blow Ricci out of the water."

"Is the point I been tryin' to make," Dex replied, totally wiped out, and more disgusted with his lot than ever before.

Cobbs watched Dex another moment, looking as if he was about to hit him with another round of questions. Then he seemed to change his mind, pushed the chewing gum from the back of his mouth with his tongue, and spat it out onto the pebbly ground.

"Good riddance to one God Almighty asshole," he said.

• • •

Ricci splashed above the water just when he'd felt he couldn't exhale any longer and would drown within feet of the surface.

Exhausted and gasping, he floated on his back and swooped air into his lungs. Thus far he was feeling no symptoms of decompression sickness, but that didn't necessarily mean he could dismiss it as a serious concern. The first indications were usually a bone-deep pain in the joints of the arms or legs, and could take minutes or even hours to become apparent. Still, he had fair odds of getting away clean. The nitrogen gas in the bloodstream that caused the bends when you ascended too rapidly after long descents—decompression stops being meant to give it time to dissolve through respiratory processes—tended to accumulate in fatty tissue, and he'd worked hard to stay in peak shape for more reasons than just impressing women at the gym.

He took a few moments to recoup, aware he couldn't spare too many more. Not safely anyway. The skiff was nowhere in sight, but it was almost certain the water was being scanned for signs of his reappearance—though he did not yet know whether it would be from the island, the skiff, or both. Whichever, he wasn't going to let himself be spotted.

He glanced around get his visual bearings, then double-checked them on his compass, having no idea how far he'd drifted from the dive site, or which direction the current might have taken him in. He quickly found that he was near the mouth of the cove and within a hundred yards of its southeastern flank. The skiff wasn't anywhere in sight, not that he'd expected it would be. To the contrary, he thought he could guess where Dex must have brought it.

His breath slow and almost regular now, Ricci allowed himself another twenty seconds to recover his strength, reached into his satchel for the eight-inch J snorkel he'd separated from his spare oxygen canister before ditching it, and put the mouthpiece between his lips. Then he turned facedown and lowered his head underwater, blew into the snorkel to make sure its airway was clear, and began to swim toward shore, his legs loose and straight behind him, his fins stroking smoothly, gliding unseen beneath the surface of the bay.

It was, he thought, a bad run of snake eyes. He'd been set up twice in as many days, and on both instances had felt bound to confront his opposition when it was their two against his one—only this time he couldn't count on Pete Nimec popping out of nowhere to even the odds.

Crouched low in a clump of juniper bushes perhaps five yards behind the jut of rock he'd noticed from the skiff, Ricci had just heard Cobbs and Dex working out a cover story to account for his "disappearance." Simple, but it didn't have to be anything more: Bumptious, know-it-all city boy Ricci had been diving for weeks without letting modest, conscientious local boy Dex properly check and maintain his scuba equipment, and since a tender couldn't do his job if the diver insisted on being foolhardy, Dex had given up trying to argue the point with him. Divers had gotten into bad fixes before through their own carelessness, and it would surely happen again in the future.

If Ricci's body didn't turn up, that would be that. And in the unlikely event it happened to float ashore before scavenging crabs, lobsters, and groundfish picked it apart, even an honest investigator would conclude Ricci had died from an out-of-air accident due to instrument failure, based upon a post mortem exam and the faulty reading on his psi gauge. Why suspect the gauge had been jiggered with by his partner when there was no evidence of a prior falling out between them; indeed, when any of the dealers with whom they regularly did business would attest they'd seemed to get along fine as a team? And besides, considering that Dex would be handing his pile of homespun horseshit to the sheriff or one of his deputies, and would have Cobbs signing off on it, he could probably chalk Ricci's fate up to a Bigfoot attack, alien abduction, or head-on collision with the Flying Dutchman and get away with it, no sweat.

Ricci looked and listened from the concealment of the brush. In their own way they were good, he thought, the only monkey wrench in their scheme being that he was better and savvier. His mistake—and he acknowledged it was significant—had been underestimating how far Dex could be pushed. Ricci had known Dex had his weaknesses, and they'd never quite been friends, but had always gotten on all right as partners. Much as he disliked admitting it to himself, he'd started out being a cop with a deep-rooted core of positivism, and some rudiments of that attitude remained stubbornly lodged inside him despite having spent years exploring the darkest alleys of human nature. He'd been hesitant to think the worst of his partner, and had almost paid for it big-time.

Ricci breathed quietly, motionless, watching the two men stand and talk in the small, pebble-sprinkled clearing around the big rock. He had approached them through the woods at a diagonal, and was more or less behind Cobbs, who was turned toward the beach, with Dex facing inland in Ricci's general direction. While they had been ironing out the main points of their little deception, he'd put the finishing touches on a plan of his own, and it too was pretty bare. Cobbs had a weapon—not the sharpshooter's rifle Ricci had speculated about earlier, but a Remington pump, which at close range could pack an even deadlier wallop—and so would have to be taken down first. This time there was no truck door to pin his sorry ass in, but the shotgun would only be a problem if he had the chance to use it.

As for Dex . . . he was unarmed, and would be easy.

Surprise and the ability to hit fast and hard were then Ricci's best assets. He'd abandoned his scuba tank, fins, and mask in the woods, and left himself wearing only the dry suit and knife rigs. The urchin knife would be of marginal use offensively and was in its scabbard. The pointed, double-edged blade was in his right hand. That baby had the meanness in it.

A breeze fluttered through the woods, and Ricci eased partially out of his crouch using the rustle of leaves, branches, and weeds to cover the sound of his movement. When the wind died down he stopped, then waited for another gust to stir the foliage and stole forward, falling back on his SEALs training again, obeying tried and proven fundamentals of stalking one's quarry. Registering one leg in front of the other. Touching the ground with the ball of his foot and slowly lowering his heel while scanning for rocks, fallen leaves, anything that might trip him up or be disturbed by his weight. Shifting direction every few steps so that the brush wouldn't sway unnaturally and attract attention.

The wind quieted. He paused. The two men were still talking. Cobbs's back was now less than three feet in front of him through the brush that constituted Ricci's self-designated skirmish line. Another draft of wind and he would launch from his concealed position, tackle Cobbs from behind, and hopefully disarm him before he could get off a single shot.

It was the squirrel that screwed things up.

". . . want to make it look good, you ought to wait another couple hours, then phone in a diver emergency to me *and* the sheriff's office," Cobbs was saying. "I'll handle it like any other—"

He stopped talking and gave Dex a questioning glance.

Dex had suddenly cast his eyes toward the maple tree on which he'd noticed the munching squirrel a short while before. Already on heightened guard because of his and Cobbs's near proximity, it had been startled from its perch and abruptly gone bounding up the tree amid a loud rattle of branches, dropping the seed pod it had been clutching in its obvious fright. This instigated a sort of chain reaction, the commotion sending a jolt through Dex's tightly wound nerves, prompting him to jerk his head up toward the squirrel, then drop his gaze to the creeping junipers below it—and just a few feet behind Cobbs—to find out what could have sent the little animal fleeing

That was when he saw a dead man about to spring from between two of the bushes in a semi-crouch, his fist clenched around the haft of a long knife.

His face all at once draining of color, his mouth yawping open, too shocked to utter more than a wordless cry of alarm and incomprehension, he thrust out his arm to frantically gesture in Ricci's direction.

Without knowing what was going on except that something had scared the living daylights out of Dex, Cobbs spun on his heels, raised his shotgun, and brought its barrel around to where he was pointing.

Ricci was about to make his move when he heard the spooked squirrel in the treetop, then saw Dex turn to investigate its racket, his eyes sweeping up the tree, then down to land directly upon him and widen with stunned confusion.

There was no time to hesitate. Even as Dex began gesturing wildly—and a split second before Cobbs swiveled his upraised shotgun around toward him—Ricci broke from cover and came at the warden in a scrambling, straight-ahead run, ducking below the shotgun's muzzle.

The gun roared above his head, its load gouging into the tree trunk behind Ricci and flurrying the area with shaves and splinters of bark. Cobbs rocked backward from the weapon's kick, but was surprisingly quick to recover, and managed to chamber another round before Ricci could reach him. Ricci heard the *chock-chock* of the Remington's pump action and saw Cobbs swing it down at him, and charged in underneath it with his knees bent, then sprang to his full height, grabbed the middle of its barrel with his left hand, and forced the muzzle upward. Cobbs squeezed the trigger on reflex and shot a second load of steel pellets harmlessly into the air.

Without releasing the weapon's barrel, Ricci smashed his right forearm against Cobbs's neck, then hit him twice on the jaw with his elbow while jerking the shotgun around hard to the left.

Cobbs's chin snapped to the side and blood instantly began streaming from his mouth. His lips stretched into a grimace of fury and pain, he managed to hang onto the gun, but Ricci pushed close against him, using both his hand and body to keep the barrel angled upward and sideways. Cobbs hung on. Ricci had not thought he would have as much fight in him, but anger and adrenaline could give people the strength to stay committed. Still, he had to finish him before Dex got involved.

Ricci shoved against him with his chest, forcing him to stumble backward. The moment he had him off balance, Ricci jammed his right elbow into Cobbs's stomach and, as he doubled over with a groan, finally got the shotgun out of his hands.

A moment later Ricci dropped down into a squat and shoved his dive knife into the top of Cobbs's boot, putting his arm and shoulder into the blow, driving in the blade until all six inches of it had penetrated his foot and sunk into the dirt beneath him.

Cobbs released a howling, animalistic scream that

grew in volume and shrillness as he tried to lift his impaled foot off the ground and realized that he couldn't. His face bright crimson, the whites of his eyes enormous, he looked down at himself and saw blood swell up around the knife handle projecting from the upper part of his boot, simultaneously draining from where the blade had cut through its treaded rubber sole. His screams reached a ragged peak of hysteria and cracked apart, dissolving into moist snuffles.

"Look what you done to me!" he whimpered, and sank to his knees, looking up at Ricci, water gushing from his eyes. Blood smudged his lips and chin like grotesque stage makeup, and there was a slurry thickness to his speech that told Ricci his jaw had either been dislocated or broken. *"Oh, fuck. Oh, oh, sweet God, look what you fucking done!"*

Ricci ignored him. He had straightened up and could see the bushes thrashing to his left where Dex had plunged into the woods. So much for his helping Cobbs. Ricci whipped off after him, both hands around the shotgun he'd torn from Cobbs's grasp.

Dex's lead was slight and his panic flung him blindly through the low branches and undergrowth. He stumbled over roots, crashed against bushes and tree limbs.

Despite the relative bulkiness of his dry suit, Ricci closed the distance between them in less than a minute.

"Hold it, Dex! Not another step!" he called out, and pumped a fresh cartridge into the chamber of the Remington. "I mean it."

Dex halted under an arcade of pine branches. He was panting from fear and exertion.

"Turn around," Ricci said. "Slow."

Dex did as he'd been told.

Ricci moved forward, the gun barrel out in front of him, his finger on the trigger.

Dex stood there in a sort of half slump, still panting,

his long hair wet from sweat and pasted to his cheeks and neck. He glanced at Ricci a moment, and then cast his eyes down at some indeterminate patch of ground between them.

Ricci stepped closer, pushed the muzzle of the gun against the underside of Dex's chin, and forced his head upward.

"Look at me," Ricci said. And pushed his chin further up with the muzzle. "Look me in the *eye*."

Dex again did as he'd been told.

"First thing," Ricci said. "You're a greedy little slug."

Dex was quiet, his lips trembling. Perspiration streamed from under his watchcap.

"Second," Ricci said. "You're a would-be murderer."

Dex started to say something, but Ricci silenced him with a prod of the gun barrel.

"I can make it so there's nothing left under that hat of yours besides mush," he said. "Better you let me do the talking."

Dex shut his mouth.

They faced each other in silence. The interwoven branches overhead blocked out most of the morning sunlight and cast lacy patterns of shadow over both their features.

"We always split the take right down the middle, and that was fine by me. Didn't matter I took the chances, long as you did your job and watched my back," Ricci said. "But then you went behind it instead. Got down with Cobbs and Phipps on that pinch the other day. Fixed the pressure gauge so I wouldn't know when my tank was out of air. Emptied my spare. Rather than coming to me when Cobbs laid some heat on you, telling me so we could put him in his place, you cuddled up with him and tried to *kill* me."

Ricci was silent again. From behind him near the slab of rock, he could hear Cobbs's whimpering sobs.

"I owe you, Dex," Ricci said. "You deserve for me to pull the trigger, and better believe I'm tempted to do it."

Dex tensed, his breath coming in staccato bursts. Small blotches of red erupted on his cheeks.

Ricci held the shotgun steadily up to his chin for another second, then shook his head and lowered its barrel toward the ground.

"Relax," he said. "You, Cobbs, and all your other pals won't have to worry about me anymore. Wouldn't have even if nothing had happened today besides us striking the mother lode of urchins. Because I got an offer from somebody out of town and decided to take it. All you would've needed to do to know that was wait till this afternoon, when the for-sale sign goes up in front of my house."

More silence. Dex had a cowed, beaten expression on his face and seemed on the verge of squirming. Yet Ricci sensed he had little true remorse over the wrong he had done and only a partial understanding of its depth. In his own eyes he was a victim and that status both justified his actions and absolved him of blame. The shame in him was mostly over having gotten caught.

"Cobbs'll be okay," Ricci said. "I'm running the skiff back to the wharf. The two of you wait till maybe fifteen minutes after I'm gone, then take his boat, get him to the hospital. Anybody asks what happened to him, leave me out of your story. Or I give you my word, you'll pay."

Silence.

Ricci looked at him, and felt a sudden abhorrence that came close to making him physically sick. Then he gestured back the way they had come with his head.

"Get out of my sight," he said at last.

Dex hesitated a moment, as if he still thought there was something he ought to say but didn't know what it should be, or was afraid it might get him fouled up again. Then he simply nodded, stepped past Ricci, and started to walk away through the woods.

"And, Dex?"

Dex stopped, glanced back over his shoulder.

"Don't worry," Ricci said. "I'm sure you'll manage to live with yourself."

SEVENTEEN

VARIOUS LOCALES
APRIL 22, 2001

HARLAN DEVANE SAT OPPOSITE KUHL AT A CANE TA-
ble on his veranda, dealing out a hand of solitaire as the
engorged red sun sank through the evening sky into the
Bolivian rain forest.

"Give me your assessment," he said without raising
his eyes from the cards.

"The pulse device should fulfill its requirements,"
Kuhl said. "We are close to ready for the endgame."

DeVane turned over a card and examined it. A jack
of diamonds. He laid it atop a queen of clubs.

"The trial run seems to have made an outstanding impression on you," he said.

"Yes," Kuhl said. "The damage to the train surpassed
every expectation."

DeVane nodded and glanced up from the table.

"Your emphasis on the amount of carnage that resulted fascinates me, Siegfried," he said. "Do you know
the piece of information I find most useful after having
heard your account?"

Kuhl looked at him with absolute stillness but did not
reply. There was no sign on his face that he was con-

sidering an answer, and indeed DeVane would have been surprised and disappointed if he'd had anything to say. The most efficient predator never revealed its thinking, or made it obvious if it was thinking at all. Could anyone know the mind of a shark? A python?

"The signal light," DeVane said in response to his own question. "That you saw it come back on within seconds of the derailment indicates its circuits were left intact, and able to work normally once the disruption to the electromagnetic field ceased. Not only will the reason for the light's malfunction never be ascertained, there is no hard evidence a malfunction occurred. The cause of the train wreck will be impossible to determine or trace, and therefore we cannot be incriminated. This to me is the salient detail with regard to our larger objectives."

Kuhl's eyes were like small windows into a vast frozen reach.

"If I hadn't thought it important, it would not have been included in my report," he said.

"And I welcome your thoroughness." DeVane studied the neat rows of playing cards in front of him. There was a four of spades in one, a six of clubs in another. He flipped another three off the deck. "Of course, while there is no need for you to explain your selection of a target, I *did* admittedly find it intriguing."

"Oh?"

DeVane nodded.

"Why a passenger train as opposed to something like a freight train? I wondered. Why send human beings over that hillside rather than cattle or lumber, the accompanying loss of life being nonessential to the test?" He turned over three more cards. "And then the answer came to me. In a snap, as they say."

Kuhl said nothing.

DeVane looked directly at him. "Are you acquainted

with the paintings of Brueghel or Hieronymus Bosch?"
he asked.

Kuhl shook his head. "I've no interest in art."

"Perhaps not, but you might want to make an exception and seek theirs out anyway. 'The Last Judgment,' 'The Triumph of Death,' 'The Beggars' . . . they are works filled with marvelous deviltry, to mangle the words of a poet who admired Brueghel in particular." DeVane smiled. "Very little is known about either man, and most of their oils are undated. We know both lived in the Middle Ages, about a century apart. Who commissioned their paintings, what specifications they were given, whether they ever painted to please themselves rather than their patrons . . . these things are mostly open to conjecture. But their styles and monstrous images cannot be confused with anyone else's, and must have bordered upon the heretical in their day. One sees a Bosch canvas, one does not need a signature to identify the cruel, exacting hand of its creator. The work *itself* is signature enough."

Kuhl met his gaze.

"I don't get your point."

DeVane smiled.

"I think you do, despite my occasional tendency to be elliptical," he said. "Please accept that I implied no disrespect. To the contrary, I see you as a master of your trade, an invisible artist whose handiwork is unmistakable to the studied connoisseur. And I enjoy giving you creative leeway."

DeVane turned over more cards. Kuhl watched him, showing neither interest nor disinterest.

"I must tell you, Siegfried, my single nagging concern about our endeavor is not that we will fail to carry it out, but that success could prove a disappointment to our clients," DeVane said after a moment. "Compared to what we intend to place aboard the Russian orbital platform, the device you fielded is as a cannonball would be to a precision-guided missile."

Kuhl shrugged minimally. *A taste.*

"Havoc does have a far higher performance watershed to meet, yes, and the fact that one proved reliable is no guarantee that the other will do the same," he said. "Still, the Albanians have paid us up front. As have the cartels. We've made clear that their money is ours to keep regardless."

"I like to take the larger view. Keep our customers satisfied." DeVane paused again. "It is also my wish to see Roger Gordian's reputation and influence suffer for all this. UpLink's growing presence in so many of our pipeline nations arguably represents our greatest threat. The economic and political stability his operations brings to those states is bad for business, and what is bad for business must be eliminated. Think of the trust he stands to lose with his global partners should we deliver on our contracts . . . and consider the embarrassment to *us* if we don't. There are huge dividends at stake on both sides."

Kuhl nodded once.

"A weapon's effectiveness cannot be absolutely proven until it is deployed," he said. "But we know that the engineering difficulties that beset its prototypical antecedents—namely the lack of an adequate, rechargeable energy source, and susceptibility to their own radiation—have been solved. The sun itself will function as an incomparably powerful generator and allow long-range, focused targeting from space. And the exotic metal alloy developed by Ilkanovitch's team has proven capable of shielding the device's components from its intense, repetitive production of broad-frequency microwave beams. Ilkanovitch's documentation of the Russian testing is backed up by the evidence we've seen of its potential."

"You are referring to the railway 'accident'?"

"And to the crash of the 747 commuter plane in Los Angeles some months back. American investigators attributed its explosion after takeoff to a spark in the conductive wiring inside its center fuel tank. This was true. But the cause of the spark remained undetermined in official reports, and the abrupt retirement of a senior FBI official who publicly speculated that it might have been a microwave pulse was swept under the agency's very large carpet." Kuhl paused. "Again, I am convinced beyond doubt that Ilkanovitch's claim of responsibility is genuine . . . and Havoc is many, many times more effective than the ground-based device that ignited the fuel tank. Imagine the destruction of not a single plane, but of dozens with the targeting of a major airport's air traffic control system. Imagine the chaos that would arise from the total disruption of civil electronic systems and communications grids in a city such as New York or London. Havoc will achieve superb results. It will make the entire world hostage to our demands."

DeVane looked at him.

"Tell me what you've learned about Gordian's proposed reinforcement of the Cosmodrome."

"It's as we foresaw. My intelligence is that he's succeeded in convincing the officials at Baikonur to let him provide additional security. Much of the support is being brought over from the UpLink ground station in Kaliningrad, though he is drawing upon other assets as well . . . all meant to prevent anything from interfering with the shuttle's launch."

"So he is playing into our hands. Without being aware of our true goal, thinking we mean to *cripple* the ISS program, his security measures will be misdirected."

"Exactly."

DeVane looked at him another moment, then nodded. "Good enough," he said. "You have sufficient manpower in Kazakhstan to implement our strike?"

"Yes," Kuhl replied. "With added elements leaving from our base in the Pantanal tomorrow night."

"Those men will be transporting the device, I take it?"

"Yes."

"Then let us be expeditious and move within a few days," DeVane said.

"Yes."

DeVane turned over his last three cards and nodded with satisfaction, his smile lengthening, his lips parting slightly to show his small, white front teeth.

"Aces, Siegfried," he said, "We're all aces."

As the sun was setting in Bolivia it was blazing an ascendant track through the Kazakhstan sky halfway around the world, where the latest stream of UpLink helicopters and transport planes had begun to arrive at the military airfield in Leninsk, some twenty miles south of the Baikonur Cosmodrome.

His hand visored over his eyes to shield it from the desert brightness, Yuri Petrov stood looking out at the tarmac as a wide-bellied Lockheed transport made its final approach. He scowled. Perhaps he ought to feel something like gratitude for the assistance he was receiving from UpLink, but instead he felt . . . what? Outrage was more than he could muster these days, and he had worn indignation on his back for so long it was like an old, threadbare shirt. How could it be otherwise?

He was the director of a Russian Space Agency that was propped up by American loans and subsidies. The Baikonur facility that had been the launch site for every manned space mission Russia had conducted, and the town of Leninsk that had been established as an outpost for its defense and supply, had since 1994 been leased from the sovereign state of Kazakhstan—once part of the Soviet Union—for over a hundred million dollars a year, much of it apportioned from the American hand-outs. And now the Voenno Kosmicheskie Sily, or Military Space Force, that was garrisoned in the town had been subordinated to a private American security contingent under the rubric of "mutual support" at the direct order of President Vladimir Starinov himself, who many believed had become not merely indebted, but *indentured,* to Roger Gordian after UpLink's people saved him from assassination the year before—and whose regime had been taking continuous political fire for blatantly kowtowing to American and NATO interests.

Petrov's scowl deepened. Why bother raising the Russian flag over the installation, emblazoning Russian decals on the spacecraft that launched from it, or stitching Russian patches onto the spacesuits of the cosmonauts that rode into space aboard those craft? Why not confirm what was already all too evident to him and stamp the stars and stripes, or better yet the U.S. dollar sign, onto the brow of every person who worked for an agency that had once been at the forefront of space exploration, sending the first satellite into orbit around the earth, the first unmanned probes to the surface of the moon and Venus, the first *human being* into space?

Now Petrov watched the Lockheed taxi easily to a stop in an unloading area across the airfield, where ground crews and wheeled freight conveyors were already rolling toward its freight door. He was aware of the almost subliminal drone of more aircraft winging in above the steppes, while above him another transport bearing UpLink insignia entered its landing pattern. The palletized loads of weapons, armored patrol vehicles, and other heavy lift had been arriving along with large complements of operating and service personnel for over forty-eight hours, and would continue to arrive right up until the launch later that week.

Petrov found himself wondering how the American

populace would react if their government invited a Russian paramilitary force with tremendous surveillance and fighting capabilities into the heart of their nation, imposed fewer practical restraints upon their use of weapons than the average citizen was asked to accept, then allowed them to usurp control of a military policing operation from indigenous army units. Would that not be seen as compromising America's internal security? As a threat to the very underpinning of its national sovereignty? Would it be *tolerated*?

He dropped his eyes and stuffed his hands into his trouser pockets. There could be no greater proof of America's global hegemony than those planes in the busy sky.

How could he describe how he felt?

He searched his mind for the right word and finally nodded.

Castrated.

That was it. That was *perfect*.

Damned fortunate for him that his wife had lost interest in sex some years ago. His head bent, his shoulders slightly stooped, Petrov strode toward the small terminal where he would prop himself up to give a gracious, politic reception to the current batch of newcomers from UpLink.

Welcoming them where they very well might be needed, but were most assuredly not wanted.

"—don't know why you keep coming here to visit, Annie. You aren't around for someone's time of dying, it isn't like missing your train or a dentist's appointment or the early-bird sale at Wal-Mart. There's late and there's late, and if you think that puts a heavy load on your shoulders, think of how it felt for me."

Annie is back in Room 377 of the hospital, sitting at the bedside of the man in the carrot-red flight/reentry suit. The man with the Vaseline-smudge face who is and isn't her husband. The room is dark, the lights off, night outside the window behind her. The only illumination is a soft glow coming from the equipment—she's gotten used to seeing it change from hospital instruments to a space shuttle console to the front panel indicators of an F-16 with almost every glance—on the far side of his bed.

She shakes her head. "I didn't know, they said there was time—"

"And you had a training session to conduct," he interrupts with a chuckle like the sound of someone stamping down on dry twigs and broken glass. "How convenient."

"That isn't fair," she says, an imploring note in her voice. "I was going to come back in the morning. You knew I was coming back. You knew. And then they called . . . they phoned me . . ."

"Yeah, yeah, we've been through this same old song before. Sudden heart attack, smoke in the cabin, with a heave and a ho, they just had to tell you so." He produces another brittle expulsion of laughter that dissolves into a chain of hacking coughs. "Might've made it easier for my Annie to digest, you know how the Juiceman says to drink your bromelain before bedtime. But to be honest, there's not much difference from where I'm lying. There's late and there's late and you missed our date—"

She shakes her head. "No, don't say that again—"

"You can't stand hearing it, lassie, then why not put on your tweed cap and head on over to Erlsberg Castle? That's got to be better than this here barn hop," he says with a mock Scottish brogue. His hand comes up and points in her direction, the burned, sloughy flesh dangling off his finger like strings of half-dried glue. "Or you can always use the ejection seat. Handle's right in front of you."

And it is. It is. Annie thinks she can remember pulling a plain wooden armchair up to the bed, is sure she can, but it suddenly becomes clear she's mistaken, she is in a McDonnell Douglas ACES II ejection seat, the same type that launched her out of her burning F-16 over Bosnia. She acknowledges this discovery in the same unstartled way as she does the endlessly transforming instrument panels, and the smeary blotch of grease in front of—Mark's?—face, making it impossible for her to discern its features. She is in an ejection seat, okay, all right, an ejection seat. Belted into the safety harness, the recovery parachute container above the headrest against the back of her neck, the data recorder mounted on the side of the chair to her left over the emergency oxygen bottle . . .

The yellow ejection handle in front of her.

"Do it, Annie. Bail!" the voice from the bed says in what almost sounds like a dare. "We both know how it works. Catapult will ignite in, what, three tenths of a second? The rocket sustainer less than a tenth of a second after that. Five secs later you'll be separated from the seat and floating down nice and soft in your 'chute."

"No," she replies, her own forcefulness catching her off guard. "I won't do it."

"Easy enough for you to say now, but just wait. There's smoke in the cabin! Smoke all around us."

Again, Annie is hardly surprised to find that he is right, has actually gotten used to these snap announcements of his, which have begun to remind her of hearing a video jock on MTV or VH-1 introduce the weekly hit list. He knows what's cuing up, he's always on top of the game, and if he tells you that there's smoke, you better believe you're about smell it.

Just you wait a second.

At first it is white, vaporous, and odorless as it tapers up from underneath her seat, like the sort of dry-ice

*smoke produced for theatrical effects. But it rapidly
darkens and thickens, rising in dirty gray billows that
fill her mouth and nose, threatening to overcome her
with its choking stench.*

*"Go on, Annie, what are you waiting for?" the man
in the bed asks in his familiar gibing, goading tone. He
props himself up on his pillow, thrusts his seared-to-the-
bone finger at her through the smoke, and wags it in
front of her face. "Reach for the lever and you're up
and out!"*

*"No!" Annie is even more forceful, more adamant
than she had been a second earlier. "I won't, you hear
me? I won't!"*

"Cut the crap and reach for it," he snarls. "Reach—"

*"No!" she again shouts back defiantly, and then
pushes herself off the seat against the resistance of her
buckled harness straps and does reach out—though not
for the eject lever. No, not for the lever, but for his
hideously burned, reddened hand, taking it between both
of her own with careful tenderness. "We're in this together, and that's never changed. Not for me."*

*The smoke wells blackly around her now, congealing
so Annie can no longer see the bed only inches in front
of her, or the man lying under its sheets. But she can
still feel him, can still feel his hand in hers. And then
she realizes with a jolt of surprise—the first she's experienced in this latest twist on what some small portion
of her sleeping mind realizes has become a recurrent
nightmare—that he isn't pulling it away.*

"It's all on the tape, Annie," he says.

*His voice now clearly that of her husband, but without
the sneering, disdainful quality it has had in each previous version of this scene.*

"Mark—"

"On the tape," he repeats.

Kindly.

Gently.

Oh, so heartbreakingly gently from behind the shroud of smoke, reminding her of how he had been before the cancer, how she had come to love him, how much about him she had loved what seems such a very long time ago.

"You already know everything you need to know," he says, all at once sounding as if he has moved further away from her.

Then Annie realizes that is exactly what is happening. She feels his hand slipping out from between her fingers—feels it slowly, inevitably slipping into the black. Try as she does, struggle as she does, she can't seem to hold onto it.

Hold onto him.

"Mark, Mark—" She breaks off in a fit of coughing and gasping, her lungs crammed full of smoke. Wishing she could see him in the blinding smoke. Wishing, wishing she could just hold on. "Mark, I—"

Annie awoke with her arm outstretched and her fingers clutching at empty air. Awoke in her darkened bedroom, sweaty, trembling, and breathless, her heart tripping wildly in her chest. The trailing edge of her inarticulate cries—cries that, in her dream, had seemed to take the form of her husband's name—were still on her lips.

The dream, she thought.

Once again, the dream.

Annie reached over to her nightstand for the glass of water she had brought in from the kitchen before climbing into bed, took a drink, another, a third. She swept the hair back off her forehead, released a long, sighing breath. Thank heaven she hadn't startled the kids with the noise she must have been making.

She sat there for several minutes, pulling herself together, letting her heartbeat and respiration slow to a normal rate. Then she put down the now-half-drained glass of water and pressed the illuminator button of her Indiglo alarm clock.

3:00 A.M.

She had fallen asleep less than two hours ago after poring over the written transcript of the *Orion*-to-LCR communications, concentrating on the final transmissions from the flight deck. It was obviously what had precipitated the dream this time around, just as reading the newspaper story about *Orion* had originally brought it on. Which made, what now, *four* occurrences in less than a week?

"Shit," she muttered aloud. "Better find a way to clear your head before hitting the sack or you're going to burn out fast, Annie. Listen to some music, watch those *Seinfeld* reruns on TV, anything besides taking your work to bed with—"

Her eyes snapping wide open, her heart pounding again, she straightened with such an abrupt jerk that her headboard struck the wall behind her with a bang.

Mark's words to her in the dream . . . those *last* words.

She could recall them as if they had actually come from his mouth and not her own subconscious mind. As if he were repeating them from beside her in bed at that very instant.

It's all on the tape, Annie. On the tape. You already know everything you need to know.

She switched on her reading lamp and grabbed up the bound pages of the transcript from where they lay on the nightstand, unaware that she'd barely missed knocking over her water glass in the process.

Everything you need to know.

"Oh, my God," she said into the pin-drop silence of the room, slapping the transparent binder onto her lap and opening it with a jerky, almost violent flick of her hand. "Oh, my *God*."

EIGHTEEN

FLORIDA
APRIL 23, 2001

NO MATTER HOW HEAVY ANNIE'S WORKLOAD AT THE JSC, she'd routinely driven the kids to school every morning rather than hustle them off with their nurse-maid, and she hadn't wanted that to change while they were in Florida. When the phone rang she was helping them pack their book bags, impatient to get under way, having jumped out of bed, showered, and dressed almost immediately upon awakening from her dream long hours before sunrise.

She motioned for them to keep packing and snatched up the receiver.

"Hi," she said. "This is Annie."

"Good morning," a man's voice said at the other end of the line. "My name's Pete Nimec. I'm from—"

"UpLink International." She glanced quickly at the wall clock. Seven-thirty. Some people had their nerve. "Mr. Gordian called yesterday to tell me you'd be coming to Florida, and I'm very appreciative of your assistance. Hadn't expected to hear from you so soon, though."

"Sorry, I know it's very early," he said. "But I was

hoping we could get together for breakfast."

"No can do," she said. "You caught me as I was practically heading out the door, and I need to get to the Cape—"

"Let's meet there," he said. "I'll bring the coffee and muffins."

She shook her head.

"Mr. Nimec—"

"Pete."

"Pete, I've got a million things on my plate this morning, one of which is tracking down one of our more quirky volunteer investigators, and I haven't got time—"

"I can tag along with you. If you don't mind. Be a good way to gain my bearings."

Annie glanced out the terrace door and considered his proposition. Bright sequins of morning sunlight glittered on the blue Atlantic water, where a small recreational sailboat was tacking along parallel to the beach. Dorset had promised a view, and a view she'd gotten. She wished she were of a mind to enjoy it, to try spotting those dolphins and manatees that were supposedly frolicking around out there.

"I really don't think that's advisable," she said. "You may not realize how hectic and crowded it gets in the Vehicle Assembly Building. There are dozens of people scrambling around. Sorting, examining, whatever. It can be pure chaos."

"I'll stay out of everybody's way. Promise."

Pushy guy, she thought. *Just what I needed.*

"Look, there's no sense in dancing around this," she said. "Some of the things I'll be doing today are highly sensitive. I realize we're both on the same team, and it isn't that I'm trying to keep any secrets. But right now I'm following up on a hunch that involves some highly technical particulars—"

"All the more reason you can trust me to stay out of

your hair, since I won't have the faintest idea what I'm looking at," Nimec said.

"I'd still rather we try for later," she said. "Maybe we can arrange to have lunch—"

"Mom, Chris keeps calling me monkey-face!" Linda shouted from the living room.

"That's 'cause she untied my shoelaces!" Chris rejoined.

Annie cupped a hand over the receiver.

"That's enough, you two, I'm on the phone," she said. "Your books packed?"

"Yeah!" In unison.

"Then go into the kitchen and wait for Regina to give you your snack money."

"Chris called me monkey-face ag—"

"Enough!"

"Hello?" Nimec again. "You still there?"

Annie uncovered the mouthpiece.

"Sorry, I'm getting the kids ready for school," she said.

"Understood, I've one of my own. A nine-year-old."

"You have my sympathies," she said.

"Lives with his mother."

"She does then," Annie said. "Where were we?"

"You were about to invite me to the Cape in exchange for me springing for lunch later on."

She sighed in acquiescence. Roger Gordian *had* sent him, after all. And what harm could there be in letting him come?

"I'm not sure that's quite my recollection, but okay, we can meet at the official reception area in an hour. With one stipulation."

"Shoot," he said.

"This is my show, and nothing's to be disclosed to the press, or anyone else, until I explicitly give the okay. Acceptable?"

"Sounds fair to me."

She looked at the clock again.

"Mommee!" Linda cried from the kitchen. *"Chris said I stink like a monkey's butt!"*

"See you at eight sharp," Annie said, and hung up the telephone.

The "quirky" volunteer Annie had mentioned to Nimec was a twenty-five-year-old research scientist named Jeremy Morgenfeld, whom she was able to reach on her cellular after depositing the kids at school—and just in the nick of time, Jeremy explained over the phone, since he'd been about to set out on his catamaran and had intended to remain incommunicado for the rest of the morning, his usual habit being to work no more than four hours a day, Monday through Thursday, beginning neither a moment sooner nor later than the stroke of noon. The living definition of a prodigy, Jeremy had graduated from the Massachusetts Institute of Technology a month before his sixteenth birthday with a bachelor's degree in aeronautical engineering, and had later gained four master's degrees in that and other related fields, as well as three *doctorates* in the physical and biological sciences. By the age of twenty-one he had started up the Spectrum Foundation, an independent think tank financed almost entirely by the sale of its own diverse technological patents, with a small percentage of additional grant money coming from MIT in exchange for participation in several joint projects, which included what he was presently describing to Nimec as magnetohydrodynamics—

"Plasma theory," Annie said. "You'll have to excuse Jerry. Every now and then he likes to remind people that was once the exclusive subject of a MERF study."

"That an acronym for something?"

"The Mensa Education and Research Foundation,"

she said. "They're interested in measuring the upper levels of intelligence . . . identifying the cultural, physiological, and environmental determinants of people with genius IQs."

"Nature or nurture," Nimec said. He was seated between them on the KSC tram, crossing from the reception area to the Vehicle Assembly Building. "The eternal debate."

"Look, I'm not into making anybody feel dumb," Jeremy said. Nimec guessed that was an attempt at being charitable. "But getting back to MHD, Annie's definition is much too broad. It's kind of like how every gerbil's a mammal, but not every mammal's a gerbil, you know? Plasma theory covers everything from the creation of the universe to these weird electrical surges in space I call Kirby crackle—after Jack Kirby, the comic book guy who outclassed all the megabucks special effects you've ever seen in sci-fi movies with only a pencil, an art board, and his imagination. Talk about genius." Jeremy paused. "Anyway, MHD's about the behavior of plasma in a magnetic field, which can lead to *majorly* immense practical applications. Power from atomic fusion, for example. It's the cleanest way known to generate energy, assuming we can figure out how to build reactors that are big and powerful enough to do the job on a mass scale without turning them and everything *around* them to melted slag."

"Better stop," Nimec said. "You're scaring me."

"Why's that?"

"Can't talk about it." Nimec kept a straight face. "Childhood trauma."

Jeremy raised his eyebrows.

Pleased, Nimec sat back and regarded him with his old cop's eye for noting standout physical characteristics: straight brown hair worn in a step cut, gold wire-framed glasses, smallish chin, teardrop-shaped whisker under his lower lip. Wearing a Boston Red Sox baseball cap backward on his head, a Red Sox T-shirt to match, baggy khaki shorts, and Nike sneakers sans socks.

Nimec gestured to the insignia on his shirt.

"Take it you're a Red Sox fan," he said, seeking a bit of common ground.

Jeremy nodded. "I have a place on Sanibel Island about an hour's drive from where the Sox do their spring training, and fly down to watch them get primed every year."

Nimec gave him a curious look. "Sanibel's a couple hundred miles south and west of us, isn't it?" he asked. "You told me that you were going out on your cat' when Annie contacted you this morning . . . how'd you make it here so fast?"

"Easy," Jeremy said. "Got a place in Orlando too. I've been staying there since Annie asked me to help with the investigation." He leaned forward and gave her a wink. "My girl beckons, I come running."

Annie smiled a little. "Jeremy and I met about three years ago when he arrived for payload specialist training in Houston."

Nimec tried not to sound surprised. "You," he said, "were an astronaut?"

Jeremy adjusted his glasses. He seemed suddenly uncomfortable.

"Not exactly," Annie interjected, moving in for an obvious save. "Non-NASA payload specialists fall into a unique category and are chosen by a sponsoring organization—usually a concern that's arranged to perform a set of low-gravity experiments or launch some orbital hardware aboard a flight. These would include chemical and pharmaceutical companies, educational institutions, military contractors, and communications outfits like your own."

"And the Spectrum Foundation?" Nimec said.

Annie nodded.

"At the time Jeremy was doing a study on crystal formation."

"Crystallization *patterns* under varying environmental, thermodynamic, and thermochemical conditions," Jeremy said. "Here's an example: Everybody's heard the old saw that no two snowflakes are alike, but that's one of those sucky oversimplifications that always gets corrupted into a popular fallacy. Way back in the nineteen-thirties Ukichira Nakaya, a brilliant professor from Hokkaido, charted all the basic forms of snow crystals, and the temperature and moisture conditions that cause them to occur. His work laid some of the groundwork for research by another high-wattage Japanese scientist named Shotaro Tobisawa, who studied and described the crystallization of various chemical substances under controlled-implosion conditions." He ran a fingertip down over his small tuft of beard. "Another example: Drop a nuke of a specific megatonnage somewhere, you get a predictable, unvarying type of mineral and atmospheric crystal formation in equally specific zones radiating from the blast epicenter. We've known that since Los Alamos. But the kinds of research I've been talking about are just the first steps toward understanding these phenomena. It's one thing to know *what* set of conditions will result in a certain kind of crystal geometry, and another to figure out *why* they do. That fascinates me, because it leads into a whole area of physical law that's virtually uninvestigated. Nobody thinks much about it now, but in the future when we get to areas of deep space exploration like terraforming or genetic adaption to other planetary environments, that sort of knowledge can be applied toward—"

"Jer," Annie said. "We're moving off-point."

He frowned, shrugged.

"They said I wasn't a team player," he said.

Nimec looked at him. "Who's *they*?"

"The director of the National Space Transportation System, plus his two deputies, plus the associate administrator of the Office of Space Flight. An amorphous group of gods known to us mortals as the Lords of the Great Kibosh," Jeremy said. "The only NASA exec who spoke up for me was Annie, but even she couldn't duck their lightning bolts."

"Didn't you say payload specialists fall outside government management?"

"Subject to final approval by the agency," Annie said. "Jeremy being somewhat unorthodox in his ways, certain people at the top came to feel he might develop personality differences with his crewmates, and that those differences could blow up out of proportion in the extended confinement of a shuttle mission."

"They thought I was a total pain in the ass, is what Annie's trying to tell you without offending me," Jeremy said. "You know that payload specialists don't even have to be American *citizens*? But somehow I can't go up for a miserable ten days without driving everyone else aboard to either leap into the void or dump *me* out of the cabin without a spacesuit. At least according to NASA."

Annie smiled fondly and reached over to pat his arm.

"Jeremy could have handled it, and the crew could've handled him," she said. "The upside to the whole affair is that he and I got acquainted, and have stayed friends ever since."

"I'm here for you, babe," Jeremy said, pitching his voice down to an exaggerated macho tenor.

The tram stopped to discharge its three passengers on the east side of the VAB. Annie was the first off, and as she led the way toward the huge building's guarded personnel entrance Nimec picked up on an abrupt change in her demeanor. There was a tension beneath the surface he could almost feel her struggling to control, a hurriedness to her step that hadn't been evident when they'd left the reception area for the tram. Whatever was on her mind was something she'd chosen to keep to herself, and he could only admire her poise and composure in doing so.

The floor of the high bay area was as chaotic as she'd warned him it would be, but it was the organized chaos of people faced with a serious and complex task, and operating under intense pressure. He'd known it in combat, known it at police crime scenes, known it all too frequently since joining Roger Gordian's operation; it was part of the game he'd played throughout his entire professional life. What struck him in this instance, however, was the absence of accompanying background noise, the purposeful silence of the men and women Annie had drawn together for her team, some in NASA coveralls, others in civilian clothes, dozens of them scurrying everywhere around and past him. Their silence, and the sheer amount of debris that had been collected here. As his eyes swept the enormous room, he knew it would have been impossible to fully comprehend the annihilating magnitude of the explosions that had wracked *Orion* on the launchpad without seeing these remains firsthand.

Nimec surveyed the feverish activity a while longer, then realized Annie and Jeremy had already gone on ahead, walking side by side, leaning their heads together in private discussion. He started after them, but on second thought decided to hang back. Though he'd met her a scant half hour ago, he already suspected Annie Caulfield had good reasons for whatever she did. And he had given his word not to crowd her.

He watched them walk up the broad transfer aisle stretching away before him and climb onto one of the movable work platforms, where four or five investigators were gathered over several large sections of the space-craft. Annie spoke with them briefly, projecting an easy, gentle authority—paying close attention to their comments, patting one woman on the shoulder with the same sort of open, unself-conscious warmth she'd shown Jeremy on the tram. Nimec again found himself singularly impressed by her bearing.

When the group left the platform a few moments later, plainly at Annie's request, she and Jeremy hunkered into what reminded Nimec of a palaeontologist's crouch and began shuffling amid the wreckage, occasionally exchanging comments and pointing things out to each other.

After a bit Nimec figured it would be okay to join them.

Annie acknowledged him with a nod as he reached the foot of the platform, and then waved him over, continuing to inspect one of the shuttle fragments. A soldered clump of tubes and valves in a cracked, scorched housing, it was attached to a component that, though also burned and dented, nonetheless retained something of an identifiable bell shape. Nimec thought he could make an educated guess about what it was, but didn't, not aloud anyway, wanting to give them some more breathing room.

Finally Annie glanced up at him from her crouch.

"You're looking at what's left of a main engine," she said, confirming his hunch. "The shuttle has three of them below the vertical tail fin. It's no secret that the recorded dialogue between *Orion*'s flight deck and ground control tells us a red warning light went on at T minus six seconds, and indicated Main Engine Number Three was overheating."

He nodded. "This it?"

She paused before answering, then said quietly, "SSME Three was essentially vaporized in the initial blast. SSME Two, which was situated right beside it at the aft end, is being partially reassembled from what little of it we've been able to recover. You're looking at SSME One. I'm not sure why, but it's been left relatively intact. The engines are in a triangular configuration, and this would have been at the apex, so maybe its position above the other two allowed it to escape the worst brunt of the explosions in some way. That'll be determined. What's important to me right now is that we *have* it to study."

"These mothers feed off a potent mixture of cryogenic liquid hydrogen and liquid oxygen," Jeremy said. He was bent over the opposite side of the engine bell. "Annie'll correct me if I'm wrong, but I think the propellants in a shuttle engine generate 1.7 million newtons—that's equivalent to, what, about 375 thousand pounds of thrust at sea level. Makes it the most efficient dynamo of a power plant ever built. On the other hand, the ignition of hot hydrogen gas can be savage unless it's precisely regulated. Remember the *Hindenberg*."

"Which means exactly what regarding *Orion*?" Nimec asked.

"Getting back to the shuttle-to-ground communications record, it's apparent that a problem developed with the flow of liquid hydrogen fuel," Annie said, her face solemn. "Again, this is information that's been very widely circulated in the media, so I doubt I'm saying anything you don't already know. One of the last things Jim . . . *Colonel Rowland* . . . said to the controller was that LH2 pressure was dropping. Then he broke off for a second."

Nimec had listened attentively, but felt a little baffled. "If I'm following this at all, you're implying a reduction in liquid hydrogen pressure may have caused the *increase* in engine temperature that in turn sparked the fire.

But I'd think it'd be the other way around—less fuel, less burn."

"Yeah, sure, unless the pressure drop is in these here strands of spaghetti," Jeremy said. He gestured toward one of the clumps of mangled tubing behind the engine bell. "They channel the LH2 into the walls of the engine nozzle and combustion chamber before outletting them to the preburners—"

Nimec raised his palm to stop him.

"Whoa," he said. "Back up a second. I'm still not clear on how less equals more in this instance."

"That's 'cause a very important word I used to describe the state of the liquid hydrogen must've slipped past you," Jeremy said. "Namely *cryogenic*."

Annie saw Nimec holding back his irritation at being patronized.

"As Jeremy said," she broke in, "the SSMEs operate with a high level of efficiency. That's in part because the propellants are used for multiple purposes. To remain in a liquid state hydrogen has to be kept supercold . . . to give you an idea of *how* cold, bear in mind that it vaporizes at any temperature above minus 423 degrees Fahrenheit. As a solution to the problem of critical engine overheating, the designers of the SSMEs found a means to divert some of the liquid hydrogen fuel throughout the engine with a system of ducts before it finally makes its way to the preburners. There's a pair in each of the main engines, and their function is to ignite the very hot hydrogen vapors that result from the combustion process *before* they can accumulate and ignite in the engine bell. If you ever watch a video of a liftoff in slow motion, you'd can see the preburners shooting the gas out below the bells as thousands of tiny fireballs."

Nimec looked at her. "So you're telling me that a significant dropoff in LH2 pressure would have caused the engine to overheat and the preburners to fail . . . leading to an explosion of the free hydrogen vapors in the engine bell."

"That's what *Jim* was telling us. Or trying to. He would have known where in the engine the liquid hydrogen pressure had critically decreased just by looking at a gauge on his instrument panel. But with everything happening so fast . . . the cabin filling with smoke . . ."

"He never finished saying what he wanted to."

"Which was that the LH2 pressure was dropping *in the preburner ducts.*"

Their gazes met. Nimec saw the moist, overbright look in her eyes, realized she was fighting back tears, and found himself on the verge of reaching out with a comforting hand. Instead he stiffened, caught wholly off guard by the impulse.

Turning to Jeremy, he said, "When we were on the tram you mentioned the difference between knowing what happens given a certain set of conditions, and understanding why it happens."

Jeremy visibly wavered.

"I was talking about snowflakes," he said.

"Then talk to me now about explosions," Nimec said. "What do you think made the LH2 pressure drop? And if it occurred in Engine Number Three, why are there fused cooling ducts in Number *One*? How could the identical problem simultaneously occur in at least *two* of the three separate engines?"

Jeremy looked to Annie, still hesitant. He was waiting to see how much she wanted to share, and would say nothing more without her okay. Nimec decided he liked him a little better for it.

"The other night I came here after everyone else was gone, just to do some thinking," Annie offered at length. "I'd had a tough day wrestling with the press and needed to get my head straight. . . ." She trailed off a moment, then shook her head. "But that doesn't matter. What *does* matter is I stayed a long time. Much longer than I expected, in fact. Walking around, looking over the pieces of wreckage we'd started to assemble. When I saw this engine, I noticed that the internal damage seemed far greater than the damage to the exterior of the housing. And started ask to ask myself the same things you just asked Jeremy." She paused again, exhaled. "I've requested assistance from the Forensic Science Center in San Francisco. It's at the Lawrence Livermore National Laboratory, I don't know whether you're familiar with them—"

"They did evidence analysis on the Unabomber case, the Times Square and World Trade Center bombings in New York, probably hundreds of other investigations," Nimec said. "UpLink's had a relationship with them for years, and I've worked with them personally. The LLNL's the best group of crime detection and national security experts in the business."

She nodded. "They're sending a team of analysts with an ion-store/time-of-flight mass spectrometry instrument."

"Which means you're looking for residual by-products of a blasting material," he said. "IS/TOF-MS allows the trace-particles analysis to be done right here in this building . . . avoids deterioration that can take place by transporting the sample to a lab."

"Yes."

Nimec mulled that over for a while.

"In acts of sabotage, you have to work quickly and on the sly and that's how errors are sometimes made," he said. "If you're good at destruction, you know that the way to take the possibility of a foul-up into account . . . to anticipate and keep it from happening . . . is to be redundant. Get your hands into three engines, though all you need is one to go bad. If I'm reading you

right, then whatever made Engine Three—and maybe
Engine Two—overheat was supposed to have done the
same with Engine One, but didn't. Or at least not to the
extent intended."

"That's a reasonable explanation, yes, if we assume a
deliberate and successful effort was made to destroy
Orion." Annie breathed. "We'll see what the mass spectrometry and FSC analysts give us. Meanwhile, Jeremy
believes it likely there *was* such an effort."

"More than likely," Jeremy said. "I'd bet anything on
it."

Nimec looked at him.

"What makes you sound so definite?"

"Remember a second ago, when I was talking snowflakes, and you wanted to talk explosions?"

Nimec had already gotten enough of a feel for Jeremy
to realize the question wasn't rhetorical.

"Uh-huh," he said.

"Well, it happens we were already on the same page.
An offshoot of my work in thermodynamic crystal geometry, which involves various types of controlled explosions, has been an interest in *blast* geometry."

"Somehow," Nimec said. "I had an inkling."

"I know you did."

Nimec gave him a nod.

"Tell me what you've got, Jeremy," he said. "Why so
definite?"

"In simple language," Jeremy said, "a certain type of
chemical reaction equals an explosion equals a pattern.
And to me the splay, burn, and scoring patterns in this
engine had to have been made by tiny thermal charges—
could've been something like noncommercial RDX—
that were meant to destroy the hydrogen fuel turbo-
pumps, but only partially did the job."

Nimec considered that a second and nodded again.

"Thanks," he said.

"S'okay." Jeremy put his hand on the ruined engine, peering at Nimec through the lenses of his wire glasses. "You want to come around this side, I'll show you what I mean."

A comradely overture.

"Yeah," Nimec said. "That'd be good."

"There's something I kept to myself at the VAB," Nimec told Annie half an hour later. "Wasn't sure how much to say in front of Jeremy."

They were having coffee in the KSC commissary, his offer of lunch scaled down because of her packed schedule, Jeremy now on his way back to Orlando.

She watched him intensely over her cup.

"Go on," she said.

"In some instances terrorists will want to leave a footprint of sabotage without taking credit for the act. It's been an increasing trend over the last decade. Lets them have it both ways—they put the fear into you without bringing heat down on themselves."

Annie kept her eyes on him.

"You think Main Engine One wasn't meant to be destroyed? That the attempt was just supposed to look as if it were botched?"

"I think it's a distinct possibility."

She was silent awhile. Then a pale little smile touched the corner of her lips. "That must have occurred to Jeremy too. My guess is he wasn't sure what to say in front of *you*."

"Could be." Nimec noticed himself noticing her smile and redirected his eyes toward the tabletop. What was with him? They were colleagues and these were inappropriate circumstances for such things. Weren't they? He was looking at her again before he knew it. "He's certainly smart enough."

Annie quietly drank some more coffee.

"Two questions," she said. "Would UpLink find it acceptable if I inform the press that we are now cautiously progressing along a line of inquiry that *may* link *Orion* to the incident in Brazil?"

"We wouldn't have a problem with that," he said.

"Next question," she said. "If it was sabotage, do you have any idea who may be responsible?"

He thought a moment, then made a decision.

"I think we could very soon," he said. "Our outfit has a small satellite ground station in Pensacola. I'm getting flown there from Orlando by a corporate jet at four o'clock this afternoon. We're conducting an operation you may want to observe."

She chewed her lower lip contemplatively, holding the coffee cup, steam floating up in front of her face.

"I need to get home to the kids."

"It's a short trip," he said. "I'll arrange for the plane to take you back soon as we're finished."

Silence.

Annie took another drink from her cup, then lowered it onto the saucer.

"Count me in," she said.

NINETEEN

IT WAS 2:00 P.M. PACIFIC DAYLIGHT TIME, APRIL
twenty-third, in San Jose, California.

It was 5:00 P.M. Eastern Daylight Time in Pensacola,
Florida.

It was 6:00 P.M. Brazilian Daylight Time in the central Pantanal.

It was 3:00 A.M. the following day, April *twenty-fourth*, in Kazakhstan.

The variations in dates and time zones made no difference to UpLink International's Hawkeye-I and -II hyperspectral high-resolution imaging satellites, nor to the relaying and data-processing equipment used to establish a real-time downlink to receiving stations in each locale—these only being machines, as Rollie Thibodeau readily pointed out to Megan Breen from behind a notebook computer on his hospital tray.

To the *people* involved in this synchronized monitoring operation, on the other hand, the whole process of coordination was a howling, troublesome bitch.

As Rollie was also free and quick to note.

• • •

Tom Ricci rubbed his eyes. Had it really been less than seventy-two hours since he'd left Maine, its deepwater urchin beds, and the reclusive life he had cultivated for over two years behind? Something like that, he guessed. So much mental and physical distance had been covered between then and now, it was hard to keep track. There had been the flight to San Jose, his meeting with Roger Gordian, the formal offer from Gordian to join UpLink in what had to his surprise become a position—its official title being Global Field Supervisor, Security Operations—that he would hold *jointly* with a guy named Rollie Thibodeau, who, if memory served, was the other candidate for the job mentioned to him by the high-and-mighty Megan Breen back in Stonington. There had been his acceptance of the offer despite reservations about working in partnership with Thibodeau, someone he'd never met, someone very much liked and preferred by Breen, a woman toward whom Ricci had taken an automatic *dis*like, which impression had seemed in his eyes to be a two-way street filled with bumps, potholes, and inevitable collisions. Only Ricci's fidelity to the commitment he'd given Pete Nimec had overcome his second thoughts about agreeing to the modified proposition in Gordian's office.

All of which had preceded his express shipment to Kazakhstan, a severe, inhospitable place populated with equally severe, inhospitable Russian military and scientific personnel whose antagonism toward him was more than a little reminiscent of his old friend Cobbs. They were indignant about his having taken command of site protection at their Baikonur Cosmodrome prior to the space launch. They had bristled at his front-line deployment of Sword patrol units and defensive systems. They viewed his assistance as gross interference, and had let him know it at every possible turn.

He wondered how much worse his reception would

have been if they'd known this was, more or less, his first day on the job.

Fatigued and out of joint, his biological clock in jagged contention with the time displayed on his wristwatch, Ricci sat at an onboard vehicle computer in the trailer that was his mobile command center and logged onto UpLink's secure intranet server via cellular modem, waiting for pictures from space that his instincts told him were about to reveal complications that would make every problem he'd encountered since his arrival in Central Asia—if not since his farewell urchin run with Dex—seem piddling by comparison.

Soon after the transmission began, those instincts proved themselves to be right on the money.

"This ground station's part of our Geographic Information Service division," Nimec was explaining to Annie. "Our clients include real estate developers, urban planners, map and atlas publishers, companies involved in oil, natural gas, and mineral resource exploration . . . a whole range of businesses that can benefit from high-res topographic imaging data. Essentially, though, the profits we earn from those contracts go toward defraying expenses the GIS piles up doing gratis work to satisfy Gord's altruistic drives."

They were alone in the first of several rows of theater-style seats climbing toward the rear of what could have been mistaken for a small movie screening room, but for the technical staffers at horseshoe-shaped computer workstations to their left and right. A large flat-screen display covered most of the wall in front of them.

"Spy-eye time as a charitable donation," she said. "That's a new one to me."

Nimec looked at her.

"You remember that child abduction in Yellowstone about six months ago? The little girl, Maureen Block,

got snatched out of her parents' camper? The guy who
did it was some survivalist nutcase, held her in a lean-
to made of timber and leaves. She was found by park
rangers after sweeps from Hawkeye-I penetrated his
camouflage, captured infrared images of the girl and her
kidnapper while they were in the shelter."

Annie put her hand up to her forehead.

"I think," she said, "I've just embarrassed myself."

"No reason you should feel that way," Nimec said.
"Our involvement was never disclosed. We've worked
with local police departments, the FBI, NSA, you name
it. This isn't quite classified information, but it *is* for the
most part held confidential by the various agencies."

"At whose preference?"

"Everybody's," Nimec said. "It's pretty well known
how competitive law-enforcement organizations can be.
They like taking their pats on the back for closing cases,
and we're glad to let them. It tends to eliminate any
inclination they might have to see us as sticking our nose
in where it doesn't belong and reject our assistance. It
also has the fringe benefit of keeping the bad guys off
guard." He paused, quietly watching the techs key up
for the satellite feed. "There's a whole range of other
situations we help out with, besides. The birds can detect
toxic chemical concentrations in soil runoff, plot out the
extent of oil spills, pinpoint the specific types of mineral
depletion in agricultural areas to give farmers a heads-
up on potential crop failure . . . it goes on and on."

She looked impressed. "If I may ask, just what *are*
your satellites' capabilities?"

"Confidentially?"

She nodded, and gave him a faint smile. "If not quite
classified."

"Hawkeye can zoom in on objects less than five cen-
timeters across and scan on over three hundred spectral
bands, which matches anything the spooks at the Na-

tional Reconnaissance Office have at their disposal. Same goes for the speed and accuracy of our analysis— and we hope to have *moving* real-time pictures within a couple of years. Also, the telemetry images we're about to see here are going out over our corporate intranet to be viewed by members of our security team on three continents and examined by photo interpreters in San Jose." He gestured toward the headsets jacked into the armrests of his seats. "These provide an audio link for anyone who's got a request for the analysts, or wants a particular area enlarged, enhanced, or identified. You may want to listen in."

Annie got a quick flash of herself playing host to Roger Gordian and Megan Breen in the LCC firing room at Canaveral what seemed an eternity ago, pointing to the lightweight phones on her console.

"When the event timer starts again you'll want to put them on and eavesdrop on the dialogue between the cockpit and ground operators."

A chill ran down her spine.

Nimec noticed her far-off look. "Anything wrong?"

"No," she said. "Just kind of dazzled by the scope of this operation."

Nimec knew she was lying, but dropped it, although he couldn't dismiss his peculiar interest in what was on her mind.

Then, from one of the techies, a wave.

"Get ready," he said. "Show's about to start."

Some 2,500 miles northwest as the crow flies, Roger Gordian was in a room identical to the one in which Pete Nimec and Annie Caulfield were seated, watching, as they were, the first satellite images stream down from Hawkeye-I above Brazil. Filling the row to either side of him was the group of satellite recon specialists Nimec had mentioned to Annie, most former employees of the

NRS and its PHOTINT section, the National Photographic Interpretation Center.

Over the previous twenty-four hours, Hawkeye-I had made a series of low-resolution passes over an area describing a radius of about three hundred klicks around the ISS installation in Matto Grosso do Sul, its field of reconnaissance determined by the results of a computerized vector analysis seeking those areas of highest probability from which the raid of April 17th might have been staged. Entered into these calculations were wind conditions on the night of the attack, approximations of the HAHO team's point of descent into the compound, estimates of their maximum range of travel, flight controller logs from known airfields, likely sites for *concealed* airfields, intelligence about regional criminal and political extremist enclaves, and a galaxy of other data deemed pertinent by Sword's electronic surveillance experts.

After reviewing the computer analysis and initial flyby imagery, the photo interpreters had systematically narrowed their interest to two geographic areas: the alluvial plains and savannah of the Pantanal, and an overlying region of rocky, semiarid escarpments called Chapada dos Guimarães.

It was the highlands that came to attract their most intense scrutiny. Magnification of the images registered what appeared to be an ad hoc runway in a massive table formation at the Chapada's western edge—some fifty kilometers from the ISS facility, and well within the bounds of a radar-eluding aircraft launch and HAHO drop. Further examination revealed the snaking, deliberate track of a roadway winding up the precipitous sandstone walls of the plateau. Light reflection patterns in the visible spectrum showed the definite earmarks of mechanical objects on the formation's broad, flat top and in a narrow draw cut into the base of the slope—guessed to be fixed-wing aircraft and wheeled vehicles from their shapes and dimensions.

⋅ These initial evaluations, coupled with a studied look at infrared bandwidth patterns coming from the grotto that distinctly showed human heat signatures, the long-wave IR "hot spots" of motorized activity, and the contrasting emissions of camouflage and growing vegetation, led to a rapid decision to target the area for the high-res, full-spectrum scan now in progress.

Gordian watched as Hawkeye-I telescoped in on the flattened plateau and relayed its digital eye-in-the-sky shots from communications satellite to ground station at trillions of bits per second, a computer-generated map grid projected over the image on the display.

"Right over there, you see those planes?" a photo interpreter beside him said. He switched on his headset and mouthed a set of coordinates into it. "What's our res?"

"We're in at slightly under a meter," a tech replied in his earpiece.

"Get us in closer, we need to see what kind they—"

"One of them is a Lockheed L-100, same damn transports we use," Gordian interrupted. "The other's an old DC-3 workhorse."

"Lots of hustle and bustle around them. I'd say a total of thirty, forty individuals."

The analyst on Gordian's opposite side sat up straight and pointed. "The vehicles lined along the slope look like quarter-ton Jeep 'Mutts,' supply trucks . . . some heavy-duty rigs."

Gordian leaned toward the edge of his seat.

"They're pulling up stakes," he said.

"Those guys in desert fatigues around the plane, how close can you zoom in on them?" Ricci said into his computer's mike.

"Give us a minute, you'll know if any of them have acne scars," a techie replied via his earphones.

He waited, his attention rapt on the screen.

It took less than a minute.

The man at the foot of the L-100's boarding ramp had short-cropped hair, an angular face with a strong, square jut of chin, and wore aviator glasses and a drive-on rag-type headband. He was clearly calling out orders, directing the upload of personnel and cargo.

"You see that one?" Thibodeau said. Hands gripping the tubular safety rail of his bed, he hoisted himself painfully up from his pillow, leaning closer to the notebook computer on his hospital tray. "You *see* him?"

"Rollie, maybe you'd better take it easy—"

"*Le chaut sauvage,*" he said.

"What?"

"Got the look of a wildcat." Thibodeau's eyes were alight under the brim of his battered campaign hat. "He's in command. An' not just of gettin' stuff onto the planes."

Megan studied the screen from the chair beside his bed.

"You think we've got the top man in our sights?"

"Don' know if he's the brains . . . but combat leader, *oui,*" he said. "I tell you, I know." He paused. "From the looks of 'em, the people he's orderin' around ain't no drug runners or guerrillas neither. They're mercenaries, for sure. Got to be the ones who hit us the other night."

Megan turned her attention back to the face on-screen.

"We better find out who he is," she said.

Thibodeau looked at her.

"*Cherie,* I think it's more important that we find out

where he an' his boys are goin' . . . an' if we can, stop them from gettin' there."

"The question is *why* they're clearing out," Nimec said into his mouthpiece.

Ricci from across the globe: "Agreed. And if they're mobilizing, what for?"

"How long before we have Hawkeye-II transmitting optical images from over Kazakhstan?" Gordian asked over the voice link.

"There's some cloud cover over the region right now," a tech said. "Weather readings indicate a slow-moving front."

"How long?"

Listening in, Annie turned from the face being close-upped on the wall and stared at Nimec.

"Kaza—" she mouthed silently.

Nimec cut her off with a motion of his hand as the satellite techs gave Gordian his answer. Then he briefly switched off his headset.

"Sorry," he said. "I wanted to hear what—"

It was Annie's turn to interrupt. "You think those people are out to stop the Russian shuttle launch? Cause the same sort of thing that happened to *Orion*?"

Nimec licked his lips.

"My feeling is they could be," he said. "The satellite pictures will tell us more."

She shook her head in anxious disbelief.

"What now?" she said. "We need to . . . are you going to contact the State Department?"

Nimec saw her hand trembling on her armrest, and took hold of her wrist.

"Annie—"

"It can't be allowed to happen again, Pete," she said. "It—"

"Annie."

She looked at him.

"We'll handle this," he said. His grip was firm around her wrist. "I promise."

TWENTY

UNMARKED, GHOST-GRAY, THEIR PROP/ROTOR WING-tip nacelles tilted at 90° angles to their fuselages in full vertical-takeoff-and-landing mode, the pair of Bell-Boeing V-22 Ospreys left their launch platforms in the ISS compound's helipad area at 7:00 P.M Brazilian Day-light Time, rising straight and straightaway through lay-ers of purple twilight at a speed of 1,000 feet per minute.

In the starboard pilot seat of the lead Osprey's glass cockpit, Ed Graham glanced out his rearview mirror and saw his wingman slot into formation off his port side. He had on a modular integrated display and sight helmet that allowed for day-or-night heads-up flight and resem-bled nothing more than the headgear worn by rebel star-fighter jocks in *Star Wars*. Beside him, the upper half of Mitch Winter's face was also hidden under a MiDash helmet.

Although they had spent many hours training in the Osprey, and proven their skill and teamwork at handling the Skyhawk chopper under fire, this would be their first offensive mission in the tiltrotor craft.

Six minutes into their ascent, Graham used the thumb-wheel control on his thrust lever to graduate the nacelles down 45° to their horizontal positions—at which point the Allison T406-AD-400 turbines behind their rotor hubs began to perform like the engines of a standard high-speed turboprop, bearing the Osprey on a westerly course toward the Chapadas as it rose to its cruising altitude of 26,000 feet.

Ferried in the spacious personnel/cargo hold of each Osprey were complements of twenty-five Sword operatives in indigo battle-dress uniforms and antiterrorist gear. They wore ballistic helmets with face shields, night-vision goggles, and digital radio headsets beneath the helmets. They wore Zylon soft body armor and load-bearing vests accessorized with baton and knife holders, incapacitant spray pouches, and other special-operations rigs. Their weapons included VVRS automatic rifles, Benelli Super 90 12-gauge shotguns chambered to accept 3-inch nonlethal rounds, FN Herstal Five-Seven sidearms fitted with laser grips, and an assortment of incendiary, smoke, and phosphorous grenades. The strike team in the wing craft also wore padded knee guards, and had rappelling ropes and pitons on their web utility belts.

It was almost one week to the day since they had been taken by surprise and forced to do battle on the defensive; since their home ground had been invaded and torn apart with mines and plastic explosives; since fifteen of their friends and brothers-in-arms had been killed or wounded by a then-unknown invasion force.

Now they hoped to turn the tables.

Pocketing his aviator glasses in the waning daylight, Kuhl felt a cool breeze drift across the plateau and dry the perspiration on his dun colored head scarf. He heard the Lockheed's turbines powering up on the airstrip behind him, turned from the partially evacuated camp in the ravine downslope, and watched as the last and most important items of payload were carried aboard the transport in plain wooden crates.

Despite how well things had gone, he was mildly ill at ease, and could not quite put his finger on the reason why. Perhaps it was just the precise and demanding timetable to which he'd needed to adhere, coupled with an impatience to get on to Kazakhstan. There was always a tightness within him before he made his finishing thrust. Yet this unsettled feeling had a somewhat different quality, and he wondered if the almost *too* smooth progression of events thus far—the absence of any outward sign that Roger Gordian's people had made substantial headway following the trail of their attackers, or were pursuing it with the aggressiveness one might expect of such an estimable force—might not be the cause of it. As a hunter, Kuhl knew the advantage of circling in silence. But he also knew that there were circles *within* circles. That a hunter at the edge of the smaller circle could all too easily become prey at the center of the larger . . .

A pair of men in khaki fatigues with Steyr AUG assault rifles slung over their shoulders—the FAMAS guns already on their way to Kazakhstan—approached him from outside the plane's cargo section.

"We've been told everything is ready for your take-off," one of them said.

Kuhl motioned toward the retrofitted DC-3 further down the ramp. It was still being packed with freight conveyed by the lines of jeeps and trucks moving between the airfield and the gully below.

"I want the decampment to continue without holdup," he said. "Make sure the pilot of that plane knows he's to leave here no longer than half an hour after we've gone. And stay on top of the loading."

The man who'd spoken to him nodded. Before he

could turn to begin carrying out his orders, Kuhl took note of the bandage around his upper arm.

"How is the wound, Manuel?" he asked in Spanish.

"Está mejor, it is much better."

Kuhl made a fist and struck it to his heart.

"A lo hecho, pecho," he said. It was an old expression he had picked up somewhere along the way. "To the chest, that which is done. Accept gladly all you have accomplished."

Manuel looked at him in silence. Then he nodded again and strode off toward the DC-3 with his companion.

Kuhl lingered for a brief while afterward, his back to the runway, staring out into the shadows as they rose from the lowlands like the waters of some dark, swollen river that had begun to overflow its banks, spreading across the lofty, sand-blown table on which he stood.

At length, he went to board the waiting transport.

Graham cursed, gazing out his windscreen into the distance. He had spotted the taillights of a plane ascending through the gloom at twelve o'clock.

"Got to be the Lockheed, from the size of it," Winter said, scanning the FLIR readouts on his helmet visor. "Of all the stinking breaks."

"Yeah." They were back down at just over six thousand feet, preparing to tip the Osprey's rotors to their vertical positions as they swooped toward the plateau only two miles up ahead.

"I can see the other one on the strip," Winter said. He pointed slightly off to starboard. "The goddamn DC-3."

Now it was Graham who checked his HUD's sensor imagery.

"You catch its IR signature?" he asked.

Winter nodded. "Engines are cranking. It's getting ready to fly."

He cranked his head around, shot a glance portside and aft. He could make out the wingman's face close behind them, his dismayed frown communicating that he'd also seen the L-100 take off.

A moment later Winter and Graham got verbal confirmation.

"What the hell do we do, Batter One?" the other Osprey's pilot asked over the radio.

Winter breathed.

"Forget the big bird, Batter Two, we'll take the nest as planned," he said, and pulled throttle.

Hard.

Manuel knew the sound of helicopters. He had hidden from them in El Salvador when, eighteen years old and woefully naive, he had joined the Marxist FMLN in their failed revolutionary campaign. Years later, while a paid soldier of the Medellin cartel and the guerrilla armies that emerged after its downfall like countless tiny snakes issuing from the belly of a slain dragon, he had played cat-and-mouse with the Black Hawks, Bell 212's, and Cobras flown by U.S. Special Forces and Marine Corps personnel in Colombia . . . and once or twice, had successfully assumed the role of the cat and swiped them out of the air. He knew the sound of helicopters, had heard it throughout Latin America as he had sold his services to whoever could meet his price, and was able to differentiate between them with his eyes closed.

However, the rotor aircraft he suddenly heard now, descending through the near-total darkness that had settled over the plateau, was unlike anything in his experience. But for the speed at which it was vertically dropping, he might have mistaken it for a large plane.

He stood outside the DC-3, looking up, listening along with the others who had frozen on and near the cargo ramp. His heart thumped in his chest. They were close, close, almost overhead—

Then he saw their winged shadows fall over him in the remaining daylight and, raising his Steyr bullpup, waved for his men to scatter.

Graham was about to deploy his landing wheels when he heard the first bursts of submachine-gun fire rattling against the cockpit floor.

Not this time, you fuckers, he thought.

He dipped the Osprey's nose slightly and turned toward Winter.

"Release a couple of Sunbursts . . ."

Which were folding-fin, high-velocity rocket projectiles fitted with combination phosphorous/smoke warheads in launch tube pods below the Osprey's wings. Their purpose was to blind and confuse, although the rockets could have been capable of massive destruction had their warheads contained explosive charges.

". . . then let's hit 'em with the Peacemakers . . ."

These being elastomer-cased 40mm bullets containing a liquid core of dimethyl sulfide, a powerful sedative that is instantly absorbed through the skin and mucous membranes. Fired at a rate of 650 rounds per minute from a specially chambered nose-mounted turret gun devised by Sword's less-than-lethal-ordnance technicians, these rounds would disable first through kinetic energy, and second, by rupturing on impact to release their DMSO fill. Again, the nose gun might have easily been converted to take deadly 30mm full-metal-jacket ammunition—but a mandate was a mandate, and the Brazilians had been unyielding in the restrictions imposed upon UpLink's offensive aircraft capabilities.

". . . got it?" Graham finished.

"Got it," Winter said.

And reached for his weapons console.

• • •

Crouched over a sealed crate in the cargo bay of the DC-3, Manuel worked sweatily at its lid with a crowbar he'd snatched from a tool compartment behind the pilot's cabin. His face dripped with moisture, and he could feel the downwash of the Osprey's rotors through the bay door behind him, blasting sand and pebbles against the back of his head.

One corner of the lid came loose and Manuel shuffled quickly around on his knees to pry at another. He had managed to dash up the freight ramp and shelter himself in the plane as the first rockets from above had discharged their blinding flashes; an instant later the Osprey's machine gun had opened fire. Peering outside, he'd seen his men stagger and fall across the smoke-covered airstrip, but then had noticed they were falling *bloodlessly*. It had made him remember the robot at the ISS facility, the one he'd taken out with the FAMAS gun. Remember its dizzying lights, and the sound emissions that had sickened him to the stomach. The robot and its armaments had been meant not to kill, but rather to cripple, a weakness that had given Manuel a chance to reduce it to scrap metal. A weakness shared by the strange attack birds besieging the airfield . . . or at least by the men in control of them.

Now, as then, Manuel would exploit it.

The second corner of the lid separated, the nails that anchored it to the crate bending as they were torn free. Breathless, panting, the wound on his arm reopened from his exertions and staining his bandages with fresh blots of crimson, Manual flung the crowbar carelessly aside, slipped the fingers of both hands under lid, and then hefted it up with a grunt of exertion.

The lid came off with a splintering crack of wood.

Manuel hurriedly reached inside the crate, his hands ripping layers of fibrous packing material out by the wad until, at last, they found the Stinger surface-to-air missile launcher.

The pilot of Batter Two had remained in a circular hover-and-support pattern above the field as Batter One had alighted, lowering its aft cargo ramp to discharge its strike team.

With only a dozen or so hostiles in the runway area, most of them incapacitated by the Sunbursts and Peacemaker rounds, there was little for the team to do but cleanup work. Minutes after Batter One landed, Graham radioed up word that the field was fairly well secured.

"Thanks for the assist, Batter Two," he said. "Good luck in the valley below."

"Roger, on our way," the pilot of the airborne Osprey said, and veered off toward the ledge where it would drop its rappellers.

That was when Manuel stepped out onto the loading ramp of the DC-3 transport, the man-portable SAM launcher on his shoulder.

Manuel had little to decide in choosing his target: The Osprey on the ground had already discharged its men, and the one still in the sky was full of them.

His eye to the sight of the lightweight fiberglass launcher, his hand on its grip-stock, he angled it toward the flying aircraft and activated its argon-cooled IR seeker unit with the touch of a switch. A shaved second later he heard the beep tone indicating a lock-on, and pulled the Stinger's trigger.

His heart stroked once, twice in his chest.

The missile shot toward the departing Osprey with a *whoosh* of propellant gas.

The pilot and co-pilot of Batter Two did not see the plume of the heat-seeking missile as it streaked toward their fuselage, but the sensor pods on its nose and tail did, and instantly informed them of the threat via readouts on their dashboard and HUDs. At their low-level height above the plateau, the missile would only take a matter of three or four seconds to close, too quickly for an evasive maneuver, or for the limitations of human reaction time to allow either crew member to engage the Osprey's IR countermeasures set.

Which was why its GAPSFREE avionics were failsafed to do so automatically.

Two independent defenses awakened at once: a thermal chaff/decoy dispenser on either wing that ejected bundles of aluminum strips and incendiary flares into the air, scattering infrared bogies to confound the missile's nose-cone guidance system, and an infrared pulse lamp that accomplished much the same thing with tiny gusts of energy emitted at right angles to the fuselage.

The Stinger missile tracked yards wide of its mark to finally detonate against a blank wall of sandstone in its declining arc, harming nothing but the weeds and brambles clinging to its face.

Though Ralph Peterson had been with Sword for almost three years without ever having needed to use a weapon off the target range, his first shots fired in action would be lethal ones.

The night the ISS compound was raided, he'd been on his day shift rotation, off duty, picking up a pretty girl in a Cuiabá barroom. He'd never thought he could possibly regret getting invited back to her apartment, but that turned out to be the case just the next day, when he reported to base and heard about the raid—and about the men who had died defending the facility in his absence.

He was not going to let anyone else be murdered without doing whatever he could to prevent it.

Peterson caught sight of the guy with the Stinger an instant after the SAM was triggered and twisted his VVRS barrel control to its man-killer setting, taking no chances. Then he called out for him to disarm, noticing an assault rifle over his shoulder in addition to the missile launcher in his grasp.

The guy half-obeyed his warning and did *indeed* drop the Stinger—but only to free his hands for bringing up the rifle.

As Manuel raised and angled the Steyr in Peterson's direction, his movement a near-blur, Peterson hit him with two short bursts, aiming directly at his heart.

Blood sprayed from the center of Manuel's chest, then ejaculated from his mouth in a red gush.

He was dead before he hit the ground.

A lo hecho, pecho.

After dropping four hundred feet from the table of the plateau in its VTOL attitude, Batter Two perched on a weathered spur of cliff above the ravine, its LZ chosen after careful examination of relief maps prepared from Hawkeye-I's stereoscopic terrain images. From here its twenty-five-man strike team would rappel another hundred feet down to the floor of the trench, then wind their way between its sheer sandstone walls to the hostile camp.

The Osprey's cargo ramp opened and the rappellers, led by Dan Carlysle, debarked in hurried single file, night-vision goggles lowered over their eyes, rubber-soled boots crunching on the rocky earth.

There were five ropes, five climbers to each. Removing blade-type titanium pitons from their web rigs, the men drove them into the projecting rock with mountaineer hammers, slipped their ropes into the piton rings, fastened them with square knots, and tossed the ropes over the side of the cliff, glancing downward as they uncoiled to make sure they were long enough to reach bottom.

Gloved hands gripped the ropes. One, two, three, four, five hard tugs tested that the pitons were securely anchored. Five nods confirmed that they were.

Straddling their ropes as they faced the anchor points, the lead men wound the ropes into harnesses around their bodies—once around the hip, then diagonally across the chest and back over the opposite shoulder. This done, they began their rapid descent along the cliff wall.

They moved in a kind of springing hopskip, bodies leaned out and away from the slope, backs straight, legs spread wide, treaded boot bottoms scuffing along the furrowed rock face. Their braking hands were down, their opposite hands raised to guide them along the rope-lengths.

The satellite maps had indicated firm, hard slope along most of the decline—favorable conditions—and that was essentially what they encountered. The last ten yards were more difficult to traverse, a scree of pebbles and stones that crumbled out from underfoot in gravelly spills.

Still, they made it down fast and without injuries.

Again they gripped their ropes, this time looking upward. Again they gave five tugs to test the fastness of the ropes—and to indicate they had successfully reached bottom to those above.

Seconds later, the next group of five began their descent.

They found the base camp completely deserted. There were empty tents, some left standing, some partially folded. There was a single dusty, abandoned jeep with a flat tire. There were mounds of burned and buried rubbish, odd, scattered personal articles and pieces of equipment—entrenching tools, butane cookstoves, spools of rope, a metal bucket, first-aid kits, a disposable razor, four D-cell batteries, a pair of sunglasses missing one lens, an overturned wooden table, a commercially available Hammond map of the area with no penned-in notes or highlighted route markings.

The departed occupants of the camp had made a more or less clean sweep of it, leaving behind not a single weapon or round of ammunition, not a single clue to where they had gone.

Carlysle spat on the ground, then switched on his radio headset to contact Batter Two's pilot.

"Roger, team leader, how's it going?" the pilot responded.

"We've missed the party," Carlysle said in disgust. "That's how."

Megan helped Thibodeau settle comfortably back against his pillow, lifted his campaign hat off his head, and laid it on the table beside the bed. He looked weary and haggard, and the ward nurse had reported that his temperature was slightly elevated—nothing of serious concern, she'd assured Megan, but an indication that it was time for him to get some rest. Though she'd left a plastic cup of painkillers on his tray, he had refused to take them, having insisted on staying awake and alert until word arrived from the strike teams.

Now that it had, Megan poured some water into his glass and handed him the pills.

"Bottoms up," she said.

He grumbled something under his breath, tossed the pills into his mouth, and washed them down with a single gulp.

Taking the glass from him, Megan pressed the button to recline his backrest, pulled the sheets up over his chest, and bent to kiss him on the cheek.

"Night, Rol," she said. "I'll see you in the morning."

He looked soberly up at her.

"Them prisoners won't talk," he said. "You know that."

She nodded. "I doubt they will."

"An' *le chaut sauvage* . . . he wasn't there. Must've been on the plane got away."

Megan nodded again.

"Another thing bothers me's that we still don't know why they went to the trouble they did breakin' into this compound in the first place, use all a' that fancy equipment just to try and blow a low-security warehouse got nothin' besides spare parts in it," he said. "Can't make any sense of it, you know?"

She patted his arm.

"Sleep," she said. "It's been a long day, and there's nothing more we can do right now."

Dimming the light, she lifted her purse off her chair, and strode toward the door.

"Meg?" he called weakly from behind her.

She turned toward him, her hand on the knob.

"Somethin' goes down in Kazakhstan, you think this Ricci gonna be up to takin' care of it?"

She stood there for a long moment, then merely sighed.

"Tomorrow's another day, Rollie," she said.

Then she stepped out into the hall, softly closing the door behind her.

TWENTY-ONE

KAZAKHSTAN
APRIL 26, 2001

PERHAPS BECAUSE OF THE DARK CLOAK OF SECRECY under which Russia's spacecraft testing has long been conducted in southern Kazakhstan, the region has since the early 1950's been the scene of hundreds of unexplained UFO sightings by local peasants. Sugar-beet farmers, grain growers, goatherders, cattlemen, sinewy Mongol horse traders ... many have had stories of strange airborne vehicles glimpsed above the brown, moraine-covered steppes, some accounts accurate, others embellished over the course of time and countless retellings, a considerable number complete fabrications contrived to amuse friends and kinsmen and add a little brightness to the drowsy tedium of life in their remote, mountainous corner of the world.

The dark, disc-shaped object that went skimming over the promontories near the Baikonur Cosmodrome around sundown on April 26—a singularly overcast evening in what had been an even more extraordinary spell of damp, cloudy weather—would be spotted by the entire al-Bijan clan, from great-grandparents on down to its children, all sixty-seven of them gathered outside an ancestral home still occupied by family members to feast on grilled horseflesh, drink potent alcoholic beverages (at least in the case of the adults), dance to chords strummed on the three-stringed *komuz,* and generally celebrate the wedding of one of its daughters to the son of a well-respected and, by Kazakh standards, well-heeled livestock breeder.

In this instance, their subsequent accounts of its appearance did not require any exaggeration.

Ricci sat alone in the silence of the trailer that served as his personal quarters outside the Cosmodrome, looking over some maps of the area, liking his situation, and particularly his Russian hosts, less and less with every minute that passed. Expecting them to keep a promise of cooperation was like thinking you could hire some degenerate pedophile as a camp counselor and accept his absolute guarantee that he'd keep his hands to himself. Their original agreement to put the launch center's security under Ricci's full direction had, in the last twenty-four hours, been qualified and ultimately redefined so that he was now in charge only of *perimeter* defense, with the VKS space cops, or whatever they were called, assuming control of the facility's interior grounds protection, even prohibiting access of Sword personnel to some of its buildings. And there already had been clashes of authority at the outer checkpoints that were supposed to be his team's areas of patrol.

The duplicity had been pure borscht, reminding him of what had happened in Yugoslavia after the bombing war back in the '90s, when Moscow had no sooner cut a deal with NATO not to enter Kosovo than it had ordered a military occupation force into one of Pristina's key strategic airports. Back then, they'd had a President who'd looked and acted like a huge leech pickled in

vodka to blame for the supposed confusion . . . but what
sort of excuses were they making now?

Ricci shook his head gravely. He knew Roger Gordian
had been in repeated contact with Yuri Petrov, trying to
persuade him to stick to his original commitments. But
Ricci's own last conversation with Gordian had taken
place twelve hours ago, at which point he'd been told
to sit tight and await further news. Gordian hadn't
sounded optimistic, though, and there had been nothing
from him since—a clear indication that Petrov had fallen
victim to the hereditary Russian breast-beating reflex and
would keep thumping away until he keeled over backward. In other words, negotiations were stalled indefinitely and Ricci's curtailed functions would continue to
be the status quo until after the ISS launch was history.

Assuming it occurred without disaster striking first.

Ricci studied his map, feeling stretched thin in every
sense. His exhaustion and jet lag, the haste with which
he'd needed to organize his guard force, the ongoing
logistical problems of building it up to a reasonable level
of adequacy, Petrov's frequent curve balls and increasing restrictions upon his authority . . . the whole kit and
kaboodle was grating on him. Nor had there been a bit
of encouragement in anything he'd heard about the strike
on the terrorist camp in the Chapadas. Whoever had
been occupying that base had flown the coop aboard the
Lockheed, which had itself vanished without a trace.
And if they were as good and well-equipped as his information led him to believe, Ricci figured they'd have
a network of safe, tucked-away airfields where they
could make layover and refueling stops en route to their
ultimate destination.

And where do you think that's going to be? he
thought. *Come on, take a guess.*

Ricci studied the map, thinking they were out there
someplace close by, knowing it with a strange and im-

placable certainty he could not have explained to any other human being . . . with the possible exception of Pete Nimec. Sometimes when he was with the BPD and had worked a criminal investigation to where a bust was imminent, he'd been able to feel the accelerating energies of the thing with his nerve endings, the way he supposed animals in a forest could sense a coming storm.

They were out there, out there someplace—but where? Even the weather was working to his disadvantage. As long as the low-pressure front remained in a holding pattern over southern Kazakhstan, the Hawkeye-II satellite would be wearing what amounted to a blindfold of clouds, severely reducing its capabilities. To offset this handicap, Gordian and Nimec had shipped Ricci another of their little toys, a SkyManta unmanned air recon vehicle that looked for all the world like a flying saucer in some 1950's-era drive-in masterpiece. *Earth versus the Aliens from Zanthor.* He'd seen other drones in his military days, including the Predator, which had been in its experimental stages at the time, and was eventually given over to the exclusive use of the Air Force's 11th Reconnaissance Squadron . . . the Predator, and another UAV called the Hunter, both of which had outwardly resembled conventional airplanes.

UpLink's pilotless vehicle was in another class. While far from a scientific wizard, Ricci *was* a quick study, and his understanding based upon Nimec's apprisal was that its outer shell was called a "smart skin," a composite alloy imbedded with microelectromechanical systems— MEMS was the acronym Pete had used—which included sensors tiny enough to be carried by *ants,* and which gave it the ability to pick up infrared heat concentrations, plus near-real-time video, and most significantly under present meteorological conditions, synthetic aperture radar images that could penetrate the cloud cover hindering his surveillance efforts. Pitch black like a Stealth bomber, it had a circumference of thirty-five, maybe forty feet, making it difficult to eyeball from the ground at night. Also, something about its saucer shape, he wasn't quite sure what, would allow it to slip past ground-to-air radar arrays even more easily than aircraft with Stealth design.

The technical operators that had brought the Sky-Manta from Kaliningrad had launched it about an hour back, and Ricci was leaving it to them to keep tabs on its transmissions. If anything of interest turned up, they'd give him a shout. But what he'd needed this evening was a few hours of solitude, a chance to simply *think*.

Ricci looked at the map, running his fingertip over the topographical features of the Cosmodrome's surrounding terrain. Everywhere he looked, there were tucks and folds in the hills where an assault force with a basic knowledge of cover and concealment techniques could have been assembling for days or even weeks. And whereas they could choose the time and place to hit—and hit they would, said his own low-tech internal sensors—he was shackled by Petrov's hairy-chested exercise in self-assertion.

Shaking his head again, leaving the map on the table as he rose to brew some coffee, Ricci wished himself the best of luck trying to stop them if that hit came soon.

Dressed in the uniform of a lieutenant in the *Voenno Kosmicheskie Sily*, Kuhl rode up to the checkpoint station at the north gate of the Cosmodrome in the two-seat cabin of an MZKT-7429 military semi-trailer truck. He was on the passenger side. Olcg, a native Ukrainian with whom he had seen action in many mercenary operations, was at the wheel. In back were Antonio and four of Kuhl's best, most dedicated men from Brazil—

men who had replaced the original occupants of the truck, actual Russian Military Space Police, now dead in a ditch some miles away with bullets from Antonio's .22-caliber pistol in their heads. With Kuhl and his men aboard the trailer was the High Power Microwave cannon—tested and proven when used against the commuter train outside Sao Paulo—and its smaller but far more potent cousin, the long-range Havoc HMP device that would be placed aboard the Russian space station module. Using ISS's solar array as its power source, it would be both reusable and retargetable—allowing Harlan DeVane to virtually destroy the electronic infrastructure of any major city on earth at his remote command.

There were five sentries at the gate. Two wore the dark blue attire of UpLink's security team; three had VKS uniforms like Kuhl's—but with privates' patches on their field jackets.

Kuhl slipped his hand off the MP5K beside his seat. The Russian presence might make using it unnecessary.

As Oleg slowed the truck to a halt before the gate, one of the Sword guards approached, coming around to the driver's-side window.

"We need your identification, please," the guard said in English. Then in choppy guidebook Russian: *"Pakuh-zhee-tyeh, pa-zhal-stuh rigis-tratsiuh."*

Oleg was reaching down for his own submachine gun when Kuhl nodded slightly for him to be still, unrolled his window, and leaned his head out.

"What is this?" he said, speaking English with a fabricated Russian accent. "Do you realize I am an officer of the military police?"

The Sword guard looked calm but determined.

"I apologize for the inconvenience, sir, but my detail's been assigned security of this entry point, and if you'd just show your papers we can let you right on through."

Kuhl feigned affront and gestured toward the Russian watchmen.

"What is this?" he barked in Russian. "Am I to be insulted by these outlanders?"

The Sword guard might not have understood his words, but his tone made their meaning clear.

"Sir," he said. "I assure you this is strictly a routine check—"

Suddenly one of the Russian guards stepped up past the American, slapped his hand against the truck's rear panel, and waved it forward, signaling one of his men to open the gate.

"*Nye byespakoytyes!*" he told the driver in Russian. "Go on through!"

Oleg nodded and put his foot on the accelerator.

The Sword guard watched with dismay as the huge semi began rumbling past the checkpoint.

"Just a *minute*—"

"*Nyet!*" the Russian said, puffing himself out. "He is commanding officer of our military guard, not common criminal!"

The Sword guard looked at him, weighing his options. He *could* order his men to stand the truck down, but the damn thing was going full steam ahead, and they'd have to raise their weapons against it to do so. On the other hand, this was the third such dispute he'd had with the Russians since coming on shift tonight to suddenly find they'd crashed his party, and both times before they had bristled but ultimately yielded to his authority. Assholes that they were, he had to bear in mind they were acting on orders from higher-ranking assholes—and allowing a minor confrontation to trigger an out-and-out donnybrook would only complicate his job if something serious requiring their cooperation cropped up. Maybe it would be best to radio ahead, have the brass tussle it out, let these guys save a little face.

He turned away from the Russian and flicked on his communications headset.

Inside the truck, Kuhl had already turned on his own trunked radio and ordered his strike team to mobilize.

On receipt of Kuhl's command, the small army he had gathered in the foothills southeast of the Cosmodrome burst into hurried activity, emerging from behind artificial boulders, foliage, stone panels, and other blinds, peeling the camouflage netting off their vehicles, moving from the pockets of concealment where they had patiently hidden while going about their preparations. Often over the past week, and again earlier that night, advance scouts handpicked by Kuhl had reported back with descriptions of the launch center's eastern perimeter defenses, indicating they would be unable to withstand a direct, concentrated, lightning-fast strike. Resistance would become more intense once VKS and American reinforcements were called up from other areas of the center, but the attackers did not have to worry about penetrating it too deeply. Their objectives were limited: move in, put on a good show, move out.

They did not suspect that, in the interests of putting on the best, most convincing show possible, the scouts, under orders from Kuhl himself, had lied to them.

"Sir, we've got something from SkyManta." The young op who had come pounding at Ricci's trailer door was flushed and breathless. "Looks like this is it."

Ricci stared at him from inside the entrance, coffee cup in hand.

"What's it picked up?"

"Fifteen, maybe twenty jeeps, the controllers say the IR video's clear as day. They're heading in convoy toward the east side of the compound."

The launchpad area, Ricci thought. He hadn't wished himself luck a moment too soon.

"How close are they?"

"Two, maybe three miles, sir. There's a whole network of gullies along that way. Caves in the hills, scrub . . . it's possible they could have been hiding there for a while. . . ."

"Let's worry about the present." Ricci took a breath. "Those remote gun platforms that were brought in, what are they called?"

"The TRAP T-2s."

Ricci nodded.

"They're all in position? Exactly the way they were when we conducted firing exercises?"

"Yes, sir. Every inch of ground in that sector's covered by overlapping fire. We have at least fifteen of them just out beyond the gate—same number at each of the other perimeters—"

"Grab a few off each line, but just a few. Three, four. Leave the rest where they are. That'd bring us to about thirty guns at the point of attack. Have the additions emplaced right away."

"Yes, sir."

Ricci wanted to tell the kid not to call him "sir." He wasn't his uncle, and Sword wasn't the military. But his preferred form of address was something for later.

"Notify the firing and Quick Response teams, make sure they're all in their tac vests—"

"That's SOP, sir."

"Make sure *anyway.*"

"Yes, sir!"

Jesus, Ricci thought.

"Okay," he said. "I'm heading out to the snoopmobile to see the pictures for myself."

•   •   •

Minutes after Kuhl had gotten past the gate sentries with what amounted to a nod and a wave, the truck stopped briefly in a quiet section of the compound, where his men had placed the dish atop its trailer's roof and switched on the pulse generator. They had then driven on to within two hundred feet of the long cargo-processing facility in which the ISS service module was being stored prior to installation in the launch vehicle—a movement that was scheduled to occur the very next morning.

The concrete building was guarded exclusively by VKS troops, and only a sprinkling of them at that. None seemed interested when the cargo hauler pulled up at a moderate distance. It was one of their own trucks, and there were vehicles coming and going constantly in the days preceding a launch. Although Kuhl had been pre-pared for the eventuality of having to deal with Sword personnel, he was not surprised by their absence. One could always depend on Russian pride. That, he thought, and the impoverished economy that had ensured their facility would not be hardened against the incapacitation of their electronic alarm systems by microwave pulse, an expensive upgrade in shielding they could scarcely have afforded.

He turned to Oleg.

"Go around back," he said. "Tell the others they are to activate the cannon when ready."

The snoop-mobile was all boxed-in commotion. As Ricci entered, he saw men and women hunched over every one of the instrument consoles lining its sides, the radiance from the displays and lighted controls casting pale flickers of color across their faces.

He glanced up at a flat-panel monitor on the wall above one of the consoles, and instantly saw SkyManta's aerial IR video view of the approaching jeeps.

"Those pictures," he said, moving up beside the woman in the operator's seat. Her name tag read Sharon Drake. "They're called *near* real-time, that right?"

"Yes, sir."

Sir, again.

"How near is near?"

"What you're seeing happened less than two seconds ago."

"Putting the attack force how close?"

Sharon hit a button to superimpose grid coordinates over the image.

"A little less than a quarter mile," she said.

"Any movement near the other gates?"

She shook her head. "Not according to aerial IR scans, ground surveillance cameras, or reports from the guard posts."

Ricci thought a moment. Things just weren't making sense. Nimec's briefing had indicated the attack on the Brazilian ISS facility was a multi-pronged and precisely coordinated affair, planned around a detailed knowledge of the compound's layout. There had been airborne infiltration, scattered ambushes, the works. Though its objectives remained a question mark, there was no doubt that whoever had directed it was proficient in commando-style dispersal and distraction tactics. What he was seeing here, this column of jeeps coming at their guns, was a suicide run.

He expelled a breath. "The TRAP T-2s . . . what's the max distance their operators can stay back from the firing line?"

Sharon leaned over toward a lean, bespectacled black man at the console to her immediate right.

"Ted, I need you to tell me—"

"Sixty meters," he said without looking up from his screen.

Ricci did an approximate mental conversion. Two hundred feet, give or take.

"Notify the men at the perimeter that they're to fire soon as the jeeps are in range," he said. "I want two thirds of the weapons on lethal settings . . . we hit them with gas and fireworks first, give them a chance to back off. They keep coming, it's shoot to kill. The QR teams should be ready as our second line of defense."

Ted nodded.

"Sir," Sharon said, looking quickly over her shoulder at Ricci. "Something's happening here I don't understand."

He made a winding gesture with his hand.

"I'm getting an IR hot spot like nothing I've ever seen before from *inside* the center . . . at the north end."

"We have pictures?"

" 'Manta's nanosensor range is far beyond its electro-optical—"

"In plain English, Sharon, *please.*"

"It can detect heat and energy emissions from a distance, but video's limited to point of sight . . . objects directly below it."

Ricci ran a hand back through his hair.

"North end's the industrial section," he said. "Bring up a map of the area. I want to see exactly what buildings are over there."

Computer keys clicked to his right. Ted gestured to a monitor in front of him.

"Done," he said.

"Sir." This from another man who had come rushing over from across the trailer a second earlier. "Don't know if it's relevant to what we're seeing here, but we just got word from north sector of some friction between our people and a couple of VKS guards at their checkpoint."

"Friction over what?"

"Russian with lieutenant's boards arrives in a truck,

gets into a snit about showing us his documents, the VKS guards override our security procedures and wave him through. Same kind of thing we've been dealing with all week. We've already lodged a complaint with VKS command, but I thought you should know."

Ricci looked at him.

"When did it happen?"

"About ten minutes back.

Ricci studied the map on the screen. Yes, yes, of course. *That* fit the M.O. Fit it just perfectly.

"The cargo-processing facility," he said, leaning over Ted's shoulder. "You realize what's kept in there?"

Ted craned his head around and stared back at him for a long time before replying, his eyes wide behind his lenses.

"The ISS module," he finally said.

TRAP T-2 was another of those ubiquitous acronyms used by weapons and technology designers—the initials here standing for Telepresent Rapid Aiming Platform (Version) T-2.

As specifically configured for UpLink International, the sixty TRAP T-2s situated around the Cosmodrome consisted of a mix of tripod-mounted VVRS M16 assault rifles and Heckler & Koch MSG semiautomatic shotguns linked via microwave video, fiber-optic umbilical cable, and precision target-acquisition-and-firing software to man-portable control stations with handheld viewfinders and triggering units. The weapons platforms utilized two types of surveillance cameras: a wide-field camera on the tripod, and another on the receiver of the gun that provided a shooter's-eye perspective through its 9-27X reticular scope. Their video images were transmitted both to the firer and command-and-control centers from which the engagement was being directed.

In plainest English that would almost certainly have

satisfied Ricci, the TRAP T-2s allowed their users to hit their opposition with heavy, accurate fusillades of gunfire from locations that were secure and relatively out of harm's way, making them ideal for installation defense.

Following Ricci's orders to the letter, the Sword remote gun teams in their trailers behind the east perimeter fence waited until they could see the whites of their attackers' eyes—figuratively speaking—on the displays of their viewfinder/joystick control units before rotating the TRAP T-2's outside the fence into position, firing off salvos of 70mm smoke, white phosphorous, and CS rounds, while broadcasting a cease-and-desist warning alternately in Russian, English, and Kazakh. They had almost no hope the CS could be used to any effect, as the men in the jeeps were wearing gas masks, but were keeping their fingers crossed that the pyrotechnics would give the attackers pause.

The air around them bursting with lights and smoke, the line of jeeps slowed but did not stop.

Hands on their firing controls, the Sword gunners waited tensely to see what would happen next.

Ricci rang Petrov on his hotline before leaving the snoopmobile.

The space program director sounded in a near-panic. "What is happening? The shooting—"

"This facility's under assault, and starting *now* I intend to conduct its defense per the terms of your original agreement with UpLink. Which means—"

"Wait a moment—assault from whom? You must tell me—"

"Which means I want the VKS to stay out of my way inside and outside the Cosmodrome, and allow Sword personnel unrestricted access to all buildings we deem under threat," Ricci interrupted. "With all due respect,

Mr. Petrov, I advise you to make that happen, or the sky just might wind up falling down around your head."

As had been the case with the warehouse penetration in Brazil, the invaders gained access to the cargo-processing facility through a rear loading-bay door. What was different as Kuhl and his men went in now was that every alarm, door lock, piece of audio/visual surveillance equipment, computer—everything, *everything* that contained wires and circuits and fed off electrical current, including the light fixtures and air conditioners—had been neutralized. And because the precise calibration of Ilkanovitch's device had disrupted rather than *destroyed* the power and computer grids, most if not all of the systems would reactivate within several minutes to half an hour, leaving the intrusion undiscovered. Convinced someone was determined to halt the space station program by the *Orion* explosion and subsequent attack on the Brazilian ISS facility, the Russian and American defenders of the Cosmodrome would repel the decoy strike force at the east gate and congratulate themselves on having saved the launch vehicle.

Never would they guess that its successful launch always had been Harlan DeVane's intention. That the attacks and sabotage had been both cover for his actual plan to send Havoc into orbit aboard the ISS, and a means by which Roger Gordian's resources could be needlessly squandered, his political ties in Russia and Brazil frayed, his spreading operations in Latin America weakened and destabilized.

Their FAMAS guns shouldered, optical display helmets and visors covering their faces, Kuhl's team made their way through the ruler-straight corridor leading to the room in which the space station module was housed, following an interior plan they had long ago committed to memory. The Havoc device and antenna in Kuhl's backpack weighed only twenty pounds, and was the approximate size of a portable stereo. Planted discreetly aboard the boxcar-sized space-station module, it would not be detected by the engineers who transported the module to its launch vehicle, or the cosmonauts responsible for its linkup to the orbital space station. Once having accomplished the connection, the Russians were scheduled to return to Earth, and there would be several weeks before the first permanent crew was sent aboard, by which time DeVane would have accomplished his blackmail of Russia *and* the United States. Only the checkout engineers might have noticed it *pre*launch— and their final inspection had been conducted the day before.

There was, Kuhl thought, an exquisite symmetry to it all.

Antonio and the others close behind him, he raced forward, pushed through a door in the corridor that was supposed to be electronically locked, and glided effortlessly through another. Speed was of the essence. Though Havoc could be connected to the solar arrays in minutes, the task had to be executed, and his team's exit from the building accomplished, *before* power returned to reveal the intrusion.

Kuhl moved swiftly toward one final door, gripped its handle, and pushed it open.

The ISS module was directly in front of him on a large palletized staging work stand.

Despite his need for haste, Kuhl paused in the doorway for the barest instant, feeling a surge of momentous achievement.

Then he moved forward, Antonio and the others entering at his heels, coming up to stand beside him.

"Halt right where you are, all of you," a voice

abruptly said from his right. "Another step and we'll blow your brains out."

Ricci held his VVRS rifle out at waist level, aiming it at the man with the backpack, eyeing him steadily through his NVGs. Beside him along the right side of the room, their own rifles angled toward the door, were half a dozen Sword ops also equipped with goggles. On the left were an equal number of men.

"Drop your weapons," he said. "I hope you understand English, because you've got exactly three seconds before we open fire."

The men in the entryway did not move.

"Two," Ricci said.

His front teeth clicking together, Kuhl turned toward Antonio. It would be a pity to lose the men who were with him, but there was no choice.

"We fight," he whispered. Lying to Antonio as he had lied to the perimeter assault team. *"To the end."*

With a quicksilver movement, Antonio brought his gun up and pivoted toward Ricci, but Ricci took him down with a staccato burst to his midsection before he could release a shot.

The momentary distraction was all Kuhl had desired.

As the remaining members of his team split the darkness with automatic fire, he spun on his heels, thrust his arm out at the door that would return him to the outer hall, and pushed it open.

He was halfway through the entry when Ricci lunged from behind and caught hold of his backpack.

The man beside the TRAP T-2 firing commander stared into his handheld monitor. "Jeeps are still coming on."

The commander breathed. Didn't those dumb bastards

realize what kind of hell storm they were heading into?

"Fire at will," he said into his headset.

The attackers riding in the jeeps had not expected to come up against the remote gun platforms. Kuhl's scouts had told them that the east perimeter, now under American control, was guarded by an inadequate number of men possessing only nonlethal small arms intended to disrupt and incapacitate. The scouts had told them that the VKS was apparently convinced an offensive against the space center, if it came at all, would be launched against its industrial area—never expecting that Kuhl and his small group would *infiltrate* that sector rather than stage a mass assault there, and that the attack on this perimeter was a mere distraction that would allow Kuhl to accomplish his mission, drawing any troop concentrations away from the cargo-processing facility. Kuhl's scouts had also told the attackers that the Sword security team did not have adequate manpower to form a strong second line of defense or mount an effective counterattack.

Although the TRAP T-2s had come as a surprise to him, the leader of the attack force had assumed they had been moved into position after the last forward reconnaissance. Having never seen anything like them, he completely underestimated their precision-firing capabilities. Furthermore, the smoke, gas, and fireworks belching from the fixed platforms seemed to confirm his intelligence—relayed by Kuhl himself—that the Americans were under stricter no-kill orders than in Brazil.

Completely misled, he stuck to his plan of attack and ordered the jeeps to roll on toward the perimeter.

The Sword gunners opened up on them with everything they had, the TRAP T-2 VVRS platforms unleashing streams of deadly ammunition, angled to cover the entire field of approach with plunging, grazing, and crossing fire.

Men leaped from their vehicles as they were sprayed with bullets, many falling dead before they could make their exits, others managing to take cover behind the jeeps and return fire with their FAMAS guns. But they knew they were stalled, unable to advance, and by the time the QR squads came speeding up on their flanks, the attackers left alive were ready to surrender.

Their assault lasted just under half an hour before the Sword guards were satisfied it had been suppressed.

Exactly as Kuhl had planned.

His rifle slung over his shoulder, the fingers of one hand clutching the strap of Kuhl's backpack, Ricci pulled Kuhl toward him, keeping him in the doorway, hooking his free arm around Kuhl's chest. But Kuhl continued to press forward, fighting to escape, twisting slightly to drive an elbow into the center of Ricci's rib cage.

The wind knocked out of him, Ricci struggled to keep his arm around Kuhl, took another hard, crisp elbow jab to the diaphragm, a third.

His hold relaxed but didn't break.

Gunfire racketing behind them, the two men grappled in the narrow space of the entryway, both their rifles clattering to the floor, their arms and shoulders banging against the partially open door, slamming it repeatedly back into the wall. Then Ricci saw Kuhl reach down with his right hand, saw the truncheon in his belt scabbard, and tried to grab his wrist to keep him from getting a grip on it. But Kuhl was too fast. He pulled it from the scabbard, brought it up, half-turned again, and thrust its blunt hardwood tip into Ricci's solar plexus.

Ricci tightened his abdomen against the blow, but the pain was nevertheless tremendous. He grunted and crashed dazedly back against the door. His hold around Kuhl slackening, he somehow managed to cling to the strap that was his only remaining purchase, pulling it backward again even as Kuhl pulled *forward*.

There was a sound of fabric giving way, the strap tearing free of the stitches that held it to the pack, swinging loosely from Kuhl's right shoulder.

Slipping down his opposite arm, the pack dangled there momentarily, and then fell toward the floor between the two men.

Kuhl spun, reached a hand down to catch it, but his brief distraction had allowed Ricci a chance to recover. He brought his knee up into Kuhl's stomach, staggering him, then bent his legs to give himself some momentum and snapped a hard uppercut to Kuhl's jaw.

Kuhl's head jerked backward, but Ricci could feel him roll with the punch, and knew he'd avoided the worst of it. Ricci hit him again, aiming high, unable to maneuver in the cramped doorway and just hoping to connect with a solid hit. This time his fist smashed into the side of Kuhl's nose, and blood came spurting from it onto Ricci's knuckles.

Though Ricci could see the pain register in his opponent's eyes, Kuhl gave no other sign of weakness. Before Ricci could follow up with a third blow, he slammed his truncheon lengthwise across Ricci's side directly over his kidney, then brought it up and back for another strike, this one aimed for Ricci's temple

Raising his arm to block the swing, Ricci forced the stick out and away from himself. But his side was on fire and he was still too stunned and breathless to move. Then, through the specks of light wheeling across his vision, he saw Kuhl's left hand thrust downward again, his fingers groping for the backpack lying on the floor between them, then clenching around its broken strap.

He snatched it up and turned toward the corridor.

Gulping air, Ricci pushed himself off the door. Whatever was in that pack had to be important enough for
the other man to have paused *twice* to retrieve it when
he might instead have gotten a head start out of the
building.

As Kuhl fled into the hall, Ricci launched into the air
after him, tackling him around the middle with a force
that sent both men crashing to the floor—Ricci atop
Kuhl's back, Kuhl facedown beneath him, their legs
stretched out into the entryway and blocking the door
from swinging shut. The truncheon skittered from
Kuhl's grasp, but his other hand remained tightly
clenched around the dangling strap of the backpack.
Ricci could feel his enormous power as he fought to get
out from underneath, feel the muscles of his back and
arms working, flexing, bulging up against his chest. The
man was like a wild stallion, and Ricci knew he
wouldn't be able to keep him pinned for too long.

Pressing all his weight down on Kuhl, Ricci raised his
fist over his head, then hammered it against the hand
clutching the pack. Kuhl did not let go. Inhaling deeply,
lifting his arm back up, Ricci struck another side-fisted
punch to Kuhl's knuckles.

This time he both heard and felt the splintering of
bone. Though Kuhl again gave no outward indication of
pain, his fingers splayed open around the strap. His chest
flattened against Kuhl's back, Ricci reached out, grabbed
the pack off the floor of the corridor, and slung it over
his shoulder through the entryway behind him, the door
of which remained propped open by both men's outstretched legs.

It was just then that a hand gripped Ricci's ankle.

Blood trailing out behind him in a long, smeary ribbon,
a feeling of looseness where he'd been shot, Antonio
crawled across the floor on his belly until he was

through the doorway and, mustering all the strength left in his fingers, caught hold of Ricci above his foot. It had not occurred to him that he had been intentionally sacrificed by the man he was trying to save.

"Mi mano, su vida," he said, repeating the phrase to himself like a mantra. *"Mi mano, su vida . . ."*

My hand, your life.

Glancing over his shoulder at the dying man, Ricci tried to shake his ankle free of him, couldn't at first, then kicked out hard, his shoe bottom crunching into Antonio's face.

Antonio held on to his ankle, held on through will-power alone, pulling him backward. His lips were peeled away from his gums in a kind of rictus. There was blood smeared on his teeth, lips, and chin.

"Mi mano, su vida . . ."

Feeling a shift in Ricci's balance as he struggled with Antonio, Kuhl flailed beneath him, planting both hands on the floor to gain some leverage. Like a man doing a push-up, heedless of his shattered knuckles, he straightened his arms and heaved himself off the floor. As Ricci went spilling from on top of him, Kuhl scrambled to his feet and looked hurriedly around for his pack.

Then he glimpsed it behind him. Behind Antonio. In the room containing the ISS module.

In there with the other Sword operatives.

Kuhl saw the choices before him, and again took the one that was unfortunate but unavoidable.

"Mi mano, su vida, mi mano . . ."

Antonio's voice fading until it was barely a shiver on his lips, Ricci finally kicked free of his still-clinging fingers, sprang to his feet, and looked down the corridor.

All down its length, it was empty.

He rushed straight ahead toward the loading bay,

plunged from the darkness of the hall out into the lesser darkness of the night.

The man with whom he'd been struggling was nowhere to be seen.

Gone.

And though Ricci would search for him for the next hour, and immediately order a cordon placed around the space center's grounds, Kuhl would *remain* gone.

He had, however, left his backpack behind.

Epilogue

A SECURE CONFERENCE ROOM, UPLINK INTERNA-
tional corporate headquarters, San Jose, California.

"We've landed on our feet," Gordian said, "but let's
not kid ourselves into thinking we're on anything close
to solid ground."

At the table with him, Megan Breen and Tom Ricci
were sober.

"Our mole's still in his burrow," Megan said. "We
know now that he was familiar with the layouts of the
Brazilian compound, the Cosmodrome, and presumably
the KSC's vehicle assembly building. That he not only
revealed detailed information about the design of the ISS
service module, but also where to plant the HMP device
so it would be hidden from sight and able to feed off
the solar sails."

"Takes real access, and a lot of technical expertise,"
Ricci said. "Same for whoever did the dirty work on
Orion."

"How about the one you got the device away from?"
Gordian asked. "Any leads on him?"

Ricci shook his head. In the grounds search that had

followed the man's escape from the cargo-processing facility, his teams had found two murdered VKS guards, one garroted to death, the other with a broken neck. Ricci figured their quarry had killed them both and taken off in their missing patrol vehicle.

"Rollie holds firm that he wasn't the guiding force behind the strikes," Megan said.

Gordian looked at her. "Reasons?"

She shrugged. "He calls it a gut feeling."

"That it?"

She nodded.

"Sometimes," Ricci said, "following your gut's the best thing you can do."

Gordian expelled a long breath.

"The longer I think about all this, the more unanswered questions arise," he said. "A primary one being what the HMP generator's target was going to be once it was placed in orbit."

They all sat very still in the room's electronic envelope of silence.

"Small steps," Ricci said after a while, his voice so quiet it seemed he'd been talking to himself.

Then he noticed Gordian had turned to face him.

"That's how you count your gains," Ricci explained. "It's what I learned in the service and had reinforced when I was working the streets as a cop, and maybe almost forgot till recently. When it seems like there are ten lousy situations you can't do anything about, for every one where you can make a difference, it's all about putting your right foot forward, and just taking those small steps."

About having confidence that just being here, and alive, gives you the chance to see better times ahead, Gordian thought.

"You did a hell of a job in Kazakhstan, Tom," he said at length. "I'm glad to have you aboard."

Megan nodded, looked at him.

"Ditto," she said.

Ricci met her gaze.

"You see what I mean," he said.

The KSC staff commissary, Cape Canaveral, Florida.

Pete Nimec regarded the plate in front of him and frowned.

"Tell me if I sound crazy," he said, "but this Western omelette looks like it's made out of powdered eggs."

Annie smiled thinly from across the cafeteria table.

"What else would you expect here but astronaut food?"

"That the reason you're only having coffee?"

She looked at him.

"Do you want to know a secret?"

He nodded.

"I prefer facing the press on an empty stomach," she said. "Hunger approximating their perpetual state of being, it helps remind me what I have to deal with every day."

It was Nimec's turn to smile a little.

"Makes sense," he said.

He raised his knife and fork, took a single bite of the omelette, decided he'd had enough, and pushed the plate aside. This would, at least, be his last meal at the commissary. In about an hour, Annie was to hold an early press conference and make the official announcement that sabotage of the SSME had been judged the cause of the *Orion* fire. From that point on, the investigation would fall into the hands of law-enforcement agencies . . . and, quietly, into Sword's hands as well. Although Nimec had promised Annie he would do everything humanly possible to find out who had done the deed, and had also promised to keep her abreast of developments as they came up, his presence at the KSC was no longer needed, and he would be flying back to

San Jose the next morning. She, too, would soon be leaving Florida, for that matter, returning home to Houston.

Nimec found himself thinking—as he had more than once over the past few days—that the air travel time between the two cities was fairly short.

He took a deep breath.

"Annie," he said, "how about dinner this evening? At a real restaurant. With real food. Where we can relax. Get to be friends as well as colleagues." He paused. "It'd be fine with me if you want to bring the kids."

She sipped her coffee, lowered the cup onto its saucer, stared thoughtfully down into it.

"Friends," she said.

He nodded.

They looked at each other silently for a while.

And then Annie smiled again.

"I'd like that, Pete," she said. "I'd like it very much."

The passenger cabin of a private jet over western Bolivia.

Harlan DeVane stared out the window as his ascending plane pierced the clouds and the landscape below dissolved into far-reaching blankness.

What had happened in Kazakhstan was truly regrettable, he thought. The Colombian and Peruvian leftists had paid him a large sum of money to settle their various grudges. As had the Albanian guerrillas . . . as, unknown to them, had their sworn enemies in Belgrade. And there would have been a long line of future clients, many with sharply conflicting interests, all willing to abide by his insistence on neutrality and confidentiality. Just last week, when things had looked so promising, Iran and Iraq had *both* made generous offers meant to cause problems for each other. New York, Washington, Moscow, Baghdad, Teheran . . . DeVane was quite the egalitarian when it came to selecting his targets of destruction, and would have been leasing time on the Havoc device for many weeks to come before an astronaut team could be sent up to disable it.

He sighed. It was over, he had to concede that. Over for now. But he had never told his customers that success was a certainty, and he'd given Roger Gordian quite an initial workout, hadn't he?

Really, it was best to look at the bright side.

A world full of strife was a world full of profit, and DeVane saw no end in sight to either.